ROGUE PRINCESS

ROGUE PRINCESS

B.R. MYERS

SQUARE
FISH

SWOON READS • NEW YORK

SQUARE
FISH

An imprint of Macmillan Publishing Group, LLC
120 Broadway, New York, NY 10271
swoonreads.com

Square Fish and the Square Fish logo are trademarks of Macmillan and are used by Swoon
Reads under license from Macmillan.

Our books may be purchased in bulk for promotional, educational, or business use. Please
contact your local bookseller or the Macmillan Corporate and Premium Sales Department
at (800) 221-7945 ext. 5442 or by email at MacmillanSpecialMarkets@macmillan.com.

ISBN 978-1-250-76295-5 (paperback)   ISBN 978-1-250-30342-4 (ebook)

Originally published in the United States by Swoon Reads
First Square Fish edition, 2021
Book designed by Mallory Grigg
Square Fish logo designed by Filomena Tuosto

10   9   8   7   6   5   4   3   2   1

FOR ANGELA—
BECAUSE SHE TOLD ME TO.

CHAPTER ONE

It was the feverish gossip of the palace maids that got Aidan's attention. He was bent over the rubbish bin, just outside the kitchen. Straightening up, he flicked a vegetable peel from the collar of his uniform and stood in the back doorway, concentrating on the girls' whispers. Several princes from the neighboring planets of the Four Quadrants had been arriving since yesterday, each one more handsome than the last.

Normally, Aidan would brush off anything connected with the royal family—they were hardly his idea of decent human beings—but talk soon turned to the gifts each prince was rumored to be bringing as they all vied for Princess Delia's hand in marriage. The idea of treasures brought in by potential suitors was too tempting to ignore.

With his usual stealth, Aidan slipped into the busy kitchen unnoticed. The other staff barely gave him a second look; it was just the girls, too busy with their own chores to afford him more than a blushing glance.

He spied the deliberate care the head chef took with displaying the flowers beside the array of mini cakes—plus the ornate napkin ring. Aidan knew the valuable piece would end up in his possession by the end of the day. His reflexes were so quick, sometimes all he had to do was notice an object and the next thing he knew, it was in his pocket.

He'd spent years successfully nicking cutlery and palace trinkets during his time as a kitchen chore boy, and had amassed a substantial escape fund. He pictured the almost-full metal box under his thin cot.

He was so close to freedom! And with the headaches coming in faster intervals, he knew his time was dwindling.

The chef beckoned one of the serving androids lined up at attention, identical in their gray dresses and white aprons. "Take this directly to the guest suite in the east wing," he ordered. "It'll be my head if the prince's tray is late."

The android's lack of emotion made her the perfect victim, or rather innocent accomplice. Aidan watched her carry the tray out of the kitchen, making up a plan on the spot.

Images of a room full of priceless treasures filled Aidan's imagination as he waltzed through the bustling kitchen and down the servants' corridor. He was enough of a constant to go unnoticed, plus experience in thieving had taught him that if you looked like you belonged, everyone assumed you did.

Aidan followed the android as she took the service transporter to the upper levels of the palace. The smooth lift swooped to a stop, making his stomach rise and fall. Wordlessly, the servant made her way down the hallway of the east wing. The bright polished area was a stark contrast to his stepfather's cottage on the fringe of the Dark District. Built into the great mountain, the palace still had traces of the hard stone within the walls and floor. It was a perfect combination of technology and raw element.

But Aidan had no use for such luxury at the moment. He was focused on his new goal. The android stopped outside a door, then pressed her palm against the calling pad on the wall. The door slid open.

"Lovely work, darling," Aidan said, reaching up and touching the soft spot behind her ear. There was a click under his finger and the android froze. It was a trick he'd learned a few weeks back while eavesdropping on the royal android technician—blending in to the point of being invisible had its perks.

Aidan took the tray from her and put on his best fake smile. "Compliments of Her Royal Highness, Princess Delia," he called out, marching into the room. Then he added under his breath, "Heir to the throne, privileged daughter, and all around boring, typical spoiled royal."

He noticed the fancy clothing on the bed. The jacket was adorned with shiny buttons and a pressed collar. Voices came from beyond the smaller door across the way. He couldn't tell if it was a heated conversation or a lovers' spat. No matter, all Aidan needed was a few precious seconds to scan the room.

Then he saw it. Nestled under one of the uniforms was the silver hilt of a dagger. Aidan put down the tray, taking care to first remove the gilded napkin ring and slip it into his pocket. It was a greedy gesture, but he reasoned a little insurance never hurt.

Picking up the embellished piece, Aidan noted the inlaid jewels and deduced this was probably a courting gift rather than a weapon. *Something this beautiful should never shed blood.*

The door opened. "You there!" A partially clothed man with a short haircut stood in the smaller doorway glaring.

Aidan gave an exaggerated bow as he hid the dagger behind his back. "Compliments of the royal kitchen, Your Highness." He swept his other hand toward the tray, then did a quick twirl as he slipped the dagger into his pocket and made his way toward the door. "Enjoy the cakes," he sang over his shoulder, unable to keep the smile off his face. Not only were his days of being the chore boy over, but the ornate dagger guaranteed the last bit of cash to get him a ticket off this miserable planet. The doors slid closed behind him and he let out a satisfied sigh.

The android was frozen with her arms out front as if she were still holding the tray. "Nice working with you," Aidan said with a wink. "Forgive my hasty departure—"

"Thief!" the prince yelled from the other side of the door. "I'm calling the guards!"

Aidan scrambled for the servants' lift only to find it was on another floor. Doubling back, he sprinted down the corridor, his boots slapping a guilty echo. He turned the corner and saw the main lift ten feet down the hall. It was a risk for a servant to use it, but he had no choice. He pressed the call button, swearing under his breath as nothing happened.

The voices of the Queen's Guard echoed like rolling thunder from the far end of the hall. *How did they get here so fast?*

Aidan looked around and spied a tall alcove. Sucking in his breath, he slipped behind the life-size statue of some long dead royal he couldn't care less about. Molding his back into the curved niche in the wall, he felt the familiar twinges to both temples and knew things couldn't get much worse. Another headache was building, and this one promised to be the torturous kind that squeezed his skull to the point of passing out. And even though it meant relief, passing out now would guarantee him a lifetime in the dungeons.

Standing as still as stone, Aidan stared at the other statue across the hallway in its own alcove. He held his breath as the guards closed the distance. He estimated there were at least three of them, and all would be armed, he was certain.

From the corner of his eye, he saw the Queen's Guard come into view. Tall and imposing, the black cloaks and swords evoked a chilling respect from anyone who came face-to-face with them.

The leader paused directly in front of Aidan's alcove. The other two guards halted.

"Slippery bugger," he muttered, looking down the long empty corridor. "Take the stairs. He can't have gotten far."

"Yes, Colonel Yashin." There was a swish of capes as the guards turned and ran in the opposite direction. Aidan slowly relaxed.

The lift sounded as the doors opened. Aidan bounded inside. He reached for the main floor button, but then paused—the guards would be waiting for him, no doubt. His finger shifted and he hit the top button.

The lift came to a stop and the doors opened, revealing the launching bay. He was stunned for a moment, never having been close to this many grand ships before. Then Aidan saw a row of Queen's Guard gliders. They had fifty times the maneuvering capability of the beat-up sky dodger he skimmed over Pirate's Canyon. They were probably trickier to fly as well, but this day was apparently made for taking chances. All he would have to do was hop on one, and the sky would be his.

Before he could race to the nearest glider, a vessel on his left came to life. The door eased open as if summoning him. "A Queen's Guard Patrol ship," he whispered, equal parts awe and trepidation.

He could get much farther in a ship than an open glider, maybe even make it to another planet! No longer thinking about the metal box under his bed, Aidan seized the opportunity and eased his way inside.

He stared at the complex cockpit, suddenly overwhelmed. Anxiety set in. Aidan pulled at the collar of his shirt, frantically unbuttoning the top button. Then his hands felt the chain and the smooth disc around his neck—his medallion. Aidan touched it and closed his eyes. His mother's voice echoed inside his head. *"Always safe."*

With this new calmness, he took in his situation. "All right, you beautiful machine," he said to the control panel, scanning the array of switches and buttons. "It seems you and I are destined to have an adventure."

The general setup was similar to the smaller dashboard of the glider his stepfather owned. He was certain he could start the ship. But fly it? *Er . . . no.*

Aidan rubbed his thumb along his bottom lip, considering his next move. He knew what the future held if he didn't take this ship. He imagined his stepfather, glowering from the head of the table, criticizing Aidan's every gesture.

And never mind the sneers from his stepbrothers. There would be Drake, bulging arms and low forehead, grinning with each rude remark. Then Morgan, pale and apathetic, sitting beside his older brother, staring at the scene without comment—like always.

I'm done with them, Aidan thought. The dagger and the ship, and the opportunity they represented, were making him brave.

A jaunty sense of hope quelled his apprehension. "Machines are simple," he said, hoping to sound confident. "Just tell it what you want it to do."

He pressed what he assumed was the main power button. The

computer-generated voice of the ship was serene. "Prepare for launch. In T minus ten . . ."

There was a shudder as the ship's power thrusters came to life, knocking Aidan off his feet. The back of his head bounced off the hard floor. The computer continued to count down as Aidan fought the darkness creeping around the edges of his vision. This time he was certain things couldn't get much worse.

CHAPTER TWO

The afternoon sun stretched across the luminous tile of Delia's chamber, just reaching the edge of her pedestal. From this vantage she could see across the kingdom. The palace looked over the residences of the lords within the high walls, then the surrounding lake, and farther down she could see the raised homes of counselors and dukes. The whole area was a tiered settlement built into the massive mountain. Then lower still, private landowners. The Dark District was there too, underneath everything else.

But Delia's attention was focused on the cloud cover in the distance. She chided herself for not checking the atmospheric conditions more closely. It would be particularly miserable luck to have planned everything else, but fail because she'd forgotten to check the stupid weather.

"To the left, princess," Marta said, her metallic voice detached yet respectful. She knelt at the hem. "Thank you."

Delia conceded, turning on the spot. She could now see her younger sister, lounging on the chaise by the floor-to-ceiling windows, her finger scrolling across her infoscreen.

"Yes," Shania said to the screen. "No." Then she paused. "Hmm . . . maybe." Her face was serious, but Delia knew her younger sister's impish tone too well not to see through the sober countenance.

"Your interest in my torture borders on sadistic voyeurism," Delia told her. She felt Marta's hand brush against the end of her braid as she worked, her hair so long it nearly reached the floor.

"I'm researching the eligible bachelors that arrived last night . . . for your benefit, of course." Shania continued scrolling, and then her face lit up. "Oh, here's one! Prince Quinton of Rexula. He's good-looking, has a degree in biospheric chemistry, and says he's an accomplished competitor in battle ball." She giggled, then added, "I have it on good authority that all the men from Rexula are trained in the necessary skills of battle and proper conduct of the court."

Delia rolled her eyes. "Rexula has the largest supply of plasma in the Four Quadrants. It's his energy supply I'm more interested in than his battle ball skills."

Advisor Winchell stood over Shania, her braided hair tucked under her decorative headpiece of wallowing goose feathers. "Rexula is our closest planetary neighbor and largest trading partner." She then glided across the room, her richly patterned robe flowing behind her. The only noise was the tapping of her cane on the tiles.

Seeing that Advisor Winchell was about to meet her gaze, Delia dropped her eyes to study Marta, now quietly working on the side seam of her wedding gown. She winced as Marta took a straight pin and secured a bit of fabric in place. The fit became more constricting with each tiny alteration.

Shania smiled at the infoscreen. "Can you imagine?" she said dreamily. "Someone strong enough to fight, yet graceful enough to dance you around the ballroom?" She gave a lazy sigh.

"If you're so thrilled with the prospect of marrying a complete stranger," Delia said from the pedestal, "why don't you get up here and take my place?"

"I'd love to!"

"That's enough, girls." Advisor Winchell put up a hand to silence the pair. "Don't take this parade of suitors lightly. It has no more to do with love than any of the other matches I have overseen all these years."

"Strange," Shania said. "You've always struck me as a romantic, Advisor Winchell."

Delia braced for the reprimand, but their elderly mentor ignored Shania's remark and instead put her attention back on Delia. "As firstborn to the queen, you benefit from all the advantages that station in life affords. And as firstborn, you know you have . . ."

"All the responsibility that comes with that privilege," Delia finished. She knew the speech by heart. "Still, I can't help but feel as though I'm being bartered off like a secondhand droid . . . sorry, Marta. No offense intended."

The seamstress stayed quiet. The fabric tightened around Delia's chest, making it difficult to take a deep breath. Desperation came to the surface as she began an argument she knew she'd never win. "But why do I have to be married right away?" Delia asked. "Why can't I be one of the Queen's Guard for a few years, or learn to become a diplomat, or go to the university first, or why—"

"Why can't you stand still?" Marta interrupted. Delia felt the sharp poke of a pin, but she stayed silent.

The room went quiet—Marta never interrupted.

Delia's pulse picked up. Something like suspicion flashed across Advisor Winchell's face. Then it returned to its usual regal mask of appropriate apathy.

"Ouch," Delia said, flinching away from another pin stick. "A little less rough please, Marta."

"The intermittent fidgeting has caused the task to take fifteen percent more time to complete than I originally calculated."

Shania snorted from the chaise longue. "With so much mathematics inside that circuit board of yours, Marta, you'd be better suited to teaching at the university than making dresses."

"Sewing is my directive," she replied, her robotic voice never wavering.

Advisor Winchell turned to Shania, "You know very well that androids are forbidden to hold independent employment. They are here to serve us."

Delia stayed quiet. Marta couldn't feel the sharp, barbed tongue of Advisor Winchell. How ironic to have two of the most unfeeling women in the kingdom here while she prepared to wed a complete stranger.

A sudden wish for her mother overwhelmed Delia. She pictured the queen, her own long braid now highlighted with shades of gray. She was meeting with the council at this very moment. But if this arranged marriage was as important as everyone kept telling her, the queen should be here.

"When do we get to meet all the princes?" Shania asked. "I've heard all seven are already here."

"Seven," Delia repeated tiredly.

"Mm-hmm! There's Hagar from Lazlo—it's a small planet with only a handful of families, but he owns most of the waterway so he's adept at sailing. Then there are the twins, Maxim and Mikel from Tramsted, who obviously have no shame in doubling their chances. However, considering their fabulous fashion sense, they're certainly worth putting in the serious contender category."

Delia huffed, "I'm not going to marry a pair of twins!"

"Stop interrupting." Shania rolled her eyes. "You're taking all the fun out of this. Then there's Oskar from the Kalasta Belt—now, he's interesting, because he holds the record for weight lifting in all of the Four Quadrants. The problem is that his neck is quite large and it makes his head look absurdly small in comparison. Then there's Armano from Delta Kur, Felix from Trellium, and lastly, lovely Quinton." Shania sighed with a look of dreamy satisfaction. "The palace is turning into a wonderfully well-stocked man depot."

"You speak as if they're something to eat," Advisor Winchell reprimanded.

A panicked pulse quickened under Delia's skin. She was brave about sword skills and giving speeches to the leaders of the Four Quadrants—she was even brave enough to face Advisor Winchell once in a while.

But taking a husband?

Fear began to poke through her bored mask of composure. She sniffed, then mentally packaged the fear and pushed it far down, deeply hidden so no one suspected.

Shania continued, "Where are they keeping them, Advisor Winchell?" Her voice went up an octave. "And how will you ever choose, dear sister?"

"I will choose the man who will benefit Astor the—ouch!" Delia jumped to the side as if shocked. A pin was sticking out of her side. "Marta!"

Marta thrust another pin into Delia. "Sewing is my directive—my directive." She continued to stab the needle through the fabric, more roughly. There was a tear in the dress, a red spot appeared.

Shania screamed.

Advisor Winchell pressed the security button on the wall. "Droid emergency! Princess Delia's chamber!"

Delia pulled away, tripping off the pedestal.

"—my directive—my directive." Marta's voice became static; her hands clawed for the hem of the gown. Delia stared, amazed—then she remembered to scream.

Pulling her way free of the fabric, Delia dashed across the room, then subtly grabbed the satchel she'd hidden behind a chair. While everyone was watching Marta, she slipped out the side door and into the servants' corridor.

Years of playing hide-and-seek with Shania had afforded her a mental blueprint of every corner of the palace. She made it to the vertical transporter and hit the button for the landing bay.

She felt a temporary twinge of guilt about not telling Shania her plan, but her younger sister would never have been able to keep the secret to herself. The android technician dispatch team would be there soon, she reasoned. Besides, the glitch she'd programmed into Marta's SHEW had only a half-life of two minutes—barely enough time for Delia to escape.

Shaking, she opened the bag and put on the stolen uniform. The pilot's jumpsuit was several sizes too large. Her long braid bulged under the fabric at the back, but that couldn't be helped. She put on the helmet and slapped down the visor. She was one of the elite pilots of the Queen's Guard—at least for now.

The doors of the lift slid open. Shania wasn't kidding, there must be half a dozen new ships since last night.

The takeoff alarm pierced the air.

Delia hadn't anticipated another ship departing at exactly the same time she'd planned her escape. Regardless, she had to act now or she'd never have another chance.

She ran to the small Patrol ship she'd readied last night. Then she saw its back engines had already started to fire. Delia input the code for the door and jumped in, silently reprimanding herself for messing up the preflight timing so badly. In one move Delia locked the door and rushed forward to the cockpit.

"Argh!" She tripped, then fell onto something squishy.

There was a muffled cry underneath her. "Galaxy's sake!" a voice said—a male voice.

Delia pushed herself up on her elbow and stared at the stranger through the visor still obscuring her face. His eyes were wide and panicked. A bruise on his cheek added color to his pale face.

"Get off my ship!" she yelled.

He sat up so quickly it threw her off balance.

Delia was about to threaten him when the computer's soft voice announced, "Takeoff initiated."

There was a massive shudder. Then Delia and the stranger were thrown back as the ship blasted forward.

CHAPTER THREE

Aidan didn't have time to reply to the female pilot before his back rammed into something hard. The pull of gravity kept him in place as the ship powered forward. Through the windshield he saw the opening of the landing bay grow bigger at an alarming rate.

"Oh no!" The pilot jumped up and clambered her way to the control panel. She strapped herself in and started to manically press buttons and flick switches.

Just as the ship freed itself from the landing bay, there was a moment of gliding; then the nose of the craft dipped at a terrifying angle. Aidan's stomach twisted. The sky was replaced with a blur of darker colors as the ship began to plummet. He tumbled from the back of the ship, slamming into the copilot's chair. The pilot had her hands on the control stick, but she was still leaning forward.

"Pull up!" Aidan cried out. "We're going to crash!"

"Are you mad?" she asked. "Secure yourself in the chair!"

Aidan noticed her voice was laced with annoyance instead of fear. He could only stare out the window, gripping the sides of the chair to keep from falling into the front glass. They were heading straight for Black Lake, the water that surrounded the base of the palace. A crash at this speed would be like hitting steel itself.

Aidan heard his mother's voice, ". . . *always safe*."

Then at once, he was lifted as the pressure of the dive eased away. He slumped to the floor as the ship leveled off, sucking in gasps of air, amazed he was still alive.

"Secure yourself," she ordered him again. "Unless you have a death wish."

Yes, ma'am.

Shaking, Aidan crawled into the copilot's position and pulled the straps over his shoulders. He took in the scenery and was lost for words. They were barely skimming the water, a trick he wouldn't even try on his sky dodger.

His earlier panic was replaced with awe as the pilot eased up on the controls enough to slip over the embankment, clearing the high wall. Once they were over this last safety perimeter of the palace, the urban part of the kingdom came into view.

Most of the manors in this area were raised on massive stilts, creating whole new neighborhoods in the sky. He stared enviously as the ship glided over the sparkling buildings. The lush greenery of the gardens and decorative shrubs was a stark contrast to Aidan's home.

He was more familiar with the Dark District below, and its dim streets. The housing units built side by side reached for the sky—but not high enough to escape the shadow of the larger, more expensive neighborhoods above them. The kingdom was one of varying heights, built on stilts when land ran out. The higher your home, the higher your rank in society. The twin suns always shone on those at the top.

Gazing at the magnificent homes, Aidan was reminded of the incredible risk he'd taken—a lowly chore boy for the palace had no place inside a Queen's Guard ship. He snuck a peek at the pilot. Her visor was still down, but he could tell by her grip on the steering stick that she was comfortable in this machine. Still, he noticed the rise and fall of her chest, and saw she was breathing faster than him.

He cleared his throat and tried his hand at a casual tone. "My stop is coming up. Perhaps at the next clearing you can—"

An alarm sounded on the radar. The pilot cursed, something he couldn't quite make out.

"Hold on!" she said, pulling the controls sharply to the left. The ship dipped into darkness, disappearing under the broad platforms of the stately homes. The pilot twisted side to side, sending them into a dizzying slalom around the steel risers. Aidan saw on the radar that two larger ships were closing in on them.

"Hit the auxiliary jets!" she yelled at him.

The control board was massive, and nothing looked familiar to him. "What? Which button?" he said, panicked.

"The blue one!"

There was a multitude of blue buttons on the control panel in front of him. "Which blue one?"

The radar alarm continued to sound. The ships behind them were within shooting range.

"The largest one, you lunk!"

"They're all large!" Aidan made a split-second decision and slammed his fist on one of the buttons. The steel supports flew by in a rush of gray.

With a jubilant shout, she sent the ship even deeper into the shadows, closer to the land's surface. They weren't far from the Dark District. Aidan pictured them slamming into a row of greasy shacks with nothing left but a pile of smoking ash.

But the pilot adapted quickly and kept them in the air, barely missing the plasma train tracks that crisscrossed above the darkened neighborhoods. Aidan hung on to the safety straps over his shoulders. The radar became silent, proving the larger ships were unable to chase them in such a tight space. She altered the speed and soon they were gliding comfortably. The gentle hum of the cruising engines filled the space between them.

After a few heartbeats of silence she said, "Are you all right?"

"I'm not sure. Is it normal to have your stomach and heart occupying the same space in your throat?"

She made a sound of vague irritation behind her visor. Soon, the Dark District disappeared behind them. Aidan knew what came next: the tangled forest and then the canyon.

"So," she began. "What are you doing on a ship if you don't know how to fly?"

"That's classified," he said. "And I might ask why someone from the Queen's Guard is being chased by other Queen's Guards?"

She turned to him, and even though her visor was still down, he guessed she was trying to read his mind.

"I could tell by the radar," he explained. "It identified both ships." When she turned back to the window, he said, "Must be quite a scandal. I'm guessing you're flying solo as a result of your need to die in a ball of flames. Is that why you have no copilot?" The tops of the thorny trees reached up from below.

She stayed quiet.

"Nice day for a flight through the country," he said, taking in the view. "I love this ship, actually. I must look into getting one for myself." With the adrenaline kick easing away, a calmness settled inside his chest. The forest began to give way to thatch shrubbery.

Aidan noticed the speed drop. The pilot wordlessly eased them down into a rare clearing, just at the edge of the tangled wood. She pressed a button and the back hatch lifted open.

"Are we picking someone up? Maybe a long-lost copilot of yours?" He wiggled his eyebrows for effect.

She nodded to the door and then looked back at him.

"Honestly, your communication skills are holding you back," he said. "Also your need to remain anonymous is a bit troubling. Is that why you were thrown out of the Guard?" He snapped his fingers. "That's it! You have an unmistakable rebellious air about you." He dropped his voice and leaned closer. "I hope I'm right, because that makes you a whole lot more interesting."

"You talk too much," she said.

"Only when I'm right." He leaned back, gesturing at the expanse in front of them. "I can see it now. You're a flying ace who soared to the top of your class, but you can't stand the constraints of working for the queen. I get it . . . truly, I do. Must be tough living in all the sunshine and opulence."

She let out a long sigh as if weighing her next words. Finally she said, "You don't know what you're talking about. I'm not a pilot, I'm a member of the court. And even though it's none of your business, I'm hoping to avoid marriage."

"By stealing a ship?" he asked. "Sounds like you're running away."

"Not exactly, but . . . yes, in a way, I suppose."

Aidan blinked a few times, trying to digest this bombshell. The day was full of surprises. "This fellow you have to marry," he began. "Is he another member of the court?"

"He is royalty, yes."

"Is he cruel? Unbearably disgusting to look at or something?"

"No," she said, although her voice was uncertain. "I don't think so."

He tried to study her body language. It always served him well when trying to gauge which pocket to pick, but this woman was impossible to read. "Hmm . . . forced to live in luxury with someone who is neither nasty nor lowly in appearance," he said. "Yes, I can understand why you'd want to run away from that nightmare."

Her helmet mimicked a thoughtful gesture by tilting to the side. "Who are you?" she asked. "I don't recall seeing you before. How did you get access to the landing bay?"

"Sorry." He shook his head apologetically. "That's classified."

"At least six new ships arrived at the palace last night." Her posture straightened. "You were on one of them, weren't you?" She pointed her finger at him. "You're one of the princes competing for Princess Delia! How dare you carry on without telling me who you are!"

"She wishes," he snorted. Then he waved a hand at his modest outfit. The simple pants and collared jacket were hardly royal attire. Still, he silently expressed a small amount of gratitude that even though he was dressed like a palace chore boy, he wasn't covered in rubbish stains, which most days he usually was.

He pictured the prince's fancy uniform with the brass buttons, wishing he'd taken the jacket as well as the dagger.

The dagger! An idea started to form.

"You're right," he said, dipping his chin, feigning guilt. "I arrived on one of the ships last night, but as a worker, not a guest. After all, what kind of prince worth vying for our future queen wouldn't travel without his own trusted . . ." Then he paused—she said she was escaping!

"How far exactly are you planning to go in this ship?" He smiled, hoping it looked charming. "It would be a shame not to let it stretch its legs. Let's see how fast you can get this machine going! How about another planet? I'm quite handy to have around, plus I can pay you." Would she take the dagger as payment?

The pilot remained silent.

He tried another tactic. "And don't take this the wrong way, but someone traveling the galaxy alone is at risk and, if I may add, hints at unpopularity. You need protection."

"Protection?"

"Absolutely." He smiled again, putting a hand to his chest. "I come highly recommended. My family has been protecting royalty for generations." He even had a fancy dagger to prove it!

There was a gasp from behind the visor. Then she mumbled a few words under her breath that Aidan was quite certain were curses. "You're a bodyguard?"

He held up his hand as if taking an oath, pleased she'd helped him out with this brilliant lie. "One of the best in all the Four Quadrants."

"Then why are you on this ship? I'm assuming the job description of a bodyguard is to guard another body."

The smile froze on Aidan's face. He gave himself a mental slap. "Er, the truth is . . . my prince is absolutely awful. I loathe him so much I fear that I might kill him myself. In fact, he should have a bodyguard to guard him from me."

"Which prince?" The tone of her voice hinted she already knew the answer.

"I can't say," he whispered. "It's classified. Plus, I'm hoping to escape with you, so what's the difference anyway?"

"That's not going to happen," she replied smartly.

"I completely understand your hesitation," he lied. "And I promise we can talk all about it once we get to whichever planet we're escaping to." He put his attention back on the control panel. "Now, which button gets us back in the air?"

"You're not coming with me," she said. "I appreciate your situation, but I have bigger problems to deal with."

"You mean the handsome and rich fellow you're being forced to marry?"

A small nervous laugh escaped from her. "My mother would like you," she said. "She thinks I lack passion."

"I doubt anyone who's ever met you would underestimate your passion. Certainly not anyone who has ever flown with you." Then he frowned at her. "Sorry, who is your mother again?" he asked, as if he knew any women at all.

She gestured at the open door again. "You need to leave."

"You're letting me off here? This close to Pirate's Canyon?!"

"So?"

"So that means there are pirates close by." He stared back at her incredulously. "Obviously you've never encountered them. Then again, most people don't get a chance to talk about them since most of them don't survive the first encounter. Are you getting the picture? You're sending me to my death."

A bird began singing outside. "Pirates were outlawed ten years ago," she answered smartly.

"Yes, but nobody told them."

She checked the radar again. "I can't take you with me," she said, the plea in her voice obvious. "Trust me, the guards will pick up my signal soon."

Aidan weighed the danger of risking another flight with this daredevil or the wrath of what might be waiting for him back home. "Is there nothing I can say to change your mind?" he asked.

"If they catch me the penalty will be severe; however, if they catch us together—I can promise whatever punishment the queen has in store for me will be one hundred times more miserable for you."

Aidan mulled this over. Perhaps, he'd stretched all his luck for one day. At least he was out of the palace alive. He should be grateful for that. In addition, he still had the dagger to sell. Besides, this woman, whoever she was, seemed unstable and erratic, not exactly the finest qualities in the person flying the ship you're riding in.

"You've got a point," Aidan agreed, unbuckling his harness. He made his way to the back, but then paused at the doorway.

She was still strapped into the pilot's chair, but was turned around, facing him.

Without warning a sudden heaviness settled in his bones. "Will you grant me one last grace, then?"

She nodded.

He pictured himself sneaking around the palace, staying in the hiding places as he spied on grand rooms full of courtiers, eyeing jewelry and dropped coins. But if he knew this woman's name, he'd make sure not to steal from her. "Maybe tell me your name," he asked. "Or at least let me see your face?"

After a moment's hesitation, she flipped up her visor.

The dizzying trip in the ship earlier was nothing compared to the falling sensation Aidan felt as he looked into her eyes. He'd never seen her this close up before . . . and in person.

In the small cottage, directly above his cot, was an old infoscreen, battered around the edges with spiderweb-like cracks distorting the images of the daily updates from the palace. But even then, there was no mistaking the rich brown eyes and aquiline nose.

I've been riding with Princess Delia this whole time.

He bowed his head, partly in respect, but more so in embarrassment. "Beg pardon, Your Highness." In a daze, Aidan jumped out onto the soft forest floor. He backed up a few steps, staring at the ship. He had to admit, to land in such a small clearing took a considerable amount of skill. It was a shame they'd never fly together again.

A twig snapped behind him. Suddenly a massive bulk dropped onto his shoulders.

CHAPTER FOUR

Delia rolled her eyes. "Pirates," she whispered. Ridiculous.
Classified!

She should have demanded his name, or at least the name of the prince he was guarding.

Her hand was on the steering controls; one finger tapped a random beat. She thought about his expression when she revealed who she was. Unlike most of the young men in court, who were all nervous smiles and anxious grins, the bodyguard's reaction to her true identity was so quick, she was sure it was genuine surprise. But there was something else she wasn't used to seeing on all those other faces.

Regret? No, she decided. More like remorse at getting caught.

An alarm grabbed her attention. The radar showed a Queen's Guard ship with two smaller deluxe gliders approaching at full speed. Delia did a quick calculation. She had less than three minutes before her ship would be spotted.

A muffled cry came from outside. She listened carefully, then heard another.

Delia flicked on a tiny screen to her left. A monitor came alive with the outside view of the back of the ship. "Oh!" She hardly believed what she was seeing. Invisible hands pushed on her chest, squeezing tightly. Her eyes flicked to the radar showing the Guard's closing distance, then back to the image on the screen.

Letting out a frustrated growl, she unbuckled her safety straps and made her way to the back of the ship, easing the door open. *One, two, three . . .*

Delia jumped out and ran toward the trees, zeroing in on the figures locked in a battle.

A man with long hair had latched himself onto the back of the bodyguard, choking him in a tight arm hold, his face showing a bluish tinge. Delia pulled off her helmet and took aim. The man's eyes lifted to acknowledge what was about to happen a second before her helmet made contact with his nose.

With a cry, the man loosened his grip. He slumped off the bodyguard, his back thudding the ground. Writhing in the dirt, his hands covered his face as rivulets of blood spilled out between his fingers.

After catching his breath, the bodyguard straightened up, wiping the dust from himself. He looked at the bedraggled man on the ground, then back to Delia.

Although pale, he gave her a smile that looked just like Shania when she was making faces behind Advisor Winchell's back. "Is it just me, princess," he said, "or are you my worst stroke of luck?"

"You're welcome," she replied, jutting out her chin. There was a strange vibration under her skin that she found quite distracting.

"That's rich," he replied. "If you hadn't forced me out of the ship, I wouldn't have been attacked."

"If you hadn't stowed away on the ship—"

He put up a hand, interrupting her.

He interrupted me!

"Beyond my control, remember? Classified," he said. "Your argument is poor. But lucky for me, your aim is true."

His smug tone made her grit her teeth. *Foolish man!* She opened her mouth to refute, but he'd already turned his attention to the attacker on the ground.

"In all honesty, my friend," he said to the man. "That broken nose was a waste of natural beauty. I have nothing to give you."

The man pushed himself off the ground, one hand still covering his face. "You have no idea what having nothing means," he said. His voice was rough, but with an underlying weakness.

His desperation unnerved Delia. She looked up at the sky, expecting the Guard ship to appear. She pulled on the bodyguard's arm. "We have to leave."

His fair eyebrows rose and his smug smile appeared again.

A flush of embarrassment warmed her face. We? What in the galaxy was she thinking?

Without warning something slammed into her back, propelling her forward. Her cheekbone hit the ground with a hard smack. She saw a flash of blade and froze. A handful of her braid was pulled tight, wrenching her neck.

"Careful, Tomas!" the man in rags warned.

A knee dug into Delia's spine. Her eyes watered, but she kept staring at the knife. *Not my hair*, she prayed, *anything but that*.

"I . . . I don't want to hurt you," a small voice quavered behind Delia.

He's only a boy!

"We can give them her braid, right, Papa? They asked for something valuable, didn't they?" His grip was tight, but Delia could feel him start to shake. Adrenaline was like fire in her veins. *How dare they!*

She brought up her elbow, but before she could make contact with the boy, he was lifted off her back. She rolled over and jumped to her feet, hands ready for a fight.

"You squirm like a greasy eel!" the bodyguard said. He had the ragged, thin boy in a tight grip, his arms pinned at his sides. "And smell just as bad."

The knife the boy had used lay on the ground. She picked it up and rolled her eyes. It was so dull it couldn't even cut a mini cake in half.

"Please . . ." The man started to cry. He reached out, turning his palms upward in a pleading gesture. "We had no choice." The boy wiggled free from the bodyguard and ran to the man. They embraced each other, trading desperate sobs. The man looked at Delia. "I've been sanctioned to Delta Kur. We'll be separated."

Delia's heart pounded inside her chest. She wrapped her long braid around her arm several times, like she used to do as a little girl during thunderstorms. "Sanctioned? To Delta Kur?" she asked. She knew the desert planet needed workers for its factories. In exchange, her planet of Astor received free manufactured goods and parts for androids and machines. "It's almost a six-month-long trip. I thought it was volunteer."

"It is for some." The father wiped his face with a dirty sleeve, smearing the clotted blood across his cheek. Delia's stomach turned liquid. "My brother has an android shop there, he's expecting us . . . but only workers are given passage."

At this the boy clutched his father's shirt, trying to bury his face. His crying had subsided into tired sobs.

"My brother is the only family we have—the only chance Tomas has for some kind of future." The man's tears began again, but he ignored them. "He's a good worker, and he'll be stronger and a bit older when they arrive . . . but they still said no."

"Okay," the bodyguard said slowly. "So you ended up jumping at us from the trees because?"

"Protection," he replied. "The pirates said they'd take us on . . . take care of Tomas. But we had to prove ourselves first." He swallowed and held the boy close.

Delia's scalp stung from where the boy had pulled her hair. "There are no pirates on Astor," she said. "It was outlawed ten years ago."

The father stared at her as though she had two heads.

"They exist, Your Highness." Then he lowered his voice. "They're watching us right now."

Delia took a defiant stance, readying herself for another fight. "Or maybe this is just a ruse to create a diversion to escape," she said. "Or perhaps someone else will drop from a tree. Honestly, who taught you to fight that way?"

"Your critique knows no bounds," the bodyguard said. "These beggars are pleading and all you can—" A handful of earth exploded in the space between Delia and the bodyguard.

"It's them!" The father bent down, covering his son with his own frail body.

Another section of ground blew up, making Delia lose her balance. A glider screamed through the air just above their heads. She could barely believe what she saw. The driver had long blue hair and a matching beard. He gave a rebel yell as he hurled several small spheres.

"Bombs away!" The bodyguard dived at Delia, sending them rolling on the ground, arms and legs tangled together.

One of the black spheres exploded close enough for Delia to feel the heat on her back. With her breath stuck in her throat she stared into the face of the bodyguard.

"I suggest a hasty escape in our ship." He stood, pulling her up with him.

The pirate circled around again, purposely blocking their pathway to the ship.

"The trees," the bodyguard yelled as he made a grab for her arm. "It's our only option!"

Delia zeroed in on a black sphere on the ground. Ignoring the warning alarm in her head telling her to run, she went for the bomb. It was hot in her palm. Her thumb pressed into a groove on the side, and immediately it started to vibrate. The grinning maniac was nearing overhead. "Eat this, pirate!" she screamed, throwing the bomb straight at him.

The explosion was timed perfectly. The blue-haired pirate cursed and swerved so severely his glider nearly crashed into the thatch along the edge of the clearing. There was a yelp; then he disappeared into the sky, leaving behind a black plume of smoke.

The bodyguard stared at her with his mouth open. "Do you always choose certain death over the easier escape?"

"You're welcome . . . again," she said. "For a bodyguard you seem to require a lot of protection."

The father and son whimpered from the ground.

A quick-moving shadow made all four look up. Delia's heart sank as two Queen's Guard gliders circled, then swept into the clearing, kicking up dust. She shielded her face with her arm.

The guards swiftly dismounted and made their way toward her. She recognized the first man as the senior guard who had been serving her family for at least a decade. Honor kept her feet rooted to the ground.

"Colonel Yashin," she said, hoping her voice carried a fraction of her mother's commanding grace.

"Princess Delia," he replied, his tone soft, regretful almost. "I'm on orders to return you to the palace." Then he turned, momentarily distracted by the two desperate figures, still hugging each other. He motioned for them to come forward.

"Are you all right?" The second guard bowed to her. When he raised his chin, she found herself staring into a pair of handsome eyes. Upon closer inspection she noticed his uniform was different.

"Um, yes," she stammered, trying to place the man. "Forgive me," she said. "Are you part of the Queen's Guard?"

"Not for Astor," he said. "I'm from Trellium." His words were like a perfect march, never missing a beat.

With visions of the small but heavily militarized planet near the edge of the Four Quadrants, Delia figured out who he was. Since her mother had announced the arranged marriage she had been researching the potential candidates. Although, unlike her sister, she was more interested in the goods and services they were offering— not their romantic intentions. The image of the muscular prince on her infoscreen didn't quite capture the stern expression of the man in front of her. "Prince Felix," she said.

"Lieutenant Prince Felix," he corrected.

She blinked. "I'm sorry we couldn't meet under more appropriate circumstances."

"When the colonel received orders, I volunteered to come along." He nodded smartly, then clicked his boot heels. From the corner of her eye Delia saw the bodyguard step back as the father and son timidly made their way closer.

Colonel Yashin took notice as they approached, then made a face and put a gloved finger under his nose.

"Colonel," Delia said. "This boy and his father are in need of transportation to the preparation facility for Delta Kur. I will return with you to face the queen, but only after we've secured passage for both of them." Then she added, "After they've been given hot meals and comfortable clothing for the journey . . . and a bath."

She sensed his hesitation as he remained still.

"I am to be your future queen," she said. "Such a favor will be remembered—just as easily as the denial if you choose not to assist me."

The muscle tightened in his jaw, but he stayed quiet, and she knew she'd won. Delia continued, "You can pilot the Patrol ship with me and the two . . . uh, volunteers on board."

Colonel Yashin let out a long breath, then gave her a curt nod.

"Thank you," the father said to her. His dark eyes were wide and certain. "I will never forget your generosity."

"Yes," she said, dropping her gaze. Her stolen pilot's uniform felt bulky and ridiculous, as if she had been caught playing dress-up. "Make your way to the ship."

Looking mystified and in shock, the father and son followed the commander to her stolen ship.

"I'm certain the pair are in good hands with Colonel Yashin," Prince Felix said. "Perhaps you'll allow me to escort you back on the gliders, instead?" The prince's offer was graced with the curve of a smile.

Delia looked forlornly up at the horizon. Instead of escaping, she'd be returning to an irate monarch. The sense of victory from her confrontation with the colonel dissipated into heavy obligation.

However, even though she'd warned the bodyguard he'd have to face repercussions, she was unsure how her mother would react to his presence on the ship. He said it was classified. Perhaps she knew about it all along. More than once she'd told Delia that being queen meant holding many secrets.

Prince Felix stood by, waiting for her answer.

"I suppose," she replied. "But please keep in mind that my happenstance escort is not very good with machines and should ride with the colonel instead of taking the other glider on his own." She tried to hide the smile, unable to resist taking a jab at the bodyguard's flight capabilities, or rather lack thereof.

"Who, princess?"

Delia looked around and her mouth dropped open. The bodyguard was nowhere to be seen.

CHAPTER FIVE

A idan watched them from the shadows of the thick trees.

Earlier, he'd maneuvered his way to the edge of the clearing, and then while the princess was busy making swoony eyes with the young guard, Aidan had slunk to the closest glider. His own sky dodger was constantly breaking down, and since he had to rely on parts he scrounged from the picking stations to fix it himself, he was familiar with the basic circuitry of most fliers.

All it took was waiting until everyone's attention was on the father and son; then Aidan simply rearranged the thin cables of the plasma injector from the thruster and slipped back farther into the trees. It cost him a few thorns through the thin fabric of his clothes, but he had no choice. He wasn't supposed to be there and going through the forest on foot was impossible.

The glider was his only means of getting out of this mess. And even though he was at a good distance from them, he could see the older guard was strikingly similar to the one who'd almost caught him in the alcove, hiding behind the statue.

With a sudden panic, Aidan realized he still had the silver dagger—if the guard searched him it would be the end. Period.

For the second time that day, Aidan used his natural skills of stealth and blending in to avoid the palace dungeons. There was only one thing he excelled at more than pickpocketing, and that was standing still. He practically became one with the trees while Princess Delia and the young guard discovered that only one glider was working.

Although it was part of his plan, Aidan found it impossible not to roll his eyes when she slipped onto the glider behind the young guard, her hands resting on his waist as they waited to take off until the Patrol ship took flight.

When the clearing was empty at last, Aidan congratulated himself on such a fine plan. Still, a feeling of loss curiously shadowed his spirit as he reconnected the injectors to their appropriate circuits.

Mindful to stay low enough to avoid detection, Aidan steered the glider away from the clearing. Soon he had a bird's-eye view of the tangled forest, and within a few minutes, he was soaring over his favorite spot.

He dived into the deepest gorge of Pirate's Canyon. Large curving rows and furrows in the earth showed trails of the giant sandworms moving below the surface. One wrong move and he'd be a meal for the miserable gluttons. And yet, part of him was mesmerized by the patterns. He took a chance and flew as close as he dared. What's the point of having a Queen's Guard glider if you're not going to do a few stunts?

With barely a change in foot pressure, the sleek glider moved with his own actions. He wasn't flying the machine, he was feeling it. The glider represented a perfect collaboration of material and energy. And the engine was so smooth and quiet!

The euphoric sense of freedom was staggering. He slipped around and around the massive earthen columns made from centuries of wind and rain. The tight turns and dizzying speed made his stomach fall and rise.

Rise and fall.

The sand stung Aidan's face. He squinted tightly, then blinked several times, trying to clear his eyes.

What I'd give for a pair of goggles!

He dipped the nose of the machine down, putting it into a dropping spiral as he raced to the bottom of the canyon, relishing the wind in his hair.

He skimmed the surface, watching the patterns of sandworms. Then he noticed the bulge of sand in front of him. He held his breath as the meaty head of the eyeless sandworm launched out of the ground. With a victorious cry of escape, he pulled up at the last moment, just as a sandworm closed its jaws, snapping on the dust in his wake.

Aidan would never be able to achieve this velocity on his own sky dodger. There was a liberty to this moment he found addictive. He laughed out loud and immediately started to choke on a mouthful of sand. Harsh reality was always interrupting his best times. Then he thought of his best daydream.

Delta Kur.

A lifetime on a desert planet sounded perfect to him.

Live in the sun all day instead of scrounging out a life in the constant darkness of the surface?

Fine.

No insults to dodge?

Double fine.

And machines as far as the eye could see?

Even better.

Machines were less complicated than people. Machines might burn you or cut you if you didn't know how to work them properly, but they never made you feel undeserving or worthless. In all the burns and gashes he'd had while fixing his sky dodger or digging through the picking station piles, there was never any shame in that pain.

Delta Kur used to invoke a lightness in his heart about the new life it represented for him. When he'd first learned about the one-way tickets available for any citizen, he applied secretly, but he wasn't chosen.

Aidan wasn't vain, but he knew he was physically and mentally more capable than half the people who lined up with him at the application station. All of them were in similar circumstances; loners, not necessarily looking for a new home, but to escape the lack of one.

The teasing and berating from his stepfather when he'd returned that night was so severe he was completely convinced he'd never be strong enough. He pushed the dream away, tamping it down hard, like the muddied back alleys of the Dark District. But eavesdropping on the palace staff as he gathered the food scraps for the rubbish, he discovered you could buy a ticket. In that moment, Aidan resurrected the dream he'd buried, and he started using the skills he had to escape Astor.

He didn't always get a fair price from Griffin for the stolen trinkets, but his escape fund was steadily growing, and now he had the dagger. Surely that, coupled with the rest of the cash in the metal box, was enough for freedom.

Angling the glider out of the canyon, Aidan activated the hover mechanism and bobbed in the air. The twin suns were setting, creating a crimson band across the sky—the same color as the blood from the thief's nose.

He pictured Princess Delia swooping in, brandishing her helmet as a weapon.

Princess Delia saved me!

Another bout of laughter rose, but Aidan kept his lips closed this time, fearing a mouthful of sand. Then the lingering amazement of the memory faded. Who would he tell? Who would believe him?

He thought of the boy, Tomas. How he'd grabbed a fistful of her braid at the nape of her neck. The rest of her hair had been tucked inside her pilot's uniform. Her brown eyes were thick with terror. The knife was never near her throat—only her hair.

There was value in human hair. Some of the shops on the shadier end of the Dark District sold it illegally. The princess's hair would fetch an astronomical amount. But there was something else, a foggy memory from his childhood, something about the royal family. He winced as the headache began to grow in the back of his skull. He'd been able to fight off the first one, probably because of all the adrenaline—meeting a princess in disguise tends to distract from pain, he reasoned.

But with only the sunsets for company, Aidan knew this one was going to be bad. He peered over the side and down into the gorge. One of the sandworms poked its massive head out of the ground, screaming a death warning.

He ventured back to the city as darkness began to fall. Mindful of vengeful pirates who might be hiding in wait, he felt a bubble of panic build in his chest. If he was caught, they'd take his most precious possession, his mother's medallion, and then his life.

Aidan flew northeast, just skirting the edge of the tangled forest as the headache intensified. The throbbing worked its way from the back of his head to his temples. He would have to land soon or he'd crash, and well, what was the point of surviving this far into the most interesting day of his life only to end up dead in a crumpled heap?

Besides, he had to stay alive out of spite. He was certain no one would miss him or even come looking for him. And if they did, they'd probably pick the glider for parts and leave him there, thorny vines pushing up through his rib cage as the years went by.

A bitterness filled his mouth and heart. Tomas and his father were on their way to Delta Kur and a new life. The princess had granted passage to them so easily.

How stupid he was! Only at this moment did Aidan recognize that was his chance. He could have asked her to grant him the same grace.

The glider flew over the treetops, barely missing the two-foot-long thorns. A group of starlight bats momentarily blocked Aidan's way as they took to the sky, spooked by his sudden presence in their home.

The memory of Tomas and his father clinging to each other brought a punch of something else that overshadowed the bitterness. Jealousy.

He blinked hard, denying the tears and rush of self-pity. He increased the speed, inching his foot lower on the controls. Leaning into the turns, he saw the edge of the Dark District take form.

The glowing tracks of the suspended plasma trains zigzagged closer. He dropped speed and cruised just above a slick alleyway. He brought the smooth machine down, carefully tucking it in between two narrow buildings. No one would ever come looking this close to the picking stations for a Queen's Guard glider.

The headache was really threatening now. But Aidan only had to make it another block and he'd be all right. He turned the corner and focused on the sign ahead. It groaned on its rusty hinges. Although the lights were dimmed, the outline of Griffin's bony shoulders could be seen, hunched over his workbench.

Aidan tried the door, but it was locked. A strange silence followed as the headache took over. He felt his muscles go limp one by one, and then his vision went.

Blacker than her hair, he thought, amazed that he could have a concrete thought as he plunged to the earth.

CHAPTER SIX

"**I**nsolent child!" Advisor Winchell's voice reverberated off the twenty-foot-high ceilings. "Insufferable! Dim-witted!" Her cane hit the marbled floor with each exclamation mark.

Delia stood in her stolen pilot's uniform. It hung from her body like an outer layer of extra skin. Her feet were numb and her arms dangled heavy by her sides. When she and Prince Felix had returned to the palace, a senior guard escorted her directly to the throne room to see the queen. Instead, Advisor Winchell was waiting for her.

With her chin tucked in, barely lifting her eyes, Delia listened to the scathing rant as the light from the two suns moved across the throne room, marking the time.

She'd learned long ago to let Advisor Winchell finish her whole argument before coming to her own defense. No disobedience was too casual for the elderly woman's sharp tongue.

Once, when Delia and Shania had snuck into the royal kitchen after bedtime with the intent to have another slice of honey petunia cake, she had caught them on the way back to their rooms and kept them up until dawn, telling them legends of horror about disobedient children being punished by the ghosts of their ancestors.

Now, Delia stood in place, feeling like that little girl again. She watched the large patch of sun move across the floor, then up the ornate throne, hitting the inlaid crystals one by one. Rainbows momentarily painted the wall covered in portraits of past queens. As the lecture continued, their expressions seemed to warp from regal elegance to condemnatory glares.

"The entire fleet was put on alarm because of your unbridled spirit!"

Tap, went the cane.

"Your impulsivity put this whole kingdom at risk!"

Tap.

It was on the tip of Delia's tongue to mention the bodyguard and how she chose helping him over a quick escape. She was brave, not impulsive. She even gave that man and his son passage to Delta Kur.

"You may have jeopardized the marriage pact! Your lack of seriousness concerns the court! Astor may have lost its last hope!"

TAP. TAP. TAP.

"That's quite enough." A regal voice from the back of the room sliced through Advisor Winchell's last scolding. Delia's mother had finally arrived.

There was a rustling of silk and tempered footsteps. Then thin fingertips touched Delia's chin, tilting her face upward. She forced herself to meet the eyes of her mother. "I understand you've been busy this morning."

"Your Majesty," Delia said, curtsying automatically.

The light illuminated the queen's hair, picking up the few silver strands of her braid, elaborate and entwined with the crown on her head.

Delia always saw herself in her mother's face: brown skin, high forehead, and square jaw—features of a queen. But not today. The only thing reflected back to her at this moment was her mother's disappointment.

Advisor Winchell's posture stiffened as the queen floated past Delia and took her place on the throne. The room was silent; even the former queens in the portraits seemed to be holding their breath.

"Please explain your actions, daughter. I was under the assumption you understood the importance of this gathering we're hosting."

"I do, Your Majesty," Delia replied. "I have been researching suitable matches, determining which will benefit our kingdom the most—and likewise who I should avoid insulting."

"You're concerned about making enemies?" At this Queen Talia raised an eyebrow. The lines in her expression seemed more prominent than usual.

There was a sting of guilt as Delia worried about the undue stress she'd put her mother under, and thereby the kingdom.

The queen continued, "I'm impressed with your ability to look at all the consequences of each choice. However, this does not explain why you sabotaged a state-of-the-art android and stole an elite ship."

Advisor Winchell made a sound at the back of her throat. Her cane tapped on the floor, and Delia assumed she was silently hurling insulting adjectives in her mind.

"Sabotage?" Delia replied, her mouth suddenly dry. "I only put a glitch in Marta's SHEW."

"The stimulating humanoid equalizing widget is a complex piece of technology." The queen reprimanded her with each syllable. "Marta had to be shut down."

An unexpected force slammed into Delia's heart. "Shut down! You mean permanently?"

The queen nodded.

"But I programmed her to return to normal after a few minutes. Shut down? No, that doesn't make sense." She pictured the android who had been specially modified to serve as her royal first maid. She was to be with Delia forever.

Queen Talia tilted up her chin in a well-practiced move Delia had studied for years. There was an edge to her voice when she finally spoke. "It would seem you're not as proficient with her circuits as you think. She had a high-level clearance. Playing with it may have jeopardized the safety of the palace. Even though there has been no indication the resistance from the Dark District has organized itself beyond anything more than a gang of disgruntled ex-miners, we can never lessen our steadfast vigilance."

"Marta is not a spy for the resistance," Delia replied under her breath, flirting with the edge of defiance.

"Such audacity," Advisor Winchell grumbled.

"An important trait for a future leader," Queen Talia remarked.

Advisor Winchell dropped her gaze, looking to the side.

The rebuff was a small victory to Delia. Still, the guilt of Marta's fate pulled on her heart.

Queen Talia took in a long breath. "Your marriage means a great deal to our people," she said. "I thought that was clear."

"I am fully committed, Your Majesty," Delia replied truthfully. For as long as she could remember she had been groomed to take her mother's place when the queen was summoned by her ancestors. Just like all the former queens in the portraits on the walls, Delia knew she was one of many who had been born into the responsibility of taking care of Astor. "It is my duty to not only wear the crown, but to be the crown. I only thrive if the kingdom thrives."

A rare smile of approval graced her mother's features. "Our energy crisis could be solved with a marriage pact made with the prince from Rexula. I assume he's made your list of potential candidates."

"Prince Quinton," she answered. Delia pictured the blue planet, a globe of oceans separated by a scattering of islands, each one as diverse as the next. She'd gone several times with her mother on royal visits. When she returned she filled Shania's head with tales of water people and seaweed palaces, when actually it was rustic compared to Astor, rich in resources of the sea and the hearty people who lived there.

"He has," Delia started. "However, Prince Felix from Trellium offers military prowess if the resistance continues to grow."

"Hmm," the Queen commented, her tone solemn. "Both choices have something to offer. I wonder if there is a way to secure the plasma and the peace. Perhaps solving the energy crisis will remove the angry motivation of the resistance?"

"But what about the pirates?" Delia asked. "Don't we need protection from them?"

"Pirates were outlawed ten years ago," Advisor Winchell said, giving a tsk at the end of the sentence.

"Yes, but nobody told them."

Advisor Winchell gasped. "Rude!"

"Enough." Queen Talia put up a hand, a slight gesture that worked instantly at commanding attention. Delia studied her mother. Perhaps it was the change in the sunlight, but the dark circles that sometimes appeared under her mother's eyes were more pronounced.

Advisor Winchell remained quiet. Her respect for the queen outweighed any other emotion or motivation.

One day she will have to show the same respect to me, Delia thought. The notion gave her a momentary burst of confidence.

"You'll start meeting the rest of the suitors tomorrow," Queen Talia instructed. "The gliders will be at lakeside midmorning." There was a lightness in her tone that hadn't been there earlier. "While inspecting each prince, it would be prudent to take full advantage of your greatest asset."

"My intuition," Delia replied automatically.

"Which is?" her mother prompted.

"The guidance of my ancestors."

The queen smiled and closed her eyes, saying a small prayer.

Although Delia didn't want to bring up the fact it was her intuition that led her to steal the ship in the first place. Taking advantage of the queen's apparent mood shift, Delia said, "Even though the resistance is not a threat, maybe we should be concerned about people so starved they attack with dirty knives."

Queen Talia's brow furrowed. "What are you talking about?"

"And why are the rules for going to Delta Kur so strict? Why are we breaking up families for the sake of android parts?"

Advisor Winchell and the queen shared a look, and then both turned their attention to Delia. "Exactly what have you been up to?" Queen Talia asked.

Delia kept her mother's gaze, unable to let go of the image of the father and son. "Is there no way to improve our business relations with the desert planet? Delta Kur is one of our biggest trading partners, and yet we continue to exchange our people like they're slaves."

"Not slaves," her mother clarified. "Willing citizens who consider relocating a beneficial venture. And while I appreciate the intensity of your research into the political structure of the entire Four Quadrants, might I suggest an easier option to improve trading of goods rather than stealing ships."

"Yes, please, Your Majesty," Delia replied, resigned.

"Simply choose the prince from Delta Kur."

She groaned inwardly. "Prince Armano?" His profile picture on her infoscreen had showed a smiling face surrounded by an elaborate style of fair hair. Delia knew she had nothing in common with this grown man who enjoyed collecting various spaceship models and had memorized the entire nine seasons of *Comet Patrol*, a long running series featuring the antics of a security robot dog.

The queen smiled and continued, "It pleases me to hear you've been doing your research. Still, it's obvious by today's actions you need reminding that your immediate attention must be focused on securing a suitable match. It is essential you choose someone who benefits Astor without fault."

Exhaustion and frustration were closing in. Delia blurted out, "But why the rush? I'm only eighteen. I won't be required to do anything remotely important for at least—" She paused, unable to put a time limit on her mother's life.

"It is tradition." Those three words echoed forlornly through the throne room. "Marriage will secure the contract for life," Queen Talia said. Her tone hardened. "Leaving no room for negotiation."

"And consider the resulting heirs," Advisor Winchell added. "They will strengthen the bond more than any handshake between planetary leaders."

Delia was stunned to silence. Although she knew her life belonged to the crown, lately it had become all too real. First a husband and now children?

The throne room became too warm. Her cheeks began to burn just thinking about it. She imagined the safety of her suite and the comforting escape of her bed. "May I be excused to my room?" Delia asked. "I want to use any time left to study more matches."

The queen nodded.

On shaking legs Delia curtsied, then took her leave. She almost made it to the doorway before her mother's voice halted her midstride. Delia suspected she did that on purpose, as if she was on a leash.

"One last detail requires clarification," Queen Talia said. "Why steal the ship?"

Delia organized the words in her mind first, hoping the conviction in her heart would translate into sounds. "I was going to Rexula, to see if I could barter a deal for the plasma."

The queen's jaw dropped slightly. "Before you've even met Prince Quinton?"

"I wasn't going as a potential bride, but as a diplomat. I wanted to prove there was another way to save the kingdom than having to marry. I thought the risky action of stealing, or rather borrowing, an elite ship justified my actions . . . considering the potential benefit."

"A benefit that can be easily negotiated with a marriage contract," Queen Talia replied. "We do not break with tradition." She paused and narrowed her eyes. "Is that the main reason for stealing the ship?" she asked. "To barter a better trade deal?"

Delia felt the power of her mother's stare. "Yes," she lied.

"And now you fully understand why that is no longer necessary?"

"Yes, Your Majesty."

"Good, then I'll expect no further rogue maneuvers on your part."

Delia bowed her head in submissive agreement.

The queen let out a tired sigh. Then she motioned to the decorative doors that led from the throne chamber. "I suggest an early evening considering we want you at your best and most attentive tomorrow. Perhaps when you return to your room, you'll see this upcoming marriage in a different light."

Following the queen's ambiguous concluding statement, Delia left the throne room.

Unfocused on her surroundings, images of the day would not leave her alone; the thin boy, the murderous pirate, and the bodyguard with the hair so blond it was almost white.

He was unlike anyone she'd ever met. And there was an underlying wariness that she couldn't shake, a speck of doubt that clung to her clothes like the dust from the clearing.

"Is it just me, princess, or are you my worst stroke of luck?"

"More like the other way around," she mumbled to herself. If the bodyguard hadn't been on the ship, she would be on Rexula now asking for a meeting with the king. What harm could it have brought? At least she would know she'd done something to try to prevent the marriage.

Preventing the marriage, her real reason for taking the ship. She almost stopped in her tracks—she'd lied to the queen.

With her pulse quickening, Delia hurried along the corridor, praying she wouldn't run into any of her suitors on the way—then she immediately wondered which prince the bodyguard was running away from.

And where had he disappeared to?

She focused on the memory of the clearing and the last time she saw the bodyguard, slowly inching his way farther into the trees. There's no way he could have vanished! Then she practically smacked her forehead. The broken Queen's Guard glider! He sabotaged the machine on purpose!

Worst stroke of luck.

Delia gave her head a shake. How could she run a kingdom if she couldn't even manage a trip to Rexula and a runaway bodyguard?

She arrived at her room with a lingering sense of unease. Everything had been cleaned up from earlier. Even the pedestal had been removed. She pursed her lips, thinking of Marta, now destined for the scrap factory. She was the victim in this miserably failed mission. It wasn't her fault Delia had ruined her circuits.

At first she didn't see it, but the last rays of the sunsets hit the glass case at an angle, catching her eye with a glint.

Delia approached the glass case and carefully lifted the protective cover. This was the surprise her mother had waiting for her—the marriage crown.

She stared at the inlaid stones. Every crown told the tale of its wearer. This one had the stone representing her birth month; the light pink crystal was cut with precision that only an android could accomplish.

The other jewels represented her mother's birth month and the main mineral of Astor, once a plentiful resource, but now extremely rare. At one time, codlight could supply enough energy to run every machine on the planet for years, unlike the quickly depleted plasma they now relied upon.

Rexula had copious amounts of plasma.

Still wearing the pilot's uniform, Delia took the crown and made her way to the full-length mirror. Unceremoniously, she placed the crown on her head. Her neck muscles hardened as they took on the extra weight.

The reflection was the opposite of regal. Her face was smudged with dirt and there was a faint bruise on her cheek from when she'd been pushed to the ground by the young boy, Tomas.

There was a strange shiver that ran from her cheek all the way to the tips of her fingers. She pictured the bodyguard, wondering how far away he'd gotten on the glider.

Then she recalled something interesting he'd said. Only now did the vague suspicion finally clarify itself. It was the real reason he was stuck in her mind.

If he was a new visitor to Astor, how did he know about the pirates?

CHAPTER SEVEN

He dreamed of her again.

The familiar images were ticked off one by one as Aidan surfaced from unconsciousness; a strand of blond hair hung loose in front of her face, her voice was like gravel but soft. "... *always safe*," she said.

She smiled at him, warmly, protectively. There was a coolness against his palm, and then her chapped hands worked his fingers to make a fist. Her fingernails were crusted with black dirt.

The edges of the scene started to blur. He whispered a curse, knowing he'd wake soon.

Aidan blinked, and the room came into focus. He was on a floor, the smell of burnt plasma and grease filling the air. He groaned, pushing himself up to sit.

"You're a sight," a gruff voice said. There was a wet sounding cough. "I should charge you for medical attention."

"Such a philanthropist." Aidan slowly stood, wincing as he did. "I'll make sure to pass out in front of someone else's shop next time."

Griffin grunted in reply. His long gray beard nearly reached his belt. Small in stature, his head only reached Aidan's waist. However, he mostly spent the day perched on his high stool behind the shop counter, looking down on his customers.

Today was no exception. He sat there, arms folded in front of his chest, his bony elbows sticking out like bird wings. On the wall behind him, labeled drawers reached to the grimy ceiling.

Despite the dirt, the junk shop was well organized. Shelves held various items for resale; a plasma lamp, several timepieces, and various sizes of infoscreens. The more expensive items, such as jewelry, were under a locked glass case near the counter.

Aidan paused a moment to do a mental inventory. Whenever he woke from one of his blackouts his memory was hazy, jumbled up somehow. But then the images sharpened.

Princess. Braid. Pirate.

He remembered how close he had come to crashing the glider. Then he rubbed his jaw again.

Griffin noticed. "Your face hit first," he snorted. "Not that I wouldn't have enjoyed you getting lockjaw and being denied the pleasure of your snarky commentary. I can't believe you didn't lose a tooth."

Aidan's tongue worked around his mouth; everything was in place. "Pity, I imagine they might be worth something. Would you have paid me for them?" he asked.

"If your teeth were worth anything, I would have pulled them while you were knocked out."

They held each other's stare, then both chuckled.

"Here, lumpy," Griffin said, pushing a tin cup across the workbench. "That will warm your gut and put some hair on your chest."

Aidan wrapped his hands around the cup and sniffed. He nearly choked at the vapors. "I'm not sure my gut agrees, and I'm quite happy with my chest the way it is."

Griffin leaned in. "Ladies like a rugged man. Makes them feel safe."

"Is that why you have the door locked? Your gray whiskers are proving too tempting for the fairer customers of the Dark District?" Aidan took a sip of the drink. It burned his throat.

"How long?" Griffin asked. There was a softness in his voice this time.

Aidan moved along the bench, letting his fingers trace the pattern of the grain. Wood was rare these days. Most of the Jesper trees only grew on the palace grounds. "How long what?" he asked, pretending to be dumb.

"How long since the last headache?"

Taking another sip, Aidan made himself swallow the bitter liquid. "A few days," he answered, not looking at Griffin.

"That seemed like a bad one."

"Mm-hmm." Aidan took a longer sip. It slid down his throat and warmed his stomach.

Griffin made a curious noise.

"Yes," Aidan said. "The headaches are getting worse . . . just like my mom's."

"There are doctors—they cost a lot, but since your mom passed away, I bet there's new medicine . . ."

"Griff, stop it," Aidan interrupted him. "Let's at least pretend to be gentlemen and ignore my fatal diagnosis, yes? Great!" He put down the mug a little more forcefully than intended.

The infoscreen bolted to the wall crackled to life with a new announcement from the headline feed. Griffin snorted and made a face at the screen. "If this is news, then Astor is doomed. Stupid thing comes on every time someone farts in the palace. I tried to override the circuits but they control it wirelessly."

"I thought it was for protection," Aidan said. "In case there's a natural disaster or something."

"Natural disaster is right," he said as he rolled his eyes at the screen. The image of a well-dressed man with a trimmed mustache filled the screen. The information stream at the bottom stated he was Prince Quinton, one of the possible suitors for Princess Delia. It was like an advertisement, and they were selling him piece by piece.

Aidan usually ignored the mandatory bulletins, but this time he couldn't stop staring at the screen. He didn't think it was the prince he'd seen in the palace. Then his mind wandered to Princess Delia and the moment she told him she was escaping. An unexpected layer of guilt came over him. He'd left her there, knowing she was trying to leave. She would have been taken back to the palace to face the wrath of the queen.

Although, she did get on the glider and put her hands on the man's waist. "Do you think he's handsome?" Aidan asked.

"I like redheads," Griffin mumbled. Then he laughed so hard he was put into a coughing fit. He brought a cloth up to his mouth and spit.

Aidan looked away. A lifetime of working with dirty machinery had left a thickened layer inside Griffin's lungs.

A combination of digits was posted on the bottom of the screen under Prince Quinton's image. "What does the number mean?" Aidan asked.

"It's the odds," Griffin said. "People are taking bets on which one she chooses."

The background music changed with another image of the next prince in contention. His blond curls were in an elaborate style, practically shining. He was dressed in a decorative suit that would probably rival anything the princess might wear.

"Prince Armano," Griffin read. The disgust was hard to miss. "He looks useless. Delta Kur will probably be glad to be rid of him."

Aidan wished they could mute the infoscreen. "Seems stupid not to take the fella with the unending plasma supply," he said to his shoes. There was a hole in the toe of his left shoe. He wondered for a moment if the princess had noticed.

"Doesn't matter who she chooses," Griffin huffed. "It won't make much difference to us, will it? You think they'll be sending all that energy down here? I heard they're planning on shipping more of us to whatever planet the chosen prince comes from—free labor. Trying to get rid of the Dark District altogether, I bet. They'll plow down our houses and make it one huge picking station."

"Who told you this?" Aidan asked skeptically. The only people Griffin dealt with were thieves and homeless scroungers, hardly the most trustworthy sources of information.

Griffin lowered his voice even though no one else was in the shop. "They say a resistance is building. People are fed up with how we've been treated since the mines closed. First the queen blocks out our suns, and now she puts sanctions on the plasma, a little less energy every month or so."

Aidan shrugged in response. He had no hesitation in holding the royal family accountable, but his source of misfortune and misery was closer than the palace and had nothing to do with energy or the suns that crossed the Astor sky.

"I'm going to Delta Kur," Aidan said. "But as a free man."

"Congratulations. In five years? Because that's how long it will take you stealing spoons and hair clips to buy your ticket."

Aidan didn't bother to hide his smile. He reached into his pocket and pulled out the dagger, then laid it gently on the bench.

Whistling, Griffin picked up the ornate weapon. "Where did you get this?" he asked, his voice suddenly low and full of awe.

"Classified."

Pushing his eyeglasses up onto the top of his bald head, Griffin reached into a drawer and brought out a small lens. With one eye closed he used the handheld lens and closely examined the dagger. "Is it stolen?" he asked, still studying the dagger.

"Of course it's stolen. And we both know it's authentic, so stop with the drama and give me a price."

Griffin put down the eyepiece, but held on to the dagger. "Four shunkles."

A laugh escaped Aidan. "You're hilarious. If I hadn't already passed out, I'd be on the floor all over again. Wait, are you serious? Four shunkles! That's one fourth of the price it would have been worth last week."

"One eighth," he corrected. "Your practical math skills are terrible."

"Even worse." Aidan stared at the dagger. He'd placed so many hopes on this object.

Griffin put the dagger down. "There's an energy shortage. The price of plasma is going higher by the week. I have a business to run, inflation . . . you understand."

"Yes," he sighed, looking at his shoe again. Then he took the napkin ring out of his other pocket and placed it beside the dagger.

Griffin brought it to his mouth and bit down. "Solid," he said. "But only worth a koddy."

Aidan nodded.

Taking out a key from a chain attached to his belt, Griffin unlocked a compartment under the bench. There was the clink of money; then he placed five coins on the counter.

Aidan swept them off the surface into his hand. He jostled them in his palm, noting the heaviness. "At least that's four shunkles I didn't have yesterday," he said, putting the handful in his pocket.

Griffin produced a cloth and wrapped up the dagger, sliding it into one of the drawers along the wall behind him. "Your father was in earlier looking for you," he said.

"Stepfather."

"He left instructions for you to go home directly."

"Hmm, almost sounds like concern, but I'm sure it's because no one was home to make supper," Aidan said. "Or supply the stove with fuel or wash their stupid boots or service their gliders . . ."

The door opened, interrupting Aidan's speech. A gang of kids rambled in. From the dirty state of their clothes and faces, they'd been at the picking station all day. The tallest of them held an armload of parts.

"Have a dandy at this, Griff!" she said, laying her arms on the counter and letting the loot spill forth. "We figure it's the best stash yet! Maybe enough to buy a sky dodger!" The rest of the gang laughed excitedly, but as Griffin approached the collection, they all fell quiet.

Aidan frowned as he watched Griffin inspect every piece, turning it over in his hands. Whatever they thought it was worth, they were about to get the same disappointing news he'd received. One small item was a mechanical bird. The kids blinked back at him with large eyes. One boy in particular gnawed a dirty thumbnail, nervously switching his weight from one foot to the other.

Finally Griffin broke the anticipation and addressed the girl. "Nina, where did you manage to find nearly perfect parts from a Queen's Guard ship?" he asked her.

Her eyes grew even wider. Some of the others mouthed the words he'd just said. Obviously they had no idea what they'd found.

She sniffed, then ran a finger under her nose. "New spot in the picking station where all the garbage from the palace gets placed," she told him. "Only we know about it." She turned around, and they all nodded at her. When she faced Griffin again, her look of wonder had been replaced with a hesitant determination. "There's lots of shops around here that'd give good coin for this. We only came here first considering you're our favorite and all."

Aidan snorted at this.

"I appreciate that," Griffin said, keeping his voice calm. "You can have this back," he said, pushing the windup bird across the counter to them. "I'll take the rest though . . . for a koddy."

One shunkle was worth twenty koddys. Aidan felt the heartbreak on the children's faces.

Cradling the small tin bird, Nina bit her lip and took a sideways glance at the others. The sleeves of her sweater were short with frayed edges.

"He's giving you the best price," Aidan said. "Trust me, if you go to any other shop, you'll hear the same deal, or even less."

The children regarded him for a moment. Then Nina held out her hand toward Griffin. When he put the koddy in her palm, the others gathered around, staring at it as if they could wish it into something bigger.

As a somber unit they collectively made their way to the door. "Hold up," Aidan said. "How much for the bird?" he asked.

"It works," Nina said importantly. "All you do is wind it up and it will find the homing chip." Then she pulled out a small back disc from her other pocket, no bigger than a koddy. She frowned at him. "Why?"

"I just so happen to need one." Then he gave her one of his shunkles.

She stared at it, and then the others squirmed and screamed in celebration. Holding it up high, Nina ran from the shop, the rest in tow, probably worried Aidan would change his mind.

The door banged shut behind them.

Griffin gave Aidan an odd look. "You'd make a terrible junk broker.

You'd never make a profit and probably be out of business after one week."

"Lucky for me I'm adept at other talents." Aidan smiled through the ache in his jaw, then tossed the bird to him. "Keep it, then. You unfeeling old miser."

"Go home." Griffin caught the bird.

I have no home, Aidan thought.

Before he reached the door, Griffin called out, "It's broken." He laughed, then tilted his head to the side in a rare expression of sympathy. "Keep the homing chip," he said. "I'll work on this windup bird and send it to you when it's fixed. Maybe I'll send you a message from the resistance!"

"Don't take too long," Aidan said. He left before Griffin could read the look in his eyes. The tendrils of his last headache were fresh in his memory, reminding him the next one might be his last.

CHAPTER EIGHT

"**W**hy did you stop at the edge of the forest?" Shania's voice quavered with a mixture of delight and awe. She lounged across Delia's bed, wearing a billowing white nightgown and the wedding crown. She helped herself to another coconut ball from the platter of treats she'd asked the head baker to send up. The infoscreen rested on her lap, the monitor full of dress designs.

"Second thoughts, I suppose," Delia said, reaching for a sweet. She decided to keep the bodyguard a secret. There was no need to divulge his presence to Shania, someone who found keeping secrets such an impossible burden she actually got hives on her neck. "And I knew Mother would be irate if I'd actually gone to Rexula." She was still in her stolen pilot's uniform.

Delia then popped the treat in her mouth, letting it melt before chewing. "Were you worried?" she said, trying to bring a lightness to her voice. "If I didn't come back you would have had to marry one of the princes."

"I've already narrowed it down to my top picks." Shania held up the infoscreen as evidence. "I'll admit when you told me about meeting Prince Felix, I was incredibly jealous. Look at that jawline! He graduated from the military in the top two percent!" She squinted at the digital image. "Not the best teeth, but in time you wouldn't even notice anymore."

Delia leaned back on the bed. It was so big she and her sister barely touched each other.

"Who's *your* favorite so far?" Shania asked, reaching for another treat. "Oh, wait, you're going for more of a strategic choice rather than who will give you better-looking children, aren't you?"

"Children." Delia closed her eyes. An overwhelming wave of fear settled in her chest. "No, I have no favorite based on my research."

"Hmm, which one keeps popping up in your thoughts?" Shania was determined to get a name out of her sister.

An image of the bodyguard smirking from the copilot seat came to Delia. "I can't give you a name," she answered with a yawn.

"Don't get all sleepy on me. I want to talk!" Shania poked her sister with the toe of her silk slipper. "When Winnie found out you'd taken a ship, the feathers on her headdress almost caught fire she was so mad!"

Despite the melancholy grip on her heart, Delia smiled at the mention of the nickname for Advisor Winchell. "I do regret not being able to see that."

A plasma lamp glowed beside the bed, reflected in the floor-to-ceiling windows of her chamber. Delia tried to imagine the panic from the earlier scene with the wedding dress fitting. "Was it bad?" she asked. "With Marta, I mean."

"Mmm." Shania swallowed, then smacked her lips a few times. "Marta was stabbing the floor with the needle over and over again. I thought Winnie was going to hit her with her cane for galaxy's sake! Head of Security had to come." She licked her fingertips before choosing another sweet. "Although, that Colonel Yashin is lovely to look at, so that was a nice consequence."

"He's twenty years older than you."

Shania laughed. "Yes, and I hope my husband will be as handsome and strong when he's that old."

"And they had to take her away?"

Shania's attention went back to the infoscreen. "Who? Winnie?"

"No," Delia groaned impatiently. "Marta. Mother told me she was ruined. That she was permanently broken." She imagined the lower level of the palace, the darkened storage area for items waiting to be shipped to the picking stations. Picturing Marta in her smart uniform and prim posture seemed cruel. Delia looked at her younger sister, hoping for some kind of reprieve.

Shania glanced up from the fashion shots. "Why do you even care?" she asked.

Delia tried to organize her thoughts; something didn't make sense. When she spoke again there was a heaviness to her tone. "Even though she's not real, it's my fault she's being thrown out. I need to be responsible."

"Oh, really?" Shania laughed. "Did you fill up the ship you stole with plasma before you brought it back? Because that would have been responsible."

"Funny," Delia replied grimly.

Shania began typing words into the search field. Then her eyes widened and dimples appeared on her cheeks. "Prince Quinton is in the lead with the oddsmakers. And, may I add, he has perfect teeth."

Delia marveled at how opposite she and her sister were. Shania was robust and vivacious, full of laughter. She delighted in wearing gowns and trying new styles of braids. "If only our positions were exchangeable, then I wouldn't have reworked Marta's SHEW," she said. "And you'd be happily sneaking into Prince Quinton's chamber."

Shania squealed, unabashed. "I wonder if it's in bad taste to swoon over my future brother-in-law."

Reluctantly, Delia took in his image. Strong forehead, trimmed beard. "He has a kind face," she said.

"I wonder if there are any digital snaps of him in swimming attire or . . . oh my," she paused. "Someone works out."

Delia huffed. "Yes, he's gorgeous, I understand. Here," she said, clearing the screen. "See if there's mention of a bodyguard."

"For Prince Quinton?"

"For all of them."

"Oh! More men!" Shania said, typing quickly. Then her face darkened. "Nope. Nothing comes up. There's only a profile on the princes, not their entourage. I'll keep checking though, I know everyone has to be cleared with security." She looked up at her sister. "Why are you interested in bodyguards? What is it? Your face has a weird expression."

It's classified.

An embarrassed blush warmed her cheeks. Why was she interested? "Honestly," Delia said as she snatched the wedding crown off her younger sister's head. "I'll be your queen someday so you should get used to not asking me so many questions."

Her pulse kicked up a beat. *And not only that*, she continued in her mind, *he refused to answer me . . . twice!* Chivalry was not a prerequisite for bodyguards, apparently.

Restless, she went to the long windows that lined the south wall of her chamber, giving her an uninterrupted view of the kingdom. Instead, Delia looked up at the night sky. "The man in the moon," she whispered, thinking of the legend of her people and her own part in the legacy. It was her heritage, her birthright—her honor and her punishment. The price of having a childhood of opulence.

The moon shone down on her and with it she felt the judgment of her ancestors, as if they knew she secretly dreamed of a day when marriage would be for love and not duty. Her shoulders slumped. *I should be braver*, she thought.

Delia wrapped her long braid around her arm, then caressed her cheek with the end. The comforting gesture from her childhood did little to ease the guilt. An image of her mother's tired expression needled at her conscience. Delia tried to remember the last time they had to put an android down . . . she couldn't. Her mother was keeping something from her.

"I must find out the truth," she said.

When she turned around, Shania was snoring, the infoscreen discarded on the pillow beside her. The image of Prince Quinton was frozen in a smile.

Being careful not to wake her sister, Delia picked up her own infoscreen and took the vertical transporter to the storage level. She knew she couldn't involve the royal technicians. This was something she had to find out for herself.

With a palace full of royal suitors to appease and guard, there was no risk of bumping into security personnel down here. She slipped into the large containment area and followed the markings toward the android section.

As she turned the corner her heart almost stopped. There was Marta, her diligent and faithful maid, tilted back against the wall, already tagged for disposal. The unanimated pose to her face was unsettling. She had to remind herself Marta wasn't real. Still, there was an absence of something that had nothing to do with circuits or plasma energy.

As she'd learned in android tech class, Delia pressed her finger against the square outline just below Marta's right ear. She heard a click and opened the tiny compartment, exposing the SHEW.

With a quick look around to make sure she was still alone, Delia took the SHEW and inserted the tiny chip into her infoscreen. She accessed the program she'd designed to implant the glitch. Delia wasn't sure what she would find, but she couldn't help but feel that she was on the cusp of a major discovery.

As numbers cascaded down in patterns, Delia soon discovered nothing was wrong with Marta. The glitch she'd planted had expired, just like she'd programmed.

There was nothing wrong with Marta!

Frustrated, Delia pulled out the chip and slipped it into the pocket of her pilot's uniform. Was her mother lying to her on purpose, or had she been given the wrong information? Then there was the issue with the pirates. If Delia hadn't seen one with her own eyes today, she wouldn't think they existed anymore—but the bodyguard had known.

She pictured him escaping on the glider—the Queen's Guard glider!

A rush of anticipation made her slightly dizzy as she accessed another program on her infoscreen. As part of her training, Delia had to memorize everything about the Queen's Guard. She'd found it tedious because she mostly wanted to learn how to sword fight, but at this moment she was extremely grateful for having remembered that every glider was equipped with a locating chip.

Delia entered her security clearance and started the sweep. If the glider was on Astor, it would show up. A map of her planet filled the screen. She knew the geography by heart. The large glaciers to the north cut rivers through the mountains; then the earth dipped past the tangled forests and then to the lowest section, where the mines used to be, which was now the Dark District. Beyond that was the canyon, and beyond that was the vast southern tundra.

Multiple dots filled the screen. Most of the gliders were in the landing bay, and a few were on the perimeter, nothing odd about that.

But when she used her finger to zoom in on a lone dot apart from the others, she discovered it wasn't in the clearing where she'd last seen it.

"Gotcha." She smiled, taking note of the coordinates at the edge of the Dark District. If the bodyguard wouldn't come to her, she'd go to him.

CHAPTER NINE

Although his jaw was still aching, Aidan smiled through the pain as he flew the glider from Griffin's shop. Flying was the one thing that gave him joy, made him feel free. The night air blew through his hair, and he imagined utopia as a place where he could fly all day.

Even though it was a risk to be seen in such a highly visible machine, he knew from experience not many people bothered looking up in the Dark District. When there were only the zigzag patterns of the plasma trains instead of stars, what was the point?

He kept a moderate altitude, knowing the quiet engine wouldn't alert anyone below. In this section, shops like Griffin's composed most of the area surrounding the picking stations, but soon the apartment complexes filled the space below him. At one time the tall structures had rooftop gardens, lush and plentiful, but once the law to build on stilts was passed, the private landowners built their luxury homes higher and higher. With the platforms becoming more massive, blocking out the midday suns entirely, the gardens eventually suffered.

Now, all Aidan could make out on the rooftops were dilapidated structures that might once have been raised vegetable beds. The windows were nearly all darkened except for the occasional faint glow of a plasma lamp. The sides of the apartment buildings, however, were brightly lit. Large infoscreens were part of the structure, built decades ago when the miners lived here. They had once been used to advertise goods and services, but now they were purely sanctioned by the newsfeed for updates—just like the smaller infoscreens in every home.

Because of the lack of plasma though, the screens only lit up when there was an update.

Aidan made a face as an eight-foot-tall image of the prince with curly blond hair came up on the screen. From the numbers on the bottom, it seemed his rank had improved by a few points. He wondered for a moment how often they updated the odds and who decided which prince was more favorable. The screen went blank, taking its illumination.

A curious sensation pulled on his stomach. He leaned harder into a turn and increased his speed, slipping through the rows of buildings like he was flying around the columns of the canyon.

With the apartments behind him, he saw the smaller dwellings come into view, the simple cottages that bordered the Dark District before the mountain started.

Although almost always in darkness, Aidan's address was considered a more favorable part of the city. His stepfather's position in the Queen's Guard warranted the closer proximity to the palace.

Easing off the speed, Aidan brought the glider to an effortless landing just behind the house, close to where his own sky dodger was kept. Two expensive gliders were there as well, although not parked properly and full of dirt and grime.

A knot twisted between his shoulder blades, knowing how much cleaning he'd have to do to them tonight. By contrast his own sky dodger was in pristine condition. He removed the tarp from his machine and used it to completely cover the Queen's Guard glider. No one would guess royal transport was under the stained and cheap-looking fabric.

He gave the superior machine a small pat, knowing how much it would pain him to dismantle the glider tomorrow. Even with Griff's plummeting prices, selling the parts off one by one would make up for the loss of the dagger and be a substantial addition to his Delta Kur fund. Yet dreams of taking it around Pirate's Canyon a few more times tugged on his heart.

Dragging his feet, Aidan entered through the back door. In the vestibule was his modest bed, and tucked under that was his trunk. A shelf over his cot housed a collection of trinkets Griffin had no interest in. There was a rolled-up page from a book of poems, a rusted key, part of a chain that broke off someone's necklace, and several small glass spheres that had been used in a garden game and left behind one rainy afternoon. He put the homing disc on the shelf.

At the end of the hallway a door led to the kitchen and the upper apartment where his stepfather and stepbrothers lived. Muffled conversation came from the front of the house.

Slowly, he opened the trunk. Pushing aside his other work clothes he unlatched the false bottom. A Queen's Guard uniform, his father's uniform, with its tarnished silver buttons and medal of bravery, was neatly folded. Other than his mother's medallion, it was his most prized possession. His father never had the chance to wear the medal; it had been given to his mother after his death. Aidan had tried the uniform on once, but it was too big. He had no pictures or memories of his father, but he was certain that he had been a tall and robust man.

Aidan then lifted the uniform to reveal the metal box. He reached into his pocket and took out the four coins. There was a roar of laughter from the front room, making him freeze. The only reason he'd been able to save any money at all was because his stepfather and stepbrothers were completely unaware of its existence.

Knowing he might be discovered at any moment, he quickly opened the lid to put today's earnings safely away.

The box was completely empty.

Aidan hoped he was dreaming. He'd been saving for what seemed like an eternity. All those close calls, all that haggling with Griffin. And now with the latest inflation, it would take him years to accumulate the same amount. And by that time, he'd need ten times the money to buy a ticket to Delta Kur.

The laughter was closer this time. Aidan looked up and saw his stepfather watching him from the doorway.

"Where've you been?" his stepfather asked. He'd already changed out of his Guard's uniform and was in his loose pants and top. A stomach bulged over the belt. "Supper is late."

You stole from me! Aidan wanted to scream the words, throw them in his stepfather's face, but they only echoed inside his mind. For as long as he could remember his stepfather had two moods; neglectful or harassing. If he wasn't pretending Aidan was a ghost, he was ordering him around like a lowly servant. Actually worse than a servant, more like a servant's servant. Which, when he thought about it, he was.

After his mother died, it seemed to become official, and Aidan moved to the back room, separating himself from his stepfamily as much as he could. He had learned that being a ghost in this house was far better than getting blamed for everything.

Aidan held out the empty box. "The money?" he said, his voice brittle.

"Oh, that," his stepfather said. "I hope this teaches you not to hide money from us. Drake needed new clothes and Morgan had to get a special circuit board or something for a broken infoscreen he's working on. Plus, you didn't leave any money for the butcher. We need to eat, don't we?" Then he sucked on his front teeth. A crumb was trapped in his bushy beard.

Aidan couldn't stop looking at the crumb.

"You heard me," he said. "Supper is late."

"Yes," Aidan responded, the coins still clutched in his fist.

"Yes, what?"

"Yes, Corporal Langdon."

His stepfather insisted Aidan call him by rank. Although Aidan suspected he'd never actually made it past cadet. He'd never heard anyone speak of him at the palace as corporal, but then again, the person in charge of the royal gardens didn't need an official title.

"I'm starving!" Drake hollered from the front room. "There's nothing to eat."

"What have I said about yelling in the house?" Corporal Langdon yelled back. Then he put his attention back on Aidan. "I'll take what's in your hand as well. Drake has a running tab at the pub and they won't serve him until he pays up."

Then he should get his lazy ass a job and pay up with his own money.

Aidan glowered as he silently handed over the money, numb and hopeless.

Even as the words were on the tip of his tongue at the unfairness of it all, there was something blocking him, making him compliant with whatever they asked. It wasn't as if his stepfamily ever threatened him with violence—on the contrary, they rarely touched him and always seemed to give him a wide berth. Aidan went about his tasks in the house living two lives; the one in his head where he replied with every smart answer he thought of, and the real one, where he stayed quiet and did what he was told.

Moving to the kitchen, Aidan began to prepare supper. Within no time the cottage was filled with a tangy aroma. He poured the stew into three bowls, his mouth watering at the scent of the jaggle spice he'd picked up a few weeks ago from the royal kitchen. He served his stepfather and stepbrothers, then placed the bread on the table and filled their steins.

Without a thank-you, his stepfather began to slurp his soup. "After the robbery I was the one called to keep the area secure," he said.

Aidan turned to the stove, gripping the serving spoon, irritated at the obvious lie.

"Security was desperate to remedy the situation. I can only imagine how upsetting it must have been to invite all those important princes and then have a thief steal one of their heirlooms." He shuddered. "So embarrassing."

Aidan faced them. "Which prince?"

At the sound of his voice, all three paused. Drake pushed back his broad shoulders. He had a look of disgust on his face. "Like you'd know any," he said. His thick brows came together.

Morgan, a smaller version of his brother, looked at his bowl. He spent most of his days in the basement, tinkering with broken machines people brought to him. It was similar to Griffin's shop except he charged for repairs, while Griffin just bought items to resell. His blackened fingernails were evidence of this, but Aidan had never seen anything come out of the basement. He imagined the space under their house as a graveyard of useless machines, stacked one on top of the other.

Corporal Langdon cleared his throat. "The prince is a special guest, an important one," he said to his sons rather than Aidan. "I've been personally reassigned to guard that part of the east wing." Then he winked across the table at his eldest son. "That means my position in the garden is available for you."

Drake dipped a chunk of bread into his soup. "Guarding the gardens is stupid. I want to be a Queen's Guard."

The corporal brought down a fist on the table. "No one in this house will ever speak disrespectfully of the palace and certainly not the royal gardens!"

Drake said nothing, but the pout stayed on his face.

Morgan watched the scene from beneath his eyelashes.

He cleared his throat. "And as you know," the corporal continued smoothly, "that part of the east wing is especially important because of its close proximity to the royal library. No one is allowed inside without the proper credentials."

"Who cares about books?" Drake sighed.

Aidan couldn't help but roll his eyes. He froze when he saw Morgan had caught him. But then the younger brother gave him a half smile. It was a rare show of comaraderie.

Excusing himself, Aidan gathered his own meager meal of a hard biscuit and small tin of preserves. He escaped to his room, turned on the small plasma lamp attached to the wall, and opened the tin. Using the spoon, he spread a thin layer of red paste onto the dry biscuit.

Then he paused. There on the shelf, perched beside the homing disc, was the windup bird. "How did you get inside?" he whispered. Then a breeze brought his attention to a broken windowpane in the door. "Oh."

Aidan put down his food and picked up the bird. After getting pecked a few times, he discovered he had to stroke the beak to get it to stop.

A small compartment opened, and a rolled note fell out. Griffin's scrawling block letters filled the page.

DAGGER HAD MICROCHIP

MEET ME AT MY SHOP 2AM

DON'T TELL YOUR FATHER

Aidan was certain Griffin had no sense of humor. And he was especially certain his stepfather had no time or interest to play an elaborate joke on him.

With a wary glance down the hallway to the front room, Aidan slipped the note into his pocket. His stomach made a pitiful sound.

Forgetting about the dagger for a moment, he finished his meal in a few bites, washing down the crumbs with a can of bitter water from the tap. With all that his body had endured today, the small snack was enough to give him the illusion of a full stomach, and his eyelids grew heavy.

Lying back, he closed his eyes.

Without warning, an image of the princess sitting down to a lavish banquet interrupted his thoughts. She was probably surrounded by well-dressed suitors bestowing precious gifts. He let out a huff, certain the princess was not thinking about him at this moment. She was preparing to pick a husband.

She was preparing to pick a husband.

"As if I give a galaxy's sake who she spends her wedding night with," he whispered in the dark. There was a dryness in his throat as the heat rose to his face. He rolled onto his side. The painful throb from his jaw wiped away any thoughts of Princess Delia and her wedding night. He drifted off, no longer able to keep the exhaustion from pulling him into sleep.

✳ ✳ ✳

A loud rapping woke him. Aidan blinked a few times, the sleep clinging heavily to his brain. Someone was at the door. The outdoor plasma light detected motion and lit enough of the area so that he could make out her features.

Princess Delia!

He sat up as if shocked. The cloud of confusion lifted, only to be replaced with a sudden panic.

There was another impatient rapping.

Certain she'd figured out his true identity, Aidan feared there was a swarm of the Queen's Guard surrounding the cottage. Not only had he stolen a dagger and a deluxe glider, but he'd also lied to royalty, and if he wasn't mistaken, those offenses would land him in the dungeons.

The princess rapped again and said, "I can see you! Open up . . . please!"

There was a panic to her voice. *Not exactly the kind of tone you'd expect from someone who was about to arrest you*, Aidan thought.

Certain her noise would wake his stepfather, Aidan opened the door and stepped outside, making sure to keep her out of the cottage. "Why are you here?" he whispered.

She hit him with a stare that rooted his feet to the ground. "We have to talk," she said.

CHAPTER TEN

Why are you here?

Delia didn't quite understand it herself. How could she explain that her instinct had sent her to him tonight?

Even as she had stolen—borrowed—a Queen's Guard glider and slipped away from the palace intent on finding the bodyguard again, she wasn't exactly prepared for this part. Although he owed her answers, standing here in front of him she oddly felt at a disadvantage.

"How did you find me?" he asked. "Wait, were you actually looking for me? On purpose?" A half grin slipped into place. "I don't want to point out the obvious, but the kingdom is placing bets on your future husband, and if I'm not mistaken, I'm not on that list."

His cheeky attitude wiped away any lingering nerves she had. "After your disappearance this afternoon, I activated the signal chip built into the glider you stole. It led me here."

He glanced over her shoulder at the Queen's Guard glider she'd just landed. "Two escapes in one day?" He grinned. "Are you sure you want to be queen?"

"Neither was an escape, more like leaving without telling anyone. And alarms don't go off when someone takes a glider. I'll never be missed." Delia looked around the sparse yard and small cottage. "Why are you here? Aren't you supposed to be guarding your prince?"

"I have a few contacts in this area. The cottage belongs to a palace guard, and I'm staying here to keep a close eye on my prince." Then he lowered his voice. "He has a bit of a gambling problem and likes to frequent the rougher pubs in this part of the neighborhood."

"That seems very unorthodox."

"What can I say? He's a lunk."

"You have contacts on Astor? Is that how you knew about the pirates even though you're not from here?"

A flash of what looked like shock crossed his features, but then a smooth smile slid into place. "Yes, but I also believe in thorough research. When I found out my prince was coming here, I started reading about Astor."

Delia regarded him for a moment. She felt entirely safe, but there was something about him that triggered a suspicious notion at the back of her mind. "You sabotaged the glider in the clearing today."

"True," he answered. "I wasn't supposed to be with you, remember? I hid and secured an escape for your benefit as much as mine." Then he looked up at the sky. "So, you're not here to arrest me?"

"No," she said indignantly. "I would have sent the Guard if that were the case. I simply had to see the Dark District for myself."

He frowned at her.

Delia wasn't sure if it was the dull plasma light overhead or that she'd never looked at him this closely, but she hadn't noticed the unique shade of his eyes. They were practically crystal, but colored underneath, like when the lake was frozen but she could still see the fish swim below.

"You had to see the Dark District?" he repeated with a confused edge to his voice. "Why? Thinking of honeymooning here?"

His answer lit a fire of frustration inside her. "It's a delicate matter," she said, not bothering to keep the annoyance from her voice.

"Shh," he said, turning around and looking at the cottage. "You'll wake the neighborhood." He motioned for her to follow him to the edge of the property, closer to the trees and away from the light.

Delia walked after him, dumbfounded. She wasn't used to being interrupted. He waited for her in the shadows. With an odd skip of her heartbeat, Delia leaned closer to him. "I need someone who won't have a conflict of interest," she said. "Someone from the outside."

The air between them stilled. "What do you need?" he asked, then added, "Princess."

There was something in his voice that bordered on curious teasing. She let out a sigh, but it was more of relief than exasperation. His carefree attitude lessened the heaviness of her fears. "It's actually because of this," she said, pulling Marta's chip from her pocket. "It belonged to my android maid. It's a SHEW."

He leaned down, squinting at her palm. "A what?" he asked.

"A stimulating humanoid equalizing widget. It's the programming that gave her human characteristics. Usually androids don't blink or use conjunctions or have any other quirks . . . but Marta did. It made her seem more real." An image of Marta propped against the wall, tagged for the picking stations, hit her unexpectedly. "She is, or rather *was*, a special android. One of the most advanced ever made." Delia swallowed, then added, "She was specifically programmed to serve me forever."

"Forever?" he raised an eyebrow. "Lucky her."

Delia cleared her throat, then explained how she'd programmed a glitch into the SHEW to create a diversion to take the ship. "But because of my actions, my mother said she was damaged beyond repair and that she posed a risk to the security of the palace. But as you can see, her stimulating humanoid equalizing widget is intact."

"Of course," he said. "Anyone looking at this minuscule chip would be able to tell that."

Delia huffed at his attitude. She put the chip away. "Well, I know it works. So that means someone is either lying to my mother, or she knows something and is choosing to lie to me."

He seemed to consider what she was telling him; then he reached up and rubbed his jaw. "If you're right about the SHEW, someone is definitely lying. So maybe instead of wondering why, you should be concentrating on who."

"I never thought of that," she said. A whole new layer of worry settled on her shoulders.

The bodyguard stayed quiet, and Delia wondered if she'd told him too much. Coming here had felt like the right thing to do, but now she was starting to have second thoughts.

He looked at the sky again.

"Are you waiting for someone?" she asked. It bothered her more than she cared to admit that she had to work to keep his attention.

"Certainly not brushing up on my astronomy," he said. "Actually, if you really must know, I'm not quite convinced that you're here purely to pick my brain about the suspicious goings-on at the palace. I'm still waiting for a troop of Queen's Guard to swoop down."

She stood a little taller. "I'm here by myself."

A dimple appeared on his right cheek. "Not even a patrol circling above?"

"No, just me," she answered. A small thrill had started with the realization that she was breaking the very promise she'd made to her mother earlier. Sneaking out of the palace to meet a strange boy definitely fit the description of "rogue."

"By yourself? In the Dark District? At night?" His pitch kept going higher. "Are you sure it's safe?"

Despite the situation, she laughed at him. "If I remember correctly, I was the one who saved you from the pirate this afternoon."

"True. How did you put it again?" Then he snapped his fingers. "Yes, now I remember, you threw the bomb and yelled, 'Eat this, pirate.' Tell me," he dropped his voice. "Does the grace come naturally or was that something they had to teach you at the palace?" There was an underlying mischievousness to his words that made her want to smile, but she dared not give him the satisfaction.

She had the impression he was toying with her, and her instinct was pushing her to start firing questions. "What else can you tell me about the pirates? Are they part of the resistance?"

"Resistance? How would I know anything about that?" His voice was light, but his gaze flicked to the cottage, then to the sky, then back to her.

"We can stop with the charade. You obviously have access to information that I don't. And considering I'm going to be ruling this planet someday, that makes me very uneasy." She stiffened her resolve and forced herself to stare back.

Delia sensed she'd gotten the upper hand when his smug expression eased into a tired acceptance. He nodded. Her heart quickened, certain he was about to give her all the answers.

Looking down, he started to play with the top button of his simple shirt. "I suppose that means you really aren't here to trick me into following you back to the palace as a willing prisoner. Don't you get special royalty points for that kind of thing?"

"Why must you be so tediously ridiculous? I'm here because I'm desperate for answers. If there's anything you know, you need to tell me. I'm getting ready to choose a husband, but not for myself, for Astor." She took a few breaths; those few sentences seemed to take the last bit of energy she had.

The bodyguard studied her so intently she wondered if he was trying to read her mind.

"Your face," he said, reaching out. "It's bruised." His fingertips grazed her cheek. A crash from the cottage made them both jump apart.

The bodyguard's eyes grew wide.

"Is it your prince?" she asked, keeping her voice low.

He only shook his head, but Delia noticed the dramatic alertness that lit his features.

"What's his name?" she needled. Then she added in a more casual tone, "I just want to make sure I don't choose him, considering he's a lunk."

He snorted and the easygoing countenance slipped back in place. "If you choose him of your own accord, your brain damage is beyond repair and I'm sure you'd make another disastrous decision and finish off Astor by blowing it up."

Although it was said in jest, the very real fact that she had the welfare of Astor in her hands made the moment somber.

"Sorry," he apologized quickly. Then he looked back at the cottage again. "It's not safe here, even for a bomb-throwing princess. You should at least wear a disguise—that pilot's uniform isn't fooling anyone."

"I will be queen one day, so I should be able to go anywhere in my kingdom. Are you saying I'm not welcome here?" Then she reached out and touched his arm. "Please, you seem like someone who is part of both worlds. I need someone like you to help me." She took a few deep breaths, and then the scariest notion hit her. "It seems the people I've been trusting aren't exactly truthful, or they themselves are being lied to."

"I . . . I have some connections. I'll see what I can do."

"Thank you!" She nearly hugged him.

He took a step back, sheepishly running a hand through his blond hair.

Delia made her way to the glider and picked up the helmet.

"Wait," he said. She watched as he slipped back into the cottage, then returned to her with something in his hand. "If I do hear anything," he said, "I'll deliver a message to you."

Intrigued, Delia watched as he opened his hand and showed her a mechanical bird. She lifted an eyebrow. "A bird?" she said, not bothering to hold back her sarcasm.

"Yes, excellent observation, princess. I was worried you would mistake it for a dragon."

"How is a toy going to help?" she asked.

"This is no ordinary toy." The bodyguard held the windup bird in his palm like it was real. "This bird will find you," he continued. Then he gave her a small black disc, explaining it was the homing beacon. "I'll put the message on a microchip and place it in the storage vessel inside his chest." Then he added, "Anyone who knows how to reprogram a SHEW should have no problem dealing with that."

The compliment took her by surprise. "Thank you," she said. She mounted the glider, then slipped on her helmet, flipping up the visor. "If you're ever in need of other clothes, there's a room on the main level near the back by the kitchen where the seamstresses work. It has all kinds of uniforms of various sizes." She looked him up and down. "Perhaps you should consider a jacket or better-fitting trousers."

"You don't like my servant's attire?" He pulled the collar of his shirt. "While I appreciate your interest, I'm afraid my prince likes to look better than anyone else around him, so I can't show up all dashing and refined."

"Really? What does he look like?"

"Hard to say since I hate him. You might find him handsome though."

Delia stayed quiet, trying to reconcile everything she knew about the bodyguard. Under the simple shirt and pants she could tell his physique was one that suggested good health.

"You're staring." He smiled.

Delia stammered, "Like I said, consider adding a few garments to your wardrobe. If you're going to be around nobility, you'll need to blend in—something your vain prince will appreciate."

"And why do I need to be with the nobility?"

"Because that's where I'll be." Delia slapped down the visor and started the glider. The engine quietly powered up beneath her. Her earlier doubt had left her with a sore ego. She needed to make herself appear more regal, more dominating. "I'll be expecting your mechanical bird no later than tomorrow evening," she ordered. "With any information you gather."

He nodded as an answer, but it was obvious his attention was on the glider—not her regal power.

"And it's essential it stays our secret," she added.

Focusing back on her he said, "Of course."

She took in his full image. At first he had been jittery and unsure, almost afraid, but now a cavalier attitude seemed to be lingering beneath the wiry frame and blond hair.

She took off, sending the glider upward. When she cleared the rooftop, Delia was tempted to glance over her shoulder to see if he was still watching her, but she fought the urge and instead concentrated on what lay ahead.

By the time she'd snuck back into the palace, Delia was exhausted. She eased her way through the kitchen, making sure to take the servants' lift, then collapsed with relief in her own chamber.

Shania had gone back to her own room, but left behind her list of princes. Beside each name she had categories labeled: best smile, most handsome figure, strongest, best singing voice, and then, fullest lips for kissing.

Delia put down the list and stared at her bed—the bed she would share with whoever she chose.

It was the one truth she never shared with anyone, not even her sister. While the entire kingdom was obsessed over her marriage, Delia knew there was one area Advisor Winchell, all of her tutors, and even her mother had neglected.

Because even though she'd been trained since childhood to be queen, no one had told her anything about being a wife.

CHAPTER ELEVEN

A idan held his breath, watching her go higher into the sky, away from the surface, away from him and all this darkness. Was it his imagination or did she glance back just before she cleared the plasma trains?

His fingertips still had the memory of touching her cheek. He didn't realize she'd been hurt. It must have happened when the boy jumped on her back, sending them both to the hard earth. She'd barely even flinched, like it happened every day.

I touched Princess Delia!

Had he lost all reason? He'd seen how lightning fast her reflexes were. She could have broken his arm if she wanted. Then the reality of what he'd promised her hit him hard. "Oh, for galaxy's sake," he whispered.

He made his way back to the cottage, hands in his pockets. His fingers found the windup bird. He almost smacked himself in the face; he'd completely forgotten about Griffin's message.

Whatever was on the microchip was potentially scandalous at the least. He placed the bird in his pocket as he readied his sky dodger, his mind forming theories, each more ludicrously satisfying than the last.

The royal palace is actually being run by droids, including the queen.

An asteroid is due to hit Astor in two weeks, but there isn't a plan to save anyone, so they'll all die unaware.

There is a document from the original settlers from hundreds of years ago with a map to a secret world within the great mountain.

Aidan checked the time and realized he was due at the junk shop. He started his sky dodger, noting the plume of smoke on takeoff. Taking his machine higher, he made the return trip deeper into the Dark District, still wondering if he was about to be the victim of an elaborate joke.

Griffin came to the door, out of breath and pale as the moon. His gaze seemed wild.

"Are you alone?" Despite his small stature, Griffin roughly pulled him inside. The entire shop was dark. The only light was from the infoscreen, throwing shadows over the shelves and adding a layer of eeriness.

"Are you all right?" Aidan whispered. The mood seemed to call for a gentle tone.

Griffin gripped Aidan's wrist tighter, bringing him down, closer to his height. "You didn't tell your father, did you?" His breath was sour.

Stepfather. "No." Aidan leaned back. "What's going on, Griff?"

"He wouldn't understand, he's a palace sympathizer. He'd get us all in trouble by suns up, and probably have me sent to the dungeons for even showing you."

Without any further explanation, he took Aidan through the shop to the curtained-off archway in the back. Aidan had never been to this part of the store before; it was strictly off-limits. Then Griffin unlocked a hidden door and began to descend a rickety stairway.

A cloud of moldy air hit Aidan in the face. He followed Griffin into a subterranean room. "How long has this been here?" he asked, ducking his head to clear the low ceiling. The walls were composed of layers of solid rock. A huge map of Astor was nailed to one wall.

"It was here when I bought the place," Griffin said, turning on a plasma lamp. "Used to belong to a mine manager. He used it as a wine cellar." He let out a desperate chuckle. "Poor lunk probably died not even able to buy water."

A desk with several computer screens was set up. There were small containers filled with microchips that looked similar to the one

Princess Delia had shown him. Another organized container held miniature versions of the tools Aidan used to fix his sky dodger.

Griffin began to explain. "Working down here hides the signals," he said. "The Queen's Guard is always monitoring our systems for rebel activity."

A prickly layer of panic sent goose bumps down Aidan's arms. "What are you hiding? Wait, are you working with the resistance?" He added a nervous laugh at the end, hoping to coax a more reasonable explanation.

But Griffin's answer did nothing to quell his fears. "Not officially," he said. "Small things here and there."

"I don't understand. I know you're not a fan of the royal family, but I didn't think the resistance was really a thing?"

"They're growing. The monarchy can't last forever. Besides, it makes sense to help them out; it can't hurt to have friends in the right places. I like to think of it as insurance." Griffin went to the desk and sat down. He opened a drawer and brought out the silver dagger.

"I was polishing the handle when it came apart," Griffin said, still in a hushed voice. "And this fell out." He used a pair of tweezers and held up the chip to Aidan. "I ran a decoding program on it."

The air in the small room grew thick. "What is it?" Aidan asked.

"A message from the resistance." He paused and looked at the chip, then up to Aidan. "They're planning something big, something that will change the course of Astor's future."

Aidan was reminded of Delia's speech about choosing the right husband. "Is this about the upcoming royal wedding?" he asked.

"No," he said, but he still looked worried. "It's the queen. She's in danger."

Aidan stared at the small device, trying to absorb what Griffin had just told him. "What? When? How?"

He shook his head. "There are no details, they only mention a secret weapon. I couldn't decode all the files." Griffin ran a hand down his long beard. "I'm not sure what we should do."

"We?!" Aidan took a step backward.

"You brought it to me! You're partly responsible."

"No, thank you." Aidan put his hands up. "You're the rightful owner now. Besides, how do you know this is legitimate? Your decoding skills are legendarily lax, and how stupid would someone be to put the chip inside a silver dagger?"

Griffin picked up the chip and put it in Aidan's hand. "I'm returning this, free of charge. I don't want it in my shop." Then he stood and began to push Aidan up the steps and out through the front of the shop and to the door.

"You're right about me," Griffin said. "I'm an old miser, not a revolutionary. It's not that I don't think dissolving the royal family would benefit the Dark District, but I don't want blood on my hands."

"And I do?" Aidan called out over his back as Griffin pushed him out to the street.

"Then figure something out!" he hissed, slamming the door shut.

Aidan heard the bolt slide across.

He stood motionless, staring at the door. A scream from several streets over moved him into action. The Dark District came alive at night, but not in the best fashion. Mindful of the gangs that wandered about looking for easy targets, Aidan made his way to the alley.

Then figure something out!

A shadowed figure was hunched over his sky dodger. "Hey!" Aidan picked up a stone and threw it, meaning to scare away the kid. Then the shadow stood up and turned.

"Uh-oh," Aidan whispered.

The blue-bearded face of the pirate grinned back at him. "Ain't this karma?" the pirate drawled. He reached into his pocket and pulled out a black sphere.

Aidan turned and ran directly into two more pirates who were blocking his escape. The stench nearly knocked him out. In a flash his arms were pinned behind his back while the other pirate landed several massive fists to his gut.

There was a tightening of his throat as the edges of his vision grew dark.

* * *

When he blinked again, the alley came into focus, but only partly. His left eye was swollen shut. He took a breath and winced as his hand grabbed his right side. There was no blood, but Aidan suspected a rib or two might be broken.

He pushed himself up, grunting with the effort. Apart from the stabbing pain in his side and a swollen eye, everything else seemed intact. His old sky dodger was gone though; only a few bits of metal and cogs were scattered on the ground where it had been. It appeared the pirates had stripped the machine of every last salvageable part.

An odd sensation of loss came over him. Flying that sky dodger was his respite from his dreary life. Besides the collection of trinkets, it was the only thing he could call his own. Except of course . . .

Panicked, Aidan felt for the chain at his neck. Miraculously, his medallion was still there.

Shuffling his way home, he kept his head down, fighting off nausea. His jaw was aching again as well.

Thankfully the cottage was still dark. He collapsed on his bed, certain he'd fall asleep immediately, but his mind had other plans.

Then figure something out!

He reached into his pocket and took out the microchip. With his other hand he pinched the medallion between his thumb and finger. It always grounded him. Then his mother's voice came through.

Always safe.

He wondered what his mother would tell him to do.

If he kept the information to himself, the queen could be in danger. But still, Griff might be wrong. He was a junk broker, not a tech whiz. Then he pictured the stone room and the computer screens and small tools.

Aidan put a hand to his side; his ribs didn't hurt as much now. He was living on borrowed time anyway. The next headache might be his last, and if he died tomorrow, he'd have nothing left, no legacy.

It was an easy decision. He had to tell Princess Delia.

Tucking the microchip back into his pocket, Aidan finally closed his eyes, bones aching and heart full of worry.

But as he settled to sleep, a thought slipped into his mind—the owner of the dagger.

Whichever prince was in that room was either the intended recipient or a conspirator passing along the message. Regardless, Princess Delia had a spy sleeping in her palace.

CHAPTER TWELVE

"I think you'll find the military capabilities of Trellium are far superior to those of any neighboring planet in the Four Quadrants," Prince Felix said, carefully folding a cloth in half.

Delia could make out the sharp pleat in his jacket. His buttons kept catching the sunlight, distracting her. Then he bent over and started to polish the nose of his machine. Deluxe gliders lined the edge of Black Lake. The shimmering reflection off the water made all the courtiers squint.

"Oh, yes?" Delia responded, one hand shielding her eyes from the glaring midday suns. The weight of the transmitter stored in the pocket of her silk trousers was a constant reminder of her activities last night. She had no idea when a message would arrive from the bodyguard, but she felt it best to be prepared. Yet, as the morning lagged on, she started to doubt herself.

Maybe the windup bird was broken?

Maybe the transmitter was faulty?

Maybe the bodyguard was lying?

She'd talked to most of the princes, but none of them had ever been to the Dark District. In fact most of them didn't know it even existed. The twins, Maxim and Mikel, gave her identical looks of confusion behind their sunglasses. Their naturally curly hair had been straightened in similar styles. Prince Hagar shrugged, then tried to steer the conversation to sailing and wondered if there were any fish in Black Lake.

"There is no militia more loyal or fierce than my own," Prince Felix continued, still bent over, polishing the flier. Delia wasn't sure if he was sweet-talking the machine or her.

Then she felt a nudge to her side. Shania stood there holding a heat-shielding umbrella, staring at Prince Felix's backside. She winked at Delia and showed her the mini infoscreen in her palm.

Shania had added a new category to her rating list of top picks. Delia rolled her eyes.

Unable to stifle her laughter, Shania snorted out loud.

Prince Felix stood upright. His chin dipped in a curt bow. "Princess Shania," he said. "I trust you are well this fine day."

"Just enjoying the view, Prince Felix." Shania beamed back. "You're going to outshine the suns if you keep polishing like that."

His expression was serious. "A smart soldier keeps his equipment in top working order."

"Oh?" Shania exaggerated the length of the word. "Do you polish your equipment every day?"

"Yes," he answered, steadfast. "Every proper soldier on Trellium has been trained to do so."

"So admirable . . . so disciplined," Shania cooed. "Do your hands get blisters, though?"

He frowned and looked down at his palms, then back up to Shania.

She continued, "If my sister chooses you for a husband, perhaps she can help polish your equipment?"

"Serving in the military has strengthened every part of me," Prince Felix said, his tone purposeful. "I take every task to heart to complete myself, no matter how small."

"Small?" Shania giggled.

Delia's ears burned. "Th-Thank you for the delightful conversation," she stammered to Prince Felix. "I'll let you continue your prep for the hunt."

He nodded to both of them, then clicked the backs of his heels smartly before turning back to the glider.

"Good luck," Shania called out over her shoulder. She linked her arm through Delia's as they walked up the slope toward the gardens. "His hair is perfectly parted and so precisely trimmed. How does he do that? Do you think he brought his own stylist?"

Under the shade of her younger sister's umbrella Delia finally found her voice. "If Mother heard you speak like that you'd be locked in the library until you were thirty."

Shania sighed. "I'd still find something romantic in there, I'm sure." She pinched her sister's elbow. "Honestly, Prince Felix might be the one. Think of how much fun suppers will be! Although the children might suffer, I suspect he doesn't know how to play anything except war."

Delia remembered his arrival at the clearing. She was curious to see how he'd do against pirates.

"You're smiling! Why are you smiling? Are you thinking about his equipment?"

"At least pretend to be somewhat reserved," Delia sighed. "And no, I wasn't thinking of his . . . equipment. I have to picture each of these princes as a partner. And while his interests appear lacking in variation, there is something fiercely protective about him."

They stayed quiet as they walked up the ascending tiers of the garden. Delia had been instructed by Advisor Winchell to make a sincere effort in chatting with all the princes today before the hunt.

Most she regarded with polite interest, but others, like Prince Felix, who were on her radar as a serious choice, she spent more time with. Although, she felt no romantic inclination toward any of them.

"Princess Delia!" a thickly built man called from the tier below. His shirt was undone partway and he was covered in sweat. A huge boulder had been unearthed beside him, and one of the royal gardeners was carrying a sapling to the newly formed hole.

"Is he helping the gardener?" Shania squinted.

"Hello, Prince Oskar." Delia waved back. "Aren't you going on the hunt?"

He shook his head. "No, Your Highness. I prefer the ground." Then he put his hands on his hips and looked around. "Right, I'll just carry on, then."

Delia continued down the path with her sister as Shania whispered, "The flirtatious methods of men from the Kalasta Belt are odd, indeed."

"Trying to figure out men is exhausting." Delia yawned into the back of her hand.

"Don't you dare let Winnie catch you yawning!" Shania warned. "She came by your bedchamber last night and woke me up. I lied for you, said you were in the bathroom with an upset stomach due to all the nervous butterflies about today."

"She accepted that as truth?"

"I've been lying to her for years." Shania waved a hand in the air, disregarding her concern. "So, where were you last night?"

Delia grinned. "Classified," she said. She had to look away from her sister's prying gaze.

They reached the top tier. From this vantage the royal garden spread out below them, sections of varying heights connected with stone pathways. The brilliance of the flowers seemed electric under the suns.

They turned a corner in the pathway and stopped in their tracks. Shania sucked in a breath. "Speak of the monster."

Advisor Winchell strode up to the sisters. Her countenance of quiet authority was softened by her colorful headdress. Today it was decorated with the red and yellow feathers of the larkspire, a soulful bird that nested in the marshy areas of the Black Lake.

"Greetings, Advisor Winchell," Delia and Shania intoned together.

"I believe the main goal of this gathering is to ensure the future queen finds a proper husband." Advisor Winchell then took the tip of her cane and placed it between Delia and her sister, slightly pushing them apart.

"I'm helping keep score," Shania said, a pout close to the surface. A pointed stare from the advisor made Shania drop her gaze. Then she grumbled under her breath. "You won't have to work as hard to marry me off." She turned and flounced down the path, the umbrella twirling behind her.

Advisor Winchell began to stroll along the garden. "Let's talk," she said, gesturing with her cane at the pathway lined with blooms. Delia tagged along, dreading the coming lecture.

She took in the courtiers wandering the gardens. It seemed everyone was determined to show one another up with their outfits. From the gems entwined in the fabric to the bright colors of their garments, no one was taking a chance at being overlooked. She searched for the bodyguard in his simple clothing, knowing he'd stand out.

"Have you made good use of this morning?" Advisor Winchell prompted. "Anyone of interest yet?"

Delia continued to scan the view. Royalty from neighboring planets and territories crisscrossed the tiered gardens at the base of the palace, some with pages in tow, others with members of her mother's court.

"Prince Oskar seems very . . . helpful, and Prince Hagar is interested in our aquaculture. Prince Felix's discipline is admirable. Then there are the twins from Tramsted, although I can't tell them apart yet." She let out a deflated sigh full of obvious reservation.

"Hmm." Advisor Winchell paused, then focused on one particular person gazing at the roses. His flaxen curls were pulled back in a tie. "And what are your thoughts on Prince Armano?"

"I spoke with him quickly at the beginning." Even though she tried to cover the disappointment, the tedious dullness came through in her voice. "He offered to read my palm. My true love is close by, apparently."

"Oh." She put her lips in a hard line.

"Then he gave me an autographed picture—it was already in a frame."

"I see."

They walked in silence for a few steps, and then Advisor Winchell said, "You seem overwhelmed." Her fingers clutched the top of her cane, the knot of the tree molded perfectly into her palm, creating the illusion that the Jesper wood was an extension of the advisor herself.

Delia was reminded of how long she'd been serving the royal family, almost six decades.

"I'm trying to pick the person who will determine my happiness for the rest of my life," she answered.

They stood at the low stone wall, looking down on the hedge maze, the lowest tier of the garden before it gave way to the lake.

Advisor Winchell huffed. "*You* are the person who determines your own happiness. You need to start thinking like a queen."

"I'm not being selfish or romantic. I know that I'll only be happy, or rather content, if I make the choice that is right for Astor." Her gaze went over the lake and past the stilted homes of the nobility, but as hard as she tried, the Dark District was impossible to see from the palace.

Advisor Winchell nodded toward the lingering figures leisurely making their way to the gliders lined up at the lake's edge. "Many people don't have the luxury of so many choices."

With a sense of bewilderment, Delia instinctively looked through the crowd for Shania. Her younger sister's usual flirtatious gestures were in full display; the head tilt, the high-pitched laugh, the one hand going repeatedly to the neckline of her dress as if hiding a tantalizing secret. She was speaking with one of the princes. Even from this distance Delia could tell it was Prince Quinton.

Unlike the others, he was actually dressed in proper hunting gear, full leather and studded gloves. Another young man joined Prince Quinton's side. He had a similar style of dress, although his black hair was longer, held in place with a small knot at the back of his head. He bowed to Shania.

Delia turned to Advisor Winchell and said, "Mother has made it clear which choices will benefit our kingdom the most."

"The queen is wise," she said, nodding. "She has worn the crown for longer than you've been alive, princess. You would do well to listen to her."

"What if she's wrong?" The lingering doubt about the pirates and the resistance was an idea firmly implanted in her brain, impossible to ignore. Delia sensed Advisor Winchell's annoyance. She braced for the next scathing comment.

But when the Advisor spoke there was an unexpected calmness in her voice. "You were such a rambunctious child, never paying heed. Always looking up. Do you remember? You couldn't understand where the moon went in the morning—even then you had a strong connection to your ancestors." She smiled. "Only when Shania was born did you finally stop and find the world around you more interesting than gazing at the heavens."

Together, they turned and took in the mountain peak that rose high above as an extension of the palace. Taking advantage of its natural protection and the abundant water source from the glaciers, the palace had been built into the side of the mountain after the great eruption.

Delia knew the ancient tree that grew at the base of the summit would be covered in white blossoms this time of year. She had always felt safe there.

Advisor Winchell's uncharacteristically nurturing comment confused Delia and even left her a little unsettled. She sighed, "I wish our home was not dependent on someone I just met. I hate relying on a stranger."

"In times of confusion, you must be quiet, you must listen for the voice of our ancestors. Simply ask, and they will tell you. Deep down you will know the truth when you feel it."

Delia stayed quiet, but the questions in her mind seemed too big. *Who should I marry? Who will help Astor the most? Who can I trust to help me?* "I don't feel anything," she said, feeling deflated. She once again looked for the bodyguard in the crowd, knowing at least he might have a few answers for her.

"You are young," Advisor Winchell said, her critical tone surfacing again. "But you already have everything you need to lead your people. You are a direct descendant of Arianna, the first queen and child of the moon. We belong to the moon. It gave us life."

Delia gave her a smile. "I wish I could marry the man in the moon instead."

Advisor Winchell made a gruff sound. "Have you learned nothing from all that tutoring? The moon lives inside you." With her wrinkled finger she pointed to Delia's thumbnail. "See the crescent image? Look at your hand. You have crescents on all fingernails, as only a true queen does."

An unexpected wave of gratitude filled all the tired and empty spots inside her. "Thank you, advisor," she said.

"Don't bury me under compliments, princess, I'm only stating a fact." She took in a deep breath and stood to her full height. "I will let your mother know this event is proving fruitful. And that you're enjoying the possibilities of choice."

Delia frowned, thinking of her mother's tired expression in court yesterday. "Why isn't she here?"

"The shaman is seeing to her needs at present." Then before Delia could question her further, the advisor resumed her walk along the path.

Shania's voice floated close by. Delia turned quickly, catching the toe of her boot on the edge of the stone walkway. She stumbled backward, hitting the ground with a thud. A curse escaped her lips.

A strong voice said, "Princess, are you all right?"

Delia looked up at a kind face. His brown eyes were wide with concern.

"Oh . . . thank you." She accepted his outstretched hand and stood, grimacing at the ache in her backside. "There's a loose stone, please be careful. Um . . . sorry."

Shania was grinning, eyes shining with tears of laughter. "Prince Quinton of Rexula, may I present my sister, Princess Delia."

It took every muscle in Delia's body not to roll her eyes. Instead, she smiled demurely and tidily bowed her chin.

Shania continued the introductions. "And his page, Niko . . . also of Rexula."

He gave Delia a curt nod, his expression like stone. He shared the same physique as Prince Quinton, but his deeply set eyes and golden hued skin were unique. Judging by his muscle tone and staunch demeanor, Delia assumed Niko was also in charge of Prince Quinton's safety.

"Welcome," Delia said. "I'm pleased to have you as guests at the palace."

"Thank you," Prince Quinton said. "The natural beauty of your land and the hospitality of your people are unparalleled. I am very much looking forward to today's activity."

"I'm glad to hear that," Delia said. From the corner of her eye she noted that Niko's steely gaze was unwavering. "Luckily the migration of the wallowing geese was early, and the timing proved particularly favorable."

He smiled. "I'm afraid I've never tried hunting fowl alongside them in the sky; however, I understand you're quite an ace when it comes to flying."

"We're taking the double gliders," Shania said. "I'm riding with Niko."

At this, Niko's expression opened into something similar to a smile.

Prince Quinton cleared his throat. "Perhaps you would like to ride with me?" he asked Delia.

"I'm . . ." The transmitter in her pocket started to vibrate. Her eye caught a black dot in the sky that seemed to grow larger. "Oh dear!"

She stammered as the trio frowned back at her. "Oh dear, I . . . I think I'm going to have to skip the hunt. I prefer to wait here to see who comes back with the biggest catch." Her gaze darted back and forth between the ever-growing dot and Prince Quinton's brown eyes.

He gave her a crooked smile. "A contest, then?" he said. "And would that entail a prize for the winner?"

She took a step back. "You'll have to wait to find out." The flirting was forced, but she continued to smile. The horn sounded, signaling the hunters to the gliders. She watched as her sister was escorted by Prince Quinton and Niko.

The dot was now definitely taking shape, and seemingly headed straight toward her.

"Princess Delia!" Prince Armano called to her from the upper tier. He waved a handkerchief.

Ignoring him, Delia looked around wildly. There were too many people close by. She couldn't be caught picking a mechanical bird out of the air.

Making a quick decision, she rushed down the stone steps that led to the lowest tier of the garden. The opening to the maze loomed ahead, the hedges over ten feet tall and three feet thick.

The perfect hiding place.

Delia ran into the maze and began to track her path to the center. Like the palace, she knew the route by heart. Every few turns she paused to catch her breath and look up. The bird was definitely getting closer, she could even make out the flapping of its wings.

Prince Armano called her name from a few hedges over. Panicked, she hurried along, knowing he'd get lost many times over before he ever found her.

Arriving at the center, Delia took in the monument of the first queen, Arianna. The statue never failed to give her a sense of awe. It was so lifelike she often wondered if the sculptor encased a real woman.

Goose bumps peppered her arms.

There was a clicking noise behind her. She turned to see the bird was flying straight toward her. She screamed and flung herself behind the statue, dodging the missile. It turned and flew at her again, its beak threateningly sharp.

After several more circles around the statue with Delia shielding her face and head from the mechanical threat, she realized what the problem was. Quickly fishing the transmitter out of her pocket, she threw it on the ground. Immediately, the bird went to the same spot, gave one last chirp, and stilled.

With wild strands of hair stuck to the side of her face, Delia cursed and picked up the bird with a sigh.

"Do they teach you that kind of language in royal etiquette class, princess?"

The bodyguard stood with his arms crossed, an amused expression adorning his pale features. There was a patch over his left eye.

Delia's pulse picked up. "You!" she said.

CHAPTER THIRTEEN

Aidan absorbed the image of the princess. No longer in an oversize pilot suit, she now wore yards of layered silk creating a billowing blouse that tied around her waist and a pair of fitted slacks that showed off her figure.

He swallowed dryly, suddenly at unease, wishing he'd made use of the seamstress's room as she had suggested. Although he was wearing a simple jacket without any tears, many washings had rendered it somewhat dull. *A few fancy buttons would be nice at a time like this*, he thought. At least he'd managed to swipe a pair of Morgan's old boots this morning. They were rugged, but at least they didn't have a hole in the toe.

She stared at him with her mouth open. He couldn't decide if she was going to yell at him or not. "How . . . ?" she began. "When . . . ?"

Cautious relief relaxed his arms. "I don't remember speaking being this much of a challenge for you." He grinned. "Are you all right?"

A momentary scowl lined her features. "I'm perfectly fine. Exactly where I should be, actually. But where have you been? Your prince was parading all around the garden unprotected."

"Classified," he said. "Besides, I have it on good authority that the palace supplies guards for their garden."

She huffed at his answer. "I can't help but wonder what kind of prince hires a bodyguard who is never around."

Aidan noticed her eyebrows came together in a frown that was far too elegant to render a serious threat. He marveled at the perfect symmetry.

Princess Delia took a step closer, her critical gaze sweeping from the top of his head to his hastily polished boots. Her attention lingered on the eye patch.

"Unfortunate result of my prince's excessive gambling skills. Some people have no sense of sportsmanship." Then he lifted the patch slightly, so that she could see the deep purple. At least the swelling had gone down considerably.

He had decided to keep the pirate attack a secret, since it created too many questions. Better to keep up the charade of the fake prince.

"This happened last night? In my kingdom? That's positively barbaric." Her chin tilted upward. "You must give me the names of the men your prince was gambling with so that I can alert the Guard."

"That's a bit intrusive. I haven't demanded any details about your whereabouts last night after you left me."

Her cheeks flushed, and for a moment she seemed frozen, but then she put a hand on one hip. "I command you to give me names."

Aidan just smiled at her attempt to order him around.

Her mouth became a hard line. "Withholding information from royalty might be considered a crime against the palace."

Aidan ran a hand through his hair, lifting his bangs, exposing the eye patch fully. "Do you think it makes me look mysterious? I thought if I had another run-in with pirates, I might be able to convince them I'm one too."

One of her perfect eyebrows lifted. "That's rather closed-minded of you to assume that every pirate has an eye patch," she said.

"No more closed-minded than a princess who assumes every bodyguard owes her full disclosure."

There was a quick gasp of shock. Then Princess Delia regained her voice and said, "You're in *my* maze, sir!" Her expression changed to a more questioning look. "How did you find me?"

"You're assuming I was looking for you," he replied. "Really, you need to address this infatuation with me."

She scoffed at this.

"The bird," he admitted, nodding to the windup mechanism still in her hand. "I wanted to make sure it found you. I was afraid others might think it's a game bird and try to catch it. It's not every day you see a clockwork bird."

"True." She looked at her hand. "And I appreciate you taking extra care with this. Most people use the infoscreens to communicate." Then she took a step closer to him. "Am I to assume this means there is sensitive information in this message?" He heard caution in her voice.

"Yes," he said. "But the microchip is encrypted . . ."

The princess shook her head and placed a finger to her lips. Then she furtively slipped the bird into her pocket. Aidan knew she wanted the microchip, but he didn't want to leave her to open it on her own and read about a secret weapon that may or may not be used against her own mother.

She wandered over to the statue. Aidan went to her side but stayed at a respectable distance. He gazed up at the woman's stone face. The young queen's hands reached toward the sky. Her braid traveled down her back and coiled at her feet.

"Worshiping at the altar of yourself?" he asked, working to keep the moment light.

There was a quick laugh and something that suspiciously sounded like a snort. She said, "You think this is me?"

"Long hair, regal countenance, a wistful gaze of longing." He shrugged. "Or maybe that's just when I'm around."

"You're insufferable," she replied, but there was a smile under the insult. "This is Arianna, daughter of the moon and the first queen of Astor."

Aidan nodded. Of course he knew who the monument was in honor of, he just wanted to keep them in the conversation. The only person in his life who seemed to enjoy his company was Griff. And even though the pawnbroker was a friend, being with Princess Delia made him feel important, like he mattered.

The quiet of the garden and all its earthy scents descended upon them, creating a calmness.

She took in a slow breath and then smiled. "When my younger sister and I were little, we would play here, pretending Arianna was our third sister. We left her gifts, cookies and posies at her stone feet. Every time we returned, the offerings were always gone, proving to our young hearts that she was real."

Aidan smiled, imagining how magical that must have seemed. Then he thought of his stepbrothers and wondered if there was a time when they might have played like that as boys—but there were no memories like that.

He noticed three words at the base of the statue, written in raised stone letters: Bravery, Wisdom, Love. A wrench of loneliness pulled at his chest. "You're lucky to have a connection to your past, your family."

"Yes," she started. Then her voice became solemn, defeated-sounding. "But sometimes the burden of heritage outweighs the privilege."

Aidan stayed quiet, pretending to study the statue. It seemed each of them had let a small secret out to the other without intending.

The moment was interrupted by a rustle on the other side of the hedge, followed by the unmistaken sound of Prince Armano calling out, "Princess Delia? I'm coming for you!"

"Oh no, anything but him," she grumbled.

"Do you want me to distract him while you climb the hedge?" Aidan teasingly offered.

Wordlessly, she turned to the monument and pushed three raised letters from the words at the base of the statue: B, W, L.

There was a thick clunk. The statue rotated at the base, revealing a spiral staircase descending into the ground.

Princess Delia went down the first few steps, her body disappearing up to her shoulders. Then she stopped and turned to him. "Hurry up," she instructed. "Come on!"

Without waiting for a second invitation, Aidan followed her, ducking his head inside just as the statue slid smoothly back in place.

Blackness descended instantly.

"Um, princess?" Aidan whispered, his hand groping for a railing to hold.

"There is nothing to be afraid of," she said. "Ten steps to the bottom is all it takes. And once you reach the bottom, the light will come on. You can count to ten, can't you?"

"Nice to see the darkness doesn't diminish your natural charm."

He heard her huff as her footfalls increased. Then thankfully, the area was illuminated. Aidan followed her off the steps, his mouth dropping in awe.

"You're impressed," she said with a hint of pride.

Aidan took in the scene before him. The long passage was a smooth, curving tunnel, illuminated by the evenly spaced plasma lamps. Inlaid in the stone walls were thousands of small tiles, creating a riot of colorful designs. The princess watched him as if waiting for his approval.

"What is this place?" he whispered.

"These tunnels were carved by hand by the first ancestors," she said. "They were originally used for protection, in case they had to flee from the palace. Some of the tunnels lead all the way to the Dark District."

He looked around him. The tunnel was as wide as it was high, just several feet above his head. Every inch was decorated in tiles. "It feels," he started, "sacred, almost."

She smiled. "This is where my ancestors left their greatest legacy—the legend of Astor's creation."

Aidan was still enraptured by the perfectly sculpted tunnel. He pressed his hand against the curved wall. He could swear there was a vibration.

"Do you know the story?" she asked. "You mentioned you'd done research before coming here."

"Your creation legend? Only some of it." Then he grinned at her, still on a high of having her invite him to come along with her in this dark and secluded spot.

She glanced to the wall, almost a little shy. "It's the first mosaic of the legend," she said. There was a funny hitch to her voice.

Aidan sensed she was nervous. "It's beautiful," he said honestly.

She gave him a small smile. "It's detailed along this whole section, but I can narrate for you . . . if you like."

Yes, I would like, he thought. *I would like very much.*

He gave her a slight bow. "I'd be honored. Should I take notes?"

"No. Just try to keep your smart mouth shut and listen."

CHAPTER FOURTEEN

"Long, long ago," Delia started, just as her mother had done the first time she brought her into the tunnels, "the first family that landed on Astor was of royal descent from a far-off planet. They were the last of their tribe and with them they carried their most precious cargo: their children and a chest full of jewels. They found a lush homestead close to the mountain. The father declared himself king of this beautiful land."

She snuck a glance at the bodyguard from the corner of her eye as they moved to the next mosaic. He was fully concentrating on the images it seemed, and not at all aware of how close their hands were to touching. Delia cleared her throat, hoping she didn't sound as dull as her history tutor. "The king wanted a house to reflect his great fortune, so he and his sons cut down all the trees, leaving the forest bare."

At this he turned to her. "Greedy and proud." He shook his head. "I don't think this will end well."

Hiding her smile, she moved him to the image of a girl with long dark hair—an image that could have been her. "His youngest child, a daughter who was wise beyond her years with hair that reached the ground, warned him the forest was home to many creatures and what he was doing was stealing. He laughed at her and said she knew nothing of the powers of nature."

Delia led him down the tunnel as it naturally curved right and then left. The next image was the most dramatic, with the huge palace and bright, colorful gardens. "The king wanted to fill his house with running water and crystal clear pools for his garden, so he and his sons stole the supply from the waterfall. But his daughter warned him that the land needed the water too."

Delia took a breath and held it, something deep inside of her starting to bloom. "Again, the father laughed at his daughter. Next, he wanted his grand home to be brilliantly lit, so he and his sons stole the sun and kept it inside the palace."

She paused, and her voice took on a softer quality. She could see the bodyguard was now staring at her instead of the mosaics. "His daughter begged him to return the sun, because the moon would be lonely without his brother. But the father said the planet's purpose was to give them everything they needed, because he was the king. He then patted her on the head, telling her she was meant to be beautiful, not to think."

The bodyguard whispered, "I definitely feel a sense of foreboding."

She hit him with a look. "If you're going to make fun of my ancestors, you can leave. I'm sure Prince Armano would enjoy reading your palm."

"On the contrary, princess. I'm much more interested in the past than the future." He waved a hand at the next mosaic. "Please continue. I promise no more interruptions, and I will save all my questions for the end."

Delia continued. "After a time, the sun became weak with loneliness for the moon. It could no longer shine, and the world filled with darkness. With no sun, the winter came early and stayed. The water froze, filling the house with shards of ice. The strong wooden beams were no match for the expanding ice and they split apart. The glorious shrine to the king's wealth fell in on itself, leaving a miserable pile of catastrophic wreckage."

Pausing at this junction of the story, she let the silence fill the air; her favorite part was coming up. "When the sun escaped the confines of the palace, it flew back into the sky. The moon was overcome with joy and embraced the sun so tightly that it split into two smaller identical orbs. But the moon was worried the suns would be stolen again, so he hid them deep inside the mountain."

She concentrated on making her voice sound more regal. "Without shelter or a means to warm themselves, the royal family suffered through the never-ending winter. One by one the sons died, until it was only the father and the young daughter left. She kept them warm with her long swaths of hair, while her father tightly clutched his chest of jewels. Then one night, the daughter asked the moon for help."

Taking in the next mosaic of the moon and the girl, Delia looked down at her hand, seeing the crescents on her fingernails. "The moon heard something sincere in her voice. He promised to help her in exchange for her most prized possession." She looked at the bodyguard. "Do you know what that was?" she asked him.

His face opened up in surprise. "Um . . . no."

She motioned to the next image. "The daughter knew the only thing that had kept her alive was her hair, so she offered it to him. The moon scooped her up in his arms and kept her safe, while the planet below froze, killing everything on its surface.

"All the while the two suns burned brightly inside the mountain, until one day the heat was so great the rock turned to liquid and blew off the top of the mountain. The hot lava formed new fertile soil for the forests, and its heat melted the great islands of ice. Soon water flowed again over the land."

A smile broke out on his face. Delia intensified her energy. "The suns took their place in the sky next to their brother the moon, giving energy and warmth to the planet once again. Over the years, the seeds of the forest grew into tall trees and the creatures returned.

"When the moon saw the planet was fit for living, he woke the daughter, now a grown woman. From the hair she'd given him, he made a braid of three thick strands. One strand for each of her unique qualities: bravery, wisdom"—Delia swallowed dryly and looked away from the bodyguard—"and love.

"Using this braid as a ladder, she was able to climb down from the moon to the summit of the great mountain. Seeing she was worthy, he returned the braid to her, but had inlaid it with stars from the sky. He gave her the new name of Arianna, meaning most wise, and made her queen. He then bestowed upon her the power to pass down her wisdom to her firstborn daughter, and in turn to her firstborn daughter, and so on, as it has been for centuries."

They came to the last mosaic of the great tree. A woman with a long braid held a bundle. "This is the great tree," she told him. "It actually exists behind the waterfall. After the era of ice, the first seed to take root grew into this tree. It's the oldest living thing on Astor."

She hesitated, all too aware of his close stance. In the thick air she detected the faint smell of soap. "The legend says the first queen, Arianna, was named by the moon under this very tree. So, in keeping with that tradition, each royal child has been named under the tree during the full moon."

She realized her voice had taken on the tone of one of her tutors, as if spouting facts and not something that was connected to her. He remained quiet, and she wondered if the legend sounded silly. Delia tried to imagine what she would think if she were hearing it for the first time.

When he spoke, his tone was sincere. "Including you?" he asked.

Delia was once again struck by how pale he was. *The man in the moon*, she thought. "Of course," she said. "And my sister too."

His expression was open and kind. "And someday your own daughter?"

She blinked back at him, and a warm sensation rose up her neck. "Or son," she answered. Then, because her hands felt useless at her sides, she took a long strand of braid and wrapped it around her arm a few times. "It's also the place where I'll be married," she added quickly. There was a lump in her throat, making her voice sound off.

"Sounds like you're taking a shine to the idea of getting married."

"No, not really. I'm just stating a fact."

"I see."

Delia was unsure how long they stood there, staring at the mosaic tiles. A peculiar melancholy mixed in the air. Wordlessly, she started walking; he followed behind at a slower pace.

The passageway took a gradual turn and soon they came to a three-way split. "This one leads to the lakeside," she told him. "This one is a dead end, and this one," she pointed to her right, "takes us to the palace."

"Your ancestors carved these by hand? The width is a perfect circle the whole way along, even when the tunnels curve. How many tunnels are dead ends?" he asked. "I'm just curious. Aren't you curious?"

"About the dead end tunnels? No. It's the result of the mountain shifting generations ago." She put a hand in the pocket of her trousers and felt the windup bird. "Regardless, the tour is over. I have a microchip to decode." She turned, but he stayed in place.

"And you don't want to find out what's on the other side?" There was an impish quality to his voice.

"The rest of the tunnel is on the other side." Regret began to settle in. Why had she invited him down here? She didn't even know his name. And whenever she asked, he kept giving her the same reply—it's classified. However, she'd brought him down here instead of leaving him in the maze, so she had no one to blame but herself.

Frustrated, Delia huffed and started down the tunnel that led to the palace. "And it's irrelevant, since they don't give princesses bomb-making classes on how to blast through the rock. I'm afraid I'm one of those princesses who uses logical solutions instead of blowing things up." She quickened her stride, not bothering to check if he was following her.

The bodyguard's voice echoed down the tunnel. "Eat this, pirate," he said in a high-pitched voice.

"That's a horrible impersonation," she said, still walking. She fished the bird from her pocket and started to inspect it. She tried to pry open the compartment with her fingernail.

"Sorry," he replied, dropping into step beside her. "I was just reliving one of the most interesting moments of my life. Truly."

Her thumb slipped and the bird came to life. A yelp escaped her lips. The bird flew out of her hands and hit the side of the tunnel, landing on the floor with a metallic clunk.

"You're trying to kill it!" He bent for the bird at the same time as Delia, and they collided.

"Ouch!" she cried out, holding her forehead.

"For galaxy's sake," he whispered, taking a step backward. They stood, scowling at each other. The bird was in the bodyguard's hand.

"I was only trying to open it," she said, reaching for the bird.

He moved it out of her reach. "Allow me," he said. "I had no idea royalty were so hard on their things." Then he gently stroked the beak with his finger. A slot on the belly popped open and the microchip fell into his palm.

Delia snatched it quickly. "Finally, let's move along."

"You're welcome," he sighed.

They reached the end of the tunnel where a steel door was in place. Without any further instruction, Delia opened the massive door with a groan. "There shouldn't be any guards down here."

The rock foundation gave way to marble flooring and bright lighting.

After a careful glance in each direction, Delia told him, "I can lead you to the regular vertical transporter that will take you to the main floor of the palace; I'm sure you know your way by now. And I'll take the servants' lift."

She waited for him to acknowledge the plan. When she turned around, she saw he'd stopped a few feet from her, paler than usual. There were beads of sweat on his forehead. "Or maybe you should call for the shaman. Are you all right?"

"Fine," he said as he grimaced through his teeth. "Just a post-beating twinge." Then he coughed into his fist and doubled over. When he straightened up, there was blood on his hand.

"You need help!" She rushed to his side.

"I'm fine," he stammered. "I'll double back and take the tunnel to the lakeside. I just need some fresh air."

"Fresh air? Don't be ridic—"

From the end of the corridor a conversation echoed down to them. "We weren't prepared for this development. Are you certain?" The voice was low, not much higher than a whisper, but Delia recognized it instantly.

Advisor Winchell.

Adrenaline surged through her. She closed the metal door, leaving it open just enough. The bodyguard slumped to the floor. He cried out a muffled curse.

Cautiously, Delia peeked through the cracked opening. Advisor Winchell came into view with the Head of Security, Colonel Yashin.

"Who else knows?" The severity of Advisor Winchell's voice sent a trickle of ice water down Delia's spine.

"Only the inner circle of the court," he said. Then he added, "And of course, the shaman."

"Good."

"Should we tell Princess Delia?" he asked.

"No. It was her mother's choice to keep it secret."

Their voices faded as they made their way down the corridor.

Delia's mind reeled with questions.

CHAPTER FIFTEEN

An intense throb gripped Aidan's side.

"We have to get to the lift," Princess Delia told him with urgency.

Aidan felt her tuck in close, then roughly grab hold of his waist, pulling him off the wall. With a grunt, he stood, leaning against the wall for support. Aidan bit back a yelp.

The princess practically dragged him down the rest of the hallway. They passed the main vertical transporter and instead took the smaller servants' lift, hidden around the corner. She was talking to herself, but he couldn't hear specifics, just hisses and huffs. And if he wasn't mistaken, a curse or two.

Without loosening her grip on him, she touched a button close to the top of the panel. As they smoothly rose, Aidan concentrated on breathing, every movement feeling as though he was being stabbed. He tasted the bitter copper of his own blood. He wondered if this was what would happen before the last headache. Would his brain actually hemorrhage and leak out? The notion took his mind off his cracked rib.

The numbers counted higher as they continued to rise. "Where are we going?" he asked quietly.

"My bedchamber."

"Bedchamber?" His voice noticeably changed.

They came to a stop, making Aidan's stomach swoop. When the doors opened with a whisper, Princess Delia stretched her neck out, looking right and then left. Her grip around his waist tightened as she led him around the corner, then across the hallway and into her room.

Aidan was blinded by the reflection of sunlight off the marbled floor. He squinted against the glare as Princess Delia moved him along. There was a change in direction and he felt his knees bump into something soft.

"Sit down," she ordered, although he noticed her voice was softer than before.

As his eyes adjusted, Aidan took in his surroundings. Floor to ceiling windows lined one entire wall. The room was richly furnished, but not cluttered. He perched on the edge of a plush bed that seemed far too large for one person. His body sank softly. The only sound in the room was the rustle of silk as she moved around the foot of the bed to the other side.

"What exactly do you have in mind?" he asked, more suspicious than intrigued.

"I couldn't very well leave you in the tunnels. I'm going to look at your injuries, but first I need to get this microchip decoded." Princess Delia stood by the bedside table and reached for her infoscreen. "I only feel safe downloading whatever is on this chip to my own computer. Winnie and my mother are keeping something from me on purpose."

He stayed quiet, watching the glow of the screen play off her features. She looked worried, but there was a stubborn set to her jaw. Princess Delia took the chip and slipped it into the device. "My decoding program will take a few minutes."

Aidan could see her impatience, so he decided to stay quiet. Besides, the bed was lovely and she might consider sitting beside him. When Aidan woke with a purple eye that morning, the last place he'd seen himself ending up was here. He had imagined the princess would take the bird, and then maybe toss him a shunkle or two before waving goodbye.

But here he was, inside her bedchamber. He thought of all the dapper princes in the gardens, trying their best to show off for her attention. And it was him, the lowly chore boy, who she'd invited along. A smile crept through the pain.

Princess Delia took the clockwork bird out of her pocket and gently placed it beside the infoscreen. Then she turned her attention to Aidan. Her gaze went to his side, where his hand was still pressed. "Take off your jacket," she said.

"We barely know each other, princess."

"You're hurt. I need to see how badly. Come on, at least it will give me something to do while I wait for that file."

Aidan began to unbutton the jacket, mindful of the mending he'd done to a rip in the collar. "What kind of qualifications do you have to supply medical care?"

"I worked as an apprentice to the shaman all last year." She tossed his jacket to the other side of the bed, where it landed next to the bedside table. Then she began to unbutton his shirt. Her mannerisms were controlled—not at all jittery like every cell in *his* body at the moment.

"And is that usual practice for royalty?" he asked, trying to distract from the way his heart was pounding under her fingertips. He was certain the sensation of her almost touching him was as thrilling as the real thing.

Her cheeks started to glow. "It was punishment," she told him. "The result of me practicing glider jostling with the Queen's Guard." She opened the shirt and lifted it off his shoulders.

The cool air on his bare chest sent a shiver over his skin. Aidan stared at her incredulously. "Glider jostling!" He'd seen the sport and the bloody results of sparring at such a velocity. He thought it had been banished due to the tragic accidents. "How did you manage to be allowed to practice with them?"

"I dressed as one of them, of course." She gasped at the bruise on his side. "How have you managed to be so cheeky with this injury?"

"Just naturally tough, I suppose." He tried to puff out his chest, hoping it looked muscular.

She moved her hand along his lower ribs, gently pressing in every few spaces. "Does that hurt?" she asked, focusing on his side. "Do you feel anything when I touch you here?"

"Definitely." He cleared his throat.

Keeping her hand on his side, she raised her gaze. "It must be a hairline crack in the rib. I don't think anything is broken, but it doesn't explain why you coughed up blood."

"It seems to have stopped." Aidan made no motion to get off the bed though.

"Still, you need to be taped up. And for galaxy's sake, take that eye patch off."

"I thought it helped with the healing." He slipped off the patch and placed it on the bed beside him.

"You should have ice on it." She went over to a tall chest across from the bed. Pulling out the top drawer, she gathered a few supplies, then returned. Head bent, she began to tape his side, taking care to make sure each piece was the same length.

When she was finished, Aidan took a deep breath, and it didn't hurt as much. "Thank you," he said.

She kept her hand on his side for a moment as if trying to heal him with her touch.

He felt it was working.

Then all too soon she removed her hand, and with it the warm sensation. She leaned back, assessing her work. "That should do for now, but I really think you should see the shaman. I'm still concerned about the blood."

He stayed quiet about the headaches, although he wondered if that meant she'd inspect his head for bumps. Aidan started to imagine what her fingers would feel like combing through his hair.

"Are you feeling faint?" she asked. "You look a bit dreamy in the face. When was the last time you took something for the pain?"

"I've taken nothing," Aidan managed to say.

"Nothing? At all?" She studied him. "Well, no wonder you're making faces and collapsing!" With an air of disbelief, she glided across the floor and disappeared through another doorway. There was a clinking sound, followed by running water; then the princess reappeared with a glass and a small white tablet in her palm. "Take this," she said. "It will help with the inflammation."

Nodding, Aidan took the pill and finished the entire glass of water.

It was so clear and sweet, nothing like the dull-tasting stuff from the tap at home.

"Thank you, princess," he replied quickly, feeling foolish for forgetting his manners.

"Stop calling me that," she sighed. "Delia is enough. I'm more than my title, sir." Then she paused. "And you are?"

"A grateful recipient."

"I mean who you are. I don't know your name."

"Of course not, I didn't give it to you." A warm comfort eased into his side. Aidan was amazed the medication could work so quickly. His eye had stopped throbbing as well.

Those perfect eyebrows came together. "Are you being coy on purpose?" she asked.

He smiled, almost drunkenly. "I like to think my mysterious ambience makes me more enjoyable to be around. I fear once you know my name, you will grow bored and move on to the next bodyguard."

The corner of the bed lowered as she sat beside him. "You could at least give me the name of the prince you work for. Then I could call on him and he'd tell me."

"Better yet, why don't you marry him and that way I'll always be around."

The medication had taken away almost all of his pain and replaced it with a sense of brash invincibility. He worked to keep a straight face as he counted the seconds before her rebuttal.

They stared at each other, the time slipping away unnoticed. Aidan imagined the air becoming thicker between them—a line had been crossed.

She broke eye contact first. "A name . . . please. So I can address you properly."

Aidan heard something new in her voice, a genuine plea perhaps. "There is one name I can give you," he said. "Aidan of Doberon." He was shaking inside, having claimed the smaller sister planet of Delta Kur as his homeland.

"Pleased to meet you, Aidan of Doberon." Then she dropped her gaze to his chest. "That's a unique piece," she said, staring at his medallion.

A lump the size of a dried biscuit sat in Aidan's throat. "My mother gave it to me before she died," he said. "It used to belong to my father."

"And he's passed on as well?"

"Yes."

"I lost my father too. Although I don't remember much of him. When I was very little, he contracted a rare disease after a trip to the Kalasta Belt." She looked out the window and seemed to stare into the distance. "So, you're all alone?"

"No, I live with my stepfather and his two sons." Aidan's shirt was lying beside him. He considered reaching for it. "But I've left them back in Doberon. They have no interest in coming here."

That got her attention. "Are you starting a new life here?" she asked, turning back to him.

"You sound hopeful, princess. Sorry . . . Delia." Saying her name by itself, without the title, felt like a secret intimacy.

"Hopeful?" She crossed her arms in front of her chest. "Another suitor is the last thing I need. In case you haven't noticed, I'm to be wed shortly." She laughed at the end, but it came out as a dry chuckle.

"Have you made a final decision?" his voice went high. Aidan cleared his throat and leaned back into the pillow. "I'm only asking because of my own prince. He's been watching the newsfeed and is hurt he hasn't even made the top three with the oddsmakers." Then he added, "Prince Quinton was in the lead this morning."

She looked down. "He'll be able to provide Astor with as much plasma as we need."

"In exchange for what though?" Aidan asked. "I mean, besides the fantastic honor of having you as his wife and all that entails." He allowed himself to steal a glance at the bed they were sitting on.

A smile graced the edges of her mouth. "Why would you assume I wouldn't be enough?"

"Any man worth marrying would consider you enough; however, it's apparent from your lack of enthusiasm for the union that this is not based solely on congeniality. If they're promising plasma, what is our planet giving them in return?"

"It's complicated, but you're right, there are . . . other benefits. Wait, you said our planet, not *your* planet."

"Interesting." He leaned closer. "When you're suspicious of someone you do this thing with your eyebrows and it's so disarming, but in a charming way, of course."

She hit him with a stare. "The truth, please."

Aidan smiled, but his lips were shaking. She was much too smart. "Maybe I feel so at home I forget I'm not from here. Um, Delia . . . the microchip?" He nodded toward the infoscreen. "I'm sure it must have decoded by now."

But the princess would not be distracted. "Why are you really here?" she demanded. "There is no gambling prince, is there? I checked with all the princes this morning, and none of them have ever visited the Dark District, let alone even know it exists."

"All this time you knew, and you said nothing?" He tried to sound accusatory but inside his heart was racing.

"Why do you think I invited you into the tunnels? I need answers!"

Aidan felt like he was getting punched in the stomach all over again, except her words were more painful than any force behind the pirate's fist.

"And to be brutally honest," she continued, "I'm tired of people keeping things from me."

He slouched. Of course she wasn't interested in *him*, only getting answers. And now that she had the microchip, she'd have no more use for him. Still, like a true thief, he wasn't ready to give up on this adventure yet. "I only told you half a lie. I am a bodyguard, but not for a visiting prince. I was hired by someone on your staff. I wasn't given a name; it was all very confidential." Aidan was amazed how easily the lie came to him, like he'd been working on it subconsciously.

"Hired by someone from the palace?" She laughed, but sounded nervous. "Who are you supposed to be guarding?"

"Someone who is in grave danger. You."

She was quiet for a span of three of Aidan's racing heartbeats.

"That's why I was on the ship," he interjected quickly. "I'd been watching you. I knew you were planning on taking it."

She tilted her head but stayed quiet.

"I can tell by your eyebrows that you're still unconvinced, but sincerely, what makes more sense, me being on the ship you just happened to steal by random coincidence, or because I'd been hired to protect you?"

"That's all too convenient. Besides, you haven't been exactly saving me, more like the other way around."

"I was supposed to be undercover, remember? I simply let you think you had to save us."

"And how can I believe what you say this time?"

He glanced at the infoscreen, a heavy sense of obligation cooling his excitement. "I know some of what's on that file. The resistance has a secret weapon and they're planning on using it against the royal family."

She let out a nervous chuckle. "What kind of weapon?"

"I don't know, that was the part that needed decoding, I think. Honestly, the information comes from a reliable source, someone I've known all of my life."

Her face paled. "How did *they* know about the resistance?"

"There's always talk in the Dark District," he sighed.

"A secret weapon?" The princess pursed her lips together. Aidan could almost see the gears working in her brain, trying to find a loophole. "I wonder if that's what Advisor Winchell and Colonel Yashin were discussing."

"I have no information that would confirm that," he said. "But you deserve to see that file. That's why I made sure it found its way to you."

There was a gentle ding from her computer. Delia tapped the screen and the file filled the monitor. She frowned, and then her face lost all its remaining color. "Oh no," she whispered. "This is . . . this is horrible."

CHAPTER SIXTEEN

Queen Talia's inner chamber seemed dead quiet. Even the soft prayers of the shaman had been absorbed by the heaviness in the air.

Delia stood ten feet from the foot of her mother's resting chair, the respectable distance for anyone addressing Her Majesty. Unlike the throne room, this area was the queen's personal space, furnished with more traditional pieces constructed from the natural resources of the planet. The intricate details of the Jesper wood chair had been carved by the royal woodsman for her grandmother, the queen's predecessor, nearly eighty years ago.

As a child, Delia would sneak in and run her finger along the bumps and smooth designs. The familiar braid symbol of three intertwined strands ran along the high back and legs of the piece. She remembered the feel of the wood under her touch, believing that being queen would fulfill her and that she'd grow into its purpose— that it was her destiny.

Heavy lidded, without changing her stone-like expression, the queen brought the tip of the pipe to her mouth and closed her lips. There was a moment of stillness, and then tendrils of smoke snaked upward from her nostrils.

Delia stood in place, confused as to how her mother could be so casual. She had barely been able to keep her tone even as she had spilled out the information she'd found in the file. Her knees shook from fear at addressing her mother so brazenly. "There is an underground community who wants to overthrow the monarchy!"

The queen took another delicate drag of the pipe, then placed it on the granite pedestal. She nodded to the shaman, who quieted his vespers and stepped back, hands clasped in front of him, head down. "And this information comes from a reliable source?" she asked.

A sense of calm eased over Delia. Her mother was exhibiting a rare show of confidence for her opinion. "Yes," she said, handing her the infoscreen. "The chip was a message sent by the resistance, but it was intercepted."

"By whom?" the queen asked, not lifting her eyes from the device. The light reflected off her face, highlighting cheekbones that seemed more prominent than usual.

"Someone from the Dark District who is too afraid to be identified." A sliver of worry started to wedge its way into her reasoning. Delia practically held her breath as her mother looked over the evidence.

Her mother continued to read silently, but Delia noticed that the mask remained in place. How could she not be alarmed?

"And who decoded the encrypted file?" the queen asked, eyes still down.

"I did, Your Majesty." A flush of embarrassed pride warmed Delia's face, despite her work to keep her expression blank. She knew from experience that the queen expected perfection. Assuming she was in favor usually led to saying too much, resulting in a stinging remark from her mother, a little something to keep her mindful of her duty.

But when her mother finally put down the infoscreen, all the queen had as an answer was a tired sigh. "In the future," Queen Talia said, "make sure your reason for interrupting vespers is warranted. I hope you'll show more restraint and reason as queen."

Delia blinked a few times, unable to reconcile her mother's reaction. Finally, she blurted out, "The resistance is creating an android that is far more sophisticated than any before. This is more than a simple SHEW that gives mannerisms and intonation to a robot, this is about using a machine to take the place of a human—not as a worker, but as a true replacement . . . maybe even to replace someone already alive. Someone who has power!" She stopped there, unable to say the idea out loud. It was too gruesome.

The shaman closed his eyes and began to hum a soft prayer. She wondered if she'd just made a mistake in not waiting until her mother was alone. However, his calm demeanor mirrored the queen's bored attitude, and Delia started to suspect the secret file was some kind of experiment to see if she was capable of leadership.

Was this all just a test set up by my mother?

With a careful, more restrained manner, Delia said, "This means there could be a plan to slip an actual android into the palace without us knowing."

Her mother put up a hand, "Anti-royalty sentiment is nothing new." There was an undetermined disappointment to her voice. She took another taste of the pipe.

Delia bit back the impatient curse that lurked dangerously close to the surface. Why wasn't her mother assembling the Guard or making plans to hold an emergency meeting with the royal council? The lack of panic was driving her crazy. She wanted to scream.

The queen took in a breath and rested her attention directly on Delia. "This message is ten years old," she started, her voice no longer lazy, but full of calm purpose. Then she held up the infoscreen for Delia. "The date is clearly encoded at the beginning. I even remember reading it the first time."

A complicated mesh of relief and shame knotted inside her chest. How could she have been so stupid to miss that? An amateur's mistake! Delia bit the inside of her cheek.

"It's real, of course, but it's also expired. We took the proper precautions at the time, and obviously this radical cell never fulfilled this pact." The queen reached for her pipe and took another long drag.

"But why was I never told of this?" Delia asked. She'd begun to grow light-headed. The aroma of herbs from her mother's smoking layered the moment with a cloud of doubt.

An unexpected smirk played at the corner of her mother's mouth. "You were eight years old at the time."

"I see," Delia whispered to herself. A vague shame settled on her shoulders. Everything her mother said was right. She'd been too quick to jump to conclusions without checking the message thoroughly. Her lack of faith in her mother had morphed into suspicion. She couldn't believe she'd become so paranoid.

The queen tilted up her chin. "And although I appreciate the initiative you've shown, it has led to assumptions and rash decisions— not unlike your handling of Marta. I hoped a lesson had been learned from that episode, but it's apparent that it has not."

Queen Talia put both hands on the arms of the chair and pushed herself to stand. Her expression wavered. The shaman took a few steps toward her, but the queen put up a hand, stopping him. Then she stretched to her full height, regal attitude filling the room.

Delia stayed in place as her mother closed the distance between them.

"It was a clever plan," the queen continued. "But the technology isn't there."

Delia dropped to her right knee as her mother approached. She stared at the floor, seeing images in the granite cut from the mighty mountain. Her mother's voice washed over the top of her head.

"Marta was the most advanced android in the Four Quadrants, and no one would mistake her for a human."

Delia remained silent. Had she been wrong about her diagnosis of her personal maid as well?

A soft hand cupped Delia's chin. She looked up into her mother's eyes and was relieved to see sincerity in her expression. "Stand," she softly commanded.

Now eye to eye, Delia saw the toll that commanding a kingdom had taken on her mother's face. Lines stretched out from the corners of her eyes, and her skin was waxen and pulled across high cheekbones. She was looking at her future self, she realized.

"I wonder if Marta being taken from you has left more of an absence than I had anticipated. Is this why you're looking for conspiracy theories? Are you afraid?" Queen Talia paused a moment and a softness graced her features. "I'm breaking my own rule by telling you this, but since your mental health is suffering and is putting your judgment at risk, I want to assure you that I have taken extra precautions in the palace. What with the influx of representatives from the Four Quadrants in anticipation of your engagement, some we have congenial relations with, and others a more strained relationship. Therefore new security measures are in place—specific to your safety, actually."

"Extra security measures?" she said, thinking of Aidan, waiting in her bedchamber. "I'm assuming you're referring to my new secret bodyguard." She'd left him dozing on her bed, sleepy from the pain medication. Delia was about to mention this, but decided to stay quiet, certain her mother would not approve.

The queen sighed and looked up to the ceiling as if praying. "Yes," she said. "But clearly he hasn't done a very good job at staying in character. You weren't supposed to know his true purpose."

The urge to say his name was strong. Delia wanted to discuss him and what they'd experienced together—how he was making her see Astor with new eyes—but she was intrigued by her mother's forthcoming attitude and information. She asked, "And do you have all the information about the underground community of rebels?"

"Yes," she replied. "The resistance is an old organization, but their resources are infantile. Still, we keep an eye on their activity."

"Then I should know everything you do, Your Majesty. As you pointed out, I'm no longer eight years old."

Queen Talia waved her hand toward the large infoscreen mounted on the wall and spoke a command. The monitor came to life at the sound of her mother's voice.

An atmospheric view of their planet came into focus. Delia knew the geography by heart. The land was mostly covered in rugged peaks, and large glaciers to the north cut rivers through the mountains; then the earth dipped past the tangled forests down to the lowest section, where the mines used to be, which was now the Dark District. Beyond that was the canyon and the vast southern tundra.

"The supply of codlight from the mines ran out decades ago," the queen said. "Since then we've had to use other sources of energy from outside our region. Our society may be technologically superior to that of Rexula, but we've grown dependent on their plasma supply."

"I know this, Your Majesty," Delia said.

The infoscreen zoomed in on the Dark District. "The anti-royalty sentiment is homegrown," the queen continued. "This area was once bustling with miners and their families, but now it has turned into a den of lethargic despair and waste. People there no longer work or take pride in this region. It's a breeding ground for criminal activity and unrest."

The screen filled with images of rough men prowling the dark streets, fights breaking out, and gangs of young people howling and rushing the plasma trains.

"Each shipment of plasma from Rexula is smaller than the one before," the queen said. "They're withholding on purpose, asking for more in exchange. We've had to cut back on consumption to make it last longer. This means fewer plasma trains running and fewer hours of light for each household." Queen Talia pursed her lips. "Rationing is always met with resistance," she said.

Delia tried to absorb everything her mother was showing her, but something felt unbalanced. The soothing herbal smoke in the room started to become suffocating. Her royal braid pulled twice its normal heaviness, giving the sensation that she was being swallowed by the granite floor itself.

I am the crown.

I am the kingdom.

I am the tradition.

How can I fix this?

"But there is a solution," Queen Talia said. Then she smiled and Delia was suddenly a child again, racing through the hallways of the palace, or making plans to sneak cookies from the kitchen, or concocting a scheme with Shania to steal Winnie's favorite headdress.

"Marry the right prince."

Delia nodded, and the faces of all the royal suitors went through her mind. She felt as if she were wearing a necklace that got heavier as more jewels of responsibility were added, pulling her spirit down. She imagined being bent forward so far that her nose touched the floor.

Queen Talia placed a hand on her shoulder, then ushered her toward the door. "Prepare for the banquet," she commanded. "Your sister is already in your room picking out your gown."

"My room!" An alarm went off inside her. Ignoring the queen's frown, Delia gave a final rushed curtsy, then bolted out the door and down the hallway.

CHAPTER SEVENTEEN

The white pill had not only taken away Aidan's pain, but any power he had to stay awake. He fought to keep his eyelids open as his body was claimed by the soft bed.

Delia had told him to wait until she returned, but Aidan knew his lie wouldn't hold once she'd talked to the queen. His brain was trying to get him to stand, but his body wasn't cooperating.

Several times already, he'd drifted off only to jolt awake, thinking he'd heard the fast footfalls of the Queen's Guard about to burst into the room and drag him away to the dungeons . . . or maybe they'd skip the dungeons and execute him instead. He could imagine the look on his stepfather's face.

Then a horribly pathetic idea occurred to him—he wouldn't even be missed. There would be no remorse. Not one tear, not one regret, not even an intake of shocked breath when his stepfather learned of the demise of the son he never loved.

The somber thought wiped away the euphoria. He blinked slowly. Why were his eyelids so heavy? He blinked again, but his eyes stayed shut this time. An image of the princess . . . of *Delia*, appeared. The unfathomable depth of her brown eyes stared back. Every time she looked at him, he felt like he was tottering on the edge of the universe, about to trip and spill into the galaxy, suspended in space forever.

How long ago had she left? One minute? An hour? Aidan had no idea.

The sound of the bedroom door opening jolted him awake again. But unlike the other times, footsteps actually came into the room.

"—all extremely vexed that you weren't even waiting for us by the lakeside when we arrived first!" a girl's voice sang out. "With the largest wallowing goose, I might add. And you'll never guess—" She stopped so suddenly her dress swirled around her still frame. She stared at Aidan, her mouth half open.

She had Delia's coloring and similar long hair, except her braid was more intricate. She brought with her a waft of fresh air and fragrant blossoms. Even through his medicated haze, Aidan recognized the younger princess from the infoscreen bulletins from the palace.

A basket hung from the crook of her arm. She slowly raised a finger and pointed it at him. Aidan prepared for her to scream. Instead she said, "You're not my sister."

"And neither are you," he chuckled. "Aren't we a couple of geniuses?" Then a shred of common sense seemed to make a connection in his hazy brain. He needed to escape before she alerted the guards. He put a hand to his bare chest, over his heart. "Begging your pardon, Princess Shania, obviously I'm in the wrong room."

Aidan swung his legs over the side and pushed himself to stand. His head swam, and he immediately lost his balance, falling backward onto the bed again.

"Oh!" She came to the edge of the bed. "Oh no. Are you all right?"

He felt her slap his cheeks a few times.

"Don't die! Don't die!" she said.

Throwing up one of his arms in a blocking maneuver, Aidan pushed himself up to sitting. "Please stop hitting me," he said. The bed took her weight as a few pillows were slipped in behind his head.

When she eased back Aidan noticed her eyes were sparking. "You're not here by mistake." Shania pointed to the bandaging on his side. "That's her handiwork. I'd recognize my perfectionist sister's first-aid skills anywhere." Her tone was playfully accusatory.

"Isn't she though?" he replied quietly as if Delia were across the room and trying to listen. "Was she always like that?" he asked. "Even as a little girl? This room is immaculate."

Shania put a hand to her mouth and laughed. Her eyes went to his bandages again, and the stare seemed to linger. "Wait," she asked, her voice full of awe. "Did she do that to you?"

It took a few moments for Aidan to realize she meant the rib injury. "What? This? No."

"Oh." Her gaze moved to his face. "The eye, then?"

"No." He shook his head. "Not that either."

"So what happened to you?" She put a hand on her hip and leaned to the side, creating an interesting curve of her silhouette. Then, because Shania hadn't screamed yet and Aidan was enjoying the relaxation of the medicine, he simply shrugged.

"Long story," he said. He noticed his shirt crumpled beside him and reached for it. "But let's save that for another day. I really should be going."

She was by his side in an instant. "No, no, no, no," she said, gently putting a hand on his shoulder, keeping him in place. "Obviously you're still getting treatment. You've been injured, and if my sister left you shirtless on her bed, then that's where you should stay."

Aidan watched dumbfounded as the young princess moved about. Her dress billowed behind her as she picked up the forgotten basket and began taking out items, placing them on the bed. There were several small plates, all covered with crisp linens.

"Cook had a few things left over from the banquet preparation," she said excitedly. It took a few moments, but she set up an impromptu picnic between the two of them. She pulled back the cloths to reveal what Aidan recognized as the pastry chef's specialty: tiny cakes with sugared flowers mimicking those in the royal garden. He knew the finished product took at least a week in preparation and decorating. His mouth watered as a sweetness filled the air. In all his shifts in the kitchen, he'd never dared to snatch up one of these delicacies.

Shania picked up a small pink cake with a purple flower on the top and popped it into her mouth like it was only a biscuit crumb. "So," she said, already reaching for another cake, a dark brown one this time. "I know you're not one of the princes, so who are you? And why are you in my sister's bedchamber?"

Aidan stared as she consumed another tiny cake. "Um . . . classified," he answered.

"Here," she lifted a plate of white cakes toward him. There was a curious topping, like it was rolled in snow. "At least tell me about the black eye. Was it a fight? I bet it was over a girl. Am I right?"

"Pirates," he said. Aidan took one of the white cakes and brought it to his nose. Oh! He hoped it tasted half as good as it smelled.

"Pirates!" Shania's eyes grew as large as the plates. "I thought they were outlawed!"

"Ask your sister." He smiled. "She actually threw a bomb at one." Then he took the smallest bite possible, wanting to make this last.

An explosion of gleeful sounds escaped Shania. She put a hand to her chest and laughed as though it came all the way from her silk slippers. "Really?" she sighed, once the giggles had subsided. "She never told me! That sneak!"

"Truly!" He grinned back. The first bite of the sweet melted on his tongue. "I wanted to run and hide, but she was determined to stay and fight."

An expression of admiration and awe lit her features. "That's amazing." Shania licked her fingertips, then took another cake. She winked at Aidan. "You've been having adventures together, then?"

"Mm-hmm," he said while chewing. He was concentrating on eating the cake slowly to enjoy the moment, but he could no longer fight the urge and he inhaled the whole thing. He reached for another.

Biting her lip, Shania looked to the side. "Is this your eye patch? I like it." Then she picked it up and slipped it over her own eye. She struck a pose. "How do I look?"

"Dangerous," Aidan said, popping the white cake in his mouth. Then he closed his eyes and groaned. "What am I eating?" he said. "It's amazing! Forget plasma, give everyone in the Dark District these cakes."

She laughed. "Haven't you ever had coconut before?"

He chewed languidly and then swallowed. "Co-co-nut?" he repeated.

Shania leaned forward. "Where did you come from? And are there more like you?"

Aidan reached for another cake. "I like these so much," he said. Then he nodded to the glass of water on the bedside table. "And I like that white pill your sister gave me."

Shania angled her head, studying him from a new direction. "That's interesting," she said. Her voice had an underlying impishness. "Did you know those pills are also used by the guards when interrogating prisoners? It's impossible to lie when you're under the influence. I wonder if that's why she gave it to you."

A faint coolness changed the air in the room. "I only took one," he said, putting down the white cake he'd just picked up.

"I'm only joking!" she snorted. "Do you really think my sister would drug you? What a scandalous notion!" There was a pause, and then she leaned closer to his ear and whispered, "Why are you really half-dressed and in my sister's room?"

A shiver traveled all the way down Aidan's body. He was distinctly aware of her close proximity. From the corner of his eye he could see her intense expression, one that reminded him of the kitchen cat when it had cornered a mouse by the rubbish bins. He took in a breath and answered her with one word. "Classified," he said.

There was a grunt of exaggerated disappointment as she moved away. "You're no fun," she said, taking a yellow cake this time. "Let's play a game. I'll try to guess who you are by asking you questions that you can only answer with a yes or no."

"No."

"We haven't started yet," she said with a pout. "Oh, you're a terrible tease! It's obvious you're new to the court, but you're not one of the princes or even working for one of them. I would know, I've memorized all of their portfolios."

He looked at her incredulously. "All seven?"

She chewed. "Mm-hmm."

"Name them."

Without hesitating, she swallowed, then started, "Hagar, then

Maxim and Mikel—I tend to think of them as a package deal. Then we have Armano, who is rumored to have brought enough wigs to require a second ship for the journey. Also Oskar who smells like the woods, but not in a bad way. Then Felix, and last, Quinton."

"Impressive recall skills," he praised. "Who will she choose? You're her sister, you must have some inclination of where her heart is leaning."

"Her heart?" she huffed. "My sister is all about duty. She'll probably pick the most boring one." Then Shania reached for another cake and held it up to her face, inspecting it. "I can't wait for my turn," she said matter-of-factly. "But my qualifications in a husband are quite different from my sister's. I'll be picking the man whose kisses make my eyes roll into the back of my head."

"That sounds impractical. You'd be blind and bumping into everything."

Snorting a laugh, Shania had to wait before her chuckles subsided before eating the sweet. She sighed thoughtfully and picked up her infoscreen. "However, let it be known that I feel for my dear sister. Look at the choices, though." She passed the infoscreen to Aidan.

He took the device, noting how much more advanced it was than the busted one he had bolted to his wall back at the cottage. "I see you've designed your own rating system," he said, scrolling through the princes.

A moment of jealousy stung his heart when he came to the image of Prince Quinton. "What do you think of him?" he asked Shania, hoping there would be some unsavory characteristic about him they could laugh about.

She tilted her head. "He's lovely, actually. Handsome, polite, and he has the most charming page, Niko. I can see my sister being happy with him, I think."

A stillness descended over Aidan. He'd never once considered how he'd feel after Delia married. But sitting on her bed and spending time with her had somehow created a small hopefulness in his chest. It wasn't like he actually thought they could be together—even friends would be impossible. Still, there was an odd spark, deep inside, that would not dampen.

Shania took the device from him. "But this one!" she practically squealed. "He clicks his boots at the end of every sentence. Such a quirky trait! He must have special clicking material in his heels, because it sounds like a giant robot eating a metal sandwich when he does it."

Then she stood up and demonstrated. She said in a gruff voice, "When may I show you my big gun, Princess Delia?" Then she clicked her heels.

Aidan laughed. "Go again," he prompted. He was enjoying her bringing down the prince.

In the same gruff voice she said, "It's essential for all Trellium men to eat a well-balanced breakfast before going off to war! Click, click, click!" She mimicked the heels clicking. Then she came out of character. "At least he's nice to look at," she sighed, handing the screen to Aidan.

The laugh stuck in his throat as he looked at a close-up of the man's image. "This is Prince Felix?" he asked.

"What's wrong?" Shania asked. "You look like you just saw a ghost pirate."

This was the man he'd taken the dagger from, he was sure of it. "When did he arrive on Astor?" he asked as his voice shook.

"He was here for certain yesterday, because he went with Colonel Yashin to search for Delia. Why?"

Aidan's stomach twisted. This was the man in the clearing, the one who she rode back on the glider with! "I have to speak with your sister," he said, pushing himself off the bed.

"No, please don't go!" Shania moved quickly, blocking his way, her hands going to his waist. "Besides, she'll be upset if I let you leave when she specifically asked you to stay."

"I can't wait. We must find her now. Please!"

Shania leaned closer. "Who are you?" she whispered.

There was the sound of the doors sliding open, then rushed

footsteps. Aidan looked over to see Delia standing before them, eyes full of confusion. Her chest rose and fell quickly as if she'd been running.

"What's going on?!" Delia's voice reverberated off the walls.

"We were having a picnic," Shania said, still keeping her hands on his waist.

Aidan stepped away from her, suddenly aware of his state of undress.

Delia's nostrils flared. "A picnic?" Then she shook her head. She put her entire attention on Aidan. "You have to go. I'm grateful for everything you've done, but it's been rendered moot."

"You're making him leave?" Shania stomped a foot. "But he's injured and there are a few cakes still left to eat. And . . . and . . ." She looked around the room as if hunting for inspiration. "And we'll need his opinion on which dress you should wear tonight."

"No!" both Delia and Aidan said in unison.

Shania glanced between the two of them. Then she picked up her infoscreen and started tapping it.

Delia went to her bed. In a smooth motion she gathered up Aidan's clothing and handed it to him. "Take the servants' lift, you won't be seen." She turned him around and pushed on his back.

His feet were shuffling under him before he knew what was happening. "Wait, please," he said. He almost tripped a few times.

"I apologize." Then she helped him button up his shirt. "Imagine how that would look if you left my room only partially dressed." She stared at his chest as she spoke.

Shania stayed on the spot, but she craned her neck, listening.

Aidan whispered to Delia, "It's about the microchip. There's something I've discovered!"

She fastened the top button, then slipped the jacket over his arms as well. "Me too," she said. "But it's no longer any of your concern. That information was ten years old. There's no threat. Thank you, but if you'll excuse me, I have to get ready for the banquet." Then she met his eyes for only a fraction of a second before activating the doors to open.

Aidan watched as she checked to make sure the way was clear. Then she ushered him out.

"Regardless, we need to talk privately." Aidan touched her elbow.

She slipped away from his touch. "You are my bodyguard," she said. "Nothing more. I cannot risk taking any more false information to the queen, I looked like a fool. It's not all your fault; I allowed myself to be easily convinced. However, it's better for everyone involved if you go back to being my secret bodyguard, and I return to focusing on picking a husband." She took a breath, then added, "I hope you understand."

Then the doors slid closed, leaving Aidan standing in the corridor all alone.

CHAPTER EIGHTEEN

D elia turned away from her sister's intense stare and busied herself by straightening out the bed. "You've gotten cake crumbs everywhere," she said.

"Yes, that seems like the most natural topic for us to discuss. Never mind the gorgeous man who happened to be in your bed, and happened to be shirtless, and happened to have all kinds of wonderful stories about you fighting pirates." Shania finished the last cake. "Sorry about the crumbs, though."

Ignoring her sister, Delia went to the large wardrobe. She opened the wooden doors and pretended to take a great interest in her gowns. She could feel her younger sister's stare burn through her back.

"I have it on excellent assurance that green is Prince Quinton's favorite color," Delia said, hoping that talk of fashion would distract her younger sister.

Shania stood beside her. "And what is the favorite color of our blond mystery man? He seemed to really enjoy the coconut cakes. Perhaps you should dress in white."

Delia continued the fashion quest. "And yet, color isn't the only consideration," she said. "I shouldn't underestimate the suggestive cut of a bodice." She pulled out a dress and held it up for Shania's approval.

"You hate pink." Shania took the dress from her sister and hung it back up. "Now stop this nonsense, you can't hide your heart from me."

"My heart?" Delia crossed her arms in front of her chest. "Don't be absurd."

"I've been watching you interact with over half a dozen men, and none of them ever put that shade of red in your cheeks." She put a hand on her sister's shoulder. "I know you have to keep some things secret from me, just as Mother keeps secrets from us both—but I'm your sister! Please! At least tell me his name!"

"You're impossible," Delia sighed. Aidan was her secretly hired bodyguard put in place by the queen, but Shania couldn't keep a secret for all the cakes in the kingdom. Still, if she knew a little bit, it might not seem as scandalous, and her younger sister would get bored of the topic soon. "His name is Aidan," she said. A small thrill traveled down her spine. Delia paused, noting the effect that just saying his name out loud had on her.

"Aidan," Shania repeated dreamily. "Suits him."

She scoffed at her sister. "Don't get all swoony, he's only here because of all the princes. He's extra security, but he's undercover." Delia studied her sister's jubilant expression and realized a calming tactic was called for. "So you can't talk about him to anyone, it may jeopardize his safety . . . and ours."

She nodded. "Understood. But can I talk *to* him?"

Typical Shania, looking for the loophole. "You won't see him again," Delia answered. "He's rather elusive. Oh, don't pout, it's his job to be hidden."

"Do you know where he comes from? I wonder if there's an abundance of plasma. Or what if his planet has something Rexula needs and then we can still get our energy source and you might be able to consider marrying Aidan and then—"

"You're being foolish," Delia interrupted. "Obviously he has nothing to offer, nor is he even considering entering a marriage contract . . . oh! Look, stop derailing this conversation into some romantic nonsense. I don't wish to marry Aidan! I don't wish to marry anyone, but as future queen I have to pick the man most likely to benefit Astor." Her voice had risen enough to bounce off the walls. Her sister's face lost all its sparkle. Delia paused and took a deep breath.

"I'm sorry," Delia said more docilely. "I'm just nervous about the banquet tonight. Can you help me pick out a dress? You know I'm hopeless at this kind of thing."

"Of course." Shania smiled, her usual verve returned. She moved in and practically pushed Delia out of the way as she arranged the hangers along the rod, pausing every few moments to critique each dress.

A wave of gratitude spilled from Delia's heart. Her younger sister's future was as much influenced by this marriage as Delia's. The queen's words came back to her.

Marry the right prince.

"Rumor has it Prince Quinton is saving himself for his true love," Shania said, smirking. She held the end of a sleeve, stretching it out, studying the intricate designs on the cuff.

Blinking out of her despair, Delia stared at her sister. "Excuse me?" she asked.

"He's never dated any girl." Shania pulled the gown out and held it up against her sister, giving them both a critical eye. "I wouldn't exactly call this a true green, but there's an underlying hue that complements your skin tone. And the beadwork on the neckline and cuffs are the perfect example of elegant excess. Still, I need to see you in it. Try it on."

"How do you know he's never had a girlfriend?" Delia asked, taking the gown and moving behind the dressing screen.

"Niko told me. He has a wealth of information about Prince Quinton. They've been together for the last three years. You should talk with him." The next part of Shania's sentence came through the dressing screen in a salacious whisper. "I bet he'll give you all the tasty tidbits about your future husband."

Delia rolled her eyes as she slipped on the gown. "Niko is too busy scowling at me."

"He was perfectly pleasant with me on the hunt today."

"Besides, what do I care? Prince Quinton can have a dozen lovers as far as I'm concerned." Delia emerged from behind the dressing screen and stood in front of her sister for inspection.

"Tragic," Shania said, shaking her head.

"Really?" Delia smoothed the fabric. "I thought it was a good choice."

"Not the gown." Shania came behind her sister and began to button up the back. "The dress is perfect. I'm talking about your tragic attitude. How can a future queen rule a kingdom if she can't rule her husband in the bedroom?"

Delia rolled her eyes again.

"Your braid will fall out if you keep pulling that face."

As a reply, Delia gave the most exaggerated eye roll she could manage. Then she turned to the mirror. She took in the perfectly fitted gown with the intricate beadwork at the neckline—Marta's handiwork. Would she be happier right now if she hadn't sabotaged Marta's SHEW? For all her preplanning and worrying, she'd ended up in the same place she started. Trying on dresses to meet her future husband.

With one exception—Aidan. He told her they had to meet privately, that he had something to tell her about the microchip, even after she'd told him the information was old. What else could he know that she didn't?

"I heard Prince Armano brought his own team of stylists," Shania's voice broke through. Her words had returned to their usual excitement whenever there were dresses and men involved. Her attitude was a perfect opposite to Delia's feelings.

The crease on the bed caught her attention. Delia walked over and spread her hand over the cover, smoothing it away. The pillow still had the indent of Aidan's head. Unable to help herself, she smiled secretly, thinking of the inside pocket of his jacket and what she'd slipped inside.

Will he find it before the banquet tonight?

It wasn't unreasonable to assume he'd be there. He was still her secret bodyguard. And just because she couldn't see him, didn't mean he wouldn't be there, carefully watching her. Maybe they could still meet somewhere privately . . .

"You're blushing." Shania grinned. "Nothing could be more obvious than a bride staring at her bed."

"Do you think Mother and Father had a happy marriage?" Delia asked. She knew her own parents had a contracted engagement—still, they had been acquainted with each other since childhood. Her father had come from one of the wealthiest families within the court.

Shania shrugged. She was so young when he died, she didn't have many memories of him. "I don't think it was an unhappy union." Then she gave her sister a sweet smile, no hint of teasing. "I can't imagine anyone not loving you. Even if you're strangers at first, two similarly kind people will make each other happy."

A quiet sigh left her lips. "Thank you."

"Interesting." Shania lifted an eyebrow and her usual impish expression slipped back into place. "This is the first time you haven't outwardly refused, gagged, or made a face at the idea of marriage." She waited, then asked, "Has our lovely Aidan changed your mind?" She poked her sister in the ribs.

"No." Delia pushed her away playfully. "And don't call him our lovely Aidan."

✳ ✳ ✳

It took nearly an hour for Delia to greet all the families of the court and then finally the princes and their entourages as they entered the great hall for the banquet.

Prince Hagar smiled at her, his eyes blue and sparkling like water. A double stranded necklace of colorful shells hung to his waist.

"That is so beautiful," Delia said.

He lifted the strand with one finger. "On Lazlo, the shores are covered with these shells only one time during the year. Each shell has its own legend."

"Which makes the piece even more precious."

His cheeks flushed. Then he leaned closer and said, "Perhaps you'll own one just like it someday." He strode away, the shells clicking softly.

"I like a man who is also a wind chime," Shania remarked smartly.

Queen Talia watched from the throne, nodding elegantly as the courtiers passed. Shania, in perfect opposite fashion, became more energetic—not missing an opportunity to whisper a handsomeness rating in Delia's ear as each prince went by.

Princes Maxim and Mikel arrived in matching black jackets with fur trim and heeled boots. Their brown hair was curled this time. Delia mixed up their names. "How will I ever tell you apart?" she asked genuinely. She wondered if it would be rude to ask them to wear tags.

Both princes looked at each other and smiled slyly. Then one of them replied, "Perhaps that's a discussion for a smaller or rather more intimate audience, Your Highness."

Shania watched them leave to find their seats, her mouth slightly agape. "My galaxy," she breathed. "I believe they've just raised the bar."

"Princess Delia." Prince Felix gave her a quick dip of his chin. "You look exquisite this evening. I brought something very rare from Trellium I'd like to share with you. I understand you're seated next to Prince Armano, but I'm hoping you can join me in dessert later."

"Join you in dessert?" Delia had an image of sitting in a large bowl of cream and berries with Prince Felix staring at her from the opposite side of the rim.

Shania snorted and poked her in the side.

His face remained stoic as if he were answering a math question instead of proposing an invitation to share food. When she remained quiet he added, "You can't expect Prince Armano to have you all to himself this evening."

As always, his expression relayed not even the smallest hint of interest. Then again, Delia wondered how much of her reluctance showed through her forced smile.

She curtsied. "I'd be delighted."

Click! His heels signaled his leaving. With a quick nod to Shania he marched his way farther into the grand room and down the long dining tables.

Delia watched him with curiosity. Around the room she saw the Queen's Guard, but at regular intervals she noticed the uniforms of Trellium's military. Her mother had hired a secret bodyguard, but had she also engaged extra military protection?

A wedge of unease pushed its way into her logic. If she chose Prince Quinton, would Prince Felix feel rejected to the point that he would retaliate with weapons? She not only had to choose the right man, but she had to make sure she didn't reject the wrong one.

Prince Oskar appeared and bowed awkwardly. He definitely seemed more at ease doing arduous labor than the pleasantries of court. "You look lovely," he said, glancing over her shoulder. Then he focused back on her and nodded. "Let me know if you'd like to converse later."

"Yes, I suppose so. And thank you for helping with the gardens today."

He bowed again, then made his way to the side of the room. He turned and stood with his back to the wall, hands clasped in front of him.

Finally, the queen stood, addressing the room. Staring directly at Delia, she hinted at the grand announcement that would be made during the celebration of the Full Moon Festival. "A union that will solidify our place of honor in the Four Quadrants as the most lucrative, and assuredly the most envied, of our neighboring galaxies."

From the periphery of her vision, Delia noticed Prince Quinton. She looked his way and smiled. He dropped his eyes. A quiet panic started deep in her bones. All this time she had been hesitant about the match. She had never considered she'd have to win him over.

CHAPTER NINETEEN

Aidan made it down to the tunnels without being noticed. Again, he marveled at the perfect symmetry of the underground passageways.

When he came to the junction, Aidan took the path that led to the lakeside, not eager to bump into Drake, who by now was probably napping under a shrub somewhere, sleeping off a hangover from the pub.

It was a ridiculous irony that his stepfather regarded his eldest and most useless son as having all the potential. Aidan kept his train of thought firmly planted with his family. He must put the princess from his mind.

He had no more excuses to see her again, and from her actions in the bedroom it was obvious she had no need for him any longer. Acknowledging that he was, in fact, now thinking about the one person he was desperate to forget, he kicked the rock wall of the tunnel.

He swore through gritted teeth. "Much better."

Limping through the doorway at the end of the passage, Aidan emerged onto a secluded shoreline section of Black Lake. He watched the door slide closed behind him, blending in seamlessly with the natural rock.

The moment couldn't have been more symbolic.

Leaving the airy beauty of the palace behind, Aidan made his way to the plasma trains, wishing he had his old sky dodger. He hoped at least the pirates would use it for parts to fix their own gliders, which was slightly less horrible than imagining his machine ending up in the picking station.

The suns were soon shut out as the train dipped under the magnificent lawns of the stilted mansions. The gray slowly turned to black as he descended lower into the Dark District. The surroundings matched his own depressive emotional descent. He had half a notion to visit Griffin, but he was behind in his chores.

Although his spirit was as low as the dusty ground, his heart nearly skipped when he arrived at the back of his cottage and noticed the tarp was still undisturbed. He went over and pulled back the cover, relieved to see the Queen's Guard glider was still intact and in place. He'd have to start taking it apart later tonight, after the others had gone to bed. Then he'd sell the parts to Griffin in small bundles at a time, trying to make the most profit. He was resigned to restarting his Delta Kur fund; what other choice did he have?

Aidan entered the cottage, tossing the threadbare jacket on his bed. He also slipped off the boots, just in case Morgan noticed. While not as gruff as his older brother, Morgan's cruelty lay in his refusal to even acknowledge his existence. Many times Aidan had tried to start a conversation, only to have him leave the room. No explanation, not even a snide remark. Just neglect.

And even though he was grateful he didn't have to spend too much time with his cold stepbrother, the sting of being constantly ignored hurt far more and far longer than any insult from Drake.

He went into the empty kitchen and began to prepare the evening meal. His stepfather and Drake wouldn't be done with their shifts at the palace for several hours, giving him enough time to make it look as though he'd been completing chores all day long.

Most people in the Dark District only had access to packaged food, but since Aidan's stepfather was a guard, he had his pick, or rather was the last one on the list to pick, from whatever vegetables were left over from the chef's garden.

He peeled the root vegetables and readied the plasma stove. Since they only had enough supply to use the stove for an hour, this was the only hot meal of the day. Aidan cleaned the floor and washed up the dishes left by the others. The aroma of the roasted supper began to fill the small room.

A blast from the infoscreen mounted to the wall made him jump. His heart kicked up a beat. It was an announcement from the palace news feed. An image of Queen Talia seated on her throne filled the picture.

She stood and addressed the crowd. "The Full Moon Festival will have especially significant meaning for us this year. It is the hope of this monarchy to continue our viable reign and assure the kingdom we are here to serve the greater good for all of our people. I hope to share tremendous news of a promised union."

The camera focused on Delia. Aidan couldn't breathe. She offered a weak smile and then turned her attention to the middle of the crowd. Her smile faltered, and then the screen switched to the newsfeed as information regarding the upcoming ball scrolled across.

"What are you thinking?" Morgan's voice broke the silence.

Aidan spun around, unsure how long his stepbrother had been standing there, watching him. He had a cloth in his hands, wiping his fingers. There was a smell of burnt plasma in the air.

"What are you thinking?" Morgan repeated the question, but stayed on the other side of the room. There was something new in his expression that Aidan couldn't quite pinpoint.

"I don't know," Aidan replied, still a bit dazed by Morgan's appearance. Only when his stepbrother's gaze moved to the screen did Aidan realize that was the longest he'd ever held eye contact with him.

Still watching the infoscreen, Morgan asked, "You don't feel anything . . . different?" His voice rose on the last word. Then he put his focus back on Aidan.

"No. What difference does it make to us who she marries?" Aidan turned away pretending to be busy at the stove. He could feel Morgan's stare burning a hole in his shirt. He must know about Delia! He waited for the insult to come . . . or perhaps a threat. Yes, a threat to tell Corporal Langdon would be more likely. His stepfather would consider it blasphemous for Aidan to even think about Delia, let alone sneak up to her bedchamber.

He considered the royal family close to godlike, while Aidan was no more than a speck of dirt under his boot.

"Aidan?" Morgan prompted.

"Supper will be shortly," he answered. "I'll call you when it's ready." He kept his back to him while he wiped out the already clean sink.

There seemed to be a lapse of a thousand seconds before he heard Morgan's footsteps fade out of the kitchen. There was the click of the basement door opening, and then closing again. Aidan's hands shook as he prepped the table. Morgan had never uttered so many words to him in such a short time. It couldn't be a coincidence, could it?

He heard Morgan under the floorboards using one of his tools. There was a loud buzzing, but then he heard him talking. It sounded like he was arguing. A loud bang made Aidan jump. The machinery stopped, but Morgan continued to talk to himself. Then he swore. Something heavy hit the basement wall. Then there was silence.

Aidan gave the basement door a furtive stare. He made sure to keep his senses tuned into the lock turning open.

It was another hour before the sound of his stepfather's glider announced the arrival of both him and Drake.

"Grand news!" Corporal Langdon bounded into the room out of breath. He looked past Aidan and zeroed in on the pot on the stove. Taking off the lid, he leaned down, but then his happy expression melted. "Roots again?" He sounded disappointed. The lid went back down with a clank. "Hardly a supper fit to celebrate Drake's advancement!"

Walking around Aidan, he yelled out Morgan's name. "Come here! We're celebrating!"

"What's the news?" Aidan lined up the dishes and began ladling the food.

Drake made a face as if he were smelling rotten sandworms. "You spoil everything," he muttered. Aidan wasn't sure if he meant the food or simply Aidan's existence in his field of vision. He laid the three dishes on the table, making sure to pour the ale into his stepfather's stein first.

The basement stairs creaked, followed by the door opening. Morgan arrived, his expression bearing the same deep concentration of earlier, but a little less intense. His gaze moved back and forth between his father and brother. "Drake has made the Queen's Guard?" he said dully. "Stunning."

The Queen's Guard? Drake can barely tie his own shoes! Astor is doomed. Aidan watched Morgan from the corner of his eye, wondering how he had even guessed such a preposterous event. It was more ludicrous than his own adventure today.

Corporal Langdon stared down Morgan. A warning flashed across his eyes before it vanished. He then slapped Drake heavily on his meaty shoulders and laughed. "He *will* be stunning in his uniform! And it couldn't have come at a better time, what with the Full Moon Festival approaching."

Morgan went to the table and sat at his place.

"Princess Delia will announce her engagement at the ball," Corporal Langdon said. His body dropped onto his chair, making the floor shudder. "Every important leader will be there," he continued, practically gushing. "It will be a historic moment for this family." Despite his earlier remark about the meal, he started eating with gusto. "Only the important households get invitations," he said around a mouthful.

A snort escaped from Drake. Then he caught his father's eye and dipped his chin.

Aidan scooped out the last piece of vegetable and dropped it into a small dish for himself. He started to make his way to his room.

"One more thing," Corporal Langdon called out to him. "I forbid you from going to Griffin's shop anymore." He pointed the spoon at Aidan. "He says terrible things about the palace. There are rumors he's part of the resistance. No child of mine will do business with such lowlifes."

I am not your child! Aidan screamed in his head. Instead he nodded. "Yes."

"Yes, what?"

"Yes, corporal."

The fine pinpricks of a headache started. Aidan put a hand to the right side of his head. He noticed Drake's elbow nudge his stepfather. "Excuse me," Aidan said, escaping to his room.

He sat on the small cot and downed his piece of supper in one bite. Turning on the plasma lamp, he focused on the shelves above his bed. He touched each item, remembering when he'd gotten them. Then he put his attention on the latest acquisition.

The delicate cake was somewhat crushed, but its coconut aroma brought a plethora of images. It was cruel, actually. Daydreaming of Delia when he knew he'd never be that close to her ever again.

He popped it into his mouth, letting it melt, thinking about Shania's infoscreen and the image of Prince Felix. Even if the message that came from the dagger was ten years old, Delia should know it had been in his possession. If only he'd had more time to explain to her.

Aidan thought of the Queen's Guard glider hidden under the tarp. His heart started to pick up. He could slip into the palace airspace easily, maybe even fly up to her balcony. Maybe even offer her a midnight ride. He closed his eyes and imagined what it would feel like to have her sitting behind him with her arms around his waist.

There was a roar of laughter from the kitchen. "Him? At the ball? Wearing his kitchen garb?" his stepfather snorted.

Reality punched him in the gut. It didn't matter if he had a state-of-the-art glider—he was still a chore boy wearing his older brother's rags and holey shoes.

The jacket he'd tossed on the bed earlier caught his eye. He picked it up and assessed the poorly sewn collar. Had she noticed? He slipped on the jacket and imagined it was a fine coat, rich in color like the ones the princes had worn today on the lawn. His mind told him it was foolish, but he told his mind to "shut up, thank you very much."

Aidan did a mock pose, pretending he'd crashed the ball, and was imagining the look of surprise on Delia's face. "I came back for my eye patch," he'd tell her, making sure to add extra cheek to his tone. He put a hand in his pocket, still pretending.

Then he paused. His fingers touched something. He pulled out the familiar small black disc. Tripping back over the details of the day he tried to remember putting it there, but he couldn't.

"Sneaky princess," he whispered. A smile took over his face, a real one this time. She must have placed the homing device inside the pocket when she gave him back his jacket as she rushed him out of her bedroom. He was momentarily in awe of her skill. Then a thought occurred to him, one that made him feel like he'd eaten a hundred coconut cakes.

There was only one reason she would give him back the transmitter—she wanted to see him again!

CHAPTER TWENTY

During the feast, Delia barely tasted any of the numerous courses, all beautifully served on the finest dishes. Prince Armano and his nonstop conversation buzzed around her like a bug she couldn't swat away.

For the last hour she'd endured him retelling all of his favorite episodes of *Comet Patrol*, starring the robot dog.

"They actually use a real dog," he said, using his fork to push around the last piece of roasted wallowing goose in the sauce. "Except they give him a voice, which of course would never happen if you had a real robot dog. But if they did exist, I would very much like mine to also speak three languages and sing." His flaxen curls were done in an elaborate updo, and Delia was certain he'd spent five times the amount of time and preparation for this evening that she had.

The plasma chandeliers caught the embedded crystals in his sleeve, sending a frenzy of reflected dots of light over Delia's face. She kept squinting at him as he spoke, his hands gesturing with each sentence.

Delia's attention swept the perimeter of the grand room. Curiously, it was Prince Oskar she saw first, standing off to the side, his gaze orbiting the room just as hers was. Who was he looking for?

She, of course, was hoping to catch sight of Aidan. Even though she'd told him they should never meet again in private, they could certainly share a glance across the room. He was still her bodyguard, after all. She hadn't thought of her safety before this—certainly not when she was stealing a spaceship—but seeing him now would give her a little peace of mind.

Her gaze landed on Prince Felix, who also happened to be looking her way. She had the feeling he was locking on a target. Unblinking, he raised his glass of wine in her direction and brought it to his lips.

The gesture was so unlike his characteristically brisk manner that she couldn't help but watch him. When the glass came down he revealed a curve of a smile.

". . . and my collection of miniature spaceship models of the galaxy rivals that of the esteemed Duke Archibald," Prince Armano said, his voice close to her ear.

She recoiled somewhat, then carefully turned to face him. "I'm sorry, who?"

Prince Armano's jaw dropped. "Duke Archibald is regarded as the master of antique miniatures of the Four Quadrants."

"A master?" She couldn't keep the bored sarcasm from her voice.

His face showed the insult had hit.

"Although," she said, her voice softer, "I'm quite sure your collection of miniatures is fine and would be very interesting."

"I was hoping you'd say that." He pulled out a small infoscreen from his inside pocket. He brought up images of tiny spaceships, some held in his hands, others beside his smiling face.

Delia prayed to her ancestors for an intervention. Unfortunately, they ignored her silent plea. "Pardon me," she said, standing. "I'm suddenly unwell, a headache from all the stimulating conversation."

"Let me accompany you back to your room."

"No!" she said, a bit too forced. "A simple walk outside is what I need." Then she added, "Alone."

She made her way to the balcony and was grateful the moment she stepped outside. Although it had been a lie she told to displace herself from Prince Armano's company, the freshness of the night air was soothing.

Moving to the stone railing, she looked out over the gardens bathed in the soft glow of moonlight. The sounds of the feast were muffled behind her. Delia was exhausted by the whole charade, cloaked in elaborate dresses and manners.

"I'm not sure what is more beautiful." Prince Quinton came from the shadows to stand beside her. "The royal garden in the daylight of the two suns, or at night with the subtle illumination of the moon."

Delia started at his sudden appearance, then composed herself. "How was the hunt today?"

He smiled and dropped his chin before answering. "I returned first," he said. "With the largest wallowing goose, I might add."

"Congratulations," she replied. "I regret not being there to witness it."

There was a hint of a dimple. "My motives were purely selfish, princess. If I recall correctly, I was promised a prize by you."

She stumbled a few words together, "Oh . . . well. I, um . . . a prize?"

"Rest easy," he chuckled. "I'm more than pleased to be spending this unexpected moment with you. And I'm sure you'll agree, the situation we find ourselves in on this lovely evening is unique." He took a step closer. "You know why I am here, princess. I wish to marry you, but I am not the kind of man who hides behind grand gestures or is ignorant of the real reason you are choosing a husband. So please, go ahead and ask me anything. I promise to answer truthfully."

There was something sincere in his voice. Delia enjoyed a rare moment of ease and was encouraged by his candor. "Why do you want to marry me?" she asked.

"As you know, the bond will strengthen trading between our planets." He put a hand on the railing and stared at the grounds, looking beyond the maze. "More importantly though, I'm looking for a new start," he said. "Rexula has many resources and its beautiful shores are unparalleled, but the planet is backward in some ways . . . or at least in the ways that are meaningful to me."

"In regard to technology?" she asked. The large mammals that ruled the oceans on Rexula had fatty tissue that contained plasma. The process to procure the precious element was uncomplicated yet labor intensive, and a sour odor filled the air. "I visited the first time with my mother when I was five. The unending sea scared me—I was used to mountains. And the plasma factories made me plug my nose. But I loved the people, they were very nice to us."

"So true, the method to obtain plasma is simple—unchanged for hundreds of years, but the by-product is unfortunate." He made a face. "Sometimes I think the smell is inside me, that it clings to my soul."

"Really?" She moved in closer and inhaled. "You smell nice to me."

"Thank you," he said. "You're sweet to say so." Prince Quinton appeared moderately satisfied, or maybe it was a look of relief, but either way his next sentence came out smoothly. "A couple in an arranged marriage have just as much chance at being happy as two partners who find each other by happenstance."

His matter-of-fact approach to their situation was comforting to Delia, and yet she couldn't help but feel slighted. "I find it hard to believe that fate is so concerned with one couple that it uses everything in its power to put them together," she said.

"Precisely."

His answer pleased her. Still, there was something missing. "What are you passionate about?" she asked.

Color lightened his cheekbones. Before he could answer, Prince Armano emerged from the doorway.

"There you are!" he said, his arms opened wide. Delia wondered if he expected her to run to him. Instead he went directly to Prince Quinton. He handed him a small note folded over many times. "There was a messenger asking for you; had your manservant running all over the banquet hall, I dare say. Seems of the utmost importance."

Prince Quinton took the note and opened it. His expression was solemn, and then his lips formed a straight line.

"Is there an issue?" Delia asked.

"Do you have to return home early?" There was an underlying hope to Prince Armano's question.

"No," he replied, tucking the note into his jacket. Then Prince Quinton bowed to Delia. "But I have already taken enough of your time. It's been a pleasure," he said. Then he disappeared through the curtained doorway and back into the banquet hall.

"I thought he'd never leave!" Prince Armano said, blowing air out of his cheeks.

"Who was the messenger?" she asked.

"A young lady, actually." Then Prince Armano lowered his voice and leaned closer. "I confess, I read the note."

There was a strong smell of wine on his breath. Delia fought the urge to put space between them, but her curiosity won. She dropped her voice and added a hint of playful gossip. "I'm all astonishment at you! Please tell me, what did it say?"

"Only two words." He winked. "Maze. Midnight."

"That's it?"

"It seems Prince Quinton may have a lovers' rendezvous planned." He laughed with a hand over his mouth. "Terribly sloppy of him to bring along his lover—not to mention poor taste."

Prince Armano shifted his stance and maneuvered closer to her, nudging her side. "As you know, princess, Delta Kur is far away and I've been waiting many months for this very moment. Allow me the honor of officially offering you . . ."

"Forgive me," Delia interrupted, faking a yawn. "I'm quite played out from all your joyful company. Tomorrow will be a better time to continue this very important conversation, for which I want to be at my most attentive, Prince Armano. Please be at your leisure." She waved a hand toward the entrance to the banquet hall, still full of guests. Then she gave him a simple curtsy and hurried back into the palace.

After reaching her bedchamber, she began to pace the floor, trying to ease her frazzled nerves. The princes were proving to be too complicated to figure out. The only one she was sure about was Prince Armano, and he was definitely a no.

And where was Aidan? Was he more injured than she thought?

Images of him lying in the tunnels somewhere, bleeding internally, haunted her. She spied the clockwork bird on the nightstand. After she wrote a quick note, she placed it inside the bird, then took it to her balcony and set it free. She frowned as it headed straight over the maze, away from the palace, and into the night.

Why wasn't Aidan on the premises?

A knock at the door interrupted her thoughts.

"Come in," Delia said, expecting Shania to arrive with an info-screen full of her latest stats. Instead, Prince Felix stood at attention in the doorway, holding a tray with a covered dish.

"You promised me dessert," he said, making his way past her and onto her balcony.

Wordlessly she followed him outside, partly in shock, but more out of curiosity.

Holding the tray in one hand, Prince Felix pulled off the cover of the dish to reveal a bowl of glistening red fruit.

Delia took in a quick breath. "Rubis berries!" Her mouth started to water.

He smiled and it softened his sculpted cheekbones. "Trellium is not only known for our superior military power, but is also the only planet in the Four Quadrants that can grow and sustain the rubis bush."

"I haven't had one in years." She started to reach for the dish, but he pulled it away from her reach, closer to him. "Are you going to eat the whole bowl in front of me?" she teased.

"I sense I'm not making my intentions perfectly clear. I'm not only here as a representative of my planet, but also as a man." He seemed to stand a little taller. "And I'd be amiss if I didn't tell you that I am prepared to love Astor and its people as I love my own home."

He took a step closer to Delia and dropped his voice. "As I am already in love with its future queen. And I vow to be a most attentive husband in every way you wish."

Delia could scarcely breathe. Her pulse was in her throat. Who would have guessed the hardened military soldier was all fiery and romantic underneath? She was certain Shania would have fainted at this point.

Prince Felix continued, "There is a belief that this fruit acts as a . . . how should I say, enhancement for couples." He then picked up a berry, gently pinching it between his thumb and finger, and placed it against Delia's lips.

The fruit was soft and sweet and melted on her tongue. Then he leaned down and kissed her, his lips barely touching her mouth before pulling away.

My first kiss, she thought dully. The moment was so much less spectacular than she'd hoped or even imagined.

He gave her that smile again, the one that seemed natural and not dictated by protocol. Then he gave her the bowl. "I'll let you enjoy the rest," he said. "I hope you'll think of me with each berry you relish."

And since her brain was still trying to compute all that had happened today, she simply said, "Thank you."

With a click of his heels, Prince Felix left as quickly as he'd arrived, leaving Delia holding a dish of promises.

It was another hour, and nearly all of the berries, before she could focus properly. She checked the time and changed out of her gown and into something more suitable for eavesdropping. It was nearly midnight, and there was no way she was going to be crashing Prince Quinton's secret meeting dressed like a princess. Just before she left, she slipped the few remaining rubis berries into the small pouch on her belt, wary Shania would sneak into her room and steal them.

Following the secret tunnel, Delia emerged from the spiral staircase, taking care to listen and make sure Prince Quinton wasn't there. She climbed out into the center of the maze and gazed up at Queen Arianna's statue. She closed her eyes and tried to listen to her ancestors.

Which prince should I marry?

But her imagination could only conjure the last time she'd been in this spot with Aidan. She wondered if the windup bird had found him yet.

". . . you promised me!" a voice hissed on the breeze.

Delia moved to the hedge. She could barely make out the silhouette of a couple through the branches.

"Just a little longer," Prince Quinton replied, soft but insistent. Then there was the sound of a kiss.

Delia's heart was in her throat. Prince Armano was right!

She squinted through the bushes, but Prince Quinton's back blocked whoever he was with.

The other voice answered, their words thick with tears, nearly inaudible. "It's killing me."

"You must be strong," Prince Quinton urged. "We have to hold it together for only a few more nights. Trust me."

There were more tears, masking the voice. "I thought I could handle this, but seeing you with her is worse than living in secret back home."

"Shh," Prince Quinton soothed. "I love you." The conversation was interrupted with more kissing. A hand with thin fine fingers combed through the back of Prince Quinton's hair as the kiss deepened.

As the kissing continued a bubble of curious longing grew inside her chest. It was the kind of kiss that was full of passion and promise—certainly not the briefest brush against the lips.

Prince Quinton spoke again. "Everything will be just as we planned. In a few days I will be king of Astor, and then we can be together forever."

CHAPTER
TWENTY-ONE

Aidan had been watching the sky for the last two hours. The plasma trains screeched above him as they skimmed into their stations. He had one hand in the pocket of his jacket, keeping hold of the homing device while he gazed upward through the lines of plasma trains that zigzagged overhead.

He understood this was a useless exercise. The bird would find the transmitter, even if he was inside the cottage, but he didn't want to raise suspicion with another broken windowpane. And besides, his stepfather and Drake were still in a boisterous mood, making the small cottage unbearably loud and suffocating. Even Morgan had escaped to his basement workshop.

Plus, there was the fact that just because Delia gave him the transmitter didn't mean she was sending him a message right away . . . or ever for that matter.

Still, he rationalized, the walk would clear his mind. A headache was slowly growing, but he found being outside was a helpful distraction.

He began to play with the idea of selling the Queen's Guard glider to Griffin in order to buy a new outfit for the ball. Just once, he thought, it would be nice to see her in a social setting and not while acting as a rogue. The hope was there, deeply buried.

Aidan shook his head. He was losing all logic and reason. Why should he care about how she saw him? She had a palace full of princes to choose from, and soon she'd have a husband.

He kicked a rock across the street. Then his pocket vibrated.

With his heart hammering inside his chest, Aidan saw the silhouette of the bird high above. He took out the transmitter and gently placed it by his feet. The bird landed, zeroing in perfectly on the transmitter. He allowed himself a rare laugh, remembering how the bird had chased Delia in the maze.

Picking up the mechanism, he stroked the beak and retrieved a piece of paper. Her handwriting was lovely and it took him a few moments to decipher the loops and swirls of her letters. He was used to reading typed words on the infoscreen.

Meet me where the glider is hidden. I need to speak with you. Not safe to be inside palace walls.

Aidan checked up and down the road, expecting to see Drake covering his mouth, fighting back laughter. This was too easy. Someone was setting him up.

However, if there was a chance he'd see her again in person, Aidan knew he'd take it, no matter what the risk. "What do I have to lose?" he whispered. Because this was what his life had become, a daily exercise in risk and reward.

He hurried back to the cottage and waited in the darkness for what seemed like a lifetime.

Then there was the unmistakable sound of a glider swooping overhead. She swiftly landed in the shadows, out of sight. The plasma engine made a soft ticking sound as it cooled. There was a sigh, and then footsteps came closer to him.

She was wearing high boots and a long fitted jacket that ended above her knees. Her cheeks were flushed and her eyes full of fire.

"You got my message," she said.

He snickered. "I thought we weren't going to meet anymore?" Aidan had no idea where the haughty tone was coming from. Inside he was a jumble of nerves.

She answered him with her own string of questions. "Is there some reason you're not at the palace?" she asked. "Considering you're

149

supposed to be my bodyguard, wouldn't being closer to the body you've been hired to protect make sense?"

Switching to defense, Aidan said, "Sometimes the right security is all about being in the right place at the right time. Even if that means not being close to the body I'm supposed to be protecting."

Delia jutted a hip to the side. "You like to twist my words."

"And you like to escape your palace. This is three times now and that's only since I met you. Shouldn't you be organizing a wedding?" The teasing came easily.

"It hasn't made it to that point yet."

"Are you saying an engagement isn't imminent?"

She shrugged. "I'm still considering my options."

"And is meeting me in the middle of the night one of your options?" He laughed nervously. "Just kidding. Go on, you were saying."

"I'm tired of being lied to, Aidan," she said. The statement came out tired, sad. "Something is going on in the palace. Every time I figure out an answer, another lie pops up and I'm more confused than ever."

"What have you discovered?" he asked. "You told me the android plot was ten years old."

"Even though I foolishly went to my mother before examining the chip more closely, I'm still bothered by the fact my maid was put to scrap when there was nothing wrong with her. And why is Prince Felix one way one day and entirely different the next? And why does Prince Quinton seem so authentically charming but then turn out to be a snake?!"

"I can't comment on any of those issues, but I do need to tell you that Prince Felix may be involved in the resistance. The information I shared with you was found inside a silver dagger that had been taken from his room in the palace."

A look of disbelief crossed her face. "How do you know this?"

"My source confided in me, and he is someone I trust implicitly."

There was defiance in her stance. "Why didn't you tell me this when you gave me the microchip? Are you doing this on purpose? Are you trying to put an unfavorable light on Prince Felix? Did someone tell you to try to influence my choice? What if I want to marry Prince Felix?"

"Do you want to marry Prince Felix?" The words practically choked him.

"Of course not! I don't want to marry anyone. I only want what's best for Astor."

They stood staring at each other, an argument brewing under the surface. Aidan could have told her everything at that moment and come clean with his true identity, but it was clear she wasn't finished with him yet. She had come to him, sought him out especially.

She went to the glider and came back with two folded cloaks. "I need help," she said. Her tone was less insolent now.

Aidan eyed the clothing. "This looks intriguing."

Delia put on one of the robes and pulled the hood over her head, shielding her face, completely disguising herself. Then she tugged at the cloak, making it hang straight to the ground. "I require a tour guide," she continued. "And since you're the only person I know who is familiar enough with the Dark District, I thought we should go together." She tossed him the other robe.

"You didn't even ask if I had plans for tonight. How can you assume I'll go along with you?" Still, he put the robe on.

"I need to see the Dark District with my own eyes, not through an infoscreen. I've heard much about the picking station. I think we should start there. Do you know where it is?"

Pausing, Aidan considered lying. He was not expecting this request, but she was looking at him with such earnestness, he couldn't refuse her. "Um . . . yes. I think so."

He pointed them in the right direction and they began the walk. The robes helped them blend in with the various vagabonds still trolling the streets at these late hours.

She spoke to him from under the hood. "I'm about to make an irreversible decision that will affect Astor's future."

"Not to mention your own happiness."

"Irrelevant," she sighed. "A lot depends on what I see tonight,

Aidan. If I'm going to be their queen, I'll need to look them in the eye. Plus, I'm partly interested to see if I can find Marta."

Aidan steered them across the street from a clot of men all stooped over something, their heads nearly touching. "I've been thinking," he started. "Marta could be programmed to do anything you wanted, correct?" He took them down another alley.

"Yes." Delia used the hood to cover her nose and mouth. He noticed the stench as well and knew they were getting close.

"Why didn't you program her to pretend to malfunction instead?"

"Not an option," she said, her voice muffled behind the material. "It's against her fundamental logic. That's why I had to put a glitch in her SHEW to escape the dress fitting. She would never agree to pretend to have an episode."

He thought of another option. "Would she have let you leave though, and even helped you with the ship? If you commanded her to do so?"

"That never occurred to me," she said, her tone surprised and deflated at the same time. "I suppose I wanted to do it on my own, or maybe I didn't want her to get into trouble. I didn't even tell my sister."

They took the last turn, and the entrance to the picking station was directly in front of them. Aidan could make out the silhouette of the higher piles in the distance.

He knew every inch of the picking station by heart. He mainly came to find parts for his sky dodger, or in desperation to find something to trade for coins from Griffin.

"Where do we start?" Delia asked. He could tell she was overwhelmed by the size of the area.

"You're assuming I'm an expert in hunting for missing androids in picking stations."

She waited, then said, "Where do you think she might be?"

He snuck a glance at her and was rewarded with a smirk. "Finally. I've been waiting for your sarcasm to surface. I've missed it." He felt like a king when her smirk turned to a full smile.

They started making their way to the top of the first hill, carefully choosing where to step. She lifted a scrap of metal and used it to move the bits underneath.

They climbed again and moved around more pieces. He saw a few gadgets that could be traded in Griffin's shop, but he kept going, content to play the part of her bodyguard.

By the time they'd made it to the second pile, their robes and hands were covered in black dirt and grease. He was reminded of Morgan's fingernails.

Delia straightened her back and sighed. He suspected she was about to call it quits, but instead she said, "I've been wondering about something. You knew I was going to steal the ship, because you'd been watching me, like you were hired to do, but how did you know when I was going to steal it?"

Aidan couldn't think of an explanation. He knew their time together was dwindling. She'd be picking a husband soon and he'd never be with her again. The truth came out before he had a chance to reconsider his words. "I'm the one who stole Prince Felix's dagger," he started. "And when I was running away from the guards, I went to the landing bay intent on taking a glider, but then your ship started automatically so I jumped inside."

She rolled her eyes at him. "You're a terrible liar, you know that." She picked a new path and he followed her in silence.

"You're right," he finally said. "I had been watching you. After you left the ship, I climbed on board, intent to wait until you returned. I had to sleep there overnight, thanks." He winked at her. "You'll make a ruthless queen, Delia. I don't know why you're so worried about spies and such. I can't imagine anyone fooling you for long."

She snorted. "If your acting skills were as poor as your flirting skills, I would have figured it out much . . ." She stopped midsentence, staring at something over his shoulder.

Aidan turned and followed her gaze. The children he'd bought the clockwork bird from were off to the side. The tallest one, Nina, was focused on them.

His cloak and hood were hardly enough to fool the children. He put a hand on Delia's arm. "If you want to keep a low profile," he whispered, "I suggest we leave them to continue with their search. Besides, I hear these children can be territorial. They might bite us." He made a face.

"Are you obtuse?" she asked bluntly. "It's the middle of the night and instead of sleeping in a warm bed, these children are picking through trash."

"That's why it's called a picking station." He pulled on her arm again.

"How can you be so cold?"

"How can you be so blind? This didn't start tonight. The mines have been closed for decades. These children aren't sleeping in warm beds because they need money to buy breakfast instead." The words were out before he had a chance to regret them.

Delia shook her head, causing her hood to fall back.

Still watching, Nina nudged one of the gang.

Aidan said, "We need to go . . . now!"

Together, they ran all the way back to the cottage. She leaned on the glider, her face wet. Wiping a sleeve across her cheek, Delia finally looked at him and said, "I couldn't eat all the food on my plate tonight." There was a pause. "No wonder there's a resistance in the Dark District. If I were them, I'd want to overthrow the palace too."

Aidan wished he could pull her into an embrace and tell her everything would be all right. Instead he said, "Your ignorance is hardly a crime."

She ran her finger along the seam of the cloak, appearing to contemplate what he'd said. "I've lived in luxury my whole life. I knew that I was being groomed to become queen one day. I always thought I was a martyr, giving up freedom to serve the people. But I haven't suffered, not like those children." She sniffed. "I spent my childhood running through the lush maze, leaving treats at the altar of a stone statue, while all along the Dark District has been living in constant shadows, never seeing the sun." She looked at Aidan. "Only one thing can grow in the darkness—a rebellion."

"But you gave Tomas and his father a chance at a new life," Aidan said. "Surely that counts for something."

"There's only one way to bring the Dark District into the light," she said thickly. "I must marry. And soon." She pressed her lips together as if holding back more information.

Something that had been deeply buried inside of Aidan was starting to push through. He took a step closer. "And you're sure there's no other way?" he asked.

She shook her head.

He tried a different approach. "Then I suggest you do something selfish before you marry. When was the last time you truly enjoyed yourself?"

She cleared her throat. "When I was flying the ship, and you were screaming with fear."

"Bloodthirsty princess."

They both laughed.

"All right then." He gestured toward the glider. "How about a replay? At least try not to kill me this time."

"Right now?"

"Well, you're soon to be married, and I don't ride around with other men's wives, so I suggest we make this our final adventure."

She dried the last of her tears, then mounted the glider. He took his place behind her and strapped on the goggles she handed him. He wasn't sure what to hold on to.

"Don't be stupid," she said. "You know I like to go fast. You better hold on to me unless you want to end up dead."

"Lovely," he said. "You really need to think about brushing up on your interpersonal skills."

She hit the power and they lifted off. Aidan instinctively gripped her waist and leaned forward, pressing his chest into her back.

If Delia minded the extra weight, her flying skills didn't hint at it. Soon, the Dark District was far below them and a wide sky full of stars filled the view in front of them. Aidan could make out the first chasms of the canyon.

He began to relax, but then she dipped the glider at a sudden angle. Aidan clamped his lips on a scream. He'd just put the most reckless pilot he knew in charge of his life! She laughed as she made several swooping maneuvers. One hard turn to the right nearly tipped him off.

Without warning, there was a thud against the back of the glider. Aidan turned to see a much larger ship in the distance with several smaller gliders in front, heading straight toward them again. The glider that had hit them closed the distance quickly. He recognized the driver. It was the blue-haired pirate who had bombed them in the clearing, the same one who had stripped his glider.

The pirate raised a sword into the air with a battle cry as he rammed them a second time.

CHAPTER TWENTY-TWO

The massive lurch from behind thrust Delia forward, jamming the hand controls into her ribs. A scream escaped her lungs as she practically flipped over. There was a sickening sensation of her feet being above her head. Somewhere in that moment she realized Aidan had nothing to hold on to but her.

The glider toppled nose first into a downward spiral. Instinctively her right hand worked the thrust, and a powerful burst of speed righted the craft.

Every cell in her body was vibrating with fear. There was another powerful slam from behind. Aidan yelled something, but she couldn't make it out. Turning the craft in a tight circle, Delia saw the cause of the trauma.

A large ship loomed over them, while two smaller gliders zoomed around like anxious hornets. The pilots on the smaller vessels were brandishing swords and belting out a battle song. One of them came closer and launched a small object.

"Bomb!" Aidan yelled.

Heat filled the space above them, followed by a quake in the air. The glider shuddered in the wake of the explosion. She added more power, increasing their speed. The ground was coming closer. She'd have to pull up soon or she wouldn't be able to come out of the dive in time.

"Six o'clock!" he screamed.

The features of the canyon blurred. With only the light of the glider to guide her, Delia made a sharp right followed by a quick left, then another right. She continued the zigzag pattern, but the other gliders were unrelenting. "Tenacious bastards," she growled.

Aidan gripped her tighter as another explosion blistered the air beside them. Suddenly the glider lost speed and they began to roll onto their left side.

"Don't let go!" Her whole body twisted inside itself as the sickening plunge to the earth began.

The free fall lasted an eternity of two seconds before they were stopped with a violent shudder. Two gliders were on either side of them, practically wedged together.

Delia's breath came back as they were steered toward the bigger ship. At first the prow resembled a sea-maid, but as they neared she saw the statue was composed of bones.

"They mean to take us," Aidan said, between his own rushed breaths.

"At least they didn't let us die," she replied.

"No . . . not yet."

The master pirate ship reminded Delia of something from one of Winnie's terrifying bedtime stories. Unlike the sleek and clean Queen's Guard ships she was used to, this one was a ramshackle machine put together with mismatched parts. But surprisingly, every surface was shined to perfection, no hint of grime.

* * *

Delia stood on the outer deck with Aidan by her side. They were deep in the canyon, hovering above the dusty ground, low enough to avoid detection by the Queen's Guard and high enough to avoid a potential attack by sandworms.

The crew surrounded them, some squatting on the floor, others standing with weapons. All of them stared with the same unsavory anticipation. A bottle began to make the rounds. The one with the long blue beard who had crashed into their glider licked his lips. He had a bun loosely knotted at the top of his head.

The captain walked up to them in a jaunty fashion. A gold ring through his nose caught the moonlight. He had a long red coat with brass buttons, trimmed in black velvet. It made him stand out as something magnificent. His hand rested on the hilt of the sword in his belt. "Princess Delia." He gave her a salacious smile.

She nodded and counted only three teeth in his mouth. "If you wanted to show me your fine ship," she said, "all you had to do was send an invitation to the palace." She felt Aidan stiffen beside her.

The captain's smile fell. "You're not here for a tour, little queenie." He used the sword tip to lift the back of her braid from her neck. He leaned close and inhaled. "Oh, how I've dreamed of this moment!"

Delia fought the urge to kick him. "I had no idea pirates were such cowards," she said. "Killing a woman with no means to defend herself is hardly something worth dreaming about."

The captain burst into laughter. He doubled over, holding his stomach. The crew joined in, a few spitting in turn.

He paced a circle around her and Aidan, the tip of his sword flirting with the cuffs of their jackets. "Despite what the resistance thinks, your hair is worth more than your life," he said. Then he added with the quirk of an eyebrow, "I'm no dupe though, I'm not about to do the dirty work for those floundering fools. I have no interest in ruling a kingdom that's dying."

"The resistance?" Her heart began a new terrified pounding.

He widened his arms to the crew. "We're pirates! We're in it for the loot!"

This was met with a raucous cheer. Delia turned to Aidan. His expression was surprisingly calm. He shook his head quickly as if to say, stay quiet.

"And the braid of Princess Delia is . . . as they say, and forgive the paraphrasing, the mother lode."

Hot anger boiled in her veins. She struggled against the chains around her wrists, certain her ire for this pack of heathens was enough to break the steel. "Then fight me for it!" she challenged.

"Delia, no!" Aidan said. There was an unmistakable panic in those crystal-like eyes of his.

"Fight me fair," she said to the captain. "Each of us armed. If you win, you may have my hair. If I win, you grant my friend and I our leave."

The captain stared lasers through Delia, then curtly nodded. "Agreed," he hissed.

Within seconds the manacles around her wrists were opened and someone pushed her in the back, making her stumble toward the captain. She fell into his arms and the roar from the crew was deafening.

Delia pushed off his chest and regained her balance. He laughed and tossed her the sword from his belt. She caught it easily and stepped into position.

Although her legs were shaking, the familiar stance was comforting. She had been dueling since she was a little girl, and the choreography was like a dance to her. Unbeknownst to the captain, she had been sizing him up since they boarded the ship and already had a strategy planned to play on his weakness. The limp on the right side was a good place to start.

She afforded a quick glance at Aidan. His usual paleness was even more pronounced. She gave him a smile, hoping that it conveyed her full confidence. She knew this would be a great moment to tease him about later, how she had to rescue her own bodyguard—again!

A sharp whistle brought Delia's attention around. The captain stepped back and ordered the crew to unlock the grate in the floor. The look of terrified anticipation on the crew's faces put Delia on alert.

A low wet snarl echoed from the dark chamber. Then fingers clawed at the edge, then another hand, then another . . . and another. Delia counted six hands before the creature pulled itself onto the deck. It was a man, bare chested and wearing only thread-worn pants, with six arms coming out of his sides. A loop of chain was attached to his ankle, with the end disappearing into the hole he'd just emerged from.

"You've heard of the lost tribe of Zennith, yes?" the captain asked Delia. "Tookah is the last of his kind . . . unfortunately. Never in the Four Quadrants will you find a more skilled warrior." Then he wrinkled his nose at the man monster. "I'd breed him if I could, but the women keep jumping over the side of the ship to their deaths."

There was a burst of laughter from the crew.

Delia thought she noticed a look of despair on the man.

The closest pirates tossed him weapons: a dagger, a plasma hatchet, and a sword. He caught them without taking his eyes off Delia. In a matter of seconds, she was staring at her opponent—it would be like fighting three men at once.

Aidan swore. "That's cheating," he yelled to the captain.

"I'm a pirate," he answered. He looked at the creature. "Tookah," he ordered. "I care not if it's quick and painless or long and sufferable, but please leave the last cut to me." The ease with which the captain ordered Delia's death was an icy blow that nearly made her collapse. The enormity of her fear moved into every crevice of her heart.

"Delia!" Aidan screamed. But she had no time to look at him as a clash of metal against her sword wrenched her arm back. Tookah, the man monster, stepped back and readied his next blow, this time with the plasma hatchet—its blade glowing red hot.

Delia knew just one swipe of that blade and her flesh would never recover. Still, she pushed her fear aside and let her training take over. Her body reacted automatically, blocking his sweeping arch. They fell into a rhythm, clashing and stepping around each other. He was toying with her, she knew. Yet, she used the fight to test him.

The first rule her instructor taught her was that everyone had a weakness.

Grunting, she focused on the deadliest weapon. She slashed at the handle of the hatchet and it flew out of his hand, spinning along the deck. Several crew shrieked and jumped out of its path. A wine bottle smashed, causing more swearing. Delia took advantage of the distraction and slashed one of his six arms. Green blood dripped from the wound.

He came at her again, one hand stabbing at her chest with the dagger while the other held the sword above his head. She swiped a high kick, making contact with his knee; then she grabbed the chain attached to his ankle and tugged hard. He cried out and stumbled. His other hands pushed him back up. He seemed to hesitate.

The captain screamed out an order to fight to the death.

With tired arms, Delia struggled to keep up her speed. Her leather jacket was heavy. Sweat gathered under her arms and inside her boots. She was pushed down, but felt Aidan's hands under her as he lifted her back up. "You can do this," he said as his chains clinked against her sword.

She ran at Tookah. Another blow and she relieved him of his sword. He stared as it flipped end over end, surprise crossing his grimy face. From the corner of her eye she saw the plasma hatchet. Without hesitating she dived, then rolled, picking up the powerful weapon in her free hand. She rushed at the creature, planting a kick to his chest. He spun on the spot, then fell on his back. Holding the sword tip to his throat, she put her boot on his stomach. In her other hand, the hatchet was poised for a deadly blow.

His eyes did not hold the fear she expected to see, rather there was a plea in his expression.

"Please," he said. "Kill me." Then he dropped the dagger, the last weapon in his grasp.

There was complete silence among the crew. Bodies stilled, but all eyes darted toward the captain. He slammed his boot on the deck, then spit out the longest laugh.

"I'm in awe of your skill, princess." Then he gave her a bow with such flourish she could have sworn he was Prince Armano in disguise. He stood straight again and regarded her and Aidan. "We may be thieves and vagabonds, but every true pirate respects a good fight. I dare say, Astor is in good hands, your royal feistiness. Go ahead, kill him. Finish the duel."

This was met with a snorting of approval from the rest of the crew.

Delia looked back down at Tookah, his eyes still pleading. Then she raised the plasma hatchet over her head and brought it down with all her might.

There was a collective gasp as the blade easily sliced through the iron manacle. Delia laid down the sword and the hatchet, then offered Tookah her hand, helping him to his feet. He shook off the loose chains.

She addressed the crew. "I am Princess Delia, firstborn of Queen

Talia, ruler of Astor and direct descendant of Arianna, the first daughter of the moon. And I grant this man his freedom." She turned to Tookah. "As long as I'm alive you will always be free on Astor."

It was so quiet the occasional shriek from the sandworms far below was crystal clear. She turned to the captain, who already had a wine bottle in his hand.

His weathered face regarded her with a look of malice. "A bold move for one so young," he said. Then a smile overtook his grim expression. "Something I admire." He uncorked the wine with his scant teeth, then held it up, giving a toast. "Stay as my guest and drink, for tonight is a new beginning!"

Shaking inside, Delia stared at the captain. Then she felt Aidan's fingers as he slipped his hand around hers, their palms pressing together.

CHAPTER TWENTY-THREE

Aidan wandered the open deck of the ship, running his fingers along the various pieces of scrap machinery that made up the mechanical collage of the prow.

"Aye," a scratchy voice came up behind him. "Captain has paid ya a great honor by sparing yer lives. Be a pity to have to throw ya overboard to the sandworms if we caught ya stealing."

Turning around, Aidan looked into the eyes of the blue-haired pirate. "You took apart my sky dodger after you attacked me outside Griffin's shop," he said. "I just want to know if it's still flying as part of this ship. I just want to see that it's still purposeful."

"Purposeful?" He rolled his eyes and took a swig from a bottle. "Never had the chance. The other fellas came along and scared us off."

"Scared you off?"

He pointed a gnarled finger at Aidan's black eye. "Oi! That wasn't there when I leaved ya. Ask those other fellas. They knew ya, called ya by name they did."

An unease settled deep inside his bones. "What did they look like?" he asked.

The pirate scratched his chin. "Hmm, one was kinda big-ish and the other was not so big, but not so small either. Hard to describe folks when they don't have a peg leg or a tattoo."

Aidan tried to remember, but he'd only seen the pirates that night. "So they have my glider?" Aidan asked.

Far off there was the unmistakable hiss of a sandworm. All heads swiveled in the direction of the noise. The captain barked an order, and the vessel rose another twenty feet.

Aidan saw Delia speaking with the six-armed man. There was a black bird on his shoulder. She smiled at him and seemed to be intently listening to every word he said. A sense of tragic pride pushed against his chest, making it hard to breathe. She was more than a girl who knew how to fight, she was going to save the whole planet—regardless of her own happiness.

He used to think she was a spoiled royal brat, but watching her battle was the single most exciting and terrifying spectacle he had ever witnessed. He pictured himself as an old man, retelling the story, describing how the blades clashed and the sound reverberated off the bottom of the canyon. And how the great ship hovered thirty feet off the ground with plasma torches around the outer deck, making it look like a floating halo. Then he paused, because he knew he'd never grow old.

Still, he was grateful. And it didn't matter that his headaches were getting worse, or that he was pretending to be a man he wasn't, or that she had to marry someone else. They had this moment, and it could never be taken away.

Quite simply, he was with her and that was all that mattered. His only regret was that he was powerless to help her solve Astor's energy crisis without an impending marriage.

He looked up, trying to memorize the sky full of stars. A brief twinge of pain near the back of his skull warned him a headache was on the cusp, slowly building in intensity. A gust of wind blew through his hair.

"He howls tonight," the pirate muttered, looking out over the railing of the ship.

"Who? The sandworms?" Aidan heard a gale whistle through the canyon.

"No, the greedy king." He put down the empty bottle and pulled out a pipe. After tamping down a pinch of dried leaves, he clamped it between his teeth. "Don't ya know about the creation legend? Kinda stupid to be flying around with the princess and not know the legend of the lost treasure."

Aidan backtracked through the mosaics, trying to remember mention of a treasure. "You mean the moon and the girl with the braid, Arianna."

The pirate took a small wooden dowel and lit the end from the nearest plasma torch. Then he touched the flame to the bulb of the pipe. He sucked back a few times, letting the leaves catch. "Yup, the same one." He threw the piece of dowel over the side, then leaned his elbows on the railing.

Aidan said, "But the king died when the planet froze over, only the daughter survived."

The smoke from the pirate's pipe rose up from his mouth like a ghost. "Aye." He nodded. "Most people think Astor is dying, but it's not so. She's only sleepin' . . . waitin' for the right one to wake her, to unearth her greatest treasure." He worked the pipe a few more times.

At the mention of treasure Aidan's heart sped up—typical for a pickpocket. He sensed this could be important. "Treasure?" He worked to keep the excitement from his voice. He was pretty sure the pirate wouldn't be sharing all his secrets.

"Aye, just as the legend says." He looked up to the stars as if reading the story from a book written in the sky. "After the daughter offered the moon her hair, he pulled her up into the sky to be with him, where he kept her safe. Down below, Astor froze."

"Yes," Aidan said. "And everything on the planet died . . . including the king." He studied the pirate's lined face and was beginning to wonder if the old goon of a bandit was toying with him.

"No." The pirate's voice took on an eerie tone. "He had a different fate." The wind died down, it too anticipating this new part of the legend. "Thinking he should have been saved instead of his daughter, the greedy king demanded favor from the moon. When the moon asked for his most prized possession, he turned away, clutching his chest of jewels. Tired of the father's selfishness, the moon transformed him into the wind."

The plasma torch flickered above them as the breeze picked up again, throwing shadows on the pirate's face. He continued, "The king was a ferocious wind that howled and rolled over the bare land, spinnin' in the dirt until it caused giant ruts in the earth. Down, down, down deeper the king blew into the earth spinnin' his anger, making spirals of dust, creating a deep chasm."

Aidan felt every hair on the back of his neck stand. He stayed quiet, not even daring to blink and miss a part.

"When he saw what he'd created, the greedy king took his jewels and hid them deep in the canyon and there they've laid for centuries." The pirate ended the story with a satisfied nod, then put the pipe back between his teeth.

Aidan leaned over the railing, looking down below. "You really think there's treasure in the sand?" he asked.

The pirate gestured to the north. "Aye, the mountain exists, the two suns exist . . . the canyon is right below us, boy!" He pointed the pipe at Aidan. "Truth lies in the most unexpected places." It came out as a hissed whisper. "I come from a family of pirates, my grandfather was one of the last miners in the Dark District."

"You've been looking for this your whole life?"

"Why do ya think they call this place Pirate's Canyon? Aye, I can see it in yer eyes. Yer strugglin' with logic, but yer heart wants to believe. Hmm, I know that look well." He turned his gaze toward the unending sky. "Think of what it will mean to the people of the Dark District. We'd be able to give them somethin' they lost decades ago."

"Their livelihood?" Aidan guessed, thinking he meant the miners.

"No, boy. Hope."

Aidan studied the pirate's profile. "I greatly misjudged you."

A quick sound of amusement slipped out from the corner of his mouth. "Most people do." Then he held out his hand. "Name's Nazem."

Aidan shook his hand. "It's a pleasure. I'm Aidan." He paused a moment, then added, "Although, you can understand my prejudice, considering you threw a bomb at me."

"I missed on purpose." The pirate leaned over the railing, pointing to a section of the sand with his pipe. "See the curved paths? They move in patterns, but never the same spot. They dive down too, you know. I reckon there's miles of sandworm tracks down there."

"So all you have to do is find a way to get rid of the sandworms and you can start digging?"

"Yup," Nazem sighed. Taking his pipe, he smacked the bulb on the railing. A puff of soot escaped and was picked up by the wind. He tucked the pipe into his pocket. "Not that easy. We've tried plasma bursts, bombs—even dropped a glider into the mouth of one when it was jumping up to eat the ship. Nuttin' happened though. Not even a scream. Those things are indestructible."

Aidan grew quiet. A notion hidden inside of him was trying to come to the surface. He thought of the mosaics in the tunnel.

Nazem's usual scratchy voice turned almost dreamlike. "Aye, the man who uncovers the treasure of the greedy king could change a lot of lives—change his own destiny."

CHAPTER
TWENTY-FOUR

"Thank you," Delia said to Tookah. "I know you weren't fighting with your full strength."

They sat on an overturned crate. A layer of sand carried on the wind had covered the other half. They had segregated themselves as the rest of the crew drank and cavorted about the ship. "And I stand by my word," she said. "You are free now. I will instruct the Queen's Guard to keep an eye on you."

"No need to enforce your offer," he said, his voice smooth and articulate. "What the captain said is true, I am the last of my kind. And although it may seem strange, I do feel at home with these scoundrels. I will stay with them until I am called elsewhere."

She looked at him incredulously. "But you were their prisoner. They kept you chained up and locked in the brig."

"And now I am one of their crew and will be covered by the pirate code as any other man aboard this ship."

"You could come to the palace, though. With your fighting skills you'd be an asset to the Queen's Guard."

He put up one of his hands and shook his head. "I am in the company of other castaways of society. I have made friends here." At that moment a blackbird rested on his shoulder. With one of his other hands he pulled a small sack from his pocket and began to feed the animal small crumbs.

Delia thought of the berries she had in her pouch. "I am sorry," she said. "To be the last of your kind must be lonely."

"Loneliness is a state of mind, Your Highness. I can find common ground among others easily. And I still have my skills. I always have my home close to me because it is inside of me."

"You mean your skills as a warrior?"

He chuckled softly. "Let me show you." While one hand fed the bird, his other hands started to draw lines in the sand. With only his fingertips, Tookah created a scene for Delia.

She watched in amazement as the picture came alive. He even managed to give definition and a sense of movement. "I see a mountain," she said. "And a field of flowers, and oh, is that a bird?"

"It is my home," he said, a soft tone of satisfaction.

"You're . . . this is," she stammered and laughed at the same time. Then a gust across the bow wiped the scene clean. A sound of exasperation escaped her lips.

He laughed. "I always have home with me," he said, putting a hand to his heart and another to his head. All the time the first hand was still being attentive to the bird.

"You're a genius," she said.

"I was an artist and a sculptor . . . and a builder. I find beauty in everything."

"You sound like my sister."

"Is she an artist too?"

"No, she's a romantic. She sees beauty in most things too . . . people, actually, of the male persuasion."

"Romance," he whispered the word, then smiled. "Romance sounds enjoyable."

Delia felt her cheeks burn. "I'm not sure about that."

Tookah tilted his head, studying her, then focused on something over her shoulder. "You should join your pale friend, he looks like he needs rescuing." He nodded in the direction of the blue-haired pirate who was in deep conversation with Aidan.

She watched Aidan, amazed at how much happened to her when he was around. Then he turned and looked at her. Everyone else on the ship disappeared, leaving only them. She wasn't sure how long they stayed that way. The pirate said something else to Aidan, then hobbled away, leaving him alone by the railing.

When she turned to Tookah, he'd gone and joined a group passing a wine bottle around.

Pushing herself off the crate, Delia walked across the deck on shaking legs, her nerves still buzzing from the events. She was five steps away from Aidan when the captain rushed between them.

He addressed Delia directly with another exaggerated bow. Then he thrust a wine bottle in her hand. "A token of my admiration, Your Highness."

Delia took the gift, and for a moment considered smashing it over his head. She was still suspicious and even wondered if this whole scene was a ploy.

"Thank you," Aidan said, coming to Delia's side. He was all smiles and politeness. Then he made a show of rubbing his wrists, now freed from the chains.

She snuck a glance at his profile. There was a subtle defiance she'd never noticed before.

The captain addressed him as an equal. "I will give you and the princess passage to wherever you chose."

"Home would be nice, thank you." Delia's shoulders relaxed somewhat.

The captain raised a heavy black eyebrow. "Home? As in the palace?" He made a tutting noise. "Not possible, too close for comfort, what with us being pirates and all that."

"The edge of the Dark District, then," Aidan offered. "We have transportation waiting for us there."

The captain nodded, then motioned to the bottle in her hand. "Rest easy for now, but in the meantime, drink."

"How can I refuse such a generous offer?" Delia replied. She glanced over and saw a crowd of pirates had circled the Queen's Guard glider, tools in their hands, no doubt discussing how to start dismantling it.

Knowing they were still at the mercy of the captain and his crew,

Delia allowed him to lead her and Aidan to a quiet area of the ship near the bow. She sat cross-legged, putting her back to the windows of the observation deck, thankful he let them stay outside.

"You don't mind sharing the bottle with each other, do you?" the captain asked. There was a suggestive quality to his question that made her blush. Giving another exaggerated bow, the captain took his leave.

"Who knew pirates could be such cordial hosts?" Aidan said, watching the captain swagger away.

Delia uncorked the wine and took a tentative sniff. The vapor was enough to make her eyes water. She blinked a few times until her vision came into sharper focus.

Aidan sat beside her. A plasma torch cast a warm glow over their area. A few flies circled, then started to fly into the light. There was a ping and the fly zoomed away only to return again to repeat the poor choice. "I wonder what a normal day with you is like?" he asked.

"This is my normal," she said. Feeling ambitious and wanting to show off, she tilted back the bottle, letting her mouth fill with the liquid. It burned at first, and then she swallowed. The cough was immediate, but she held it down and took another swig. She laughed at Aidan's expression, then passed him the bottle. Delia pretended to be interested in the stars, but all of her attention was directed on his raising the bottle to his lips.

He paused. "You know this will probably kill us, which means everything we've done up to this point will be for nothing."

"You're stalling. Drink up."

After a halting start he took his first sip and nearly spit it back up. "Oh, lovely," he coughed. "It's unfortunate we don't have roasted wallowing goose to fully appreciate this fine bottle of what is probably pirate piss."

"Aidan!" She slapped his arm. The release of nervous energy from the buildup of adrenaline made her loopy.

Keeping eye contact, he took the bottle and drained a generous amount. Wincing, he said, "I'm no expert, but this may have been the last thing that fellow drank. I certainly feel like arms could grow out of my sides." He motioned to Tookah, now putting a bottle up to his own lips while the crew encouraged him to guzzle it down.

Delia scooted closer to Aidan. She let their knees touch. "I told him I would hire him as a Queen's Guard but he prefers to stay here as a pirate." Then she smiled slightly. "He told me I'm the hardest person he's ever fought."

"Sounds like he's an expert in warrior princesses, then."

"Warrior princess," she repeated, unable to hide the smile. The flies continued to dart into the torch, one by one. Delia said, "Did you know it's not the light that draws them, but what they perceive to be beyond the light?"

"I thought they just wanted to get warm."

"You're hilarious," she said, only half as cynical as usual. "The fly is driven by instinct. Biology is convincing the fly to move toward the light, even though the light in some cases represents certain death." She stopped talking when she noticed he was staring at her.

A pool of warmth started inside her and spread outward. Aidan's paleness in the moonlight made him luminous. She was about to tell him this, but instead she said, "You and that pirate were having a long discussion. What were you talking about?" Then she grew brave and touched his elbow. "Wait, are you joining the crew?"

He smirked at her. Then his expression smoothed out, becoming serious. "He told me there's treasure in the canyon. It comes from the creation legend with the king being turned into the wind. Have you heard of that version?"

She rolled her eyes. "That's only a fairy tale," she said. "People like to add on to the story to make it their own. They invent what they need to hear the most."

Aidan moved closer to her, and his eyes had an intensity behind them that made it almost impossible to look away. "But it's worth researching, isn't it? You could have the Queen's Guard out here looking for the treasure. If you found it Astor would be able to buy as much plasma as they wanted, and anything else. Then you wouldn't have to marry . . . or at least you wouldn't have to marry anyone you didn't want to."

His eyes were so full of hope they nearly mirrored Delia's own fantasy. It would be so easy to get swept up in his version.

"The king's chest of jewels is not real," she said. "I wish it were. I'd be down there now, digging with one hand while I fought off the sandworms with a sword."

"I'd pay a million shunkles to see that," he interrupted.

"But it's not real," she repeated.

His gazed dropped to the bottle. "Are you sure?"

"Yes," she sighed. "I only know the story because Winnie used to scare Shania and me with it to make sure we'd stay in our rooms at night after being tucked in. She told us the king was the wind and he was always looking for princesses to steal to replace the one the moon took." She closed her eyes and took a measured drink.

"Are you sure? Deep down, at the very bottom of your soul, where you know the truth lives . . . are you sure? Because it would solve everything!"

She wiped her mouth with the back of her sleeve and placed the bottle in his hands. "I'm sure," she said. The wine sent a warmth all the way to her toes. "Now help me finish this pirate piss before they throw us overboard." She stole a glance over her shoulder at the party happening on the upper deck. Some of the crew were sneaking looks down at them.

His expression was downcast. "I just thought it might be worth pursuing. It's all I have to offer you at this point."

The last sentence caught Delia's attention. She could think of a million things he could still offer her; they were all on the tip of her tongue, but she had no way to make them into words.

He lifted the bottle to his mouth, then put it back down. "Thank you," he said.

She stared at his lips and saw the wine had changed them to a deeper color. "You're welcome," she replied, partially distracted. "For what exactly?"

"Saving my life by fighting the six-armed man. It would be a shame to die on such a lovely night. I'm not sure I'll ever witness another fight quite as spectacular."

He was teasing her, but there was something in his voice that made her melancholy. Sometimes when he looked at her, she could feel it, even from across the ship. But now that they were closer, the intensity from him had slackened.

Or had she imagined it in the first place?

Confused, Delia stared at the moon and wished she could interpret its silence. There was an urgency in her veins, a growing impulse she tried to understand. In the stillness she became thoughtful. "Do you wonder if you're on the right path? If you're making the biggest mistake of your life, or are we all just tumbling independently and it doesn't really matter what we do?"

"No." He tilted the bottle all the way back. The last drop hit his lips. "Every decision makes a difference. Think about Tomas and his father. If you hadn't sent them to Delta Kur, Tomas would probably end up being a pirate with this crew of outcasts. So, yes, your actions make great changes in the universe, Delia." He regarded her with a steady gaze of what she hoped was admiration. "There is no greater power than the power of choice."

Delia held her breath. Her gaze focused on his mouth, and she wondered if his lips would taste like the wine.

He ran a hand through his hair, then let out a heavy sigh. "I'm sorry," he said. "I've spoiled the party. Forget what I said about buried treasure. We should be celebrating your victory." Aidan raised the bottle. "To your bravery, Princess Delia."

"It's easy to be brave when you're holding a sword and a plasma hatchet," she replied. She stared as he wiped his thumb across his lower lip. Her heart was pumping inside her ears.

"You should see yourself through my eyes, then, because I think you're the most fearless person I know." He put the bottle down with a hollow thud. "My apologies, I seem to have finished this. I wonder if we should have another bottle. After all, when will we find ourselves on a pirate ship again?"

"Indeed," she whispered. *Fearless. I need to be fearless*, she thought.

"Do you want another bottle?" he asked, starting to stand.

"No," she said, patting the spot beside her. "I have something better." Delia reached into her pouch and pulled out the small clutch of berries. She poured the last handful into her palm.

Aidan slid back down beside her. "You were holding out on me," he said.

"Think of it as dessert," she said. Her voice had an underlying quiver she hoped he couldn't hear. "These are rubis berries. Have you ever tasted one?" She stared at the fruit, hardly able to look him in the eye, worried she'd falter.

Pinching a berry between her fingers she said, "They are absolutely . . . exquisite," she sighed. When she looked up, Aidan wasn't staring at the berry, he was staring at her. Before she lost her courage, she leaned forward and kissed him.

CHAPTER
TWENTY-FIVE

Aidan had barely registered the pressure of her lips on his when she leaned back just enough to study him. Her eyes were wide and full of surprise as if he'd kissed her instead of the other way around. Yet, she stayed close enough so all he would have to do was inch closer and the kiss could continue.

And he wanted to kiss her again, more than anything. But this was real, not a daydream, and he was petrified of saying or doing the wrong thing.

Perhaps the kiss was a thank-you, he reasoned. Perhaps the wine had warped her judgment. Or maybe she was in shock after almost crashing the glider and fighting Tookah.

These thoughts coursed through his mind in a matter of milliseconds as they stared at each other. Her eyes gave away no hints. But then she reached up and pressed the berry to his lips, making him open his mouth. The fruit was more intoxicating than a hundred bottles of pirate wine. Dropping the rest of the berries, Delia put her hands on either side of his face, fitting her mouth against his.

The kiss felt like he was falling, like that first ride in the spaceship when they met. A thrilling, terrifying drop that started in his chest and pulled tight. It was slow at first, but the hesitation only intensified the sensation. Aidan's eyes closed when their tongues touched, and he was certain nothing would ever feel this real.

The world disintegrated around them, so only they existed. And everything he'd ever done seemed to have led to this moment of tasting the wine on her lips and the berry on his tongue. Aidan was on fire and shaking at the same time. He felt her move in his arms, pressing closer.

An explosion of raucous cheers and bellowing yowls came from the upper deck and behind the glass of the observation windows. The pirates raised bottles in their direction. Delia dropped her chin and turned away from him, her cheeks glowing a fiery blush.

Then her hand found his and squeezed tight. She tucked into his side and they stayed that way until the pale lights of the Dark District emerged from the darkness. Aidan wished the trip would never end, knowing that as soon as they touched land, he would have to tell her his true identity.

Nazem escorted them to the surface on one of the makeshift pirate gliders. Aidan saw it was a mismatched machine of various parts. He let them off in the alley just a few streets over from Aidan's cottage.

He nudged Aidan, handing him a small device that fit into his palm. It looked like a miniature bomb. He said, "If those fellas try and rough you up again, just press that button. It alerts the ship with your location."

Aidan tucked the small sphere into his pocket. "Pirate protection?" he said.

Nazem winked. "Pirate code." Then he lifted off, quickly disappearing into the night sky.

Aidan nodded, his heart still thumping from Delia's kiss.

Wordlessly they stuck to the shadows. When they reached the cottage, Aidan pulled back the tarp to reveal the Queen's Guard glider. He waved a hand at the machine. "I believe this belongs to you," he said, careful to whisper.

She gave him a confused smile. "You're the most interesting bodyguard," she said. "Surely you're not going to make me order you to escort me back safely." Then she reached out to him.

He tried to smile but the emotions of the night had robbed him of his courage. It was suddenly too devastating to have to tell her the truth. How she'd look at him! He could handle never kissing her again, maybe, but to see the disgust and hurt on her face when he confessed his identity would tarnish this memory forever.

Delia's smile faded. When she spoke again her voice was so soft Aidan could barely hear it above the wind. "You haven't said anything since we kissed."

Hearing her say the word "kiss" was almost as intoxicating as the act itself. His arms hung useless at his sides; the cruelty of the situation made him weak.

Aidan finally said, "I feel like the heavens crashed around us and we are the only two wandering around its ruins. I am surrounded by my own personal utopia where words have become meaningless. I am at a loss . . . a complete and incurable loss to express how much I want you."

As the truth slipped from his lips, he barely had time to apologize for spilling his heart so daringly at her feet.

Delia rushed to him, pressing herself against his chest, murmuring a soft plea across his lips. He held her tightly and kissed her in a way that erased any doubt of his sincerity. The embrace lingered, and it was bittersweet.

The night air grew cold around them, but Aidan ignored the elements, his senses consumed instead with Delia; the feel of her racing heart beating under his palm, the scent of her hair as he kissed her neck, the vibration of her voice along his earlobe while she whispered his name.

It was almost too much to absorb, too much to experience.

Delia was the first to step back. "Do you know the small shore at the south edge of Black Lake?" she asked.

"Yes."

"Meet me there tomorrow when the suns are the highest at midday. I have no idea what I'm doing, but I know I have to see you. Will you be there?"

Aidan smiled. Having her this close was like holding the suns. "Said the plasma torch to the fly." The promise of another day with her was irresistible.

Her kiss had erased all logic. How could he let this continue? It was impossible for them to be together. Then, as if he needed another reminder, the headache that had been skirting the edges all night made a move, reaching its fingers from the back of his head, gripping tightly.

It had never come on so quickly before. He concentrated on breathing, praying he wouldn't pass out in front of her.

Mounting the Queen's Guard glider, Delia slipped on her helmet and gave him one last glance before she lifted into the sky. Aidan watched as the light on her glider grew smaller, far above him. There was a pull on his heart that continued to stretch painfully as she disappeared from view.

Only when he turned and shuffled his way to the back of the cottage did he fully grasp the anxiety. "I won't be content until I see her again," he admitted to himself. But what difference would it make? She had to marry one of the princes. And yet . . . he closed his eyes briefly, remembering her kisses.

In this conflicting state, Aidan opened the back door, hoping to make it to the cot to sleep off this massive headache that threatened to be the worst yet.

A thought made him stop short. What if this was the headache that ended it all? He should have gone with her. He wasn't afraid of dying—okay, maybe a little—but he was more worried she would never know what happened to him.

He pictured her waiting at the lake.

"Out all night?" A formidable silhouette moved out from the shadows. Aidan's stepfather leered at him.

"Obviously." The sarcastic response was out before Aidan could censor his impulse. Another rush of pain made him wince. He pushed a finger to his temple.

From behind their father, Drake and Morgan emerged from the shadows.

"What's wrong with him?" Drake whispered. There was a fear in his voice.

"Ask him where he's been," Morgan said to his father. It sounded like an order.

"None of your business," Aidan replied to him directly. "And while we're in the mood for an inquisition, why did you steal my sky dodger? Don't deny it, you've probably ripped it apart and are selling it piece by piece from the basement." He turned to Drake. "And are you the one responsible for my black eye?"

Corporal Langdon took a step closer to Aidan. There was a small crease between his eyebrows. "Interesting. You've never talked back before."

"Why is that interes—" The word died on Aidan's lips. All the energy in his body evaporated. He dropped to his knees, then fell forward, his cheek smashing into the floor.

Blackness encroached from the edges of his vision as he saw three pairs of boots approach.

"Take him to the basement," Morgan said matter-of-factly.

Then Aidan passed out.

CHAPTER
TWENTY-SIX

Delia felt lit up from the inside. Aidan had infused her with an intangible spark. She was certain stars would tumble from her hair if she shook out her braid. The kiss had changed everything. It was the first time she'd felt something so deeply rooted and unwavering. There was an invincibility building in her soul.

The smile was still in place as the vertical lift ascended to her floor. Her cheeks ached from the permanent grin.

I kissed Aidan! And it was wonderful and amazing and I can't believe it's possible to be this happy.

Then she found a name for her newly enlightened state: hope. And she would in turn give hope to the people of the Dark District.

Delia thought of the children in the picking station who had no time for school. She imagined all the books in the palace library, just sitting there. They must invite the public into the palace! They must make it accessible to everyone!

She was ecstatic with the endless possibilities. The doors to the lift opened and she twirled out into the hallway.

"It seems you have your secrets too, princess."

Delia halted, staring at the figure leaning against the door to her bedroom. Shock gave way to anger as she remembered her last image of him. "Actually, Prince Quinton," she said smartly, "it is you who has explaining to do."

He bowed slightly and put a hand on his chest in an apologetic gesture. "I was forced to leave you earlier this evening, which troubled me greatly." He stood to the side, motioning to her door. "Perhaps we can talk in a more private setting," he said.

Instead of outright accusing him, Delia chose to stay quiet, knowing that she had the advantage. As she led him into her room she raised her chin, like she'd seen her mother do a thousand times, and hoped for the same authoritative effect.

The twin suns had started to rise, filling her room with a golden hue. Delia perched on the corner of her bed, then nodded for him to begin.

Prince Quinton took in the surroundings with a silent apathy. "I have a proposition of a rather delicate matter," he started.

"Marriage?" Her tone was full of sarcasm.

"In a sense," he said. "We will be queen and king in name, but not in the bedroom. I assure you, I will honor that promise."

His answer was the last thing she was expecting. Delia tried to decipher his every mannerism. "Why would you promise such a thing to me?" she asked in a straightforward manner. "What kind of queen would I be if I couldn't live my life authentically? And how am I to produce an heir if my own husband won't—" She glanced at the bed, surprised she couldn't say it out loud. Shania would be squealing with laughter if she could see this scene.

"I want you to have as many children as you want . . . just not with me." Prince Quinton's expression was serious and solemn. He pressed his lips together. "That's why I'm here. I'm proposing you keep a lover."

Her jaw dropped.

Prince Quinton said the next few words to the floor. "It's common practice among many royals. I didn't think the idea would be so scandalous for you."

"You, sir," Delia started, "are ahead of the game. I know your secret."

All the color instantly left his face. Now Prince Quinton was the one who looked shocked.

"I heard you and your mistress in the maze," Delia said. "But your midnight tryst is only part of your deception. Regardless of how many young women you keep hidden away in your bedchamber, I might also wonder why you assume you'd become king so quickly after we're married."

"I was simply referring to my title after we're married. On Rexula that's the tradition. If I'm to remain a prince even after we are wed, I don't care."

There was something genuine in his expression that made Delia consider what he was saying. She noticed his eyes were red with dark patches underneath. He had been up all night as well, but instead of fighting pirates and kissing until the suns rose, he was waiting for her.

"But you don't deny having a lover?" she asked.

"Niko," he said, his words sounding exhausted, desperate. "It was him I met in the maze."

"I . . . oh, I see." Delia absorbed what he'd just confessed. "I never considered you and Niko could be a couple." Even though Delia knew of a few similar relationships within her own court, it was the furthest image from her mind when she spied him in the maze.

"That's the problem." He laughed bitterly. "No one ever does."

Delia tried to imagine how her life would be if she agreed to what he was proposing, but it seemed impossible. "We'd all be living a lie," she said.

He faced the long windows, watching the suns rise together. Hues of orange and pink scattered across the sky. "Believe me," Prince Quinton said. "I know what it's like to live a lie. What I'm proposing to you is that we do what's best for our planets without sacrificing our hearts."

When Delia spoke she heard her mother's voice. "My heart has never factored into this decision."

Prince Quinton's furrowed brow smoothed out. "Then I envy you, because you'll never know the anguish of a broken one." His posture caved somewhat, giving the impression he'd used his last bit of energy. Then he gave her a slight bow and left.

For the next hour Delia paced the length of her room as the rest of the kingdom woke. She closed her eyes and tried in vain to hear her ancestors, but they stayed quiet. Memories of kissing Aidan kept interrupting her concentration.

She considered going to Shania, but she knew her sister would ignore any sound logic and go straight for what the heart wanted. Delia knew what her heart wanted, and now she had a possible solution to get it—but was it the right solution for Astor?

There was only one person she could ask.

Once again Delia was in her mother's inner chamber requesting an audience.

As the shaman mixed a concoction of tea, Queen Talia was in her bed, propped up on pillows. She was cooling herself with an elaborate fan of wallowing goose feathers. "This is unexpected," she said as Delia took her post the required ten feet away.

"You can imagine my own surprise, Your Majesty. Prince Quinton is offering a marriage in name only so he may keep his present lover."

There was a crash of porcelain on the floor as the shaman froze. A gap of silence followed. Then he bent over and slowly picked up the shards, placing them in a cloth.

Her mother regarded her. "What is your instinct telling you?"

Delia swallowed. "Our marriage is more or less a business transaction, and perhaps this is a solution that will satisfy at least one of us romantically."

The shaman looked to Delia, then back to the queen. A few forgotten pieces of the tea set remained on the floor.

Queen Talia put up a hand. "In accepting his offer, you obtain the plasma Astor so badly needs, but you will be undermining your own authority. I understand you have no romantic connection with him; however, as his queen you should be his greatest confidant and most trusted ally. I suspect that will be this lover instead."

All of Delia's prior anxiety morphed into heavy embarrassment at her failure to see what seemed so obvious now. "I see," she replied. "He will be loyal to the one he loves first . . ."

"And you second." Queen Talia's face softened. "Remember, it's healthy for a leader to not trust anyone more implicitly than herself, but your husband must instill confidence in you, and not be concerned with making another feel empowered. Tell me, if the ancestors are silent for you in this matter, what else are you basing your choice of husband on?"

Tucking her chin down, she replied, "I am basing this choice on fear."

Queen Talia pressed. "Fear of what?"

Delia was amazed at her mother's ability to pull the answers from her even when she didn't know them herself. "Fear of choosing the wrong husband and therefore ruining the kingdom."

Queen Talia picked up her fan and began to cool herself again. "Contentment comes from wisdom and making choices that are based on logic. That is where you will find your true fulfillment. Immersing yourself in your emotions is a luxury a queen cannot afford. The sooner you learn this the better."

The shaman passed the queen a cup of tea. She took a sip, then smiled over the rim to Delia.

"I wish I was more confident like you, Your Majesty," she said tiredly.

Queen Talia gave a quick laugh. "Do not confuse confidence for courage. It is when our heart is most afraid that true bravery appears."

"Then I suppose I lack that as well," she said. "How can I be a leader if I can't lead with certainty?"

The queen took another sip of tea. "Most people are unaware of their courage until it is tested. When the time comes, you will know what the right action will be."

Her mother's calm words washed over her with a soporific effect. Delia imagined sleeping forever as soon as she lay down. "And how will I know for sure if it's the right thing to do?" she asked.

The queen put down her tea. The early morning light illuminated the tired lines around her eyes and mouth. When she spoke her voice carried the clout of all the ancestors. "Because it will most likely be the hardest."

CHAPTER TWENTY-SEVEN

Drip. Drip. Drip.

Aidan blinked as his small room came into focus. He was lying on his stomach, staring at the sink. The dripping tap matched his throbbing jaw. He did a mental inventory and was surprised to find his rib wasn't sore. And other than his jaw, he actually felt energized. The headache that had promised to do him in for good was gone as well.

He stood and looked at the small mirror above the sink. His eye had healed completely. The strips that Delia had so expertly applied to his side were still there, but when he put a hand over the area and pressed, there was no pain. He pictured the white pill she had given him. "Miracle," he said.

The cottage was quiet. Aidan checked the infoscreen and saw it was nearly time to meet Delia. A layer of guilt settled over his shoulders. He had to tell her the truth today. Absolutely. No excuses this time, even if it meant ruining the last bit of time they'd have together before she chose a husband.

He moved about the small room, looking for a clean set of clothes. He might have to settle on his usual uniform. The outfit from last night still had sand ground in. His eye caught the shelf above his bed and he saw two new additions: the cork from the bottle of wine they shared, and one of the red berries she'd dropped on the deck. He didn't remember putting them there last night; still, he smiled as he touched each one.

"You've got a fine museum started." Morgan stood in the entrance to the kitchen. Then he took a step closer. "Why do you collect those things? What's special about them? Are they useful to you?"

Aidan was unsure how long his stepbrother had been there. This new inquisitive version of Morgan was troubling. He was used to the one who never talked to him, who treated him as if he were invisible.

"I have to go out," Aidan simply said, trying to ignore the way his heart was panicking under Morgan's stare. He grabbed his uniform of a loose shirt and straight slacks.

"You're working?" he asked, but his voice stayed even, as if he already knew the answer.

Aidan tightened his belt, then on impulse took the clockwork pigeon, slipping it into his pocket. "Um . . . an afternoon shift. The androids are taking on more responsibilities." Then he added with a nervous laugh, "I hope I don't lose my job to one of those things."

"Why are you taking the bird?" Morgan asked. He took a step closer. "Seems odd for you to be interested in a child's toy."

A flashback of Morgan standing over him the night before sent an odd chill over his skin. There was an urge to run away as fast as possible.

Take him to the basement.

Aidan shrugged as he reached behind him, searching for the doorknob. "It's nothing, just a funny little thing Griff gave me."

Morgan raised an eyebrow. "Father told you to stay away from him. He won't be pleased to learn you've disobeyed him."

His back bumped up against the door. "It was from before, it's broken actually . . . I have to go or I'll be late." He turned and fought with the lock a few times before he could open the door and leave the cottage. He didn't look back, not wanting to see if Morgan was standing there watching him.

Still a bit unhinged, Aidan's mind wandered as he made his way toward the outskirts of the palace. Part of him was convinced last night was a dream.

The plasma trains were slower than normal, making him late.

They took him farther into the sky, toward the stilted manors and away from the ground. He missed his sky dodger. The dull ache in his jaw was distracting, but he was grateful the eye had healed. He wondered where all this vanity was coming from.

It was at least an hour after the time she specified, but when Aidan reached the spot on Black Lake, she was waiting for him.

She was wearing a flowing top that showed off one shoulder, a long skirt, and her high boots. Her smile was more radiant than the suns.

"You came," Delia said, her eyes dancing. Then her gaze lowered to his uniform.

"I'm in disguise," he said. "I wouldn't be a very good bodyguard if I dressed like one, would I?"

"And your eye is completely healed?"

"Must have been the berry."

She laughed and took him into her arms. "I was certain last night was a dream when I arrived and you weren't here."

"I'm sorry. If it's any consolation, my heart and mind never left you."

"Come," she said, leading him up a precarious footpath around the lake. Her braid swayed back and forth, grazing her calves. Aidan heard the roar of a waterfall grow louder. They turned the corner and saw the cascading water.

"It's from the glaciers," Delia said, her voice echoing against the rocks. "Our royal ancestors made the dam that created the lake. When the palace sanctioned the developments on stilts, they were able to use this supply via aqueducts."

Aidan was mesmerized as the pathway, now wet with spray, led behind the falls. He followed her along the very edge of the rock face, the pathway uneven and precarious.

Several minutes later they stepped out into an oasis. At the summit of the mountain stood a grand tree, its limbs stretching so far it blocked the entire sky.

"Is this the tree from the legends?" he whispered.

She stood in front of him with an expression of pride. "I wanted to bring you here because every important declaration in the royal family has happened on this very spot. Every naming ceremony, every wedding, every funeral . . ."

Aidan was afraid to blink, afraid to miss any of this.

Her voice faltered. "This tree and I are very alike; neither of us can escape the kingdom. We are rooted to the palace by obligation. And I always accepted that destiny, albeit without a sense of passion. But since I met you, I feel like I'm not confined anymore, that there is a whole new world of possibility. For the first time in my life I feel empowered by my position. I can make a difference, I can help the people who live in the Dark District, especially the children. And that . . ." She halted her speech, then instead of finishing the sentence, kissed him.

Aidan breathed her in, letting the moment linger. A pained sigh came from the back of his throat. How could he empower her? He'd been lying to her the whole time.

He tilted up his chin, breaking off the kiss. "I have to tell you something," he said.

"Wait." Delia put a finger to his lips. "I didn't get a chance to say this last night . . . I want you too."

The air stilled around them. Aidan could hear the whisper of every leaf on the great tree. He felt like he was part of something much greater than himself. "I had no idea life could be like this," he said.

She sighed in his arms, then pulled him to sit down beside her. They leaned against the trunk. Aidan took the pigeon out of his pocket and let it rest on the ground. A blossom from the tree spiraled from the branches above and landed on its beak.

"I'm wound up so tight I feel like I'm ready to burst," Delia said, taking his hands in hers. "I have something I want to ask you, but before I do, I need to tell you my reasons."

Aidan was certain his madly thumping heart would crack his ribs all over again. He'd let her speak first. It was a selfish move, but he couldn't deny himself one more second with her before he told her the truth.

She seemed to be building up the courage as she looked at their clasped hands. "I always thought I was brave, that taking on the responsibilities of my training in a serious manner meant I was mature and capable. And I never wavered on any decision because every decision I made simply meant measuring the benefit for Astor against the risk. The crown and my own soul were the very same."

Delia paused and let out a shaking laugh. "And I thought I would be more than able to choose a husband if I applied that same logic." Tears began to fill her lower lids. Still, she continued, her voice getting stronger. "But I have learned that being brave is doing the thing that scares you the most. And I am most afraid of failing, Aidan. I have hardly slept since I last saw you and even though everything seemed monumentally complicated, I realized it was only my fear clouding my good judgment."

Aidan felt her squeeze his hands. He had no idea where she was going with this, but he was terrified and in awe of her at the same time. He tried to memorize the way her braid lay over her shoulder and draped down her arm, resting in a coil in her lap.

She blinked, and two tears rolled down her cheeks. He ached to comfort her, but she shook her head and kept him at arms' length. "So, I've decided who I will marry."

Aidan had a sensation of slamming into the face of the mountain. Everything had gone numb. He may have even stopped breathing. She brought him here to break up with him. The revelation stunned him into a dull silence. Still, there was a small part of him that realized he'd gotten off lucky and should be grateful to have been in her life for a few days.

Even though he could still see the tracks of her tears, Delia's expression had turned serious, determined.

"I am a descendant of Arianna, daughter of the moon. Our braids are sacred," she began. "Made of three strands representing bravery, wisdom, and love." The color rose in her cheeks as she picked up her own braid. "And for that reason, only the bride may choose who receives the honor of unbraiding her hair on her wedding night."

Aidan was swept up in a vision of Delia standing in her bedchamber with only her long hair covering her body as she handed her husband the end of her braid.

"I want that man to be you, Aidan," she said.

He was stunned. She proposed to him. There was the distinct sensation of his mind shutting down and then trying to start over again, like rebooting an old android.

Her hopeful expression began to melt into confusion, bringing him back to life.

"I'm sorry," he said. "I'm simply waiting to wake, because this must be a dream."

"It's no dream," Delia said. Then she moved into him, her arms encircling his neck as her lips found his mouth.

The kiss took him over completely. Aidan felt it everywhere. His body had become one large heartbeat. There was an urgency to the moment that made him dizzy and focused at the same time. His hand moved to the back of her neck, fingertips tracing the pattern of her braid—the braid he would unravel on their wedding night.

Their. Wedding. Night.

How had it come to this? A small voice whispered from the depths of his subconscious. It was insane, not to mention cruel that he still hadn't told her the truth. He'd kept postponing the revelation, rationalizing that their time together was limited, selfishly unwilling to risk losing another second of her company. But the kissing! He was useless to resist. The kissing was intoxicating and yet he suspected only a hint of what they could experience together.

It took all his strength to pause the moment. "Are you certain?" he asked.

She leaned back, one hand on his chest. "Your heart is beating as fast as mine," she laughed. "And yes, I've never been more sure of anything in my whole life."

Aidan felt instant relief. Her confidence soothed his panic, hushing that persistent voice. She wanted to marry him, and that was all that mattered right now. Then she kissed him again and it was another eternity before they broke apart, breathless and clinging to each other.

A few blossoms floated down, resting on top of them. Leaning back against the tree, they laughed and sighed like they'd had too much pirate wine. Aidan was giddy and void of worry, but he wanted there to be some token to make it official. He reached to the back of his neck and unclasped the chain. "This is my most prized possession," he said. "I want you to have it. It only makes sense to give you something if we're to be together."

"Your mother's medallion," her voice was soft. "Are you sure?"

He fastened it around her neck and traced his finger along the chain all the way down to where the medallion rested on her chest. "This is the first time I've ever taken it off," he said.

She put her hand over the gold disc. "I will always wear it."

This time Aidan started the kiss. There was no hesitation as they fitted into each other's embrace. The ground under the tree was soft as they lay down. Breathy promises mixed with the scent from the blossoms made him light-headed. And he took it all in, helpless to stop and listen to logic.

Her lips grazed his earlobe, and he knew he would never feel this exhilarated again. Aidan made the choice to keep the charade going until the very end, no matter how many sleepless nights it would cost him, no matter how much it would hurt when she discovered the truth. This memory, this moment was worth it. "I'm truly alive," he whispered against her skin as he kissed her neck.

"You're the best bodyguard I've ever had," she sighed.

Aidan pushed himself up on his elbow and stared at her. "How did you do it?" he asked. "How did you persuade the court you could marry your own bodyguard instead of a real prince? And what will this mean for Astor?"

"Marry?" she faltered. "I never said we would marry. The man I'm choosing will only be a husband on paper, not in my bedroom." She squeezed his arm. "I'm asking you to be my lover."

It was like crashing his sky dodger into a nest of sandworms. "A lover? Instead of a husband?"

She nodded. "In secret," she said.

The great tree loomed over them like an impending storm. "No." Aidan sat all the way up. "No," he repeated. "I've lived my whole life being only two things, used and invisible. You've shown me what freedom feels like." His voice was quiet, like he couldn't believe his words.

"I can't do as you ask. This will have no meaning," he said, touching her braid. "How can I unbraid your hair when our relationship is a lie? How can it still be sacred?"

Tears choked her words. "Please, our feelings are true, it won't be a lie. I cannot choose between you and the death of my planet! Please! Our feelings will be enough. Don't you want me?"

Her plea made the ground feel like it was tilting on its side. "Yes! More than the air, but . . . I can't." He stood and put a hand on the trunk to steady himself. "I can't be with you if I'm hidden away like something you're ashamed of."

Delia put her face in her hands.

Aidan went over everything she'd ever said to him. "You never considered marrying me, did you?" he asked.

She stood and took him by the shoulders. "I never wanted to marry anyone! But I want to be with you. Please, it's the only way. We'd be a couple in every sense. You could still be my bodyguard, no one would ever suspect . . . please!"

"I . . . I can't be your bodyguard." He shook his head and backed away. "It's not meant to happen." Aidan turned and ran back along the pathway. The sounds of her crying followed after him as his feet slipped on the wet rocks.

And he knew that he was wrong. He'd fooled himself into thinking falling in love with her would be worth the pain, no matter how severe.

Feeling the agony of his heart splitting in half—he knew he was wrong.

CHAPTER TWENTY-EIGHT

Delia was lying on her back, staring up at the underside of the great tree. Everything was coated in a desperate, confusing haze. Not only from her unending tears, but from the conflicting emotions. She was full of misery one moment, knowing she'd never feel his kiss again, and then her mind attacked her heart for being so selfish, so childish.

So incredibly stupid.

Aidan had ignited a dormant resolution within her, a fresh perspective on her future—a hope for something more.

And when they'd kissed, a hidden universe exploded inside her body and heart.

Delia blinked and another row of fat tears trailed down the side of her face, one slipping into her ear. The wind picked up, moving the leaves. A blossom landed on her cheek. She left it there, her limbs too heavy to move. It seemed the earth was reaching up and claiming her body.

Bury me, she thought, *for the only part of me worth living has died*, but she knew she couldn't stay much longer.

The back of her blouse was damp from the ground and she was certain her braid was full of blossoms, but she didn't have the energy to shake the debris from herself.

On the ground she saw the clockwork bird. Most of her was numb, completely detached from the scene, like she was a spectator. Still, she took the tiny mechanism and carried it in her pocket.

As Delia took the route along the lake, her eyes focused on nothing in particular. Only one thought repeated inside her mind. *I am lost. I am lost. I am lost.*

She entered the palace and made her way up the main lift. *No bodyguard to smuggle through this time*, she thought desperately. Then a horrific idea occurred to her. She would have to ask her mother to fire Aidan. She would have to make up a story, of course. Regardless, there was no way Delia could ever face him again.

A fresh wave of hot tears threatened. Instead of her own chamber, she hurried to the one person she felt safe crying in front of.

Shania took one look at her sister and pulled her into her arms. She sat them down on her bed, the billowy coverlet eased around them. Delia thought she had cried out all her tears, but in her sister's embrace a whole new level of heartbreak resurfaced and the tidal wave of sobs began.

"What's wrong?" Shania asked, her voice panicked. "I haven't seen you cry like this since . . . well, never."

In between sniffs, Delia relayed the story of Aidan. Her sister's eyes kept getting larger with each revelation until they took over her face. When Delia finished, she hiccuped and slumped against the pillow her sister had propped up for her.

"I can't even begin to imagine," Shania started. She went to the bedside table and picked up a plate of treats. She placed it beside Delia. "Here, have a honey cookie."

"I don't think I'll ever eat again," Delia whispered.

"Fair enough." Shania took one and munched on it thoughtfully. "Honestly, I can't believe you've been flying around Astor with your secret bodyguard. Me? Absolutely. But this is so unlike you, Delia."

"I know! He made me lose all reason!" Her face bunched up again. There were no more tears, but she made a miserable sound. "Being in love is horrible. I never want to feel like this again."

Shania gasped. "That's tragic! How can you say that? This is passion, Delia! This is what people go to war over."

She blew her nose. "No," she said into the tissue. "People go to war over land and energy."

"But they do it for love! If no one loved anything this much, no one would care about living."

"I cared about living before I met Ai—him." Delia couldn't even say his name out loud anymore. She groaned and sank back on the bed. "I'll be honest, I was scared to pick a husband. I was scared to become a wife, I never had a notion of what it would feel like to be connected to a man in that way. But it was different with him, it happened without me even thinking about it."

Shania reached for another cookie. "Are you sure he won't reconsider? He seemed awfully wonderful, even with his black eye. Maybe throw in a lifetime supply of coconut cakes. Not that you aren't tempting enough, but there is a chance he's playing hard to get."

"No." She shook her head. "I broke his heart. You should have seen his face. I'm certain he hates me now." Her stomach twisted.

There was a curious expression on Shania's face. "What if . . . what if you marry him anyway?"

Delia snorted. "I can't! Choosing him will solve none of our energy problems and will probably upset our major trading deals with Trellium and Delta Kur, not to mention Rexula and their precious plasma." She put her face in her hands. "It's no use. I am destined to fail somehow. I wish living with a broken heart was enough punishment, but I can't even find a compelling reason to choose one man over the other."

Picking up her infoscreen, Shania brought up her list. "All right. If I can't cure your broken heart, at least we can help you pick the best husband. You know everything about them, correct? So, let's get this done and start planning your wedding. I know you can't imagine ever being happy again, but trust me when I tell you, if Aidan—yes, you need to start hearing his name—if your connection is as strong as you think, he will come back to you."

"Really?" she whispered.

"Yes," she said, nodding smartly. "But in the meantime, you need to get engaged. It's quite exciting actually. Did you know the top three princes are neck and neck in the standings?"

Delia studied her sister. "Please don't tell me you've placed a bet."

"I'll never tell." Then she cleared her throat. "But let's focus on listing their pros and cons. Fire away."

Sitting up, Delia picked a cookie and tried to clear her mind. "Prince Oskar has the least to offer, and is oddly distracted whenever we speak. But in a weird way he's the one I'm most comfortable around."

"I can't believe you're not even mentioning how amazing his physique is." Shania rolled her eyes. "Just imagine being the one to massage those shoulders every night." She sighed and looked off into the distance.

"Prince Hagar seems kind, but other than fish and shells I don't see him able to make things better on Astor."

Shania tapped the infoscreen. "And the twins?" she asked, not bothering to keep the mischievous tone from her voice.

"Have you ever seen them apart? I haven't. I think I'd have to marry both of them or they'd cease to thrive."

"Interesting." Shania's gaze glazed over, and she nearly dropped the infoscreen.

Delia snapped a finger in front of her sister's face. "Moving on, Prince Quinton has plasma, but he's made it clear he will have a lover on the side and that if we want children, I will have to find a lover of my own."

"Okay, so a strong maybe for him."

Delia sighed. "Then there's Prince Felix. He brings a military force, and he's also declared that he's ready to start adding to the royal family."

"And don't forget that backside," Shania added. "So a definite yes for him."

"I suppose," Delia replied dryly. She couldn't imagine herself with anyone but Aidan at this point. "Maybe I'll just marry Prince Armano and let the world implode."

Shania snorted out a laugh. "Life in the palace would be interesting. He'd want there to be parties every night!"

"We would have to have separate bedrooms, because his clothes and wigs would take up too much room." Then she laughed, and it surprised her how good it made her feel.

"Did I tell you he read my palm?" Shania asked, her eyes full of mischief. "I'm about to meet my true love, but he will be the man I least expect."

"Seems to be his favorite fortune," Delia sighed. "He told me my true love was close by . . ." Then her voice dropped off, because in a way Prince Armano had been right. The stabbing pain came back. Delia curled up and hugged her arms.

"Dear sister." Shania put a hand on her shoulder. "It won't hurt this bad forever."

There was a loud rap at the door. Both women bolted upright. Shania said it first. "Maybe it's Aidan! Maybe he's changed his mind!" She rushed to the bedroom door.

Delia busily wiped the tears from her cheeks. She patted her braid a few times as she followed her sister, a prayer running on repeat inside her mind.

The door opened and Colonel Yashin's substantial silhouette filled the doorway. He was a formidable figure with a posture built up by years of victories and a strict military lifestyle, but his stance seemed to slacken as he took in the sisters' image. His eyes were red and panicked.

"Princesses," he said, with a panic to his deep voice. "Your presence is required immediately." The muscles on the side of his face were taut. "It's the queen," he said. "She's dying."

✳ ✳ ✳

The air in Queen Talia's bedchamber was thick with incense. The shaman was hunched over a smoking pot. With a ceremonial feather, he waved the scented air toward the queen. Her breath was labored, the rising and falling of her chest erratic.

Delia and Shania paused at the doorway. Dropping to her right knee, Delia addressed her mother, then stood. "My queen."

Forgetting proper etiquette, Shania ran forward, then crouched at the head of her mother's bed.

Colonel Yashin waited at attention, a Queen's Guard to the end.

Advisor Winchell stood nearby. She watched Delia approach with a grim expression, heavy with grief.

Kneeling next to her sister, Delia studied her mother's face. How had she not put the pieces together before? The grayness under her skin? The dark circles under her eyes? The fatigue, even first thing in the morning?

The queen stared back at Delia. This was the longest they had ever gone being this close without speaking.

"How long have you known?" Delia asked.

The queen closed her eyes as a fresh cloud of incense blew over her face.

"For two moon cycles," the shaman answered. He began a soft incantation. Delia recognized the prayers—a song calling the ancestors to embrace her mother's soul.

Delia had a hundred things she wanted to ask, a million words to pass between them, but her tongue was useless.

The shaman's lyrical voice floated over all of them.

Just then the queen's chest rose forcibly. She opened her eyes and focused on Delia. "There are blossoms in your braid," she said, a hint of a smile under her dull skin.

"I was at the great tree." Delia sniffed. "Asking for guidance."

Her mother pressed her lips together. They were a pale shade of blue. "You know what you have to do," she said. "The ancestors speak the truth."

Delia dropped her chin. Her mother's fingertips brushed her cheek.

Then all was silent.

Delia's regal resolve began to crumble. She put her hand over her mother's, pressing it harder into her face. Shania's sobs became louder.

There was an immediate sense of heaviness to her mother's hand, but Delia was afraid to let go. She knew the arm would drop to the bed, lifeless. She kept her eyes closed, even when Shania put her whole weight into hugging her, making her rock in time with her sobs.

The shaman began to sing a cleansing prayer.

The soft tapping of Advisor Winchell's cane echoed on the floor as she came closer to the bed.

Delia finally opened her eyes and took in her mother's face. The relaxed expression was so opposite to her usual countenance of stubborn strength.

The shaman readied another smoking pot and the air was soon filled with a sweet scent. He began the next chant—the prayer for the spirit to rise.

Delia kissed her mother's cheek. It was the first time she had kissed her since she was a little girl.

There was a quiet intake of a sob from the back of the room as Colonel Yashin tried to swallow his grief. Delia felt her sister press into her side.

The shaman continued to chant. Advisor Winchell went to Shania's other side, an uncommon display of maternal comfort as she rubbed the younger princess's quaking back. Delia looked up and locked eyes with the elderly counselor, her eyes reflecting back an unfathomable grief.

CHAPTER TWENTY-NINE

A idan's mouth was wide open. Cold steel pressed against his back teeth. He tried to sit up but an unknown pressure kept his shoulders pinned down. He stared at the ceiling of the basement, the fog lifting from his mind.

The last thing he remembered he was running from the lake, but his brain calculated that it had been five point six hours since he'd arrived back at the cottage.

Morgan breathed over him, a rancid mix of meat and brew. His face contorted with effort. There was a grunt at the same time a massive pressure was released from Aidan's jaw.

"Galaxy's sake," Morgan said, a long-handled tool in his grip. "I wish she'd designed a better way to replace these things."

From the corner of his eye Aidan saw his stepfather point a camera at him.

"Run diagnostics," Morgan said.

"This never gets old," Drake replied, grinning down at Aidan. He was holding an infoscreen and typing in commands.

Aidan saw words flow across his vision, like he was watching the captions on the infoscreen.

RUNNING DIAGNOSTICS . . . STAND BY . . .

He tried to move his head, or even blink, but nothing was working. He was completely paralyzed. Words continued to stream past his vision.

RECONFIGURING CIRCUITS . . .

Morgan's voice came through. "Are you recording, Langdon?"

"Yes, sir."

Aidan struggled to speak, but his mouth would not move.

Drake's laughter was oddly comforting. "Look how scared he is!"

"He's scared every time," Morgan added.

Something was wrong, Aidan thought. Something was very, very wrong. There was a snap deep inside him. Aidan blinked.

"He's back," Drake said.

His stepfather moved closer with the camera.

"State your name," Morgan ordered. The long-handled tool was in his grip.

Aidan's jaw throbbed. He put a hand to his cheek, expecting to feel a large lump. Then he spoke. Even though he was unaware of the answer, it came out methodical. "I am Artificial Intelligence Decoding Android Number 603." Then he paused and added, "Aidan for short."

Drake snorted. "Every time."

His chin started to quiver. Another part of his mind had taken over. Had they brainwashed him? Had they poisoned him? Had the headaches gotten so bad he'd experienced permanent brain damage?

"What's happening?" Aidan asked. But even as he asked the question, his mind, the one that was apparently in charge right now, gave the answer.

INITIATING REBOOT . . . STAND BY . . .

"No." He shook his head, trying to free his shoulders.

Letting out a bored sigh, Drake said, "I take that back, this is tedious to watch." He looked to Morgan and pleaded, "Must we do this every time, sir?"

"It's part of the protocol," Morgan replied. "You know that. We're too close to become lax with procedure." He turned his attention back to Aidan. "What is your mission, Aidan 603?"

A tremble started deep inside Aidan's chest and traveled up his throat. He could only blink back at Morgan.

"We don't have time for this!" Drake held up the infoscreen. "Just show him the video."

Aidan's thoughts moved backward. He flew through blackness into a never-ending hallway of files. He zoomed in on one that spelled DELIA. The images came to him, every memory of her replayed within nanoseconds. Aidan put a hand to his throat, and for the first time in his life the medallion was not there.

Morgan let out an impatient huff. "All right," he said, motioning to Drake. "Show him the video. Keep an eye on his diagnostics though. Any fluctuation in the life cells and we have to shut him down to preserve the energy."

"What if the last SHEW doesn't have enough energy?" Langdon said, panicked.

Morgan pulled a face. "Everything the resistance has done for the last ten years has led to this moment. He'll have enough energy to complete the task, his programming will make sure. You two need to calm down. Nothing has changed."

Aidan felt like he was living in two different heads. "What's going on?" he finally asked.

"Here." Drake rolled his eyes, handing him the infoscreen. "Every time the same routine," he mumbled under his breath. "Just watch this . . . like you've been doing for the last two months."

Aidan expected to see a newsreel from the palace, but it was his own image that filled the screen. The date at the bottom showed it was only a few days ago.

"Aidan," his image said. He recognized his voice, but there was something lacking in his expression. "You are watching this as part of the protocol for SHEW replacement. Each time your SHEW is replaced, your circuits reconfigure, erasing selected memories and updating your directive."

The real Aidan looked around the room. Drake was regarding him with a cocked eyebrow while his stepfather continued to film him. "This is a joke," Aidan said. "A cruel way to torture me."

The face on the infoscreen continued to explain. "You are an alpha style android, the only one in the universe. Gail Babineau was the engineer who designed you."

Aidan's mind opened again, searching for the file labeled GAIL BABINEAU. She was the woman from his dreams, the one who gave him the medallion . . . his mother.

The infoscreen Aidan said, "An engineer of unparalleled talent, Ms. Babineau was secretly working for the resistance to build an android capable of replacing a member of the palace in order to free Astor from its dictatorship. You are a secret weapon to overthrow the monarchy."

"But she was my mother," he said to the screen.

Drake laughed. "She built you, moron. For a machine, you're such an idiot."

Aidan put his attention back on the infoscreen. "Your prime directive has always been to save the kingdom. Trust your programmer, Morgan. And Corporal Langdon, a staunch resistance fighter, working undercover for several years."

Aidan looked at a worktable along the wall and saw a row of what he knew to be SHEWs. Each SHEW was specific to the android. All of these were identical. All of these belonged to the same android—him.

"No, I'm human," Aidan said as he put down the infoscreen. "I bleed. I bruise."

"Because of your superior design," Morgan said. "We created and cured any physical ailment you needed to experience in order to keep your cover and make your memories seem authentic."

"Create? But the blood," he said, remembering how he'd coughed it up. Delia was so worried she'd snuck him up to her bedchamber.

"A capsule you slipped inside your cheek," Morgan answered matter-of-factly.

"I don't remember doing that."

Morgan continued to explain. "You were programmed not to remember your orders. Every time we program you and replace your SHEW, it's done without your knowledge. That's the only way it would work."

A horrific reality settled over Aidan. "But my headaches?"

"A manifestation of when your battery gets too low. Your energy cells drain faster the more emotionally or physically taxing your missions. You are programmed to return to the cottage when they reach critical levels before you black out. However, there have been times when we've had to go out and retrieve you."

Aidan thought back. Even though he'd been trying to escape Astor for as long as he could remember, there was always a reason he returned to the cottage. He never considered how odd that was.

"Wait," he said, still thinking they were teasing him. "I've been working at the palace for years. I've taken all those trinkets!" He almost smiled. "Ask Griff, he'll tell you. I've been dealing with him for years." He let out a relieved curse and put a hand to his chest. "You almost had me convinced."

But the faces staring back at him didn't change their expressions. When Morgan spoke it was with a bored detachment. "Those are implanted memories. You've only been at the palace for two weeks. Griff is part of the resistance. When you blacked out at his shop, he contacted us. I arrived and replaced your SHEW."

Drake made a pout. "Had to go back in the middle of the night and fight off a bunch of smelly pirates too."

Then Morgan continued, "Griff gave you a fake microchip, by the way. It was a bad stroke of luck that you managed to intercept the real message from the resistance."

"I don't understand," Aidan said. His head felt like someone had replaced his brain. "Then why give me the microchip at all?"

"Exactly," Langdon said, his eyes dark. "Griff paid for that mistake. It cost him all his computer equipment, plus a hearty chunk out of his safe. He tried to tell us that he thought it was necessary to give you a reason to seek out Princess Delia. Oh, yes," he chuckled. "We know all about your secret meetings."

Morgan cleared his throat. "When we realized the microchip kept putting you in contact with the princess, we used it to our advantage."

Aidan tried to line up everything they were telling him, praying he'd find a snag that would prove this was all an elaborate lie. "But if there was a real microchip in the dagger that I stole, that means Prince Felix is actually involved somehow."

Langdon answered smugly. "Several planets are secretly working with the resistance. Trellium wants to make over Astor as a military base. Delta Kur is prepared to start mass production on an army of androids based on your configurations, of course. Astor is like a garden in the middle of the desert, but soon it will be the powerhouse of the galaxy," he spoke with unbridled pride. "The Dark District will become home to the most sophisticated weapon factories."

"But how are they going to . . . ? No," Aidan said. "I won't help them."

"Don't get too proud," Drake snorted. "You're plan B. If Princess Delia chooses either one of those men, the resistance only has to sit back and let Trellium's military do the rest."

"And if she doesn't?" Aidan asked, wishing he'd wake up from this nightmare already.

Langdon put a hand on his shoulder. "Then your programming will ensure the resistance gets the same results—but in a more dramatic way."

There was a hollowness inside Aidan that spread out from his chest. He saw a list of dated videos and he watched all of them. They were essentially the same, an image of Aidan verifying that he was what they said he was. Then something occurred to him. "The first one only dates back two months ago."

Drake rolled his eyes. "That's because you've only been alive . . . or turned on, since then."

"But I was a boy when my mother . . . when she died," he began. "She gave me a medallion. And I have my father's uniform and medal of bravery."

"Fake memories and simple props." Drake couldn't hold in the laughter this time. Langdon kept the camera pointed at Aidan.

"Gail was a genius," Morgan said. "She made you oblivious to the mission by implanting false memories, thereby giving you a life that never happened."

"*Was* a genius?" Aidan asked.

"She really is dead," Drake said. "I have to tell you each time your SHEW is replaced. Do you have any idea how boring that is for me?"

"Enough!" Morgan put up a hand to Drake. Then he turned his attention to Aidan. "Tell me what happened with the princess today. Who will she choose as a husband?"

Aidan's mind sorted through heaps of categorized information. The file labeled DELIA came rushing to the surface. He couldn't help but think, *I am real, I feel love, I feel heartbreak.*

Morgan's tone was more pressing this time. "Who will she choose? What did she tell you?"

The moment boiled over for him. "No!" Aidan hurled the info-screen at the wall where it shattered. "I will never help you overthrow the palace."

All three men froze.

"He's never done that before," Drake whispered. He gave Morgan an anxious look. "Why did he do that? What's going on?"

Morgan calmly ordered, "Run diagnostics."

Aidan saw the words scroll across his eyes again.

```
INITIATING DIAGNOSTICS . . . STAND BY . . .
VIRUS DETECTION: NEGATIVE
CIRCUIT FUNCTION: CAPACITY LEVEL
LIFE CELLS: 78%
MODE: CONSCIOUS
```

"Give me the last SHEW," Morgan barked at Corporal Langdon.

Aidan felt hands on his shoulders. The long-handled tool was inserted into his mouth. Everything went dark. Words appeared before his eyelids.

```
LIFE CELLS: 100%
MODE: SLEEP
```

✳ ✳ ✳

Aidan woke to see his stepfather and stepbrothers looking down at him. He had already calculated that one thousand and sixty-seven seconds had elapsed since he'd closed his eyes.

"What is your name?" Morgan asked.

Aidan answered, "I am Artificial Intelligence Decoding Android Number 603." Then he paused and added, "Aidan for short."

Morgan smiled. "What is your purpose?"

The answer came from his circuit board. He answered, "To overthrow the kingdom. To complete the mission of the resistance."

All three men exchanged looks of satisfaction. Aidan watched all of this with a vague detachment.

Morgan continued, "Yes, exactly. There is a member of the resistance on the inside, someone who the palace hired, but is actually another accomplice to aid in your mission. He's presently undercover. If needed, he will give you the verbal order that will trigger your prime directive. Once this program begins you must complete it. Do you understand?"

"Yes," Aidan's one-word answer echoed in the small room.

Drake frowned. "Won't he be suspicious when we allow him to go to the ball?"

"He'll be working in the kitchen," Morgan replied. "Plans are in place to make him a server that night. Oskar will be able to easily activate his programming if necessary."

"The timing couldn't be more perfect," Corporal Langdon said. "It's the closest we've come in all these years."

Morgan addressed Aidan directly. "You won't remember any of this, but file it away in that database of yours. The resistance is ready to rise up and take over the palace."

Aidan sensed a struggle deep inside his circuits, then felt something let go. A sweeping blankness made everything clear. He had a mission. He was built specifically for that mission.

Morgan motioned to Corporal Langdon. "Make sure you film this to show him tomorrow. We'll have to convince him all over again."

He nodded and held up the camera to Aidan.

"What is your prime directive?" Morgan asked.

Aidan looked at the camera and answered matter-of-factly, "To assassinate the queen of Astor."

CHAPTER THIRTY

Delia made her way down the garden path. Her shoes tapped a lonely beat on the stones.

My mother is dead. I am queen.

She knew these facts to be true, but her soul was confused. How could she walk along the garden calmly like she had always done? In her mind she was screaming out sob after sob. *I will never hear my mother's voice again*, she thought. The idea caught her off guard.

"Immersing yourself in your emotions is a luxury a queen cannot afford."

She kept swallowing the words until the urge to cry had dissipated. Reaching the end of the path, she arrived at the queen's favorite tier of the royal gardens. The staff had specially set up a private tribute to her mother.

Some of the flowers had been coaxed to bloom early with lanterns of plasma hung at close intervals. The shrubs were painstakingly trimmed to perfection. Chairs were placed for her and Shania to receive condolences from the courtiers, but Delia couldn't sit, she had to keep moving.

Prince Hagar stood off to the side, speaking with a lord from the court. His long hair was down and she was surprised to see it was nearly the length of his back.

Not wanting to speak with anyone in particular, she continued through the garden. The air was thick with the sweet scent of blooms. Most of the courtiers bowed or curtsied as they addressed her as "Your

Highness." Delia was relieved no one had started calling her queen yet. She wasn't ready.

Maxim and Mikel approached her from behind, one on either side of her. "We're sorry," one of them said.

"So sorry," the other echoed. They each took her hand in theirs, one twin's hand on the top, the other on the bottom. They wore long black jackets, fitted at the waist with a black handkerchief in the pocket.

"Thank you," she said, slipping away from them. "As you can imagine, we are devastated." They nodded in unison, both somber and woeful.

Delia looked for Shania in the crowd, but it was Prince Oskar standing by himself near the wall who caught her eye. He was ignoring everyone around him, but instead focusing on the distance. Then he craned his neck, taking in the sky. He repeated this pattern of scanning the area several times before he noticed her. He dipped his chin down, then disappeared into the crowd.

Hardly able to interpret his actions, Delia continued to look for Shania. She finally saw her speaking with Prince Felix. The dull expression on her face was a stark contrast to her usual effervescent self. He listened intently as she spoke, with his hands clasped behind his back. Then he stepped away, letting another courtier greet Shania.

There was something respectful in his stance that appealed to Delia's broken spirit. He turned and saw she was looking at him. There were people in between them, but Prince Felix was so tall she could watch as he made his way toward her.

"Princess Delia!" Prince Armano appeared almost from thin air and swooped in front of her with a deep bow. "My deepest and most sincere condolences."

"Thank you," she said, staring down at the top of his blond curls. There was actually a porcelain butterfly nestled inside.

He took her hand in both of his. "The garden has lost its most beautiful flower today." Then he leaned closer and dropped his voice. "I'm aware of how delicate this question may seem, but is there a chance we could meet . . . privately?" He wiggled his eyebrow when he said the last word.

"I'm afraid not." Delia pulled her hand out of his grip. "As per custom, after this we will be having a private ceremony for my mother. And as you aware, the Full Moon Festival will start the next day." She realized her voice must have given away her frustration, because several courtiers looked her way, then spoke behind their hands.

She gave him a small smile, then said, "But I will look for you especially at the ball."

Prince Armano winked. Then he put a finger to his lips. "I shall keep our secret to myself." He nearly twirled on the spot, then strutted toward Shania at the far end. Thankfully, Advisor Winchell blocked his path. Then Colonel Yashin joined them.

With her head spinning, Delia felt too warm, and the scent of the flowers was overwhelming. A strong hand cupped her elbow.

"You need to sit, I believe," Prince Felix said. His deep voice was all softness and concern.

"I'll be all right," she said. "I prefer to stand, actually. The thought of having everyone standing over me is a bit stifling at the moment."

He stepped back. "As you wish." He corrected his posture, then said, "I am so sorry this happened to you and your sister. I'm not fortunate enough to have siblings. I envy the connection you have with her."

Delia stared at him, unsure how to respond. At first Prince Felix seemed like an unfeeling soldier, all combat and strategy, but lately, the real man was surfacing. "You surprise me," she said. His expression became alarmed. "Not in a bad way," she explained. "I'm only coming to realize now that first impressions are not necessarily the most accurate."

He gave her a careful smile, then said, "I hope that means I may bring you more rubis berries in the future."

Delia's heart stuttered unexpectedly as images of Aidan caught her unaware. She brought a hand to her mouth to hide the anguish she was certain was written on her face. She forced herself to wipe him out of her thoughts. She must concentrate on the present.

"My apologies," Prince Felix said. "I did not intend to indicate a rush in the relationship, but rather the promise of seeing you again."

Nodding, she said, "I'd like that as well." And as soon as she said the words, it was like a lightbulb had gone off. Something she'd completely forgotten about. "Excuse me for asking, or if this seems a bit odd, but have you misplaced a silver dagger since coming here? I overheard one of the technicians say a droid had malfunctioned and was found with an assortment of various objects from some of the other princes." She smiled and her lip stuck to her teeth. "No one has claimed it yet and I wondered if it might have been yours."

"That's the strangest thing, actually," he said. "When I arrived there was already a silver dagger in the room. When I told the servants, they informed me that Prince Quinton's page, Niko, was originally assigned to that chamber, but then he moved to be closer to Prince Quinton. It must be his."

"I see, thank you. I'll ask him."

Then he put a finger to his chin. "That's interesting. I don't believe I've seen him since yesterday. And I don't believe Prince Quinton is here either."

"Your Highness," Colonel Yashin said as he bowed. "A moment, if you please."

Prince Felix clicked his heels and made his departure. Delia began to walk to the edge of the tiered garden, staying close to the railing with Colonel Yashin on her other side.

"The coronation will take place under the great tree before the funeral," he said. There was a heaviness to his words.

"Both ceremonies so close?" She put a hand to her heart.

He sighed. "Direct orders of your mother—one of her last requests, actually. She wanted you to be in a place of authority as soon as possible. Delegates from the Four Quadrants will be arriving soon, as well as some of their military representatives."

That got Delia's attention. "Why the military?"

His left eye twitched, and he glanced toward Advisor Winchell, then lowered his voice. "The queen and the rest of the council agreed the marriage contract should be honored as quickly as possible. There will be unrest in the Four Quadrants until you do. Astor is in a fragile state; the planet is slowly dying, our energy sources are depleted, and we are incapable of defending ourselves if another planet decides to take over." He rubbed a hand down his beard, and Delia could tell he was holding something back.

"Unrest? Take over? Colonel Yashin, if you expect me to be crowned and then marry within the next few days, I need to know everything."

He gave her a pained expression. "We have what most of the other planets envy—a strategic position in the Four Quadrants galaxy. Other delegates are eager to trade with us on one stipulation, that we allow them to build a military base on the other side of the mountain."

"No," she responded automatically. "Think of the great tree and the glacier that provides all the water. We can't disturb that area! It's sacred!"

"We would have water imported from Trellium."

"This makes no sense. We'd be selling off Astor piece by piece." She turned and saw Shania being comforted by one of the courtiers. "I can't believe my mother agreed to this plan," she whispered.

Colonel Yashin put a hand on the hilt of his sword. "We're secluded in the palace," he said. "We can no longer deny what is happening to Astor. The only way to keep it habitable is to build a military base. Trellium and Delta Kur are eager to fund this venture, but if we are not willing to enter into trade talks with them, we might be looking at war, princess."

"Our ancestors though . . ." Delia couldn't finish the sentence. She turned to him. "Is there no other way?"

He shrugged. "I wish I knew."

Delia nodded. She was inside a bubble; everything was muffled, dead.

Then he gasped. "Beg your pardon, I addressed you incorrectly." His eyes were rimmed with tears. Then he slowly bowed. "We must show a united front, Your Majesty, Queen Delia."

Queen Delia.

The words echoed through her mind as she numbly made her way along the garden path. She left the tiered garden and headed to the maze, simply walking to keep from collapsing. When she arrived at the middle, someone else was already there.

"Prince Quinton," she said, unable to muster more surprise in her voice. She took in his swollen eyes and disheveled appearance. It made no sense. "I didn't see you at the memorial for my mother."

He stood up. "No. Wait . . . memorial?"

"My mother died this afternoon." The sentence came out quietly, as if she wasn't supposed to tell anyone. The words sounded horribly wrong.

The sorrowful expression in his eyes was replaced with shock. "Oh no. I'm so sorry, princess."

"Queen," she replied, expressionless.

He cleared his throat, then made his way to her. "I'm truly sorry. Your mother was respected by many. I know the people of Astor will miss her very much. And I know you will be just as admired as your mother."

"I appreciate your kind words."

As the shadows of the late day crept across the grass, Delia glanced around the center of the maze. The statue of Arianna gave up no clues as to why Prince Quinton was here. "When I first came in you were crying. What's wrong?"

He hung his head. It looked like he was going to start crying again. "Niko left me. I told him that we'd be happier living a lie as long as we were living together, but he said it wasn't enough anymore. He said it hurt too much." Prince Quinton waved a hand at the sky, gesturing to the stars. "I didn't fight hard enough to keep him. I never knew how much I had to lose until I saw him leave. He's going to Delta Kur! I may never see him again."

Delia relived her own moment of disaster with Aidan. How much they underestimated their partners. The earlier desperation came over her in waves. "This is awful, I'm sorry."

He sniffed. "I will never see Niko again and that's my fault because

I didn't put him first. If you love anything in this world, fight for it. Otherwise what's the point of anything?"

✳ ✳ ✳

As the council looked on, Delia stood at the base of the great tree, now wearing the traditional coronation dress with the decorated fringe. Her braid had been redone to accommodate the antique crown all the other queens of Astor had worn before her. Afterward, it would be returned to its protective glass case.

Shania stood to the side, her own hair entwined with mourner's beads, dried seeds from the great tree that were hand painted by her great-grandmother's ladies-in-waiting. Each year the case was taken out and the beads were retouched by the skilled androids of the official royal jewelers.

The Queen's Guard encircled the intimate gathering. Other than the wind moving through the branches of the great tree, Advisor Winchell's voice was the only sound. She approached Delia with the elaborate crown of codlight crystals balanced on a tray in her hands. "Princess Delia, direct descendant of Arianna, first daughter of the moon, and firstborn daughter of Talia, Queen of Astor, do you vow to govern the peoples of Astor with the guidance of your ancestors?"

"I do," Delia answered, working to keep her voice steady.

"Will you solemnly promise your utmost power to maintain the safety and prosperity of Astor as her protector by our customs and respective laws?"

"I will."

"You may bow and accept your birthright," Advisor Winchell said.

Delia's mouth went dry. She knelt, keeping her chin up and head level.

Advisor Winchell passed the crown to Shania. "Your mother gave me instructions," she said, her eyes welling, but voice unwavering, "for you to crown your queen."

Nodding, Shania took the crown and secured it to Delia's head. Adjusting to the extra weight, Delia slowly stood and locked gazes with her sister.

She was only partially aware of movement around them as Advisor Winchell then began the funeral ceremony.

Shania stood close beside her and whispered, "We only have each other now."

"It will be enough." Delia watched as her mother's body was taken up the mountain to be burned at the ceremonial site. Only the shaman and a group of select Queen's Guard—her Guard now—were allowed to accompany the body to its final resting place among her ancestors.

The night was cool, but Delia didn't feel the wind wrap around her braid. Shania tucked in close to her side, the sacred text pressed against her chest. They stared at the small flicker in the distance.

The fire stood out against the blackened face of the mountain and grew to a larger flame. There was a swallowed gasp behind Delia. Advisor Winchell softly cried as she stared at the mountain.

With the sacred text shaking in her hands, Shania opened to a passage and began to read. The tears started, but she continued with the legend.

". . . and the moon kept her safe while the planet below and everything on it froze."

As her younger sister completed the story of the legend, they remained beside the tree, watching as the last lights of the pyre ignited the sky.

✱ ✱ ✱

On the way back to her room, Delia gave her mother's corridor a wide berth. The staff curtsied and whispered condolences; a few even addressed her as queen.

I will never hear my mother speak again.

Putting a hand over her mouth to stifle the sob, Delia crashed into her own room. She threw herself on the bed, hid her face in her pillow, and let the tears come.

She had no direction! Her heart was ripped into a million pieces. She tried to imagine what advice her mother would give, but no answer came.

Then she closed her eyes and reached out to her ancestors.

"If you love anything in this world, fight for it."

Delia sat upright and saw the clothes she'd worn earlier rumpled on the floor. Blossoms clung to the fabric. She could make out the lump of the clockwork bird, still in the pocket. An unexpected wave of inspiration moved her into action. She grabbed a pen and paper and started to write.

Her door opened.

"Just when I think I've cried so much I can't produce any more tears . . . I cry again." Shania came in and sat down on the bed, tucking into Delia's side. "I wish this were a dream I could wake from," she whispered. She leaned in and read over Delia's shoulder. "What is this?" There was an impish hitch to her voice.

Delia gave her sister a guilty look. "Do you believe it's possible that two people in love can accomplish anything? Even when it seems impossible?"

"Absolutely."

She handed her the letter. "It's for Aidan," she said. "But . . . what if he says no?"

Shania's eyes were bright and brimming with tears. "Then it wasn't meant to be. If he's your true love, you'll have your answer."

Delia rolled up the note and placed it inside the windup bird. Then, as a last thought, she picked up a blossom and placed it inside with the slip of paper. She stepped out to the balcony with Shania and set it free.

CHAPTER THIRTY-ONE

Aidan woke, but his mind was a disorienting blank slate. He concentrated, going backward into his last memory of Delia. As the images of their time under the tree came into focus, he instantly regretted waking. Everything was heavy, yet hollow at the same time. He wished he could fall back to sleep. You couldn't feel pain when you slept.

Delia.

It felt as though a hand reached through his ribs, cracking bones to get to his chest. Then one by one each finger squeezed until he could perfectly visualize the five puncture wounds in his heart.

It hurt. Aidan reasoned it would always hurt. But part of him hoped it would vex him forever so that he'd never forget her.

He opened his eyes and slowly sat up on his cot. A blanket was partially covering him.

This last headache had come on so swiftly he didn't even remember it. There was a kink in his neck that snapped satisfyingly when he tilted his head.

"Ow, galaxy's sake," he sighed, moving a hand to the ache in his jaw. He wondered if he had a rotten tooth.

Pushing himself to stand, Aidan ran a hand through his hair a few times, trying to get rid of the tendrils of sleep. On the shelf over his bed, the latest additions to his collection seemed pathetically symbolic. The red berry had dried up, no longer glistening. He picked up the cork and gave it a sniff; at the very least there was a hint of wine.

Boisterous voices echoed from the main room. He checked the time and saw he'd slept through breakfast. He knew there would be ramifications, but he no longer felt the automatic panic. His heart had already been broken beyond repair, and there was nothing they could say to him now that would do any more damage.

He made his way into the kitchen, but instead of facing an irate stepfather, he found all three of his family were huddled around the infoscreen on the kitchen table. It was full of images of Queen Talia.

Aidan squinted over their backs at the monitor. There were new cracks he didn't remember being there yesterday. With the sound off he scanned the words flowing across the bottom.

PALACE RECEIVES CONDOLENCES FROM ACROSS THE FOUR
QUADRANTS OVER DEATH OF QUEEN TALIA . . .

His sore jaw dropped. Immediately he thought of Delia. Then the stabbing reality that he'd never get to comfort her. He closed his eyes in shame that he left without explaining his true station in life. It was true that he didn't want to be her secret; he'd only started to be his own person since he'd known her. She'd ignited a sense of justice within him.

Still, he should have told her or at least made it clear that he would always love her. "I'm such a lunk," he whispered.

At the sound of his voice there was a jolt through the group. Drake moved away a few steps. Morgan faced him for a moment, then made his way to the other side of the table. Only his stepfather showed any signs of wanting to communicate to Aidan.

Corporal Langdon's eyes were puffy. "Such a horrible loss," he said. There was a heaviness to his voice. It was the first time Aidan could remember seeing his stepfather compromised emotionally. He didn't even recall any tears when his own mother died. Then Langdon pushed himself off the chair and pulled Aidan into an embrace.

Frozen with his arms at his sides, he felt the hulking frame of his stepfather tighten around him, then a hard slap on his back. When he stepped back, tears were trailing down his stepfather's cheeks, disappearing into his substantial beard. "I will never forget this moment," he said to Aidan.

"Nor will I." Aidan took a tentative step backward. He could still feel the grip. There was no comfort in the embrace, only the tactile sensation of being too close to a wild animal.

All three continued to stare at him. Aidan put his attention on the infoscreen, wishing they'd yell at him for not having a meal ready.

> ... OFFICIALLY OPENED TONIGHT'S FULL MOON FESTIVAL TO ALL ... AS A CELEBRATION OF QUEEN TALIA ... OUR SHARED JOY OF HER LIFE AND LEGACY WILL BRING COMFORT ...

Only when his stepfather blew his nose did Aidan realize he and Drake were dressed in their fitted uniforms. Even their shoes were shined.

"I'll be paying my condolences in person this afternoon before the ball, a privilege and an honor for all the Queen's Guard. And Drake here as well." He slapped his son's sturdy frame. "We will represent the family in fine fashion." Then he waved a hand at Aidan and Morgan. "You two don't exactly blend in with the elite crowd."

Aidan turned to see how his stepbrother would react to this snub. Usually it was three against one.

Morgan held up a card, stamped with the queen's official coat of arms. "Then I suppose this invitation to the entire household is a mistake?"

"The household?" Aidan's heart skipped a beat. "Even me?"

Corporal Langdon and Drake looked him up and down, their noses crinkled. "Do you have anything else to wear?" Drake asked.

"You know I don't." Aidan recognized it would be foolish to show up at the palace, but if he had this one last opportunity to tell Delia the truth and to apologize, he'd never forgive himself for not taking the chance.

"That's too bad," Drake said.

Morgan stood in a modest outfit with his everyday boots on. Still, it was newer and nicer than anything Aidan owned. He addressed his father. "Everything still set to go?" he asked. "Considering the announcement this morning."

Drake hissed something back, his face contorted for only a moment, but long enough for Aidan to notice.

The corporal nodded at the invitation. "You may come with us," he said to Morgan. "But unfortunately, Aidan is booked to work the kitchen this evening. The ball will require all domestic staff to be on hand." He turned to Aidan. "I'm sorry, I know this will be your only invitation to a royal ball, but it was only symbolic. No one else is bringing their household help."

Drake didn't even bother to hide his smirk.

"Come," Corporal Langdon barked to his sons. He slapped Morgan on the arm with an open hand and motioned to the door.

Drake checked his hair in the reflection of the infoscreen as he walked past. He grinned at Aidan. "Later, little brother." He faked a punch, but his smirk disappeared when Aidan didn't flinch. "Junk," he said under his breath.

The corporal paused at the cottage door. "You may be called on to serve this evening," he said to Aidan. "If you see us, please don't acknowledge that we're family. It would just create an uncomfortable situation."

The door closed behind them, leaving the cottage quiet.

The gloom set in.

Aidan sat at the kitchen table, staring at the infoscreen, watching image after glamorous image of the royal family. Why did he even think he had a place beside her?

He rummaged around and found a plain piece of paper. He'd write a letter of sympathy to Delia and slip it onto one of her service trays in the coming weeks. A strange sense of relief came over Aidan as this new plan took root in his consciousness.

Glass shattered at the back door. Aidan ran to his room in time to see the clockwork bird fly through another broken pane. He instinctively put up his arms, covering his face.

The bird landed on the shelf, right beside the homing device. Its beak was completely crushed, as if it had been tapping for days. He turned and saw that all the panes were cracked. How long had the bird been trying to reach him? He paused before picking it up. He'd left Delia in tears. It was probably a note relieving him of his kitchen duties—his ruse finally revealed.

After building up the courage, he activated the secret compartment, and a small roll of paper slipped out. His eyes danced over the words. He read it another ten times to be sure. Then he moved in front of the small mirror above the sink. "I will not be who they tell me I am," he said. "Tonight, I will be the man she sees."

Full of exaggerated hope, Aidan pictured himself entering the ballroom, but he wasn't going to be dressed as a chore boy or a waiter. He found the small sphere the pirate had given him and pressed the button.

True to his word, Nazem came into view as Aidan watched from the backyard of the cottage. He landed the glider easily. Aidan approached him, and they shook hands.

"This better be good," Nazem growled. "The wind's blowin' a warning. Somethin's in the air."

"I didn't think pirates were superstitious."

"We are the most superstitious! That's why we're so old and smart. We pay attention to what the ancestors tell us." He looked Aidan up and down. "Whaddya need?"

"A lift to the palace."

He wheezed out a laugh.

"And an outfit worthy of a princess," Aidan added.

"You want to dress like a princess?"

He rolled his eyes. "No, I want to sweep one off her feet."

The wrinkled face looked surprised. "Aye, well, you won't be sweepin' anything but the dirt off the floor in those rags." Then he made room for Aidan on the back of glider.

After Nazem flew a short distance in the air, the great pirate ship grew closer. Once the captain heard of Aidan's plan, he demanded proof. Blushing, Aidan handed over the note from Delia. As the captain read, he frowned, and then at last his features smoothed out.

He barked a few orders, sending crewmen off in all directions, then he handed the note back to Aidan. "We'll take care of what you asked for, but I won't lie, the stars have been spelling out disaster for months. Are you sure this is your destiny?"

"No," he said. "But she is."

After declining the offer of a bottle of wine, Aidan went to the front of the ship. Needing to erase the building doubt and fear, he unfolded the note and read it again, letting her voice fill the spaces of his broken heart.

You are my bravery.
You are my wisdom.
You are my love.
Nothing else matters if you are not by my side.
If you feel the same, come to the ball and
I will declare you as my husband.

CHAPTER
THIRTY-TWO

S tanding on the pedestal in the middle of her room, Delia felt like she was reliving that fateful day all over again. Except this time she was being fitted for her mourning dress. Instead of white silk, the android, Marta's replacement, was hemming a simple black shift dress.

"Adjust to the right, Queen Delia," she said, her voice halting and metallic.

Queen.

She turned, expecting see her mother, but then she understood the android was talking to her. Delia was nearly knocked out by the emotional drop of it all. The room was silent.

Shania lounged on the chair with the infoscreen on her lap, but she gazed out the window, staring at nothing. Wearing her own gown of black, she had personalized her outfit by incorporating the mourning beads into a necklace.

Advisor Winchell moved around the room, the tip of her cane practically dragging over the tiles instead of tapping its usual stoic rhythm. "I've held session with the council and we feel it would be most advantageous for you to announce your forthcoming marriage tonight."

Shania came to life, trying to catch Delia's eye. There was the hint of anticipation in her gaze.

"I hope they approve of my choice," Delia said to Advisor Winchell. She purposely avoided looking at Shania, who already had red blotches on her neck from keeping the note a secret.

But would it be enough to bring Aidan back? Or had she broken his heart beyond repair?

His words echoed cruelly in her mind.

. . . I've lived my whole life being only two things, used and invisible. You've shown me what freedom feels like.

. . . How can I unbraid your hair when our relationship is a lie? How can it still be sacred? . . . I can't be with you if I'm hidden away like something you're ashamed of.

However, Shania's romantic optimism was encouraging. And even though there had been no word from him, as the ball drew closer, Delia allowed herself to hope he'd appear.

"Their approval should not matter," Advisor Winchell answered. There was something in her tone that put Delia on alert. "You are Queen of Astor. It is accepted that your decisions are in the best interest of the kingdom." Then she added, "Your mother never sought their approval. You have to start thinking and behaving like a queen."

Shania smiled at her sister. "What will you wear for your wedding day?" she asked. "Considering the other dress was ruined."

"I have no idea." She turned on the pedestal again for the android. "But I'll need your expertise."

Marta's replacement quirked her head. "Dress is finished. Are you satisfied?"

Delia stepped down and looked at herself in the mirror. The straight style of the dress suited her. She was grateful for the high neck as it hid the necklace Aidan gave her. She self-consciously put her hand over the place where the medallion rested on her chest, pushing down a wave of emotion. "Yes."

Advisor Winchell gave her a rare nod of approval, then sent orders for one of the servants. Moments later, an android Delia recognized as one of her mother's personal attendants entered with a package.

"And now the last touch," Advisor Winchell said. "Your mother's crown."

Delia knew tradition dictated she would not wear her own crown until her wedding day, braided into place with the skilled hands of her android attendant. An image of Marta surfaced unexpectedly, adding another layer of solemn guilt to Delia's heart. She wished she'd managed to find her at the picking station.

With much less ceremony than the coronation, the android secured the tiara expertly with a multitude of hairpins. A smaller version of the antique ceremonial crown, her mother's crown was much lighter; however, the codlight and rare gems made it priceless. And yet, when the last pin was put in place, Delia had never felt so powerless.

As they made their way to the grand ballroom, Delia could already hear the music. "Guests have been arriving for the last hour," Advisor Winchell said, the hint of pride unmistakable. "Would you like me to announce your engagement, or do you have something prepared?"

"I can speak for myself, thank you. I wouldn't want you to announce the wrong name by accident," she said, trying to joke. Then she paused and turned to Advisor Winchell. "Did you hire my bodyguard? The one I wasn't supposed to know about."

She let out an impatient huff of disappointment. "That fool? Of course not, Colonel Yashin acquired his services. Your mother told me you'd discovered his identity." She gave Delia a sideways glance. "Why are you asking about him now?"

With her heart in her throat, Delia concentrated on keeping her voice steady. "I wondered if he asked to be relieved of his responsibilities."

"Relieved of his responsibilities!" she declared. "Tonight of all nights? I surely think not." She strutted a few more steps, then added, "He's in the ballroom as we speak."

"What?" Delia stopped. All the blood rushed to her head. Aidan was in the ballroom at this very moment! Did that mean he wanted to marry her? Or . . . what if he hadn't received the message at all? Delia looked to Shania, who mirrored her own anxiety.

Advisor Winchell crinkled her nose at both of them. "Colonel Yashin told me before we came down. I wanted to make sure security was in place."

"So he's here tonight because of orders?" Delia heard the desperation in her own voice.

Advisor Winchell gave her another curious look. "Are you all right? You're suddenly an interesting shade of green."

"I'm fine," she replied, pushing down the swell of panic. She started toward the ballroom doors.

Shania squeezed her hand. "You'll have to speak with him before you make your speech," she whispered. "There's no other way to know for sure."

Two servants stood on either side of the closed doors, waiting for them to approach. She knew the ballroom was full of people, but there was only one person she was thinking of.

Advisor Winchell put a hand on her shoulder. "I've been an advisor to many royals over the decades. In particular, your grandmother, and your mother . . . and now you. You have a strength none of them possessed. Do not forget that."

Delia was stunned by the praise. Before she could utter a thank-you, Advisor Winchell stepped back, taking her place—behind Delia, the new queen.

The attendants were still waiting at the entrance. Delia nodded, giving them their cue to open the doors.

Trumpets announced her arrival, making the crowd part way. She scanned the faces as they bowed to her one by one. She focused on the perimeter of the room, noting the numerous Queen's Guard standing at attention.

Delia nodded and accept greetings from the various delegates from the Four Quadrants, all the while sneaking glances to find Aidan in the crowd. "Thank you," she replied to them. And then, "It's an honor to have you here this evening."

From the corner of her eye she saw Prince Quinton dressed in his finery. They smiled at each other, but she knew it was pretend. His heart was on a spaceship bound for Delta Kur.

Prince Hagar made several members of her court part way so he could bow in front of her. His hair was pulled back this time in a tight knot at the nape of his neck. Instead of the shell necklace, he was dressed in his royal attire.

"May the tides always bring you what you need," he said. Then he stepped aside, allowing her to pass. Advisor Winchell and Shania followed her.

Up ahead she saw the sweeping stairway, looming closer, reminding her she soon had to make a speech that would change her life forever.

The twins were a few people back, heads tilted at the same angle, watching her with identical expressions of what felt like voyeurism disguised as sympathy. A chill trickled over her skin.

A familiar voice was suddenly in her ear. "Mourning suits you, my lady." Prince Armano took her hand and kissed it. "A dance?" he asked.

"Hardly the time." She pulled back, trying to smile through her embarrassment.

"Improvising protocol is so unbecoming," Advisor Winchell interrupted the couple. Delia detected the venom in her order.

"No one touches the queen," Prince Oskar said, placing himself between Delia and Prince Armano.

Advisor Winchell sighed, "Please join the other princes, Prince Armano." As he sulked away, she turned to Oskar and said, "Your cover has been compromised. You may consider yourself on duty and not an actual prince vying for Queen Delia's attention."

Oskar nodded curtly, then turned on his heel.

Delia stared at the quickly retreating back of Prince Oskar. Advisor Winchell led her through the crowd to the front of the room. "Prince Oskar is my secret bodyguard?" Delia asked her.

"Yes," she shushed her quickly. "Although not adept at the secret part." She rushed her to the front, whispering last-minute instructions to smile and speak clearly.

Prince Oskar is the secret bodyguard?!

Then who is Aidan?

Delia's head spun with questions. She couldn't focus. The encouraging smiles around her started to blur. Her knees felt unhinged.

Who is Aidan?

With her head murky, Delia shakily took the first few stairs, then turned around to address the room. The music stopped and all faces looked toward her. Shania stood in front with Colonel Yashin close by.

Delia scanned the room as a new kind of desperation sent her heart racing.

Who is Aidan?

There must be a logical answer, she thought. They'd been through too much together for it to be a simple ruse or a misunderstanding.

Advisor Winchell lightly tapped her cane. It snapped Delia out of her daze. She took in a breath and tilted up her chin. "Thank you for sharing the long tradition of celebrating the Full Moon Festival," she began. "As you know, it is a somber palace as we say goodbye to our queen, but we shall all take comfort in knowing her spirit only strengthens the voices of our ancestors as they continue to guide us."

Delia paused and took the time to look around the room. She received smiles and nods of encouragement, but no one had hair so blond it was almost white. Her soul withered inside of her.

He had not come. He did not wish to marry her. He did not want her.

She couldn't even factor in the mystery of his identity, because she could only absorb one crippling truth at a time.

I offered myself and my kingdom, and he still said no.

Her eyes fell on Prince Felix. His height made him stand out as he moved near the front of the crowd. He cut a striking figure in his dress uniform; the gold buttons blinked at her from under the plasma chandeliers.

Prince Quinton took a step forward as well, making a few courtiers move aside. His stare was intense and seemed to reflect her own desperate heartbreak.

She closed her eyes for a moment and said a quick prayer to her mother that she was making the right decision.

What does your instinct tell you, Delia? What do the voices of your ancestors say?

Images of her people being used for slave labor on other planets, one of which was so restrictive that its own prince wanted to flee, vied with the idea of a military base taking the place of their most sacred sites. But there was one image that overlapped both of these predictions: Aidan.

Whenever she concentrated on her future, all she could see was him.

Picturing the great tree, Delia began again. "My mother knew her obligation as queen was to keep the interests of the planet and its people a top priority. We live in a state of great change, and while we should hold on to our traditions, we also need to keep in step with the future. We should remember that Astor was first of the planets in the Four Quadrants to be established. And as leader I promise . . ."

An image of the children of the Dark District surfaced. She looked out over the well-dressed and overserved crowd. She never would have known the truth about the picking stations if she hadn't met Aidan.

The moon asked the girl for her most cherished treasure . . .

What do the voices of your ancestors say?

"I promise . . . I promise," she faltered.

Shania's hands were clasped tightly under her chin, her eyes glazed with anxious worry. She nodded, trying to coax Delia along.

The ballroom had grown quiet. Courtiers and delegates exchanged silent looks of confusion. The grand doors opened, causing everyone to turn.

Shania gasped. Then she looked at Delia and gave her a wild smile, practically dancing on the spot.

The crowd stepped aside for the latecomer. The pale hair and skin stood out against the dramatic red jacket as he made his way to the front of the room.

He's wearing the pirate captain's coat, she thought incredulously.

CHAPTER
THIRTY-THREE

A idan stood in the middle of the ballroom, wishing he could stop time. The look on Delia's face was one that he wanted burned into his memory forever. She was staring at him, and only him.

Once again he was certain they inhabited their own dimension where they were the only two living things that existed.

Forget oxygen and food, he thought, *she is all I need*.

He put a hand over his heart and nodded to her. She smiled. The fancily dressed courtiers took in his whole outfit. The red jacket was a bit over the top, but it fit perfectly and the buttons had been shined especially. Plus, the captain had slipped a small bottle of wine into the side pocket.

"To celebrate your engagement," he'd said with a wink.

Then the pirates gave him the refurbished Queen's Guard glider they had stolen, allowing Aidan to slip into the perimeter of the palace without raising any alarm. It was a plan built on pure guts and luck, but he'd been infused with a sense of invincibility since reading her note, and nothing would stop him from reaching her tonight.

Now he stood in front of her, trying to convey a lifetime of promises with only a look.

Delia hadn't stopped staring at him. Slowly, a blush bloomed on her cheeks. She cleared her throat and continued her speech. "Or rather, we should keep what is vital to our hearts sacred and protected. A ruler who lives empathically and rules with a genuine conviction oversees a country of sympathetic people."

Aidan took note of the murmurs from a few people. Several men in military garb were frowning. But he couldn't keep his eyes off Delia for long. Her voice was true and full of principle. If he weren't in love with her already, he was certain he'd lose his heart at this moment.

"If we're not supportive of one another," she continued. "If we do not build one another up, then we have nothing to save, nothing to keep sacred. Our planets have closely traded for many generations. There is no reason for this to change. In fact, this is a new era where anyone can rise to do great things, no matter their station in life. I want Astor to be a welcoming place of opportunity for those striving to improve life for all."

A stately woman with a wooden staff stood off to the side. Aidan noted her expression was one that bordered on awkward discomfort. Her brow furrowed as she took a calculated sweep of the room with her eyes.

"And in the spirit of freedom of choice, I shall make my first decision as queen and begin the dance with my chosen partner." She stepped away from the spotlight and he temporarily lost her in the crowd.

Even though the last message was ambiguous, the crowd remained quiet, everyone's focus trained on Delia, watching to see who she would select.

The music began, but no one paired off. Aidan swallowed dryly. It took all his willpower not to push through these gawking courtiers to find her. He strained his neck to see over their heads. Then one by one, people stepped to the side, creating an opening, and suddenly a path appeared with Delia walking toward him.

His head was full of static and his legs had gone numb.

"Good evening." She smiled and then curtsied. A respectable distance was between them. She dropped her voice, then said, "You came."

"Says the plasma torch to the fly." He ached to pull her close, but Aidan followed her lead. She hadn't clearly announced an engagement. Several of the Queen's Guard kept darting glances at one another. Aidan felt there was an edge to the moment that hadn't been there earlier.

Delia disregarded any personal space and touched his arm. "I thought I'd never see you again."

A string of murmurs went through the crowd, peppered by a few gasps. The music continued to play. Still, it was all he could do not to throw himself at her feet and pledge his eternal love. "I'm sorry," he said, meaning everything that ever made her sad. "I'm so sorry about your mother."

A flash of grief clouded her eyes. "Thank you."

Her hand lingered on his arm and because he couldn't help himself, he pulled her close and started to lead her around the floor to the music. He had no idea how to dance, but somehow the air under his feet was moving them along as if they were on a cloud.

Soon, several other couples began to dance as well, spinning expertly around them. The effect was perfect for Aidan. He could stare into her eyes the whole time, as the rest of the world rushed by. "Did you really mean everything you said in your speech?" he asked.

"I thought I had to give up everything I loved to be a strong queen, but now I see it's the opposite."

"You're the queen of Astor?" Even as he said it, Aidan recognized the stupidity of his question. Of course Delia would be queen.

"Yes. The coronation was an intimate one, done last evening."

Feeling like he was in a dream, Aidan took a moment to absorb the scene. To his great amusement he saw the stunned expressions on his stepfather and Drake as he danced past them. He gave them a satisfied smirk and it felt fantastic.

Across the room, the prince with flaxen curls stared pointedly at them. Interestingly, Aidan sensed a hostile vibe. "And your marriage to one of the princes?" he asked carefully.

She stopped dancing and looked at him directly. "I can't be queen without you by my side. I'll have to convince Advisor Winchell it will work, but I refuse to live a life based on lies. I refuse to live without love." There was a new brightness to her voice.

Although his soul was singing, there was a darkness of doubt creeping in from the edges. "Are you sure?"

"Yes!" she laughed. "Because you're here! You're here and everything will be all right." Taking his hand, she guided him through the dancers to the balcony doors.

They were almost to the exit when he stopped them. "Wait," Aidan said. He counted three heartbeats. "I have to tell you something before we can continue. I'm not who you think I am."

"That's far enough!" A thickly set man with a sheen to his upper lip put himself between Delia and Aidan. Now close up, Aidan recognized him as Prince Oskar. "Stop, you cannot go with this man. He's not on the guest list."

Aidan turned to where Drake and his stepfather had been, but they were no longer there. He wondered if they managed to tip off the other security guards.

"No, it's all right," Delia said, putting a hand on Oskar's barrel chest. "I know this man. I'm perfectly safe with him." But he remained on the spot, staring at Aidan. Delia cleared her throat. "Now, if you don't mind, my friend and I would like to—"

"Prince Oskar is right," Aidan interrupted. "I've been lying to you. I'm not your secret bodyguard. I made it up on the spot so I wouldn't have to tell you the truth."

"I know," she sighed. "At least, I know you're not my secret bodyguard." Then she pointed to Prince Oskar. "He is."

"How long have you known?" Aidan asked.

She shook her head. "It doesn't matter." She pulled on Aidan's hand and smiled at him. "Please come so we can talk. I want to know everything about you."

"Are you sure, Queen Delia?" Oskar asked, putting a hand on her arm. There was an odd sensation deep inside Aidan. He felt it grow outward, like an approaching sandstorm.

"Yes! Now please step aside."

"Understood." He stepped back. "But don't worry, I'll be close by. I am your real bodyguard after all."

She rolled her eyes and continued on her way.

"Carry on, then," Oskar said, shaking Aidan's hand. He pulled him closer with a jerk of his arm. A small gun was pressed into Aidan's palm. Oskar's voice was sharp and lethal in his ear. "Activate prime directive," he whispered.

Aidan felt a coldness cascade throughout his body. He quickly pocketed the weapon and followed Delia out to the balcony. Words flashed in front of his vision.

PRIME DIRECTIVE: ASSASSINATE THE QUEEN OF ASTOR

It was dark outside. The only light that shone down was from the full moon. She was in front of him, murmuring words he could not translate. His concentration slipped away as new data filled his thoughts.

He was acutely aware of the temperature, the wind speed, the distance he needed to be from Delia to accurately fire the gun.

Delia. Queen. Gun.

The gun was in his pocket.

A jolt ran the length of his body as the coldness enveloped him.

Her lips found his. "I need you," she whispered, almost crying. "I'm so scared to be queen. Tell me it's going to be all right. I don't care if you're not my bodyguard. We're meant to be together and that's all that matters. Tell me you want me too. Tell me we're going to make this work."

He kissed her as a reply. One hand was on her back, pressing her closer, the other reaching into his pocket for the gun. He was aware, but he wasn't in control; everything was happening without his consent.

✳ ✳ ✳

Images of being with Delia swirled in his mind, transposing over the data streaming in front of his eyelids.

PRIME DIRECTIVE: ASSASSINATE THE QUEEN OF ASTOR

He felt like he was mentally pushing a boulder up the great mountain. All of his muscles were taut. He broke off the kiss and fought every instinct in his programming to say one word. "Run."

Then he pushed her shoulder hard. His arm straightened out, the gun pointed directly at her.

Delia stumbled back a few steps. She let out a nervous laugh, eyeing the gun. As the seconds passed, her face took on a frown of confusion. "What are you doing?" she asked in quiet shock.

The gun shook in his grip. "Run," he repeated hoarsely. He shuddered. There was a sudden clutch to his stomach. Each second he delayed the mission, a torrent of agony was released into his circuits.

"Please, what is this?" Even in shock Delia was still staying calm.

Aidan yelled, "Run, Delia. Run!"

She stayed in place, her eyes the size of the moon. A single tear rolled down her cheek.

There was a tremendous snap inside his chest. He saw the gun and knew what he must do. As each electrical current pulled him in one direction, Aidan used his last bit of intent to defy his programming.

He turned the gun on himself and fired.

CHAPTER THIRTY-FOUR

Delia's scream was swallowed up by the music from inside. She stared at Aidan, the betrayal only matched by her agonizing heartbreak. He was lying on his back, eyes open and still. The gun had slid into the shadows.

Shaking, she took a few tentative steps toward his body and dropped to her knees. A tendril of smoke rose from the bullet wound through his heart. Instead of a pool of blood, the hole in his chest revealed wires and circuit boards. It was a moment before the full extent of the truth slammed her in the heart.

Aidan was an assassin.

Aidan was a spy.

Aidan was an android.

Her gaze traveled to his face. The unnatural look of his blank expression was more terrifying than any pirate encounter. She patted his cheek. It felt so real. "Aidan?" she begged softly. "Aidan?" Then louder. "Aidan? Wake up and talk to me!" He was lifeless to her touch.

The medallion came loose from the neckline of her dress. It swayed between them like a pendulum marking time.

Footsteps rushed toward her. A heavyset man in a palace guard uniform appeared, his face ablaze with color. He looked at Aidan, then to her. She could sense the gears in his head trying to figure out the situation. "What did you do?" he asked her. The accusation to his tone could not be missed.

"I . . . I don't know what happened." Delia said. She moved her hand down his chest, where a few wires poked out from the wound. She screamed and pulled her hand back, seeing the red mark from the burn.

The rotund guard watched her, and then his eyes narrowed. "I agreed to arrange your death, but I won't risk having your blood on my hands. The resistance hasn't won quite yet." Reaching down, he picked up something from the shadows. He pointed Aidan's gun toward the closest glass window and fired two shots, shattering the glass.

The music stopped. He fired two more shots, but into the sky this time. Screams came from inside the palace. There was shouting, then more gunfire. Another large glass window beside them exploded outward.

Stunned, Delia instinctively folded herself over Aidan's body. Glass began to shatter in an unending cacophony of destruction.

With ringing ears, Delia looked up. A second, younger guard with broad shoulders and a low forehead had joined the first man. His mouth hung open. "Why is she still alive?" His tone bordered on a sulk. "Stupid robot. I told you this would happen! Just shoot her and be done with it!" He made a grab for the gun.

"Shut up, Drake," the larger man said, leaning out of his reach.

Another young man came upon the scene. "Back off," he said to Delia, pushing her from Aidan. "Don't touch him, you'll damage him more!"

"Nice work with the SHEW, Morgan," the guard named Drake sneered. "You said he was perfectly programmed. But look at this mess. He has a hole in the middle of his chest!"

"Morgan!" the heavyset man barked. "Did you interfere with his SHEW?"

"Don't be so thick," the younger man named Morgan replied.

Several gliders zoomed overheard; Delia didn't recognize them as the Queen's Guard. They seemed to be in formation.

Morgan continued, "I told you he was one of a kind! We can't control what is smarter than us." He moved to Aidan's feet. "Trellium's military will be in complete control soon. Although, you two idiots only had one job to do, and it's still listening to everything we say." Then he motioned to Delia.

From the corner of her eye, Delia saw the heavyset man point the gun at her. "That crown won't protect you now." Then he bellowed, "Queen Delia is dead!"

A surge of fury coursed through her veins. She only had one chance. Grabbing her crown, she ripped it from her hair and flung it at the man's face, distracting him. Then she lunged forward, hands intent on getting the gun.

There was a giant yowl as her body connected with his. They rolled across the balcony, grunting. A hard punch landed on her side, knocking the breath out of her lungs. His puffy face leered from above.

Her heels kicked uselessly into the floor. The frantic energy she'd first felt was quickly being depleted as they struggled. She was going to be killed. This man she'd never seen before was going to murder her, right here on the balcony. Her first thought was of Shania and how she couldn't bear the idea of her sister being all alone.

No! her mind screamed. She reached up and jammed her finger in his eye.

He cried out and leaned to the side. Delia rolled out from under him, breathing hard, with her dress ripped. The gun glinted in the moonlight close to her feet. Delia grabbed it, then turned it on him. "Who are you?" she demanded. Her entire body was shaking.

"Behind you!" Quinton yelled from the balcony doorway. Delia spun around just in time to see a jagged blade swipe down toward her.

She fired a shot. The vibration of the weapon went straight to her heart. The guard named Drake fell to his side, one hand gripping his knee, the other still holding a knife.

There was a garbled scream as Quinton fought the older guard. Although large, he was no match for Quinton's lithe fighting skills. He landed a swift high kick to the man's chest, followed by repeated blows to his face until he slumped forward, eyes rolling into the back of his head.

Quinton leaned over, his hands on his knees, trying to catch his breath. "Get that dagger before more show up."

Delia looked around wildly, but Aidan's body was gone. In the confusion of the ambush the man named Morgan must have taken him. "No!" she cried out.

Another gunshot blasted through the air, followed by more screaming. Quinton retrieved the blade from the whimpering guard himself and tucked it into his belt. He reached for Delia. "The Trellium military have taken over the palace. We need to leave!"

She shook her head. There was too much to process. "I can't leave Shania!"

Shouting came from inside followed by another gunshot. Quinton gave her a pained look of desperation. "We're outnumbered and at this point I'm not exactly sure who's on our side. We'll need the element of surprise. Is there another way inside?"

She led him down the garden path. The smothered cries from the palace made her heart lurch. She imagined Shania being held at gunpoint . . . or worse. They rushed to the center of the maze, and then Delia pressed the three letters, opening the entrance to the tunnels.

The darkness of the secret passage momentarily swallowed them up.

"What's happening?" he said, his voice shaking. "Someone shouted that you were dead, and then all of a sudden Trellium's military along with half of the Queen's Guard started to fire their guns, shouting for everyone to get down on the floor."

He breathed harshly behind her as they clumsily made their way down the spiral steps. "I didn't see much in all the confusion, but I think it's safe to say Prince Felix is part of this."

There was a painful twist of her stomach at the mention of another betrayal. How could she have been so blind! "I don't care about Prince Felix," she replied truthfully. "My priority is saving my sister."

There was a surprised yelp as Delia was hit from behind. She sprawled on the hard surface of the tunnel. The lights came on to reveal Quinton gripping his ankle.

He tried to stand but crumpled as his foot gave out.

"Quick," she said, pulling him up and taking his weight. She put his arm around her shoulders and they started to walk. Quinton grunted beside her with every limp.

"What was happening on the balcony?" he asked.

Delia's confused thoughts spun like a dervish. "I have no idea. Suffice it to say I have miserable taste in men apparently." The anguish was on the surface, but shock kept it from penetrating her consciousness. She only had one thought on her mind—save Shania.

They remained quiet as they increased their speed, both in disbelief. They took the last corner at a lumbering sprint until they reached the offshoots that led to the lakeside and the dead end.

Delia swallowed a scream as they almost ran into a huffing body. Then she let out a grateful sigh. "Colonel Yashin. Please," she begged. "Tell me my sister is all right!"

Rivulets of sweat ran down his confused expression, which then warped into a menacing snarl of fury. "You're supposed to be dead."

A tremor filled Delia from head to toe. Quinton shifted against her as he reached for the knife in his belt. He threw it quickly, but he was off balance, and the blade hit the tunnel wall with a dull clank.

Without flinching, Colonel Yashin reached into the pocket of his uniform and retrieved a small sphere. Delia recognized it as a bomb like the ones the pirates had used on her and Aidan.

Aidan.

Although her mind was a scattered mess of terrorized panic, she had a sudden urge to run back to find him.

Colonel Yashin held the deadly orb above his head. "They'll find our bones scattered together! I'll be a hero of the resistance! I told them, 'Never send an android to do a man's job.'"

Something snapped inside Delia. "You're a fake!" she accused. "All this time you've been scheming to get power from my mother. I knew she didn't want a military base. You persuaded her!"

He grinned. "That's what a war hero does, dear princess."

Delia flared her nostrils. "Queen."

"Not for long." He pulled back his arm, preparing to throw the bomb. Then his eyes nearly bulged out of their sockets. His mouth opened in a silent scream. Colonel Yashin fell face forward, hitting the ground with a sickening thud. A plasma hatchet stuck out of his back.

From the shadows an unmistakable silhouette emerged.

CHAPTER THIRTY-FIVE

"Tookah?" Delia gasped.

"A pirate keeps his word," he said. There was a wet sucking sound as he retrieved the hatchet. The wound was so severe, Colonel Yashin's whole spine was exposed.

Tookah wiped the blade on his pants, then slipped the weapon into his belt. "It is not safe here," he said, picking up the bomb with one of his other hands. He pressed a small button, deactivating it, then tucked it into a satchel slung across his broad chest. "We must leave."

She eyed him suspiciously. "Are you with the resistance?"

He shook his head. "Nazem was adamant about the wind blowing a warning, so the captain ordered us to follow the pale one to the palace." He gave her a shy shrug. "We have more than one Queen's Guard glider."

"But the colonel had one of your bombs!"

"Pirates aren't the only ones who steal."

There was an echoing of footsteps rushing toward them. She saw the tip of a sword, then a blue mop of hair flopping back and forth. "'Tis a shambles up there!" Nazem arrived breathless. His hair was a mass of tiny braids, giving the impression of a continuous waterfall. He looked at Delia and then Quinton. "Where is the pale one?" he asked. "Where is Aidan?"

"Do you have a ship?" Quinton interrupted. "We need to escape."

"Aye." Nazem nodded. "At the edge of the Dark District, waiting for our signal."

"No," Delia said. "I will not leave without my sister."

Nazem sighed. "Honorable and a pain in the backside." He looked at Delia. "I'll stay with the pretty one while you and Tookah find yer sister."

Quinton eased himself down onto the ground, wincing slightly. Delia traded her gun for Nazem's sword, and then she and Tookah continued down the tunnel back toward the palace. "This will lead to the basement," she said.

The plasma lights flickered. Delia had images of the palace being destroyed. Had she lost her beloved Astor for good? Behind her eyelids, images of a military base in place of the sacred tree terrified her.

She stared forward, names blurring as she blinked away tears. Shania, Winnie, the shaman, and . . .

But she did not let herself think of him. She didn't even think of the first letter of his name. Instead, she took the memory of his kiss and buried it deep.

They finally reached the metal door. "What is the plan?" Tookah asked, the plasma hatchet already out.

A scream on the other side of the door made Delia jump. "That's Shania," she said. Without hesitating, she pulled open the door and roared into the hallway, sword at the ready.

Shania was running full tilt toward them. Each of her beautiful braids had come undone, a trail of mourning beads scattered and bouncing on the floor behind her. A shot came from the far end of the hallway. She dropped to her stomach. Several Trellium guards were bearing down quickly; the one in front had his gun out.

Delia and Tookah jumped back as the guard fired again. He quickly reached Shania and grabbed her by the arm, pulling her up to her feet. "Run away again and the next time there won't be a warning shot."

She clutched the clumps of hair to her chest, trying to keep the tangled braids close to her.

To see her sister's beautiful hair desecrated this way felt like a sword through Delia's heart. She nodded to Tookah as they entered the hallway again.

Tookah rushed into the scene, hatchet sweeping down and across, creating an effective distraction as Delia dealt with the first guard. She disarmed him of his weapon with such force she heard the bone crack under his twisted arm.

Shania collapsed against the wall and slid to the floor, her hand over her heart.

Delia turned to help Tookah only to find he'd used the butt end of the hatchet to make quick work of the three remaining guards. They lay sprawled at odd angles with bloody noses and broken kneecaps.

There was a sob from Shania. "They said you were dead," she said to Delia. Her hair was cradled in her arms, now a mass of spilled tresses.

Delia pulled her close. "Where's Winnie?" she asked.

"I don't know. One moment she was there with Prince Felix, and the next they had both disappeared."

"I have to find her." Delia stood, pulling Shania with her. "If she's with Prince Felix she's his prisoner."

"No," Tookah said. "You will be shot on sight. We need to leave the palace first. Then we make a plan."

"I can't leave Winnie behind!"

Shania put a hand on Delia's arm. "Winnie is resilient, she'll do whatever it takes to survive. And she'd expect us to do the same. The palace is in chaos. Trellium's guards have taken over and blocked off all access." She motioned to the secret entrance to the tunnels. "This is the only way out. I was hoping to escape, but this dress was not made for running."

Pushing away an image of Winnie in chains, Delia reluctantly agreed.

All three ran back to where Quinton was waiting at the junction. He had the gun propped up, and his face was pale and sweaty.

"They've blocked off the lakeside tunnel," he told them.

Nazem came from the other direction, his face telling a desperate tale. "The maze is blocked as well. I can hear 'em up there."

"Colonel Yashin must have told them about the secret entrance." Delia chewed on her lower lip. "It's only a matter of time before they realize Shania is missing and that I'm very much alive. The tunnels will be the first thing they search."

"Then we're as good as dead," Quinton said, and a hint of contempt crept into his tone. She looked down the dark tunnel to their right. The memory washed over her before she could stop it. When she brought Aidan here, he'd asked about what was on the other side of the blocked tunnel.

. . . don't want to find out what's on the other side?

She turned to Nazem. "How many bombs do you have?" she asked.

"Only one," he replied, sounding concerned.

Tookah reached into his satchel and tossed him the black sphere he'd retrieved from Colonel Yashin.

"Aye, make that two."

"Hopefully that will be enough." She looked at Tookah. "Can your hatchet cut through this stone?" She nodded to the dead end.

"It would take days."

"What if you only had to make an opening big enough to fit the bomb?"

He regarded her with a look of hope, then nodded determinedly. "Much faster."

As Tookah sliced away at the rock with heavy strokes Delia helped Nazem move Quinton farther along the tunnel. "Setting off a bomb inside a narrow tunnel might not be the best for our health if we're too close," she said.

He winced as he hobbled along. "Are all engagement parties on Astor this fun?"

Sparks flew with each crash of the plasma hatchet. The ringing of the blade on the stone echoed loudly. Delia kept looking in both directions, expecting a fresh crew of armed guards. "Faster please, Tookah," she called out.

Then there was silence.

"It's ready!" he called.

Nazem handed the bombs to Delia and she sprinted to the dead end. Tookah had fashioned the perfect pocket. She placed the bomb deep into its custom space, then pressed the small disc in the middle. At once it started vibrating.

She felt Tookah pick her up as he turned and ran back toward the others.

The air shattered as she dropped to the ground, covering her head. Coughing, she heard the others move about.

It was Nazem who spoke first. "Not bad," he praised.

Delia looked up. Through the clearing dust she saw a large hole in the wall. Tookah held up a plasma torch and looked through. "There's another tunnel on the other side!"

Voices shouted from the direction of the maze entrance.

"Trellium guards!" Shania said, her face gripped with fear.

"Quickly," Delia urged, pushing her sister through the opening first. Nazem was next. Quinton cried out as he fell on the other side. She and Tookah hurriedly followed, nearly falling on top of Quinton as they stumbled into the other half of the tunnel. Shots zinged past her head.

"Run!" Delia called out. Tookah took Quinton over his shoulder as Nazem and Shania hurried after. Delia pressed her back up against the smooth tunnel, waiting.

Just as the shadows of the guards fell across the newly formed opening, she activated the second bomb and tossed it through. An instant of stunned silence was followed by a thunderous blast.

Knocked off her feet once again, Delia waited until her shaking legs could hold her. A crater spread wide where there was once a small opening. She didn't wait for the dust to clear to see the carnage. In the eerie silence she turned to find the others, now heading down this forgotten tunnel. She had no idea where it led, but one thing was certain, it was their only hope.

CHAPTER THIRTY-SIX

I t felt like they'd been walking for days, and still the tunnel continued its slow curves to the left and then back to the right. Sometimes there was a slight incline and then an equal dip downward. Only the one torch gave them light, a glow of illumination slowly moving along the curving pathway.

With her sister by her side, Delia took the lead as Tookah followed with Quinton under his lowest arm, helping him walk. Nazem brought up the rear of the group, the hatchet in his hand as he kept glancing behind, alert for the sounds of rebel footsteps.

Delia turned to him. "The crater left behind is too big for anyone to jump over. We're quite safe."

Nazem snorted. "I could fly my glider through these tunnels. Don't think one o' those Trellium guards won't figure it out too."

A memory of flying with Aidan holding on to her waist made Delia miss a step. She held her breath until the unexpected lurch of her heart subsided.

Tookah asked Quinton about Rexula.

"And what does the water feel like?" Tookah asked. "Is it warm? Do you swim? I don't know how to swim. Is it easy to learn?"

"Water is like any other liquid," Quinton said with measured breaths. "The temperature of the water depends on many things. I don't care for swimming, but anyone can learn."

Delia stayed quiet.

"And the homes?" Tookah continued. "Is it true some homes are built right on the rocks by the ocean, so that you can hear the waves as you go to sleep?"

"Yes. It was one of the things my page, Niko, missed on this trip."

"It sounds like paradise," Tookah sighed. "I would like to paint it one day."

Quinton groaned as he limped along. Delia suspected the pain was from his heart instead of his ankle. She knew he dreaded the planet that had been nothing but a prison of lies for him.

After a while Nazem rejoined them, falling in step with Quinton and Tookah. They began to talk about Aidan. Even though they kept their voices low, their whispers reached Delia's ears as Quinton described what he'd found on the balcony. But she shut it out. She had no desire to hear the recollection of her attempted assassination. Her mind was still trying to reconcile the image of charred wires with the heartbeat she'd felt under her palm when they kissed.

Then, as soon as she was conscious of the thought, she brushed it away, silently rebuking herself for thinking of him at all.

"Prince Felix will pay for this," Shania offered. She had tried to braid some of her hair, but it only ended up a mass of tangles that she eventually wrapped around her arm, trying to create an illusion of style. "He has no idea how wicked I can be."

Delia stayed quiet. Images of Astor falling into the hands of the military haunted her. And here she was, its queen, running underground, hiding like some kind of useless sandworm.

Quinton's labored breathing was the only sound. They turned the corner and something new appeared in the torchlight, another pathway to the left, and in front of them a door that was nearly an exact replica to the one that led to her own palace.

Delia put her ear to the cold hard door and listened. She thought there was muffled talking on the other side. They all traded knowing glances.

"We have to get out of these tunnels," she whispered.

She nodded to Tookah who took the plasma hatchet and stood in the lead, hands ready to pry open the door. Delia gripped her sword. "Stay behind me," she whispered to Shania.

Tookah's arms flexed, and then with one fierce motion he opened the metal door with a slam. There was a scream. Delia stepped through the doorway.

A bright light turned on them. She squinted against the glare, her sword held in front of her.

A voice said, "One step closer and I'll make sure he never opens his eyes again."

CHAPTER THIRTY-SEVEN

It took a moment for Delia to focus. They were in a small stone room. Shelves lined the walls, filled with tools and jars of various implements. Several computer monitors were crowded along one side. There was a curious acrid odor around them.

A long table dominated the cold space with a man on either side. The smaller had a long beard and sat on a stool. A headlamp was strapped to his forehead, illuminating the tool in his grip. A tendril of smoke rose from the tip, hinting that Delia had interrupted whatever they were working on.

The small man focused on Tookah. He let out a garbled scream, but the other man put up a hand, silencing him.

"Stay quiet, Griff," the second man ordered. Then he turned and glared at Delia with a look of undisguised scorn.

Her heart nearly exploded. She recognized him as the man from the balcony. She pointed a shaking finger at him. "You!" she said. "You were there! You took Aidan!" She stepped toward him, trying to push him out of the way, but he wouldn't budge.

He had no weapon, but his stance blocked whatever was on the table. "If you want him, you'll have to kill me first."

She caught a glimpse of a red coat with black trim. "No," she whispered. Although her heart and mind had refused to combine the facts, the proof she'd been pushing away was literally laid out before her eyes.

Aidan, or what used to be Aidan, was on the table. His chest was open, but instead of blood and bone there were wires and steel.

It was Nazem who found his voice first. "Aye," he whispered. "Captain will be mighty upset about the hole in the coat."

"It's the pale one," Tookah said.

Someone put a hand on Delia's arm. "Is he dead?" Shania's voice was full of awe.

"You mean 'it,'" she replied, still staring at what was Aidan's true self. Her heart was broken and trodden down with layers of confusion and anger. There was a hole in her chest too, but instead of singed wires hers was full of a fearful spirit, unsure and terrified.

"It?" The old man named Griff gave her a hard look, his wizened face lined in a mask of anger. "He's the most amazing machine you'll ever set your eyes on."

A knife twisted deep inside her heart. "Call him by his proper name," Delia said, not bothering to keep the anger from her tone. "That machine you speak of with so much admiration is an assassin."

Morgan and Griff watched with guarded gazes.

"He came after me with the most despicable intentions," she continued. "It wasn't enough to connive to get me alone . . ." She had to stop and take in a breath. "He made me fall . . ." She stopped, the ache mixed with the devastation giving her nothing to stand on. Her whole self was crumbling.

She tried again, like forcing out a breath. "He made me believe he was real."

The room was quiet. Then Shania said, "His enjoyment of the coconut cakes seemed so authentic."

Tookah frowned, then looked at Delia. "That night on the ship, I was watching you. I thought you were in love." His blush made him look younger.

"It's impossible to be programmed to love," Griff answered in a straightforward tone, as if he wasn't bent over an android with a chest full of exposed circuits.

"Exactly," Delia said, her voice shaking on the one word. She let her eyes travel past the broken chest and up to Aidan's face. She knew she should have turned around and gone back into the tunnel, because when she looked at him all she could remember was how he'd pushed her away as he pointed the gun at her. His face had been contorted in a grimace as he yelled another warning. But now his face was still, his eyes closed. His jaw relaxed. He could have been sleeping.

"Now," Morgan said, slipping on his own headlamp. "If you don't care about him, then please leave my home. There are the stairs." He motioned to stone steps that led upward. "Help yourself to whatever you find in the kitchen and then go. We have an extensive repair job to finish."

Rage and hurt kept Delia in place. "Why are you fixing him?" she asked, taking a step toward the table, daring herself to get closer to Aidan. "So he can finish the job?"

Griff leaned back and dropped a tool on the workbench behind him. Delia saw the surface was littered with other implements, in particular a long-handled tool with a small gold disc attached to the end. A glass jar had been tipped on its side, with similar discs spilled out on the bench. They seemed familiar, but she couldn't quite place them. "What are those?" she asked, her tone sharp.

"SHEWs," Morgan snorted.

"Those aren't like any SHEWs I've ever seen." Delia was in the mood for a fight and no topic was off limits at this point.

"He's unlike any android, that's why," Morgan sneered under his breath. "Fixing him is a long shot, but I won't give up on him."

Griff's head was bent down, but his gaze flicked between Delia and Morgan.

"Don't you dare talk about him like he's a real man," she said. "You're both delusional." She pointed to his chest. "I see what he is with my own eyes."

Morgan picked up another tool. The muscles were tight in his face, his cheeks turned bloodred. Delia readied herself for a bold retort. Instead, his next sentence was one of introspection and calm. "No one knows what he is exactly," he said, looking down at Aidan. "His superior technology had foolproof programming, except no one anticipated the independent thinking."

Morgan continued, "He was programmed to kill you, but not only did he fight those orders, he took steps to prevent it the only way he knew how . . . by eliminating the threat, himself. It was a calculated sacrifice."

But Delia wasn't interested in hearing any of Morgan's praise. All she could think about was being under the tree with Aidan, how his kisses felt so real, how he'd awoken something inside of her she never knew existed. How was it possible for her to feel so deeply about something that wasn't real?

"Eliminating himself?" she laughed bitterly. Tears were close to the surface. "How can you kill something that was never alive? How much of a risk was it for him to shoot his chest, knowing you two would be fixing him later?"

Morgan sighed heavily. "Aidan didn't know he was an android."

Delia closed her eyes for a moment. She felt her lower lip quiver. Summoning up any leftover courage, she pushed back her shoulders. "It doesn't matter," she said. "There are more pressing issues to deal with." She addressed Griff. "We're in need of assistance. Our friend has hurt his foot and we're desperate to get back to the surface."

"The surface is no place to escape to now," he replied.

Without warning there was a burst of noise above them. Prince Felix's voice filled the silence. "I am calling on all people of Astor to hear this message and rejoice! The monarchy has fallen! Queen Delia is dead!"

CHAPTER THIRTY-EIGHT

Everyone looked at the steep stairway that disappeared upward. There was a pause, and then Prince Felix started speaking again.

Delia raced up the steps, taking them two at a time. At the top there was a small latch, locking the door. Delia hardly remembered hitting it with the hilt of her sword.

"For a new dawn will shine over your planet." Prince Felix's voice was sure and full of pride.

She burst through the door with her sword in front of her, ready to battle, but the room was empty. Prince Felix was not here. Instead, there was a modest kitchen and eating area. The windows were covered with dark cloth. Muffled yells echoed from outside. The only light was from the infoscreen.

"No longer will Astor want for anything."

Prince Felix's image filled the screen. He was on the balcony of the palace. Her palace! Two Trellium guards stood at attention on either side of him. Winnie was nowhere to be seen. Delia listened with a numb detachment as he detailed how Astor would become the pearl of the Four Quadrants, housing the most sophisticated and lethal military base.

"The days of your dual existence have ended. It's time to come out into the light." He spread his arms wide. "Not only will Astor be the most protected, but also the most feared and admired."

Then a vision of the new Astor was superimposed over the present planet. The Dark District was to become an industrial area, all housing removed to make way for weapon-making facilities. The canyon was to be used as the refuse dump for all the waste from the factories. The mountain with the great tree vanished, only to be replaced with the military base.

Her heart almost stopped when she saw the tree no longer there, but instead a behemoth steel structure.

"Demolition of the great tree will commence at the rising of the twin suns tomorrow morning to commemorate the birth of a new Astor." Then Prince Felix raised both his fists in the air.

The live video stopped after Prince Felix nodded to the crowd and disappeared inside the palace. The newsfeed continued to scroll across the bottom of the screen, once again, announcing officially that Delia was dead. Prince Felix and his military had successfully taken control of the palace.

"They think I'm dead," she said to the empty room. Delia felt like all of her bones had liquefied. She had no structure, no strength to even stand. She froze, like a statue, or an android whose battery had run out.

I will stay like this forever, she thought dizzyingly.

There was a clatter as her sword hit the floor. She didn't remember dropping it. Everything in her body had gone numb.

She felt like Aidan, her chest ripped open wide with its insides open for people to inspect. Her home was being destroyed and there was nothing she could do. Delia was dead in more ways than they ever suspected. She was Astor. Her whole life had been based on what was best for her home planet.

And now it was being killed.

The tree would be destroyed.

The mosaics in the tunnel would be removed. No one would know the connection to the moon. She thought of the selfish king in the canyon. "Maybe this is his revenge," she said out loud in a daze.

"What is the plan?" Tookah asked softly.

Delia turned around. She had no idea the others had followed her, she'd been so focused on the screen.

"Plan?" She laughed, but it came out sounding more like a sob. "There is no plan, Tookah." She waved a hand at the infoscreen. "Astor is fulfilling its destiny as a military base."

Quinton winced as he lowered himself into the nearest kitchen chair. Nazem and Tookah exchanged uneasy glances.

"Do you think Griff is a wizard?" Shania asked the room. "He looks like a wizard, or what I've always thought a wizard would look like. Maybe that's why Aidan seems so human, maybe it's magic."

No one said anything.

"We can leave on our ship," Tookah offered.

"Aye," Nazem said as he nodded. "Captain is staying out of the mess, but he'll risk coming back for us." He fished a small black sphere from his satchel. "Rest easy, this here is a beacon, not a bomb. They know we're here. I suspect the crew is circling until there's a gap in the patrol ships. Then they'll send a few gliders down."

"We could go to another section of the Four Quadrants and make a plan, maybe build an army," Tookah suggested to Delia. "We could leave tonight."

"Maybe Delta Kur?" Quinton suggested. There was a lift to his voice that seemed abnormal in all this despair.

Delia could barely reply. There was a hollowness that seemed absurdly heavy. When she raised her gaze, she realized they were all looking at her, waiting for her to decide.

"Do whatever it takes to save yourselves. I have nothing to offer you." She let this last sentence hang in the air. She had no words of comfort for them. An image of the statue of Arianna, the first queen, surfaced.

Bravery.

Wisdom.

Love.

Delia had lost all three in one day.

The truth was a cold slap against her face. No one would ever use those words to describe her. She was not a queen, no matter how many crowns she tried on. It was ridiculous to think she'd ever be able to replace her mother.

"I failed you," she whispered to her ancestors, picturing her mother's face. "I failed Astor."

There was a thickness to the room. It seemed to hold them in place, like water, but invisible. Shania looked about, and her eyes seemed to catalogue every detail of the modest kitchen. Then she took notice of Nazem's braids. "I like your hair," she told him, trying to keep her own bundle of hair in her arms.

Having her sister's hair unkempt and wild was another sorry sight for Delia. It seemed nothing was sacred anymore.

Nazem stood a little taller as Shania continued to talk with him. He motioned to Tookah. "He did it," he said.

Shania's eyes lit up. "Really?"

Tookah nodded, but the soft glow under his skin hinted at a sense of humbleness.

She went to him and put a hand on one of his biceps. "So many muscles," she said, in her dreamy voice. "I hadn't thought about the advantage of a man having more than two hands."

There were footsteps on the basement stairs; then Morgan appeared in the doorway, wiping his hands with a cloth. "I can give you a meal and a change of clothes if you need." He looked pointedly at Delia and Shania whose dresses were hardly proper wear for escaped royalty. Then he added, "But after that, you'll have to leave."

"We are grateful." Tookah nodded and gave him a smile.

Delia glared at Morgan. She pointed to the infoscreen showing images of Trellium's military patrolling the Dark District. "You helped this happen."

He stared her down. "And you were doing nothing to prevent it from happening."

Her mouth fell open. "Everything I've ever done since I was a little girl was for Astor! My only passion has been what was best for this planet!" She felt the hot sting of tears. "They might as well build the base directly over my dead body, because that's what it means to me when I see this."

Biting the inside of her cheek, Delia rushed out the archway and down a narrow hallway. She ended up in a small porch. There was a cot against the wall. She crumpled on the bed and let the tears come.

It couldn't be for nothing, she kept thinking. *Every decision I've ever made couldn't be meant for it to end like this.*

She wasn't sure how long she stayed on the cot, but when Shania found her, it felt like she'd aged a hundred years. Her sister's hand was firm but loving on her shoulder. "I can't stop thinking about something," Shania said.

Delia sniffed and rolled over to face her sister. "Oh my goodness, your hair!"

Shania gave a soft laugh. "Tookah is amazing! He did this in only five minutes." She patted her elaborate hairdo that was composed of many small braids. Part of her hair was swept up in a design on the back of her head, while the rest flowed down her back in a complicated design of knots.

"How did he even . . . ?" Delia was in awe.

Shania closed her eyes. "I never imagined how a man's hands in my hair would feel. So much better than having an android do my hair."

"Shania! Your brashness knows no bounds! How are we even related?"

"I ask myself that question nearly every day." Then she pulled her sister into a hug. "I'm sorry."

That one phrase seemed to encompass the entire day.

"What is it you can't stop thinking about?" Delia sniffed into her sister's shoulder.

"If Aidan didn't know he was an android, that would mean when he shot himself, he was willing to sacrifice his life to save yours." There was a thoughtful pause. "I don't know much about robots, but that seems like something someone with a heart would do. A very big and unselfish heart."

"You saw his chest," Delia said. "There is no heart."

"Just because you can't see something doesn't mean it isn't there." Shania gave her shoulder a squeeze. "Remember in the legend when Arianna gave her hair to the moon? I always thought it was because it was her greatest treasure, just like the legend says, but when Mother took me down into the tunnels, when it was my turn to see the mosaics for real, she said it was because of power. We gain power not by what we take, but by what we are willing to give up."

Delia let her sister's words soothe her. "I'm scared," she finally said. "I don't know what to do. Mother always told me my best asset was my instinct, to allow our ancestors to guide me. But . . ." She paused because it felt foolish to say it now. "They told me to pick Aidan. I sensed choosing him was the best thing for Astor." She waited for her sister to recite some quote about romance, but it was Morgan's voice she heard instead.

"These should fit." He put an armful of folded clothing on the bottom of the cot. "At least they'll do until you reach wherever you're going."

Delia sat straighter and wiped her face.

"You found his room," Morgan said. His earlier look of contempt had softened somewhat.

"Aidan's?" Delia studied the area. It was bare and nondescript, only a small window in the back door. Two of the panes were broken. Her heart felt like it was being squeezed.

Then she saw the shelf, taking in the small trinkets. "These were his?" she asked.

"He was only programmed to become familiar with the palace layout," Morgan said. "To be someone who wouldn't raise suspicion if they saw him in the hallways, a servant really. Nothing more than the kitchen chore boy. Someone who would easily slip his way to be close to the queen if need be."

Delia turned and gave him a hard stare.

Morgan motioned to the shelf. "But the trinkets, the pickpocketing for cash to buy a ticket to Delta Kur, that was all him."

Memories flooded her mind. "I don't understand," she said, thinking it sounded like the understatement of the galaxy. Her fingers lightly touched all the objects; the broken chain from a necklace, glass marbles, a rolled-up page from a book—then she saw it.

The rubis berry, now dark and dried up. And beside it, the cork from the pirate bottle of wine. She brought it to her nose and inhaled. She didn't even remember him picking it up.

Delia looked at Morgan. His prematurely lined face hinted at a life of hardship. "Tell me everything about him," she said.

For the next hour Delia listened to Morgan. She stayed quiet, making a list of questions in her mind, keeping them for when he was finished, partly afraid that if she interrupted him, he wouldn't continue.

"I was brought onto the team last year," he said. "Aidan was still in testing at that point. They had already gone through six hundred and two other versions . . . all ended in flames with overheated circuits. Gail Babineau was in charge until a few months ago when Corporal Langdon became suspicious of a telecom message he'd intercepted.

"He found out she was considering sabotaging Aidan, worried he was too advanced for our own good." Morgan hesitated, his mouth in a hard line. "After her untimely death, the project was pushed forward. She had left behind a twelve-step program where each new directive to the plan required a new SHEW to be implanted. Aidan was unaware of any of this."

Again, Morgan let the silence linger. When he spoke next, he addressed Delia directly. "Every time we replaced his SHEW, it erased some of his real memory and filled in fake ones. But there was one constant we weren't prepared for—his connection with you."

She stiffened. "He was programmed that way. He had me fooled too."

"It's impossible to be programmed to love," Morgan answered.

"Exactly," she said. "It wasn't real."

"I sense you miss the meaning of my statement," he replied. "Aidan's directive was to assassinate the queen, which we didn't realize was going to be you . . . until it was." Then a sheepish look came across his face. "I wanted to get there before the shot was fired. I foolishly thought I could stop the whole mess. You see, Griff and I started out working for the resistance, but . . . well, it seemed Aidan had changed our minds about what it meant to be a human being."

The crack in Delia's broken heart began to bleed. She stared at the wine cork still in her hand. They'd shared a kiss that night, her first real kiss, and now she realized, his as well. She put the cork back on the shelf with the other treasures. "Treasures," she whispered.

"They were to him." Morgan nodded. "When he first started bringing them from the palace I thought it was a glitch in his programming, but it continued even after his SHEW was replaced. I suppose it was because he wanted to have something of his own. Those trinkets were the only things he had."

Delia reached up and felt the medallion under her dress. She wondered where it really came from. A courtier he'd stolen it from? Something about it bothered her. It was on the edge of her memory. Frustratingly close.

Morgan continued, "He has evolved independently of any kind of programming. He is one of a kind . . . or rather was." He pulled a pained expression. "After I found you on the balcony, I brought him here because I thought this was the best place for him to be fixed. But I hadn't factored in the drain to his energy stores."

Shania had stayed quiet the whole time, but now she asked her question with a desperation Delia could feel in her own heart. "Can you save him?" she asked. "Can you bring him back?"

He looked away, and Delia thought she saw a glimpse of regret or sadness. "After I found him, I removed his SHEW. I wanted to erase his prime directive. But even if his internal circuits are fixed, he needs that component to hold the life cell energy. No SHEW, no power. No power, no Aidan. I didn't realize until I saw his diagnostic readouts. We've always replaced the SHEW, so it's never happened before. And I never anticipated that I would miss him after he fulfilled his prime directive."

"So even if you fix his circuits, Aidan will never wake up again?" Shania asked.

Morgan shook his head. "Griff and I are no match for Gail Babineau's work. Even if we had all the materials to rebuild him, he's impossible to replicate. She made sure of that in his programming.

But Griff is going to try to reuse the SHEWs we already have. None of those have enough battery life to give him much time, though."

Shania hung her head.

A spark lit inside Delia. She thought of the line of SHEWs on the workshop table in the basement room. Something triggered her memory, but she couldn't quite grasp the image. "So Aidan would need a new SHEW that was specifically made for him, correct?"

Morgan gave her a sad shrug. "There is only one person who had the knowledge to build it, and she's dead."

At once a connection was made. Delia felt an immediate sense of urgency. "I have to see him . . . right now!" She read the hesitation in Morgan's expression. "Please," she said.

CHAPTER
THIRTY-NINE

Delia followed Morgan back through the rustic cottage and down the stairs into the dimly lit basement. She focused on Aidan's boots, so still and unmoving. It took all her energy to keep calm. Fireworks were going off inside her heart.

Griff was still perched on the stool. He glanced up from his work and gave Morgan a careful gaze, full of question. Morgan simply nodded.

Delia stayed near the foot of the table, watching Griff finish the last stitch in Aidan's chest. The small tool seemed to melt the skin back in place, leaving a raised line.

When he was done, he put down the tool and arched his back. There was an audible crack. He winced and then looked up at the screen at the head of the table.

Delia saw the readout.

```
INITIATING DIAGNOSTIC SCAN . . . STAND BY . . .
VIRUS DETECTION: NEGATIVE
CIRCUIT FUNCTION: MOTHERBOARD ENERGY TRANSER FAILURE,
SHUTDOWN SEQUENCE IMMINENT
LIFE CELLS: WARNING LOW 2%
PRIME DIRECTIVE: INDETERMINATE
MODE: UNCONSCIOUS
INITIALIZING SHUTDOWN SEQUENCE AND MEMORY WIPE . . .
STAND BY . . .
```

Her heart started hammering a warning.

Morgan went to Griff's side. "I wish I knew which SHEW we should try to reuse," he said.

Griff shook his head. "The programming is too sophisticated. We might damage the circuit board permanently."

Morgan motioned to the readout. "It's happening anyway!"

Griff pointed the tool at Morgan; his tone was authoritative. "We agreed to bring him back, repair him, and then put him in secret keeping until we have the technology to make him another SHEW."

An invisible hand pushed on Delia's heart. Her ribs ached with each breath. His memory would be wiped clean! She stepped closer.

Aidan was bare chested with a long scar that ran down the middle. The stillness of his body scared her. Delia felt if she stared at it long enough, she could make his chest rise.

She realized Griff was watching her intently. "You did very well," she told him, fighting tears. "There's hardly a mark." The memory of Aidan begging her to run came back to her. He'd made the ultimate sacrifice for her.

Aidan was not made of circuits. He was more than that. He was the boy who was willing to take his own life to save hers. And not because he was trying to save a planet or complete a mission. He did it for love.

The first time he told her he loved her was under the tree. Then he gave her his medallion. She closed her eyes and prayed to her ancestors. If she was wrong, it would break her heart all over again.

She turned to the workbench and looked at the SHEWs lined up. When she'd first come into the room the small discs were unlike any SHEW she'd ever seen before. Still, they'd reminded her of something.

With shaking hands, she reached around and released the clasp of the necklace. Then she passed the medallion to Griff. "He said his mother gave it to him. It was the most precious thing he owned. I think it might be a SHEW."

Griff's eyes grew wide. He took the medallion and grabbed a lens, putting it up to his eye. "You're right!" His voice went high. He moved over to the bench and used a tiny pair of pincers to pick a smaller disc from the back of the medallion.

Morgan moved in close to Aidan's other side. He passed the long-handled tool to Griff. He cleared his throat. "The SHEW goes in place of a back molar . . . on the upper left."

"I know," Griff snapped. He placed the microchip to the long-handled device, then pulled down Aidan's chin, opening his mouth. He hesitated and locked gazes with Morgan and Delia. "You understand that if this isn't his SHEW, we risk sabotaging his circuit board forever, no matter what technology comes along in the next hundred years?"

"Yes." Delia put all her desperate hope in that one word. She held her breath as Griff inserted the long-handled tool.

At last Griff's shoulders relaxed. He leaned back and gestured toward Aidan. "The SHEW fits," he said.

CHAPTER FORTY

He dreamed of her again.

The familiar images were ticked off one by one as he surfaced from sleep. Her brown eyes pierced his soul as she gave him the smile that was only meant for him. "I want you," she whispered.

Her breath was sweet. She kissed him as she placed something long and soft against his palm. Her braid. "Only the queen may choose who has the honor of unbraiding her hair on her wedding night."

The edges of the scene blurred. He whispered a curse, realizing he'd wake soon. Determined, he tried to stay in the dream to keep hold of the image.

He sighed dejectedly, desperate to relive that moment again.

There was a jolt to his brain as he realized something was different.

Behind his eyelids a million images flashed per second. Circuits were ablaze with new algorithms. Reams of information and data were categorized and processed. A new prime directive was installed, and a file labeled CANYON was uploaded. Inside, Aidan was smiling because he finally knew all the answers.

And like taking off on a Queen's Guard glider, Aidan was pulled out of the dimness and into the light. He practiced moving his toes and fingers, and then finally he opened his eyes.

Above him the face from his dream stared down at him. "Aidan?" she said. She studied him with a frantic expression. "Do you remember me?" she asked.

He stared back at her in a dreamy, euphoric state. The last time he saw her . . .

"Delia!" He bolted upright and put his hands on her shoulders. "Are you all right? Did you escape? What happened? I'm sorry, I've never been so sorry for anything in my life." Then the full impact of the truth hit him like a sandblast to the face. "I'm . . . I'm not who you think I am." And in that moment he wished on all the stars in the Four Quadrants that he really was a kitchen boy—a human.

Her expression softened. She reached out and cupped his cheek with her hand. "I know everything," she said. "You saved my life."

Aidan couldn't tell if it was love or unfathomable gratitude that filled her eyes. Someone called out, "He's alive!" Her hand slipped away.

Griff and Morgan were watching with identical expressions of proud relief. "I have a new prime directive," he told them. "To save Astor." He turned to Delia. "The pirates are right, the answer is in the canyon! This last SHEW is like a treasure map. Gail trusted me with her life's work. She figured it out!"

He now understood the recurring dream was only made up, a backup plan to ensure he had the last SHEW to save Astor.

Delia sadly shook her head. "Prince Felix is turning Astor into a military base. He has an army. I have nothing to fight back with."

"You are the queen." Aidan leaned closer to her. "There's enough codlight to run Astor forever. And when you show up with proof, the kingdom will be yours again." Then he told her everything Gail had put in his SHEW. She listened to the whole story, wide-eyed and silent.

"It seems the legend was split up," she finally said. "The royal family claimed the first part, and the miners kept the last part."

Footsteps clamored down the stairs. Nazem's smiling face appeared first, followed by Princess Shania.

"'Tis good to see ya alive again," Nazem said. "Blinking and everything without yer wires and guts hanging out."

Shania nearly pushed Nazem out of the way. "Welcome back." She beamed. Then she looked at Aidan's chest. "The scar makes you look dangerous, much more interesting than an eye patch."

Nazem cleared his throat and addressed the rest of the room. "Captain has responded to my signal. Gliders be arriving soon to help us escape."

"Except we're not escaping," Delia told him, a regal sureness in her tone. "We're taking back Astor."

Moments later they were gathered in Aidan's small kitchen. He marveled at the group huddled around the table. Delia was full of fire and purpose as she explained to the others what they would be doing. He could stare at her for the rest of his life and never become bored. Since waking, he hadn't had a chance to be alone with her. And although she'd embraced him and cried, she still hadn't kissed him, and he had begun to accept that because he wasn't a real man, her feelings had changed.

Nazem came into the room, cheeks flushed. "Gliders are landing in the back."

Tookah helped Quinton as the others followed. Delia looked at Griff and Morgan. "And you're sure you want to stay behind?"

Griff only raised a bony shoulder. "These tunnels go all through the Dark District, Your Majesty. This is a safer place for me than on a pirate ship hovering over those sandworms."

"Besides," Morgan said. "Aidan says you'll save Astor, so I believe all we have to do is wait."

She nodded, then made her way to back door of the cottage.

"Hey," Griff said to Aidan, making him stay behind. "You might need this." He handed Aidan the silver dagger.

Morgan rolled his eyes. "He's not programmed to kill."

"Yeah, well he ain't programmed to love neither, so that's how much you know."

Aidan took the dagger and slipped it into his pocket. When he stole it, he remembered Prince Felix arguing with someone in the other room and how quickly the guards had arrived afterward. Colonel Yashin must have been the other voice, already planning the coup. "If I hadn't taken this, we wouldn't be having this conversation, would we?" he said.

Griff nodded. "I gave you the fake microchip on purpose. Langdon suspected I was trying to sabotage the rebels' plan, but I managed to avoid his full wrath. You can't imagine my surprise when you happened to bring in the one message intended for the resistance. Of all the things to steal that day . . ."

"The universe works in strange ways, doesn't it?" Aidan replied.

Griff's eyes got watery. He cleared his throat and walked back to the kitchen, head bent.

"Aidan," Morgan said softly, just a hint of a command. He held a small infoscreen. "I've been running diagnostics." He paused, then craned his neck to the side to make sure Delia had left. "The energy components are different from the others. This is your *last* SHEW, and once your life cells run out we have no others to use. I'm sorry."

Aidan automatically accessed his internal files, did his own diagnostic scan, and found Morgan was right. This last SHEW was primarily meant for him to find the treasure. At best he had roughly five hours left.

"Remember, your energy cells drain faster the more emotionally or physically taxing your missions." His expression was pained.

Aidan nodded. Instead of remorse he felt a calm acceptance. He would help Delia do the one thing she wanted most of all, to save Astor. In a nanosecond, he reconciled that a broken heart was enough to bear if he could help her fulfill this one last destiny.

"I'm sorry," Morgan repeated. "I should have done more sooner."

"You did as much as you could at the time," Aidan replied. "Thank you for being there when it counted the most. Perhaps this was how it was supposed to be all along."

✳ ✳ ✳

The pirate ship wasn't as menacing as Aidan remembered, but the captain's regard for his red coat was laced with a ferocious grimace. Aidan had sheepishly handed over the ruined garment after he and Delia boarded with the others.

Nazem tried to soften the moment. "Aye, 'tis a fine relic now. Imagine, to be the owner of the coat that started Astor's new era." He nodded enthusiastically, but the captain only grunted, handing the coat off to another pirate, barking orders to have it sewn immediately.

Delia then took over, explaining the plan to the captain. Although she'd changed into the tunic and pants Morgan had supplied them with, she looked more regal in that moment than if she'd been wearing the biggest crown. She was wearing the necklace he'd given her, but of course the medallion wasn't there.

She spoke with such authority that everyone listened with rapt attention. Aidan stared at her, watching as she explained how they solved the creation legend and what the treasure in the sand really was.

A squawk made Aidan duck, covering his head. The blackbird had been careening around the ship since they boarded. Tookah whistled and held out his top arm for it to perch upon.

When Delia finished talking, the captain wiped a hand down his weathered face. He squinted back at her. "So you're telling me the treasure that we've been looking for our entire lives is . . . sandworm crap?"

She rolled her eyes. "Yes, but I'll rework the wording for my official speech. Gail Babineau was a genius engineer, but she was also a geologist. The legend of the treasure being in the canyon is true."

He looked unconvinced.

Aidan stood by Delia, his hand brushed hers, and their fingers linked automatically. A fire of invincibility lit inside his chest. "It's the codlight," he said. "The miners thought it was an organic compound naturally occurring within the tunnels, but it was the dried by-product of the sandworms. All this time, they've been producing massive amounts of codlight without anyone realizing it."

"That's what created all the tunnels!" Delia added. "They weren't carved by our ancestors, they were old passages created by the sandworms. After the palace was built and the population grew, they were forced out and moved to the driest, quietest place they could exist—the canyon."

The plasma torches flickered. From the east Aidan saw the first few streaks of dawn. They were running out of time . . . and so was he.

The captain glanced back and forth between Delia and Aidan. "And what makes you two think you can slip into one of those tunnels below and come back with a hunk of codlight?"

"Because I know how to defeat the sandworms," Aidan said. "And it's not with bombs or fire or even water to flood the tunnels." He allowed himself to sound a bit smug. "I'll do it with the universal language, of course."

All the pirates frowned around them. Some scratched their heads. A few looked over the side of the ship at the canyon floor far below, as if the answer was written in the sand.

"The language of music?" Tookah guessed.

Princess Shania stepped to the front of the crowd and stood by him. "The language of love?" she answered.

"All noble pursuits," Aidan praised. "But alas no, I'm referring to the language of math. Gail studied the worms and came up with an equation for their patterns. It requires recalculating minute nuances in their movements, but there is a constant equivalence. All I have to do is watch them and do the calculations and then I'll know exactly when it's safe."

"That's impossible," the captain snarled.

"Not for me," Aidan simply said.

Delia added, "There is no room for doubt, captain. I have to do this. Only with proof of the codlight supply will I be able to reclaim the throne and drive the soldiers of Trellium off our planet."

The captain continued to frown. He took a plasma dagger from his belt and began to clean his fingernails.

Aidan felt his impatience grow. "This will work," he said, motioning to one of the mismatched pirate gliders, now prepped and ready at the side of the ship. It was nearly the same size as his sky dodger and Aidan knew it would be small enough to fit inside the tunnels. "All I have to do is study the sandworms' movements for a moment, wait until one of them breaches, make a quick calculation, then fly into the hole in the sand, grab some codlight, and zoom back out."

Delia turned to him, frowning. "You mean we."

He gave her a careful smile. "I'm a natural pickpocket, remember?" All this time the quick reflexes and inherent instinct to effortlessly steal valuables had been part of his programming, seeing the patterns and knowing when to move. It all made sense to him now. "Besides," he said as he smiled at Delia, "I know how to fly that kind of machine better than anyone else in Astor. The Queen's Guard glider you're used to is too big."

"Yes, but I've flown with you. You're hopeless."

"I've flown with *you*. You're reckless to the extreme."

"Great combination," Nazem said. He rolled his eyes. "I see no issue with this plan."

The captain waved them away with a flick of the dagger. "Off with you, then," he said. "But don't expect me to sail down there and rescue you. This is a fool's mission."

"The history books will note your heroic efforts," Delia replied smartly.

Aidan mounted the slim flier and slipped on a pair of goggles. He handed a pair to Delia, hoping she couldn't see his hands shake.

Princess Shania and Tookah approached them. She hugged her sister, then gave Aidan a kiss on the cheek. "Please bring her back safely," she asked him. "I can't lose her again."

"I promise," he said.

Delia made an impatient noise at the back of her throat. "I'm right here. You talk of me as if I'm as helpless as a coconut cake." She straddled the seat behind him and when she wrapped her hands around his waist, Aidan was tempted to fly off into the double sunrise, just to spend his last few hours with her uninterrupted.

Giving the dashboard a loving pat, Aidan said to the glider, "One more time." Then they lifted off, the pirate ship growing smaller as he ascended sharply.

He felt Delia take in a breath, her chest pressing against his back. And despite the countdown going on inside his circuits, he felt like the luckiest man alive.

Flying was second nature to him, and even if half of his memories of flying were implanted ones, he knew he was meant to do this. The glider weaved in and out of the columns easily. Aidan felt comfortable on the ramshackle machine.

This was my destiny, he thought, fully smiling now. He was meant to jump into that ship Delia had commandeered. Even though he was programmed to seek out the layout of the palace, something bigger had been guiding him this whole time. The universe had been working to bring them together.

The twin suns of Astor were still below the horizon, but the night sky was starting to lighten. He slowed the machine for a moment, allowing Delia to see her beloved mountain far in the distance, the summit still covered in clouds. As they hovered, he turned to her. The moon was reflected in her goggles, but he could still see the tears well up in her eyes.

He'd purposely come up this high to tell her that he loved her, but the words didn't seem big enough. If he said them now, they would get swallowed up by the wind. *So be it*, he thought. *Even if I can't be her lover, I can still be her hero.*

They hovered for another fraction of a second. Then he dipped the glider downward. When they passed the pirate ship, the entire crew, including the captain, was giving them a salute.

Aidan maneuvered them closer to the surface. It was colder in the shadows. The suns wouldn't illuminate this area until midday, but they didn't have that kind of time. He thought of the great tree, imagining its blossoms falling for the last time.

"Behind us!" Delia screamed. Aidan coaxed the glider higher as a worm lunged at them, exposing its long leathery body.

Then another reared its head in front of them. Aidan zigzagged, then rose another ten feet. He turned hard and prepared to do another fly by, his eyes already focusing on the patterns just beneath the surface. All he needed was another minute of observation and he'd have his answer.

Delia shouted another warning. Aidan steered the glider into the clear. One, two, and then three more worms breached and dived. It took six point eight seconds to calculate the safest route. Wrenching the glider hard to the left, he hit the power and targeted the closest opening.

"Hold on," he yelled to Delia. "This is it!"

CHAPTER
FORTY-ONE

Delia's stomach swooped as the glider dipped into the tunnel. Blackness surrounded them, along with an overwhelmingly pungent odor. There were only a few inches on either side of the glider to spare. The sides zoomed by at what seemed like a hysterical pace. One wrong jerk of the controls would result in a horrific crash. She shut her eyes and pressed her cheek into Aidan's back.

She said a quick prayer to the moon and wondered if it could see her all the way down deep inside the earth.

Her body molded against Aidan's, she could feel the muscles in his back react as he manipulated the glider. A sudden drop made her gasp, and she hugged him tighter. This was followed by a sharp turn to the right before they leveled off and the glider came to a stop.

Aidan whispered, "Galaxy's sake."

Delia opened her eyes and loosened her grip. She gaped at the collection of codlight along the tunnel floor. She thought of the small stone of codlight in her crown that could fuel a glider for months. "There's enough energy in this one spot to light up all of the Dark District for years," her words echoed. "This is the real treasure of Astor." From far off there was a faint chewing sound.

"Not to rush the moment of discovery," Aidan said, getting Tookah's hatchet from the back of the glider and handing it to her. "But sandworms have been known to eat a grown adult in one bite. If you don't act now, you'll be digested and turned into future codlight."

With the hatchet, Delia easily freed a sizable chunk. She carried it back to the glider in her arms like a pile of wood. "I never thought I'd be so happy to touch—"

A shriek from up ahead ricocheted off the walls as a sandworm filled the tunnel, blocking their way. Delia nearly dropped the cod-light. She climbed onto the back of the glider, one arm around Aidan, the other around the treasure of Astor.

With a nauseating flip and spin of the glider, Aidan righted the machine and they sped back the way they had come. They escaped just as the sandworm gave one last lurch, its jaws blindingly snapping at Delia's back.

A triumphant call escaped her lips. She immediately coughed on a mouth full of sand. Aidan didn't hesitate as he steered them toward the mountain.

CHAPTER FORTY-TWO

With a grimace of tremendous exertion, Aidan leaned forward and mentally urged the glider faster. The sky was turning a light blue. A pressure began to build at his temples. An alarm sounded inside his head.

WARNING: LIFE CELLS 20%

He knew the trip into the tunnel had eaten away a major portion of his battery life. Still, he calculated he had enough to get her to the great tree. He was trying to put a speech together in his mind, a gallant way of saying goodbye. A final vow of his true love that would stay with her, long after his circuits rusted out.

Morgan's warning echoed back to him. *Remember, your energy cells drain faster the more emotionally or physically taxing your missions.*

With the mountain getting closer, Aidan could see the various Trellium patrol ships orbiting high above the summit. He dipped lower—a ramshackle glider is hardly a threat. He imitated Delia's skill from that first flight by barely skimming the water of Black Lake.

Increasing to maximum speed, Aidan headed straight for the waterfall. He felt her arm squeeze around his waist. Then he turned the glider on its side and swerved behind the cascade of water. They emerged from the other side and hugged up the side of the mountain, staying in the shadows. Aidan brought them high enough that they were just above the tallest branches of the great tree. They hovered for a moment and took in the scene below.

"Oh no!" Delia gasped.

Advisor Winchell stood stoically against the trunk, kept in place with ropes. Her chin jutted out. "If you take down this tree, you'll have to take me with it!" she yelled. A circle of Trellium guards formed a border around the base of the tree; they were at attention, but thankfully none had their weapons drawn.

Aidan knew this was being broadcast to every infoscreen on Astor. He thought of Griff and Morgan watching from the cottage.

An orange glow slowly crept down the mountain as the twin suns rose. "This dawn brings a new era for Astor," Prince Felix said. He strutted in front of Advisor Winchell. "Under my direction this planet will finally rise up and show its might." The sun hit the hilt of his sword as if by purpose. "And we will no longer base our decisions on fairy tales, but on logic and military tactics." He took a swipe at the lower hanging branches. A cloud of blossoms rained down on Advisor Winchell. She cried out in anguish as if feeling the tree's pain.

Aidan brought the glider down in an instant, surprising Prince Felix and his guards. Delia jumped off before they'd come to a full stop. Aidan winced as the pressure in his head grew.

WARNING: LIFE CELLS 10%

Delia flung off the goggles and rushed toward Prince Felix, the chunk of codlight under her arm.

Advisor Winchell nearly collapsed from relief or shock, Aidan couldn't tell. But Prince Felix merely watched her approach with a devious anticipation. "Oh," he simply said. "Have you come to propose at last?" Several Trellium guards aimed their weapons at her. "Stand down," Prince Felix said, holding up a hand. "My future bride deserves your respect."

A surge of anger seemed to ignite deep inside Aidan's chest. He reached for the plasma hatchet at the back of the glider.

If I must die, I will die being her hero.

CHAPTER
FORTY-THREE

D elia dropped the codlight to the ground, then put one boot on top, standing proudly. "You're done, Felix," she said, making sure to leave off the royal title. "Astor doesn't need you or your weapons. We have a century's worth of energy."

His eyes grew wide, but then a grin spread on his face. "Which is another reason why Astor is the perfect site for a military base. Think of the bombs we'll make!" He suddenly reached for her and took hold of her wrist.

"Never!" She tried to wrench her hand from his grip.

He tugged her closer and whispered in her ear. "Don't tell me you've forgotten about the rubis berries already?"

"I've found something better," she answered smugly. "True love."

He rolled his eyes. "This is getting tiresome, either marry me or—" Then Prince Felix focused on something over her shoulder. Delia turned and saw Aidan slowly walking toward them, one hand behind his back.

"It's about time," he said to Aidan. "Kill her, please. Kill her now."

Aidan stopped beside Delia. His eyes were focused on Prince Felix, his expression like granite.

"He's not under your control anymore," Delia said.

"How did you manage to reprogram an android of his superior . . . ?" Price Felix paused, then squinted at Aidan, and then slid his gaze back to Delia. His mouth opened; then he let out a long laugh. "Oh, that is just the most . . . so, wait a moment." He pointed to Aidan. "You're in love with this thing?"

"I assure you, the feeling is mutual," Aidan said.

Prince Felix threw back his head and laughed. He gave Delia a sympathetic look. "Poor inexperienced girl. You can't program a machine to love. Besides, I'm a real man. I can give you so much more. I won't mention the obvious advantage I have over this . . ." He waved a hand at Aidan.

"You tried to kill me!" Delia answered. Then she looked him up and down. "You have nothing I want, Felix. You have no claim to the throne of Astor. You've appointed yourself by creating chaos and fear. Leave now."

"It won't be that easy." He took a few steps back, then raised his sword and took a stance. "Your own guards put me in charge. If you want Astor back, you have to prove to your people you can beat me." Then he nodded to the drone camera that was broadcasting this exchange to every infoscreen live.

"Challenge accepted." Delia turned and faced Aidan. He was paler than normal.

He held out the plasma hatchet to her. "You will win," he said. "This is your destiny."

She put her hand on his chest and could feel the raised scar underneath his shirt. "And you are mine."

As an answer Aidan simply put his hand over hers, keeping it there for another few beats of silence.

Prince Felix cleared his throat.

"Use the power of your ancestors, Delia," Winnie called out. "They are most powerful here."

Delia moved closer, with her hatchet at the ready.

"Winner takes Astor," Prince Felix called out. All the guards nodded.

CHAPTER FORTY-FOUR

WARNING: LIFE CELLS 5%

Aidan wanted to tell her that he loved her, but he knew each movement, each task, no matter how simple, drained his battery. He had to stay alive until she reclaimed the crown—there was no other way.

Delia lunged first, targeting the sword, not the man. Aidan knew the hatchet could easily slice through the hardest of elements, so mere flesh and bone would practically disintegrate with the slightest touch.

Prince Felix jumped back easily, his reflexes obviously finely tuned. He spun on the spot, bringing his own blade within a whisper's space of Delia's stomach.

Advisor Winchell started to chant, her rhythmic voice building.

The pulse of Aidan's headache moved down to his stomach, but he fought the nausea. Delia landed a high kick to Prince Felix's chest. He doubled over. She moved in again, but he lunged low and grabbed a handful of braid. Twisting it around his arm several times, he pulled her closer. The tip of his sword was at her throat.

Aidan reached into his pocket. A blackness started to creep into his vision.

Delia winced as she dropped to her knees.

Prince Felix's eyes were wild. "The royal braid is a powerful symbol in the Four Quadrants," he hissed loud enough for everyone to hear. "I will have you by my side and together we will rule this side of the galaxy. We'll be the ultimate power couple!"

Delia licked her lips. "You've missed the meaning behind the power of the braid, Felix. It's not the braid that makes the queen powerful. The power comes from what she's willing to give up—her greatest treasure." She raised the hatchet.

Prince Felix didn't have time to react. The blade of the hatchet moved in one smooth arc and found its target—the nape of her neck. Prince Felix fell back to the ground with a look of stunned confusion on his face, now holding the loose swath of braid in his grip.

Delia stood over him, breathing hard, the fringes of her short hair blowing in the wind. The hatchet now poised above his face. "Leave my planet," she told him.

Then she looked every guard in the eye. "I am Queen Delia, first-born of Queen Talia, sole ruler of Astor, and direct descendant of Arianna, the first daughter of the moon. Any man who wishes to serve in my court may do so by bowing down to me now. If not, take your leave immediately and never return."

One by one every guard came down on one knee. Delia rushed to the tree and began to untie Advisor Winchell.

A blackness quickly invaded Aidan's vision. He strained to see this one last triumphant moment for Delia. A blossom landed on his cheek.

WARNING: LIFE CELLS 2%

There was a scream from Advisor Winchell. Prince Felix had picked up his sword and was running at Delia. With the last spot of his vision fading, Aidan pulled the silver dagger from his pocket and flung it with perfect precision at Felix. It pierced his neck with a wet thud. He collapsed, face forward, limbs lifeless.

Aidan leaned back on the glider, and a numbness spread through his body. The twin suns sparkled through the leaves of the great tree. Delia was with him in an instant. "It's about time you saved me," she breathed against his chest.

His knees became unhinged and he collapsed in her arms. The colors blended and dulled. The earth beneath him felt heavy, like he was sinking into it.

"Aidan? What's wrong?" Her voice became panicked. "Open your eyes! Don't leave me again! Aidan, please!" Her next words sounded far away, more of an echo. "I love you."

That's the first time she's ever said that to me, he thought. Then everything went black.

CHAPTER FORTY-FIVE

"**H**ello, Aidan." Gail Babineau's kind face appeared behind his eyelids. She reached up and tucked a strand of blond hair behind her ear. She smiled, but there was a nervous apprehension in her expression.

"If you're seeing this, you have unlocked the secret program I encoded deep into your software, and in doing so have surpassed all my hopes for Astor's future. Like the SHEW I hid in the medallion, no one knows of its existence but myself." She paused and twisted around in her chair, looking over her shoulder.

When she faced him again, there was a sense of urgency in her tone. "As you know, you are one of a kind, and impossible to replicate. You represent my life's work. Growing up in the Dark District, I learned to despise the royal family and everything they took from us. Naturally, I became interested in helping the resistance overthrow the monarchy."

She frowned and came closer. "When I discovered the codlight deposits, I was intensely invested in the rebellion, but I had begun to question their decision to involve other planets in abolishing the monarchy. Giving them the knowledge of such a wealth of power would be unwise for Astor. I have seen what power does to people, so I reasoned the safest course of action was to store it in your software. I knew it would be safe with you."

Pressing her lips together, she took in a shaking breath. "And I fear that my hesitation has been interpreted as treason. There are whispers that I am planning on sabotaging you, that I'm a double agent for the palace, which is not true—not exactly. Regardless, I fear for my life, which is why I have designed the last SHEW for you . . . and this hidden program. I call it the Mortality Files.

"The coding allows you to refuel your life cells without the need for a new SHEW. Your own movement powers the cells with kinetic energy, storing it and then slowly releasing it as needed. However, this method of recycling your strength will become less efficient with time. You will slow down and become weaker, aging as if human, and eventually you will cease to operate. It is imperative you understand that once accessed you cannot undo the programming, no matter what advances in technology may come about in the future to give you a longer existence."

Gail reached up and touched the gold medallion she was wearing. "I have built this program, but it's still your choice. And if I'm being honest, it's to ease my conscience for taking away your reality. I knew early on you were capable of much more than I had calibrated into your circuits. I rationalized that if you proved you were capable of human emotions, you warranted to be treated as such."

A sad smile lifted her features. "I've never been in love, not really, but I suppose it's the romantic in me that put the specific trigger in your circuits. If you've earned someone's love, you deserve a real life, not a fake one designed by a lonely scientist."

She closed her eyes and nodded at him almost as if she was saying a prayer. "Goodbye, Aidan. Good luck."

The blackness returned; then Aidan found himself traveling down a hallway. He read thousands of files, then came to the last one, labeled MORTALITY. The data streamed to his circuit board in a fraction of a second. The program waited for his reply. He only had to think the word. *Yes.*

CHAPTER
FORTY-SIX

"Aidan!" Delia crouched over his unmoving body, holding his life-less face in her hands. It felt like the mountain had dropped out from under her and she was falling through space. "Please wake up!"

"Dear child," Advisor Winchell said as she came behind Delia, placing a hand on her shoulder. "His last act was to save you."

"No." Her tears rained down on his cheeks. "Not again! I won't let you go." Delia brought her face closer to his and kissed his mouth. "Please, please, please wake up. I love you."

Aidan's eyes flew open and he gasped at once, making Delia fall back. He sat up straight. "Yes," he said, looking up at the sky.

Advisor Winchell sighed a prayer.

A cry of joy burst from Delia as she wrapped her arms around his neck. "Don't ever do that again," she said, covering his face with tears and kisses.

"What," he laughed, "come back to life?"

She leaned back and studied him. "I thought you left me again. I thought you died . . . for good this time." Another stream of tears ran down her cheeks. "Are you back for certain? What's happening to you? Do you remember me?"

He smiled and there was a look of wisdom in his eyes she'd never seen before. "I am back for as long as you want me," he said. "And I have some rather exciting news. You see—"

"Wait." Delia wiped her cheeks and took his hand in hers. "Before one more second of our lives goes by, I need to ask you something.

Will you, Aidan of Doberon, firstborn of Gail Babineau, and most superior android of the entire galaxy, do me the honor of becoming my husband?"

"Says the plasma torch to the fly."

✱ ✱ ✱

"Only through change can we find opportunity," Delia said. She stood on the balcony of the palace, addressing the masses who had filled every tier of the garden. Some were well-dressed courtiers, others were from the Dark District, and there were even a few pirates milling about. Shania and Advisor Winchell stood on either side of her, dressed in their most ornamental outfits.

The mid-afternoon wind played with the hem of her cloak. It came to her knees and was trimmed with the white feathers of the wallow goose. Her hair was held in place with a headband decorated with blossoms from the great tree. She still wasn't used to the breeze on the back of her neck.

"But even though we are expanding into a new and exciting era of replenishing energy," she continued, "let's never forget it is through honoring the legacy of our ancestors that the key to our future was found. We will never lose sight of our heritage, for if we forget where we came from we will lose our way forward."

From the corner of her eye she saw Griff and Morgan looking uncomfortable in the full sunlight and next to the bright flowers. Still, they nodded her way approvingly. She noticed they were both wearing their honorary medals she'd presented to them earlier for their part in helping defeat the Trellium takeover.

"The palace was never meant to be cut off from the people," Delia continued. The longer she spoke, the clearer her voice. "From this day forward, we will be opening the palace, including the library, to everyone and filling the halls with students."

She smiled when she saw the children from the picking stations playfully nudge one another. Marta put a hand on their shoulders, quieting the rambunctious boys. Still pale compared to the courtiers around them, the group of orphans had taken on a light of their own, helped of course with meals being delivered and new clothes provided and personally tailored by Marta.

No longer Delia's personal attendant, the android had interestingly dropped sewing as her directive and had taken on the role of caregiver for the group after they had uncovered her at the picking station. The tallest, a girl named Nina, expressed an interest in learning about the Queen's Guard, especially glider lessons. She now smiled up at Delia.

"Astor will become a haven for those who crave to learn and live peacefully among the elements," Delia continued. "I propose the Dark District be lifted into the light with new housing that can span farther into the south. Plasma trains will be rendered obsolete by newly engineered transportation, all fueled by our never-ending codlight supply, making every corner of Astor accessible to anyone for free. As well, the canyon will be declared an official sanctuary for the sandworms, only tended to by official personnel trained in the art of extraction."

There was a burst of applause from Tookah, who had Nazem on his shoulders. Both were dressed in finery, their medals glinting in the sun as well. The clapping continued and grew throughout the crowd, finally resulting in a deafening cheer.

Delia reached her arms out to the crowd and exclaimed, "Long live Astor!" There was another roar of applause. After a wave to the crowd, she slipped back into the palace.

"You didn't mention the dances we'd have every month in the ballroom," Shania said, following behind. There was a bit of a pout to her tone. "I promised Tookah."

"Where are you off to in such a hurry, Your Majesty?" Advisor Winchell asked, her cane tapping along the tile.

"Did you speak to my mother with such audacity?" Delia teased. "Don't worry, Winnie. I'll be back before the council meeting, and I'll be perfectly safe the whole time." Then she winked. "I'll have my bodyguard with me."

Her sister gave a smile of approval.

Practically running, Delia took the main lift all the way to the landing bay. The doors eased opened.

"Your Majesty." Aidan leaned casually against a Queen's Guard glider. His arms were crossed in front of his chest. "I understand your speech was a real crowd pleaser." He held up a mini infoscreen.

"Thank you," she said. "You helped write it, so some credit goes to you." She stopped short of stepping into his arms and gave him a critical glance. "You found your engagement present I see."

He tossed her a pair of goggles, and then slipped on his own. "Let's go for a ride," he said. "There's something we need to discuss."

Delia's stomach dropped, but she didn't fish for information. She had an inkling of what he was going to tell her, and she wanted to delay hearing that confession for as long as she could. She climbed on the back of the glider and held on to him.

Soon they were in the sky, leaving the palace behind. Delia closed her eyes and pressed her cheek into his back. She still had nightmares of him not waking after he collapsed at the summit. He'd only been unconscious for a few seconds, but she felt her whole life hang over a bottomless chasm in those terrifying moments.

After he woke and she and Winnie were reunited with Shania, he privately told her about his dying battery, but how he now had new programming that meant he could have a life.

The days that followed were a blur of meetings with the council and the judicial court over the death of Felix and the conviction of Oskar. Prince Armano apparently had not been privy to the assassination plot, and was so incensed with his home planet's betrayal he abdicated the throne and decided to travel the Four Quadrants, intent on finding his own true love. Although Delia suspected he was probably hoping to find someone who could afford his rich lifestyle.

The other princes returned to their planets; the twins to Tramsted, and Hagar back to his beloved maritime Lazlo. Hagar had left a pleasing impression with more than a few courtiers and stated he'd be visiting Astor again in the near future.

There was little time for celebration in those first few weeks, as the cleanup from that night was significant, but they were making progress with the repairs, both structural and spiritual. It would take more than a treasure trove of codlight to earn the trust of the Dark District, but Delia was committed. There was an undeniable presence of something strong within her now, letting her know she was on the right path.

And it was all because of Aidan.

The glider slowed down and came to a gentle landing. He'd brought them to the same clearing where they'd met Tomas and his father. While sending word to the other quadrants about Felix and the newly found source of codlight, Delia made contact with Tomas's uncle. She promised to assist with Tomas's future anyway she could and extended the invitation for them both to move back to Astor, where a new home in the southern tundra would be waiting for them.

"You're not leaving me here, are you?" she said, partly teasing Aidan. "This is close to Pirate's Canyon!"

Aidan turned to her. He pushed the goggles back, resting them on top of his head. Then he reached up and gently removed hers. "You need to know something," he said.

Delia shook her head, not wanting to hear him confess what she suspected. "Can't it wait? Besides, there are more important things to discuss . . . like I asked Quinton to be on the council when he returns with Niko next year. I was able to message him on the transport ship. He said he'd ask Niko about it first, once he reunites with him on Delta Kur."

"Delta Kur," Aidan repeated, drawling out the syllables. "I spent many a night dreaming of escaping to her endless curvy sand dunes and—"

Delia kissed him before he finished. She could feel him hesitate and it scared her. Then he pulled her closer, deepening his kiss. His fingers went to the back of her neck, combing through the short ends of her hair.

"I'm sorry," she whispered against his lips. "I've denied you unbraiding my hair on our wedding night."

He sighed heavily and touched his forehead to hers. "Speaking of our wedding night . . ."

The heat rushed to her cheeks. "Wait," she said as she placed her hand on his chest. They'd been avoiding this discussion, or rather she had any time Aidan hinted that he had to tell her something before they got married. "I know what you're going to say. You've changed your mind about marrying me, haven't you?"

Aidan stammered a few times before he got the words straight. "No," he said. "My love for you is genuine. But my confession will change your mind about marrying me," he said.

"Never," she replied.

Aidan took her hand and kissed it, then pressed it against his chest. "Prince Felix was right when he told you there was something he could give you that I couldn't."

"Yes—misery, war, heartburn, depression, an early death . . ." Her voice trailed off when she saw Aidan's expression had remained stoic.

He shook his head. "Before you make any vows of marriage to me, I have to tell you something." He paused as if holding his breath. Then he said, "I'm fully functional, but I will never be able to provide you with an heir."

Delia was stunned into silence. "And?" she prompted.

He blinked back at her. "And nothing. I thought you'd want an heir. That you saw yourself as a mother, standing under the great tree, naming your child. I saw your face when you told me of the legends."

Almost giddy with relief, she linked her fingers around the back of his neck. "So much has changed since I showed you those mosaics," she told him. "And as far as children go, Shania will fill the palace, I'm sure. There's no reason to believe we can't start a new tradition in regard to rightful heirs. This is a time of growth and change, remember?" Then she smiled. "I'm not the same girl who showed you the mosaics. What I wanted then and what I want now are different."

Aidan seemed to contemplate this, then asked, "What do you want now?"

The smile overtook her face. "You. But just to clarify, you'll always be . . ." She paused, her voice dropping. "Fully functional?"

"Yes," he slipped his arms around her. "I promise you a lifetime of nights together." He started the kiss this time and as Delia sighed against his lips, she thought a lifetime of nights would never be enough. The moment lingered, sweet and exciting. It seemed everything they'd been through had finally eased away, leaving them free to be with each other.

She knew the coming years would be hard work as her planet reinvented itself. There would be times of indecision and failure, yet deep down, she knew this was the right path. And the knowledge of that was incredibly freeing.

For now, she was in Aidan's arms, truly content and deliriously happy. Delia could feel the energy of her ancestors all around them, assuring her of Astor's brilliant future.

ACKNOWLEDGMENTS

This book was possible due to the inspiration and support of many people. At the top of that list is Angela Lemmon, who finally told me, "Stop talking about that Cinderella space story and just write it already." Thank you, friend.

I owe a bigger amount of gratitude than I can ever express to the readers of Swoon Reads for helping *Rogue Princess* become a novel. I posted this story hoping to receive some helpful feedback and to meet other writers. When I received the email about publication, I was completely gobsmacked. Thank you as well to my fellow Swoon Reads authors for their support and unlimited wisdom. Being part of this group was a lovely bonus I was not expecting. You can never have enough books or writer friends.

Thank you to Jean Feiwel, Lauren Scobell, Emily Settle, and the rest of the Swoon Reads team. And thank you to the eagle eyes of my copyeditor, Linda Minton.

I am deeply grateful for my editor, Holly West, who believed in *Rogue Princess* from the very beginning and helped me uncover and polish Delia and Aidan's story into a novel I am so proud to share. Her spot-on suggestions and thoughtful contributions were indispensable as the manuscript underwent multiple transitions.

A huge shout-out of thanks goes to Mallory Grigg, art director at Macmillan, and artist Audrey Lynn Estok for producing such a stylishly beautiful cover. It was so satisfying to see the characters come to life pictorially.

Finally, thank you to my family and friends, and to Ken and our children, Ruth and Adam. You have always supported my writing and continue to provide me with daily doses of proof that nothing I put on the page compares to real life with you. Thank you.

Check out more books chosen for publication by readers like you.